Praise for Elmer Kelton

•

"One of the greatest and most gifted of Western writers."
—Historical Novel Society

"Elmer Kelton is a Texas treasure."
—*El Paso Herald-Post*

"Voted 'the greatest Western writer of all time' by the Western Writers of America, Kelton creates characters more complex than L'Amour's."
—*Kirkus Reviews*

"Kelton writes of early Texas with unerring authority."
—*Fort Worth Star-Telegram*

"You can never go wrong if . . . you pick up a title by Elmer Kelton."
—*American Cowboy*

"One of the best."
—*The New York Times*

"A splendid writer."
—*The Dallas Morning News*

"A genuine craftsman with an ear for dialogue and, more important, an understanding of the human heart."
—*Booklist*

Forge Books by Elmer Kelton

After the Bugles
Badger Boy
Barbed Wire
Bitter Trail
Bowie's Mine
The Buckskin Line
Buffalo Wagons
Captain's Rangers
Cloudy in the West
Dark Thicket
The Day the Cowboys Quit
Donovan
Eyes of the Hawk
The Good Old Boys
Hanging Judge
Hard Trail to Follow
Hot Iron
Jericho's Road
Joe Pepper
Llano River
Long Way to Texas
Many a River
Massacre at Goliad
Other Men's Horses
Pecos Crossing
The Pumpkin Rollers
The Raiders: Sons of Texas
Ranger's Trail
The Rebels: Sons of Texas
Sandhills Boy: The Winding Trail of a Texas Writer
Shadow of a Star
Shotgun
Six Bits a Day
The Smiling Country
Sons of Texas
Stand Proud
Texas Rifles
Texas Standoff
Texas Vendetta
The Time It Never Rained
The Way of the Coyote

Lone Star Rising
(comprising *The Buckskin Line*, *Badger Boy*, and *The Way of the Coyote*)

Brush Country
(comprising *Barbed Wire* and *Llano River*)

Ranger's Law
(comprising *Ranger's Trail*, *Texas Vendetta*, and *Jericho's Road*)

Texas Showdown
(comprising *Pecos Crossing* and *Shotgun*)

Texas Sunrise
(comprising *Massacre at Goliad* and *After the Bugles*)

Long Way to Texas
(comprising *Joe Pepper*, *Long Way to Texas*, and *Eyes of the Hawk*)

CAPTAIN'S RANGERS

AND

THE DAY THE COWBOYS QUIT

Elmer Kelton

A TOM DOHERTY ASSOCIATES BOOK | NEW YORK

CAPTAIN'S RANGERS AND THE DAY THE COWBOYS QUIT

A Forge Book
Published by Tom Doherty Associates
120 Broadway
New York, NY 10271

www.tor-forge.com

Forge® is a registered trademark of Macmillan Publishing Group, LLC.

ISBN 978-1-250-17794-0

First Edition: November 2019

Printed in the United States of America

0 9 8 7 6 5 4 3 2 1

CONTENTS

CAPTAIN'S RANGERS

AUTHOR'S NOTE

Between the Rio Grande and the Nueces River lay a disputed region known in the 1800s as the Nueces Strip, claimed by both Texans and Mexicans. It was a frequent battleground in an unofficial but long-simmering conflict that continued spilling blood for nearly forty years after the Mexican War officially ended in 1846. It was to a considerable degree a racial war, growing out of the same clash of vastly different cultures that had led to the Texas revolution against Mexico. Unreasoning racial hatred on both sides fostered a spirit of lawlessness which tolerated and even encouraged freebooters on both banks of the Rio Grande, men who pillaged and killed in the name of either Texas or Mexico, victimizing the innocent of both races and calling their acts patriotism.

Into this festering trouble spot in 1875 rode Captain L. H. McNelly, a complex and dedicated man of frail health but iron will, seeming to sense that he had only a while to live, and determined to bring peace in that short time if he had to kill half the people in the

Strip. A former officer in the Confederate army, McNelly had consented nevertheless to serve in the hated Texas State Police set up by the Union-dominated Reconstruction government in the hope that he could somehow serve justice despite the corrupted system. When the police were at last disbanded and the old Texas Rangers reorganized, the uncorrupted McNelly was awarded a captaincy.

In the Nueces Strip he and his Ranger company tracked down American and Mexican outlaws with equal dedication, disregarding race in a grim quest for law and order. His measures sometimes had an awful finality and may seem strong by today's standards, but they were acceptable to and expected by the people of his time, for nothing less would bring the brigands to heel. McNelly's bold raid across the border to strike an outlaw stronghold at Las Cuevas, below Rio Grande City, stirred the federal government into near panic and threatened for a time to breach relations between the United States and Mexico. But McNelly refused to back down from his tough stance and dealt a shattering blow to the border jumpers, bringing about a vital turning point in the long, undeclared war.

Though real peace was still years in coming, historians give McNelly and his Rangers major credit for the beginning of a better time.

1

They rode horseback up Austin's broad main thoroughfare toward the forbidding antebellum structure which now, ten years after the Civil War, was being denounced in the legislature as the worst firetrap and eyesore in Texas—the capitol building. There were two riders, a big man with a broad-brimmed Mexican border hat and a little man with a short brown beard. A vague military look—something sensed as much as seen, something about the way he carried himself—made it plain that the smaller man was the one in charge.

He rode up almost to the steps and swung down from the saddle. He paused a moment, his thin shoulders pinching as he coughed into one hand. His face was pale and sickly, but his piercing eyes saw all there was to see and gave a hint that behind them a keen mind was running with the whistle tied down. He handed the reins to the big man and said: "Stay close, Sergeant. I have no idea how long I'll be with the governor."

Two men idled on the steps, puffing cigars and arguing about an item in a newspaper. One looked up, frowning. "It's McNelly." He spoke in a voice the little man could not miss.

"McNelly?" The other snorted. "Ain't he the one used to work for them damned carpetbag State Police?"

McNelly gave no appearance of hearing until the big man took an angry stride toward the loafers. He turned and said, "No, Sergeant. There'll be no brawling on the capitol steps. They didn't say anything, and you didn't hear it."

The sergeant glared at the idlers but did not question the order. "Yes, sir, Captain." He watched Captain McNelly march into the building and out of sight.

The loafers felt that the order was their protection. One said, "The sergeant don't sound like a carpetbagger to me. Does he to you, Wilse?"

"Naw, he don't. Where you from, Sergeant?"

Anger stained the big man's face. He ignored the question until it was thrown at him a second time. "Arkansas," he replied curtly.

"Arkansas. Well, now, I wouldn't hardly think there'd be no carpetbaggers from Arkansas. I don't see any uniform, either. What kind of a sergeant are you, anyway?"

"Ranger sergeant. Texas Rangers."

"A Texas Ranger from Arkansas. That does beat all, don't it, Wilse? A carpetbag Texas Ranger sergeant from Arkansas."

The sergeant put one booted foot forward, caught himself and stepped back, glancing up at the open windows as if certain the captain would see him. Crisply he declared, "War's been over for ten years.

There's no such of a thing anymore as a carpetbagger. Somethin' else, Captain never *was* one. The man who says different is a low-down, yellow-bellied liar. And he hasn't got the guts to come to the Ranger camp tonight and meet me out past the picket line."

"If a man *was* to come around, who would you send out to fight him? That consumptive-looking captain of yours?"

The sergeant moved forward, fists up. The loafer jumped to his feet. "Remember your orders, Sergeant."

The sergeant's eyes narrowed, and his voice went quiet, the way the air sometimes does just before a storm breaks loose. "I'll remember my orders. But I'll also remember you two. And if you're not on the picket line tonight to find me, I'll be around tomorrow to find you." He looked as if he could drive a nail with his bare hand. The loafers decided they were moths too close to the flame.

He watched, the color still high in his broad face, as the two retreated down the dirt street and disappeared into the open door of a saloon. He led the horses to a shady place and loosened the cinches, then squatted on the ground. There he could watch both the door of the capitol building and the door of the saloon. He would be here a long time, more than likely, but the captain had said wait.

When a man followed McNelly, he learned to rest every time he got the chance, for sometimes there was no rest at all. For a little man, Captain had the devil's own endurance, except when he was suffering one of his spells.

The sergeant half dozed in the gentle warmth of the spring morning, but every movement at the capitol door caught his eye. He was sure the loafers had not left the saloon, either.

After perhaps two hours, he saw the familiar gaunt figure pass through the doorway and start down the long steps, back straight, thin shoulders held proud. The sergeant led the horses forward. He could tell McNelly was troubled by the way he chewed his unlighted cigar. The sergeant boiled with curiosity, but a man never asked the captain unnecessary questions. If Captain wanted something known, he would tell it. If he chose to keep it to himself, all hell couldn't prize it out of him. His men learned to watch him and take their cue from his actions. If he ate a good supper, they knew they could figure on sleeping. If he drank coffee and munched a little hardtack, they knew a night ride was coming up, for Captain believed a man traveled best when he rode with his belly lank.

Captain asked, "Do you have any business in Austin that needs settling before we leave, Sergeant?"

The sergeant hadn't known they were going anywhere, but then, he doubted the governor had called McNelly in to talk about the old days of the Confederacy. "That depends, sir. I take it we'll be gone before tonight?"

"My orders are to leave when I'm ready. And I'm ready."

The sergeant frowned. "Well, sir, there is one little piece of business I ought to take care of. Won't be but a minute or two. I have a small debt that needs settlin' in that saloon."

"All right, but no drinking. We've got to ride."

"No drinkin', sir." The sergeant dismounted. He held the reins awkwardly until the captain silently reached out for them. Under no circumstances would the sergeant have presumed to *ask* Captain to hold his horse. He walked into the saloon.

Two minutes later he was back smiling, rubbing

the knuckles of his right hand against his shirt. In his left hand he held several black cigars. "For you, Captain. Compliments of the bartender."

"Thank you, Sergeant. Debt all paid?"

"Paid in full, sir."

He knew better than to ask where they were going. But there were ways of fishing for an answer. "Spring like this, it could still get chilly up in North Texas. Somebody stole my coat. Reckon I ought to buy me a new one, sir?"

"We're not heading north." The little captain's sharp eyes held a rare glint of dark humor, and the sergeant knew McNelly saw through him. "We're going south."

"I didn't mean to pry, Captain."

"You had just as well know. I find the rumor is out anyway. The governor has authorized me to recruit new men and build up my force for a cleanup job. It'll be a dirty one."

The sergeant struggled against his curiosity, but he couldn't keep it from showing.

The captain could see. "We're going all the way to the Rio Grande. Our orders are to clean up the Nueces Strip."

2

They called it the Nueces River, but many of those early Texans didn't know how to spell it, for they were *gringos* and the word was Spanish, given for the pecans and other nut-bearing trees which grew in wild abundance along its banks. To Anglo ears the name sounded like New Aces, and that was how some of them wrote it.

A map of Texas shows the Nueces is born amid the Edwards Plateau, draining the limestone ridges and the live-oak flats far west of San Antonio. It runs generally south until it comes within less than forty miles of the mud-choked Rio Grande. Then, like a skittish colt wary of a tired old stallion's uncertain temper, it shies off and quarters south-eastward, ever edging away from the big river. It cuts across the horn-shaped lower tip of Texas and spills itself into the Gulf's blue waters at the northernmost point of Padre Island, a hundred miles above the mouth of the Rio Grande.

That stretch of coastal prairie and desert wasteland, that parched region of short grass and cactus, mesquite and chaparral lying between the two rivers was known in Texas' youthful years as the Nueces Strip. By treaty it belonged to Texas, but the original people living there hadn't written the treaty. Most of them hadn't even read it. They lived in easy tempo in thatched huts and brush *jacales,* in rock houses and sun-baked adobes, raising their little patches of corn, running their rangy cattle on God's own grass. They ate *gringo* beef when it came handy, for taking from the *gringo* wasn't stealing; it was an act of liberation. They worshipped their God with a great devotion and loved their families as fiercely as they hated their enemies. Though they lived in Texas, they considered themselves Mexican. They had no particular allegiance to the government of Mexico, for it changed as often as the moon, but they honored Mother Mexico because they were of *la raza,* The Race.

Since the Mexican War they had found themselves crowded more and more by the light-skinned *extranjeros,* the foreigners who came with horses and cattle, with official-looking papers and with tough, badge-wearing *rinches* on horseback to enforce the foreign words on those papers. Some of the people of *la raza* retreated across the big river to simmer in anger and futility. Others stayed, for to them the land was as Mexican as themselves, and one did not leave his *querencia*—his homeland—any more than he would abandon his mother. The more tolerant made friends with individual Anglos, though they distrusted these blue-eyed ones as a race. *Mira, hombre,* is it not widely known that the *gringo* has but two aims in this world, to rob the man and to despoil the woman? The *gringo,* in turn, sometimes found that there was no more loyal friend than a Mexican who liked you, though he was convinced that as a group the "greasers" were untrustworthy. Why, man alive, anybody could tell you the Mexicans were a cut-throat bunch of thieves and liars you couldn't afford to turn your back on.

Small wonder, then, that for decades a minor, undeclared war flared spasmodically along the Nueces Strip, sometimes fed on the one side by cow thieves and murderers who justified themselves as patriots, fighting for *la raza*; and fed on the other side by land grabbers and Mexican-haters who eased whatever conscience they may have had by telling themselves this was a holy war that had started with the Alamo.

It reached its peak in the spring of 1875. That was the year of McNelly's Rangers . . . of Palo Alto Prairie and Las Cuevas. . . .

Vincente de Zavala missed his loop at the last calf's hind legs, and chunky Bonifacio Holgúin, standing near the mesquite-wood branding fire, began to hoot at him. "*Cuidado, muchacho,* or you will rope your own neck and strangle yourself. If it were your young wife in your hands instead of that rope, you would not fumble so."

De Zavala told him in rich and fragrant Spanish to go to hell. He had been dragging these calves out by their heels. This time he built a new loop in his rawhide reata and purposely roped the calf around the neck. It bawled and pitched and kicked. Vincente's white teeth gleamed in mischief. This, *hombre,* would give that sugar-eating Bonifacio cause to laugh out of the other side of his mouth.

Tall Lanham Neal cast a quick glance at the young woman who stood watchfully by the branding irons, right hand protected from the heat by a heavy leather glove. Good thing all that hurrawing was covered up in Spanish, he thought, for much of it was ripe and gamey. But on reflection he knew Zoe Daingerfield probably understood every word. She had spent her life among the people of the Nueces Strip.

He shrugged. *If she knows what it means, it's nothing new to her. If she don't, it won't do her no harm.*

Anyway, he had tried to tell her. He had tried to talk her out of coming with the men on cow hunts like this. It wasn't for a woman. But old man Griffin Daingerfield was hobbling around waiting for a broken leg to heal, and he had declared that one of the Daingerfields needed to be out looking after the family interests. The old man wouldn't have been on that crutch in the first place if he hadn't bullheadedly refused to let Vincente take the vinegar out of a fresh and rested young horse for him. Griffin, in short, was a great deal older than he was ready to admit.

There had been only one Daingerfield son, and he had been taken by the fever the year the Yankees tried to put their gunboats up the Rio Grande to stop Confederate cotton from crossing the Mexican border. Old Griffin had tried to bring up his daughter to take the boy's place and be able to inherit the ranch someday. He had done a fair-to-middlin' job of it, Lanham Neal thought. She was a cowgirl; you had to give her that. When she got her knee hooked over the horn of that sidesaddle—hidden by heavy riding skirts, of course—there wasn't any shaking her loose; she rode like a grass burr. She knew the cow. She could even rope a little, when she had to, though roping from a sidesaddle was not widely encouraged.

The hell of it was—and this must have bothered the old man—she still looked like a woman. A pretty good-looking woman, as far as a brush-country cowboy like Lanham Neal was concerned. Maybe she *wouldn't* have caused any stampede in a place like San Antone where pretty women grew like peaches on a tree, but down here she was like a single blossom on an empty prairie. The old man had chased many a smitten cowhand away from his door, forbidding him ever to let his shadow fall there again. Lanham Neal had stolen many a long and wishful look at Zoe Daingerfield's quiet face, and now and again she looked back at him. But old Griffin never caught him at it; Lanham was careful about that.

Jobs weren't easy to come by these days; in this border country money was tight. Money was *always* tight for Lanham Neal. Seemed to him sometimes that hard luck dogged him the way a skulking wolf will trail after a lame bull, waiting to see him stumble. Seemed like every time Lanham had something going his way—something that looked as if it could work out well—luck would turn on him and kick him in the face. This job was good. Lanham didn't want to lose it, not even for a smile or two from Zoe Daingerfield.

Lanham stood aside and gave Bonifacio the honor of grabbing the fighting calf and flanking it, for it served him right. Bonifacio's heckling had needled Vincente into bringing this one by the neck instead of by the heels. Bonifacio swore profusely, threw his knee into the ribs as the calf jumped, then with great exertion brought it over and down hard on its side. The calf's breath gusted out with a harsh grunt. Lanham grabbed one hind leg and pulled it toward him, dropping on his rump and hooking the other hind leg firmly with the heel of his boot. With Bonifacio holding one end and Lanham the other, the calf was helpless.

Vincente grinned down from the saddle as he recoiled the reata. “Bonifacio, if you talked less you would have more strength to wrestle the cattle.”

Bonifacio's answer was unrepeatable. Zoe Daingerfield, unconcerned, walked out with a hot running iron in the gloved hand. She ran the letter D onto the calf's hip, then added a diagonal line that made it the Daingerfield Slash D. She carried the iron back to the fire, peeled off the glove and returned with a sharp knife. She earmarked the calf with a deep underbit, then bent over and with two strokes of the blade turned the bull calf into a steer.

Lanham looked away uncomfortably as she did it. That was a job a woman shouldn't even *see,* he thought, much less actually *do*. Lots of people would have looked at her in horror. What were these young women coming to?

If it bothered Zoe, she didn't show it. Old Griffin had trained her to look at life with both eyes wide open and not cover facts with a veil. She wiped the blade clean on an old handkerchief. “Last one, Lanham?”

Lanham was the *caporál* here, the strawboss. But *vaqueros* like Vincente and Bonifacio didn't really need much supervision. They could have done about as well without him, and Lanham knew it. He only hoped old Griffin didn't come to the same conclusion. “Yes, ma'am, we're through. Your daddy is twelve calves richer.”

“Twelve calves.” She didn't sound particularly pleased. She watched as Bonifacio opened the gate and the cattle trotted warily out in single file, a couple of the cows feinting at Bonifacio with their sharp horns. "How many of those calves will we raise, and how many will be stolen across the river by the *Cortinistas?*"

Lanham shook his head. "*Quién sabe*?" His frowning gaze trailed the cattle. They clattered off toward the protection of a mesquite thicket, where the bewildered calves would pause to lick their wounds and the cows would make a motherly fuss over them. Lanham knew that for the drive the four riders had made today, they ought to have picked up a lot more cattle. Zoe had called it. The river, that was the trouble.

The Rio Grande lay just a few miles south. A *bandido* didn't have to be skilled at his trade to swim a horse across there in the dark of night, round up whatever stock came easy to hand and take them back over. They had done it in a minor way for years and years. Now they were doing it wholesale, riding across in bunches, stealing everything that walked on four legs except the jackrabbits and the wild *javalina* hogs. In their own eyes they were more than *bandidos* now; they were *Cortinistas,* "soldiers" of the general Juan Nepomuceno Cortina.

"Dad needs these cattle," Zoe said worriedly. "They're stealing him blind and he can't afford it."

"Damn little I see that he can do about it." Lanham gave her a boost up onto her sidesaddle. This was one thing which always gave him a valid excuse to touch her. "You all set, Miss Daingerfield?"

"All set. And you can call me Zoe." She smiled.

"Not when your old daddy's in earshot."

She smiled again. "He's miles away."

That was what made it frustrating, sometimes, to work here. Lanham Neal had had saloon girls and sidewalk *señoritas* smile at him lots of times, and it didn't fever him much. He answered their beckoning fingers now and then, when he felt the need, but he held no illusions about what they really wanted. They were after whatever silver might be jingling in his pockets; it never was very much. But with Zoe Daingerfield, it was different. She didn't need what little money could be found in a cowhand's pockets, but she smiled anyway. And that roused the fever in him.

It couldn't be for his money, because he didn't have enough to buy wadding for a shotgun. It wasn't likely his looks, either, for the cracked mirror in the *jacal* where he slept told him his mouth was too broad and his nose maybe a little too big. He almost always needed a haircut, and he didn't find time to shave very often. Perhaps Zoe saw something that didn't show in the mirror.

It might have been his strength she saw. Lanham Neal had been over a lot of country the last ten or twelve years. At the age of fifteen, he had gone off hell-bent to fight the Yankees in the last futile months of the war, after they had killed his brother with Hood's army at Nashville. The first battle he was in, Lanham fell with a bullet through his hip before he ever got a good look at a Yankee. He had almost died. Long after the war was over, he started for home, penniless, walking most of the way in spite of the hip. And when he got got to where home had been, he found house caving in, family gone, the farm being worked by strangers who had taken it over for taxes in the name of the new Reconstruction government. In those first hard years after the war, a man could have swapped a good pair of boots for a farm . . . if he had had the boots. Lanham Neal was barefoot.

It had taken strength to make it through those

times. One way and another, Lanham had survived. He had squatted on new land west of the old settlements, only to have the carpetbag lawyers take it away from him once he got it broken and a good crop of cotton almost ready to pick. He had gone to mavericking cattle—picking on those unbranded calves he figured came from herds the carpetbaggers had taken over. It was a practice considered legal enough in those times. No brand, no owner. When he had accumulated a good-sized bunch of calves and yearlings, he traded them for grown steers and threw the steers in with a Kansas-bound trail herd, figuring on filling his pockets with Yankee gold at the railhead. He never got there. Jay-hawkers stampeded the cattle at the Kansas line. Lanham wound up in a Kansas jail along with most of the other drovers when they tried to take their cattle back at gunpoint. They got away from those paper-collar Comanches with nothing but the clothes on their backs and a horse apiece to carry them home to Texas.

His luck had run with a startling consistency—always sour. Everything he touched turned to ashes, seemed like.

That was one reason he hesitated to give much sign of his true feelings to Zoe Daingerfield. His luck might rub off on anybody who got too close to him.

There was another thing, too. Old Griffin Daingerfield liked him. Griffin had a head like a mule, sometimes. He was inclined to holler first and reflect later, but Lanham respected him too much to betray his trust. Griffin was one of the mossy-horned old brushpoppers who had taken this country like a challenge and had charged head-on, ready to fight man, beast, brush or weather, individually or in a bunch. Lanham figured a thing like that gave a man a right to holler once in a while. And beneath it all, the rancher had feelings for people—the ones he figured as *good* people; he made his own choices about that. Mexican or *gringo,* he sized them up individually and made his judgment. He seldom altered that first judgment. Lanham had come down to the Nueces Strip after the Kansas debacle, broke, all but barefoot again, the fever eating at him. If it hadn't been for Daingerfield and Zoe, the fever probably would have carried Lanham off for good. Griffin took the sick cowboy into his house and doctored and fed him. The only thing he had required—and he did that with looks and actions rather than with words—was that Lanham keep a fitting distance between himself and Zoe . . . no stirring of any emotions that might lead to something the old man would have to oil his rifle for. Lanham had kept that faith, though now and again it took strong measures like a sudden dip in the cold waters of a tank, or even an infrequent trip to the lamp-lighted streets of Brownsville and Matamoros.

Vincente de Zavala pointed toward the cattle as they disappeared into the brush. In Spanish he said, "It is good that we have them branded. When their mothers wean them, they might fall into the hands of mavericker."

Lanham's reply was in English. It was common for border people to conduct bi-lingual conversations, each person using the language that came easiest to him but understanding the other. "Griffin Daingerfield needs them as bad as any mavericker. Gettin' to be all he can do to hold this place together. He goes under, you and me are out of a job, Vincente. You with a young wife to feed, that wouldn't be good."

Vincente shrugged. "Food is not a woman's only need. Or a man's."

Bonifacio was staring back across the corral, his round, brown face puzzled. "*Caporál,* I thought the branding fire had burned itself out."

"It has, just about."

Bonifacio pointed. "It makes much smoke."

Lanham turned, frowning. It was smoke, surely enough, and at a glance he knew it didn't come from the branding fire. He rubbed a sleeve across his sweating face and cast a quick glance at Zoe. "Vincente, that is the direction of the house."

Zoe gasped, a cold fear suddenly rushing into her eyes.

"*Caporál . . .*" Vincente's mouth dropped open. "*Bandidos?*"

Lanham swore. "I hope not. Hang on, Zoe. We got to ride hard."

The words were wasted. She had already made the start.

Bonifacio was always the last to grasp an idea. He spurred mightily, but he never did catch up.

Vincente was saying over and over, "Maria!" It was the name of his wife. "That Cheno Cortina. That accursed Cheno!"

•

He ruled the lower river country, at least that on the south bank of the Rio, this Cheno Cortina. Juan Nepomuceno Cortina was his full name, but to the people of *la raza* on both sides of the Bravo, he was Cheno, and for most of them the name carried a touch of magic. Of good blood but unschooled, shrewd and ambitious but without mercy for those who opposed him, the red-bearded one had repeatedly gouged the greedy *gringos,* hitting them in their moneybags where it really hurt and inviting them to kiss his backside. This in itself was enough to insure his endearment to all those shoeless ones who had lost land to the *extranjeros,* to all those *pobres* who had worked hard for little pay and had felt the contempt that sometimes lurked in narrowed *gringo* eyes.

In this spasmodic border war, *el generál* for more than a decade now had been Cheno Cortina, and his soldiers had been the *Cortinista* cattle rustlers and horse thieves, bush-whackers and house burners, darting across the river unpredictably, here one time, yonder another. Quiet for months, they would suddenly make a lightning guerrilla raid, leaving a trail of fire and blood, usually escaping across the river unscathed and carrying their booty of horses or cattle, or, once in a while, silver and gold. Now and again a few hapless ones failed to make it and lay till their bones bleached white in the Texas sun. But if ever they crossed to the south bank, they were in sanctuary, swallowed up by the immensity of Mexico, sheltered by sympathetic *peons* who considered them avengers of a great wrong—people who still cursed the day the vain tyrant Santa Anna had ingloriously lost at San Jacinto and to save his own bloody hide had signed away to the Texans a birthright the Mexicans considered their own.

Now other men rode and dared and sometimes died, while Cheno Cortina waited patiently in Matamoros and pulled the strings, basking in the sunshine of the people's admiration and growing rich from his share of the Texas spoils.

Vincente de Zavala hit the ranch yard ahead of the others. "María," he shouted, eyes searching desperately through the smoke. He was out of the saddle and on the ground running before his horse slid to a stop. In front of the charred *jacal* that had been his, a woman lay still and silent. The south wind picked up dust from the hoof-churned earth and tugged at the shredded remnants of her black dress. Vincente dropped to his knees. He cried out in anguish.

Zoe saw, and her face blanched. She ran for the smoking ruin of the "big house," which in reality hadn't really been very big. "Dad! Dad!"

No answer came. Lanham saw the reason before she did. He saw the crumpled figure lying in the yard.

Zoe screamed and jumped to the ground, turning her horse loose to stand or to run, whichever he chose. He would have run from the smoke had Bonifacio not spurred in and taken the reins. Lanham handed him his own and walked to the girl. She knelt by her father, trying to shake him to consciousness. Lanham could tell by looking that it was useless. Griffin Daingerfield was dead. There must have been a dozen bulletholes in his back.

There'll be some in the front, too, I expect, Lanham thought gravely. *He wouldn't have shown them his back until he fell.*

Bonifacio tied the horses and came trotting. Lanham turned and shook his head. Bonifacio crossed himself and went to try to comfort Vincente.

Lanham looked toward the big house and saw the old man's crutch lying there in front of it. He could see the wink of brass cartridge cases, scattered about. Griffin had made it to here without his crutch, probably firing his rifle all the way. The rifle was not in sight. The raiders undoubtedly had taken it.

Lanham's eyes went to fire as he looked helplessly down at the sobbing girl. *Damn it all, what can a man say? What can he do? That luck of mine, rubbing off again.*

Pale, Bonifacio stood with sombrero in his hand beside the quietly grieving Vincente. He looked as awkward and lost as Lanham felt, for he wasn't doing Vincente any good and didn't know how to start.

Bonifacio suddenly stiffened and looked at Lanham. He came trotting, the sombrero still in his hands. Lanham reached to his hip for the reassuring feel of his pistol, for the thought hit him that Bonifacio had seen something.

But Bonifacio had *thought* of something. "*Caporál,* I just remembered. We have not seen Hilario."

Hilario Gomez was an old retainer who had already been a graying *vaquero* when Griffin Daingerfield had first come into this country. Gomez had worked for him, helped him establish himself here. Too old now to ride or to do heavy work, Hilario mostly hung around the place, doing minor fix-up jobs and giving freely of his advice, telling the hands such as Vincente and Bonifacio that nowhere today did one find *vaqueros* like those of old, like those he had ridden with in the days of his youth.

Bonifacio trotted around the yard, shouting, "Hilario! Hilario!"

Lanham's first thought was that the *viejo* might have run away at sight of the *Cortinistas*. But he rejected that idea, for despite the differences in their upbringing and their viewpoints, Hilario and Griffin had been much alike. Neither ever turned his back on trouble. If anything, they had seemed to thrive on a certain amount of it, so long as it did not come in excess. Lanham joined Bonifacio in the search.

They found the *vaquero* lying against a corral

fence near a smouldering barn. His old cotton shirt was stained with blood, and his eyes were glazed, but breath still came erratically. *"Quién es?"* he gasped. *Who is it?*

"He hears us," Lanham told Bonifacio, "but he can't see us." He spoke in Spanish to the old man, who had stoutly refused to learn English. "Be not afraid, uncle. It is Lanham and Bonifacio. We have come to help you."

"María . . . el patrón . . ." The words came through grinding pain.

No use lying to him, Lanham thought. "Only you are still alive." *And not by very much, either.*

He turned Hilario over gently and saw the two bullet wounds in the thin chest. Anyone else would have died, he thought. But they had raised them tough in Hilario's day, like the mesquite and the cactus. "Bonifacio, let's carry him down into the yard, to the shade. I doubt there's anything left to treat him with, but we'll look."

Carefully they lifted the old man, trying not to hurt him any more than they could help. They set him down beneath the broad, sheltering cover of a brush arbor that the *bandidos* somehow hadn't bothered to burn. Lanham tore the shirt away and grimaced. The bullets were still in there. He had nothing to extract them with except a pocketknife, and that would surely kill the old man. Small chance he had of living anyway.

In a hoarse voice Hilario started trying to tell what had happened. "Hush, Hilario," Lanham said. "Don't waste yourself talking. Save your strength."

The old man paid him no mind. It occurred to Lanham that he never had; Hilario regarded the younger generation—Mexican or Anglo—with no more than a quiet tolerance. He kept on talking, telling how it had been. The raiders had caught him unawares. In the old days they would not have done it, he said, but nowadays his ears had been failing him, and he was occupied with cleaning the picket-built barn. They had been upon him before he had known they were in the country. He had had no weapon, other than the pitchfork in his hands. He had run at them with that, but he had not taken three steps before they brought him down.

Through the dust and the pain, he had seen Maria dragged out of her *jacal*. She had pulled free. Yipping and shouting like coyotes after a pullet, some of the men had grabbed her. Old Griffin had boiled out of the big house, dragging himself without the crutch, firing as rapidly as he could lever his rifle. He had died in a matter of moments. María had not died quickly, or easily. The old man had pulled himself to the corral fence, but that had been as far as he could move. He could only lie and listen.

Old Hilario's sightless eyes wept bitter tears, and his gnarled hands clenched weakly as he went on about how different it would have been when he was a young man in all his strength, a man to make *bandidos* tremble for a hundred miles up and down the Rio. Lanham tried to quiet him, but Hilario talked until the last of his strength was gone. And with the last of his strength, the life ebbed out of him, too.

Bonifacio quietly crossed himself. "God was not looking this way today." Shock lay in his eyes. "I can see why they would kill Hilario, for he came at them with the pitchfork. They hated the *patrón* for his blood. But why should they kill Maria? She could not hurt them, and she was of the same blood as they."

"She lived on a *gringo* ranch. That made her one

of us, not one of them." Lanham carefully placed Hilario's limp hands on his chest and smoothed what he could of the rumpled shirt. "Been thirty years since the war with Mexico. You'd think it was still on."

Bonifacio said, "For some, it has never finished."

Lanham's eyes still burned. The smoke, he figured. He walked back to Vincente. The *vaquero's* face was buried in his woman's long black hair. Lanham touched the man's shoulder. "Vincente, this won't do you any good. We'll go and fetch some help."

Slowly Vincente's head came up. His black eyes were wet, but behind the tears lay glowing coals. "There is no help for her. Is there any help for the *patrón*, or for Hilario?"

Lanham shook his head. "They have all gone together. There is no one to help now but *la patrona* . . . Zoe."

Stricken, Vincente gazed at the lifeless olive face. When they killed Maria, they had murdered two, for she was carrying Vincente's child. Vincente's eyes were closed, and his voice was down almost to a whisper, but it carried thorns. "There will be no help for the ones who did this, *caporál*."

Zoe Daingerfield left her father and staggered across to stand by the men. Tears streamed down her face, but vengeful anger was beginning to show. "What do you mean, Vincente?"

"We will go after them," Vincente rasped. "We will kill them!"

Lanham's fists were tight. "I wish we could." But he saw little hope of it. Retribution had overtaken few of Cheno's men. "There was a sizable bunch of them. By the tracks, maybe twenty. Even if we was to catch up to them, what could we do?"

"Slit every throat we could get our hands on."

Bonifacio protested. "Against so many? We would not last three minutes."

Vincente eased his wife's body gently to the warm earth. He raised his eyes, his voice quivering with rage. "It will be a glorious three minutes. We will kill as many as we can."

Zoe Daingerfield surprised Lanham most. "He's right, Lanham. We're wastin' time."

"We?"

"They had a long start before we got here. We'll have to ride like hell to catch them."

"Zoe, you're not goin' anyplace. Leastways, not after them bandits. They'd do to you what they done to María."

"They killed my father."

"And they'd kill *you* without blinkin' twice."

Vincente began calculating. "They took the *patrón's* horses. Likely they will want to take some of his cattle, too. If that be so, they cannot move fast. The *patrona* does not go; she stays here. But *I* go. Do you go with me, *caporál?* And you, Bonifacio?"

The bitterness of it all was flooding over Lanham now. "I'll go."

Bonifacio stared at the ground, trembling like a man beneath a noose. "My mother lives in Matamoros, and my brothers. If I went with you, *el Cheno* would slaughter my people like cattle."

Vincente accepted the decision without rancor, though it was plain that Bonifacio's worry was not altogether about his family. "Then you will take *la patrona* to safety. You will go to town and bring help."

Bonifacio nodded. "Your Maria and the *patrón,* they must not be left lying here. They must be buried. Shall we wait until you come back?"

Vincente took a final look at the tiny figure that

had been Maria. "Do not wait for me. Perhaps I will never come back."

Zoe caught Lanham's hand. "I am not going with Bonifacio. My place is here, with Dad and Maria and Hilario. I will stay." Lanham started to protest, but he saw something in her eyes, something like he had seen in Vincente's. Zoe said, "Go, Lanham. Kill them! Kill as many as you can!"

Vincente swung into his big-horned Mexico saddle and spurred out without looking back. He headed straight south, with the tracks. Lanham Neal mounted as quickly as he could, but Vincente was already a hundred yards ahead of him. It took a long time for Lanham to catch up.

3

Straight as the crow flies, it would have been something like ten miles to the Rio Grande. The horses had been ridden all day, and they didn't have it in them anymore to cover the ground very fast. Lanham feared he and the seething Vincente might kill both mounts if they kept pushing them at this pace all the way to the river.

Almost simultaneously, both men saw the tracks that led away from the main trail of horses and cattle. Vincente's eyes narrowed in suspicion. Lanham swung to the ground and found a dark blotch in the midst of a flat impression in the sand. Blood.

Vincente said, "They laid a man down."

Lanham made a grim smile. "Old Griffin was always a good shot. They didn't get him at no bargain." Looking up, he pointed to where tracks of three horses led away through the chaparral. "They probably figured this one was wounded too bad to make it to the river. There's a little *rancho* over yonderway."

Vincente spat. "Galindo's *rancho*. That Galindo,

no vale nada. It does not surprise me that they go to him." Vincente's voice rasped. "If he has helped them, I will nail his hide to Cheno Cortina's own door."

Lanham knew the place. Galindo had a patch of corn, a few cattle and a herd of children. Old Griffin had mentioned more than once that the *muchachos* looked well fed; and he strongly suspected it was being done on Daingerfield beef. He had also suspected Galindo was branding his mavericks, as many as he could lay a reata upon. Some places in Southern Texas, that suspicion would have been enough to leave a Mexican *ranchero* dangling from the limb of a stout tree, for cattlemen as a class were not noted for long patience with thieves. But Daingerfield didn't work that way. Had he ever caught Galindo skinning a Daingerfield animal or putting his own brand on a Slash D brute, he would have shot him dead on the spot and never looked back. He would not do it on suspicion. "Patience," he had counseled. "Give them enough rope and they'll tie the noose in it theirselves."

The tracks led straight to the brush *jacal*. Rifle in his hand, Vincente rode almost to the door, carefully watching the dwelling. He motioned toward the tracks. "Three horses came, two left. I see a horse in that brush corral. That would belong to the *bandido*."

Lanham drew his pistol and swung to the ground, crouching. Cautious, he looped the reins around the branch of a thin mesquite. Vincente simply dropped his reins and let his horse go. It wouldn't travel far without him; he had it trained to stand where the reins fell.

The shack was of brush and mud, except for the door of rough-sawed lumber. Rifle pointed straight ahead, Vincente strode to the door and unceremoniously kicked it in. He plunged into the *jacal*. Lanham followed right behind him, heart pounding. He half expected to be shot point-blank.

Nothing happened. A frightened Mexican family huddled against a mud wall . . . a mother, a daughter almost grown, several other children ranging down to four or five years. No man.

Vincente shouted in Spanish, "He is here somewhere! Where do you hide him?"

A bed of mesquite limbs and stretched cowhide was the only furniture other than a couple of benches and a table. The bed was big enough for a *bandido* to hide under. Vincente took two strides forward and kicked the corner posts away. The bed fell. A baby squawled and crawled out from under it. Vincente was keyed to such a furious pitch that he almost shot the baby before he could stop himself. He stood numb, staring.

Lanham pulled a blanket off of the bed. Beneath it, the cowhide showed a telltale sign. Lanham glanced at Vincente and saw agreement in the *vaquero's* eyes. Blood.

Vincente whirled on the women. "Where is he?"

The women stared in terror. The children wailed.

"Where?" Vincente demanded again. He slashed out with his rifle and sent the table spinning against a wall. One leg broke off. He kicked the benches over onto the dirt floor. "Where?"

Galindo's wife collapsed to her knees in hysteria. The oldest daughter wrapped her arms around her mother and screamed at Vincente and Lanham.

Lanham said, "Galindo must've taken him out to try and hide him in the brush. We'll find him."

"Yes," Vincente said, and his voice was terrible. "We'll find him."

The sight of the terrified women and children unnerved Lanham a little, though it seemed to have no effect upon Vincente. The Mexican turned on his heel and strode outside. "There will be footprints."

There were, but too many of them. There were barefoot tracks the children had left in play, and tracks the women had made between the shack and the outdoor oven, and around the well. There were the tracks Galindo had made back and forth from the brush-covered arbor that served as a barn of sorts. Lanham looked under the arbor but saw no man.

Vincente shouted, "*Caporál,* over here."

Lanham went in a long trot. Silently Vincente showed him fresh *huarache* tracks, leading down toward a small corn patch. Following them, they saw a man coming up from the direction of the field, a hoe over his shoulder. Lanham knew Galindo by sight but no better than that. The *ranchero* attempted to give a pleasant Mexican welcome, but the anxiety was too strong not to betray him. "My house is your house." His lips smiled. His face broke out in cold sweat. "Why has God sent you here today?"

"Not God," Vincente replied tightly. "The devil. Where did you hide him, Galindo?"

"Hide who? The devil?"

Vincente rammed the rifle into Galindo's belly. "Do not play games with me, Galindo, or I will blow your guts out."

Galindo panicked and tried to dodge away. In doing it, he brought the hoe around. Vincente did not hesitate. The rifle roared. The hoe went sailing, and Galindo hit the ground on his back. Vincente dropped the muzzle as if to fire again. Lanham stopped him. "I don't think he meant to hit you, Vincente. Don't make a mistake you may be sorry for."

Vincente's face was as near white as it could ever be. "When one kills the likes of Galindo, it is never a mistake." But he raised the muzzle and stepped over the downed *ranchero,* not looking back. He walked briskly toward the field.

Lanham glanced once over his shoulder toward the *jacal.* The oldest daughter was running down toward them crying, "Papa! Papa!" Lanham could see she carried no weapon and was no threat. Galindo was rapidly passing the point of being able to raise up, much less to hurt anybody. Lanham turned and trotted after Vincente.

They came almost to the edge of the field. Vincente raised his hand as a signal to stop. He pointed wordlessly to a huge cluster of prickly pear, then toward a set of fresh footprints. The same *huarache* tracks, left by Galindo. Lanham nodded and made a sign which told Vincente to hold up while he circled around to the other side of the pear thicket. Vincente waited. Lanham moved with care, in a crouch. He could not see into the thick growth of pear, but he realized as his tongue moved across dry lips that the *bandido* might damned sure be able to see out. He remembered that time in the war when he had been shot in the hip, and the thought brought him no comfort.

A pistol fired and Lanham jumped backward by reflex. Cold dread wrapped itself around him. The bullet had missed, but he knew it had been aimed at him. He could see the curl of black smoke, but he still couldn't see the bandit.

Lanham fired once, as much by instinct as by design, and then moved fast. *If he gets me, he'll have to hit a moving target . . . moving like hell.* The bandit fired again. A puff of dust kicked up in front of Lanham.

Vincente waded heedlessly into the pear, his high-topped boots taking the thorns. His rifle roared, and Lanham heard a man cry out. Lanham moved quickly. He saw the bandit now, lying on his back in a small opening with the thick stand of prickly pear, trying vainly to raise his pistol. Black rage boiled in Vincente's face, and he cursed furiously. His rifle roared again. The bandit fell back threshing, all consciousness gone like the blowing-out of a candle, but the body still clutched at life. Vincente levered another cartridge into the breech and fired again. He fired and fired and fired, till there was not enough left of the bandit for a mother to recognize. When his last cartridge was spent and the hammer fell harmlessly, Vincente staggered back a step, crying like a child.

Lanham left him alone. He stood and waited till the outburst had run its course and Vincente stood in silence, the tears still running unashamedly down his cheeks. Only then did Lanham step forward. "You done all you could here. We better get ridin', *amigo.*"

They walked back up the trail toward the *jacal*. The girl cradled her father's head in her arms and stared at them in wide-eyed terror. "No, no!" She cried in Spanish, "Please do not shoot him again."

Best Lanham could tell, looking down on the *ranchero,* was that the bullet had gone through the shoulder. With luck, and barring infection or bleeding to death, he ought to pull through and give his wife a few more children before he crossed over finally to the other side of that much bigger river.

Vincente's hands tightened on the rifle, and Lanham thought the *vaquero* might finish Galindo where he lay. "You'll run out of shells," Lanham suggested gently.

Vincente considered a moment, spat and moved on. Lanham glanced back and saw the girl's big brown eyes set on him in fear. He had never seen that kind of fear in a woman's face before. It reached him somewhere inside and made him feel cold. He figured she hadn't understood what he had said to Vincente in English; she thought Lanham was likely to shoot Galindo after all. He spoke to her in her own language. "If he went across the Rio Grande, he would have a better chance of living to be an old man."

She trembled. "But our home . . ."

"If you stay, he may be buried here, and much sooner than he would like."

Lanham untied his horse and rode out to catch Vincente's, which had shield off a short way at the sound of the shots. When he went back, he found Vincente herding Galindo's wife and children outside. Vincente reached into the outdoor fireplace and took out a burning stick. He shoved it against the *jacal* until the dry brush began to blaze. In a moment the shack crackled with flames. The dancing fire was reflected in Vincente's bitter eyes when he turned to the chunky woman who was Galindo's wife. "If ever another bandit asks you for help, remember this day and tell him to ride on. And one thing more: if ever I should come this way again and find Galindo here, I will kill him."

He turned to Lanham and reached for his reins. "*Caporál,* I am ready to go."

Dusk came upon them before they reached the river. Following the cattle tracks, they found a limping steer the border jumpers had left straggling. Across its side sprawled a huge Slash D, branded generously, the way only a Mexican *vaquero* would do it. "One of mine," Vincente remarked. It was all he said.

The tracks led finally down the bank and into the river. Across, Lanham could see a pinpoint of firelight.

"I reckon," he said, "they got away."

Vincente shook his head. "It is but a shallow river. I have crossed it a hundred times."

Lanham knew Vincente intended to do it again. A line on a map didn't mean much to a Mexican. For that matter, it didn't mean much to Lanham, either. "You want to go, Vincente? I'll go with you."

Vincente gravely shook his head. "The fight goes on, but from here it is to be my fight, not yours."

"Griffin was my boss, and my friend."

"But you are a *gringo*. Your face would get you killed, as soon as someone saw you in the daylight and knew you were not of the *renegados*."

"There's *gringo* renegades over yonder. I've seen them."

"But they are known, and they are safe. Your face would mark you. Me, I am one of the people. No one will look twice at me."

"You're just one man. Damn little you can do by yourself."

"Each of them is just one man, too, when they separate. I will go, and I will find them out. And then, one at a time . . ." He drew his knife and ran his finger along the edge of it.

"How long do you think you'll last, Vincente?"

Vincente shrugged. "Long enough, perhaps." He stared at the flickering firelight on the other side. "I want to live long enough to spill the blood of those who killed Maria. After that . . ." He held his silence a while. "I think the *patrona*, she will need you now, *caporál.* She is strong, but she is still a woman. A woman should not be alone."

"She'll have a hard time for a while."

"It is a hard world for everybody." Vincente shoved out his hand, and Lanham solemnly took it. Vincente said, "Perhaps I will see you again on this side of the river. If not, then I will see you in hell."

"Don't be in no hurry," Lanham replied. He swung down and stood watching Vincente disappear into the night, riding downriver a way to escape surveillance when he crossed over.

4

Captain McNelly was a restless man. He had a chair and a recruiting table set up in front of the tent, but he strode back and forth beneath the deep shade of a huge old live-oak tree. In front of him, several men awaited their turn to be interviewed. Behind him, men already accepted were making camp around the wagon. Most of them were young men, some not even able yet to grow a beard. They were a varied crew, but the majority shared two trademarks. Their clothing was common, generally well worn, for these were not flush times in Texas. And without exception, each man had a six-shooter on his hip. Most of them in addition carried a rifle or a shotgun.

The slight captain chewed absently on a cigar he had never bothered to light. His intense dark eyes studied a young man who stood nervously before him. "Name?"

"Joe Benson."

"Occupation?"

"Cowboy, mostly. Farmed a little."

"Do you own that horse you've been riding? Is that your own pistol you carry?"

"Yes, sir."

"How good are you with the pistol?"

"Fair to middlin', sir. I've won some bets." He caught himself. "Not that I'm a bettin' man by nature, sir. I'm not atall."

"You don't appear old enough to have seen service in the late war. Have you had any military experience, or even been a peace officer?"

"No, sir, never did. My pa went to war, and a couple of my brothers, but I was still a barefooted young'un." He paused. "I *would* have gone to war, sir, if they'd let me. I run away once to join, but they tanned my britches. I wasn't but twelve."

It was usually difficult to read judgment in Captain's eyes. He carried a perpetual severity like some men carry a cane. "Have you ever had to use a gun against a man?"

"I fought Indians, sir, once on a trail job up through the Territory."

"Kill any?"

"No, sir. But they didn't kill me, either."

"Why do you want this job, Benson?"

"I'm broke, Captain."

"If you weren't broke, would you consider being a Ranger?"

The cowboy was slow to answer. "I couldn't rightly say, Captain. I'd think on it some."

The captain glanced at the sergeant, who sat at the table, watching. "That's an honest answer. Sign him on, Sergeant."

The next man was older. He had sat cross-legged on the ground, relaxed and awaiting his turn. He pushed slowly to his feet and walked forward with confidence. The captain's sharp eyes quickly took in the polished pistol at his hip, the broad shoulders, the hard grin in the big man's face. "I'll save you some time, Captain," the applicant spoke up without waiting to be asked. "My name's Gabe Gribbon. This is my own pistol, and that good dun yonder is my horse. I got my own rifle. I can hit a man between the eyes as far as from here to that wagon yonder, and I've done it once or twice."

The captain turned the cigar slowly in his mouth, his eyes narrowed. He had to raise his chin to see the man's face, but somehow Captain gave the impression that he never really looked up to anybody. "I take it you've had military experience, then?"

"No, sir. Happened I was in Mexico durin' the late conflict. Business down there; seemed like I couldn't hardly get loose. But after the war I come back. I was with the State Police. I had lots of experience lawin', Captain. I've handled the rough ones."

A frown started to furrow the captain's thin face. "State Police, you say?"

"Yes, sir, Captain. Just like you."

The frown deepened. "You weren't in any outfit I ever served with."

"I served under Captain Helm. He was one that knowed how to make them stand up and pay attention. I learned a lot from him. *I* can make them Meskins look sharp and speak soft, I guarantee."

The captain slowly took the cigar from his mouth and worked up spittle. He turned his head to let it go. Then his eyes met Gribbon's. "I don't have a place for you."

The man sputtered. "No place for *me*? You been here all day signin' up cowboys and plowboys that ain't ever shot a man or been shot at in their lives, and you say you got no place for a man with my experience?"

"That is correct, Mister Gribbon. Not for a man with *your* experience."

Gribbon's face darkened. "I know what it is. It's the State Police. You're down on me because I was in the State Police. But you can't tar me with that brush, McNelly, without splashin' tar on yourself. I was just a private in that outfit, but you was a captain. You was a State Policeman, just like me."

"Not like you, Gribbon. God forbid that I was ever like you. Now, I've told you I can't use you. I have other men to interview."

"You can't just . . ."

The captain's face suddenly seemed to take on full color, and his eyes went hard. "Get out, Gribbon." His voice didn't rise, but it cut like a knife. "Git!"

Gribbon outweighed the captain by a hundred pounds. He carried a pistol, and the captain's was in the tent. But Gribbon seemed to shrink under that hard, cold stare. He began backing away, grumbling. "Damndest thing I ever seen. Let the word out that they're needin' Rangers, but when a *man* shows up they don't want him. Hell of an outfit this is goin' to be anyway, a bunch of left-handed, wet-nosed kids, led by a sawed-off runt that probably ain't got the strength to h'ist a keg of whisky onto his shoulder." He turned to his horse and started tightening the cinch he had loosened while he had waited his turn. He was still talking to himself.

"Gribbon!" a firm voice said behind him. He turned. Captain stood there, a pistol in his belt. His hands were not on the butt of it, but he made a point of showing he had it. The captain pointed to a hill which lay in the west.

"How long, Gribbon, do you think it would take a man to get to that hill and ride over it?"

Gribbon shrugged. "Ten minutes."

"I'll give you five!"

5

It had been a long, cruel day, and Lanham Neal was wrung out. So was his horse. He moved back from the river as the daylight rapidly faded. It was a long way to the ranch, to Zoe Daingerfield. He dreaded the ride. Hunger gnawed at him, but he knew there would be nothing to eat at the burned-out ranch-house. He thought of the crippled steer he and Vincente had seen. At least there was beef, if he could find it before dark folded in around him.

Back-tracking, he located the animal. He noted with satisfaction that the injury was new, and to a forefoot. That wouldn't taint the hindquarters any. He was tempted to shoot the steer, but on reflection he thought he was still too close to the river to be drawing unnecessary attention to himself. He let down his rawhide rope. The steer tried to run into the brush, but it couldn't move fast. Lanham took a quick swing, dropped the loop around the horns, flipped the rope across the steer's rump and rode away fast. The steer went down with a hard thump.

Before it could arise, Lanham was there afoot, the knife in his hand.

In a little while he was riding north, a hindquarter hanging from each side of the saddlehorn, the hide still on it to keep it clean.

For no good reason he could think of, except that some inner compulsion drew him, he angled toward the Galindo place. A dozen times he had thought about the way Vincente had gunned the *ranchero* down. Lanham couldn't blame the *vaquero;* in his place and state of mind he might have done the same. Still, Lanham had been brought up with the belief that a suspect was innocent until proven guilty. The border country put a heavy strain on that kind of credo, but Lanham still had a little of it left, tattered though it was. Vincente's training, perhaps, had been along a vein much used and abused in Mexico ever since the time of the Spanish conquest: spare not the innocent, lest the guilty go unpunished.

He could see a dim glow in the place where the Galindo shack had been. Beyond it, fire burned in the outdoor fireplace. The women didn't see Lanham, or even hear him, until the dim light of the fire picked him up. The children screamed and ran for darkness. The women huddled fearfully beside a spread-out blanket where Galindo lay. Lanham didn't reach for his gun. He doubted seriously that anybody here had one; he doubted even more that they would have used it if they had it. He sat on the horse and looked down at Galindo. He did not see him move.

"Is he dead?" he asked in Spanish.

Señora Galindo began to pray, crossing herself. The girl pushed to her feet, trembling. "He lives. Did you come to kill him?"

"Don't you think I ought to? He was helping a

bandit who had a part in the killing of three people at the Daingerfield ranch today. By all rights Vincente should have finished killing him awhile ago. And I should do it now."

The girl's voice was thin. "My father had no part in it. They came, bringing the wounded man. They told my father to hide and protect him, for he could not live to the river. They said if he did not do this, they would come back and kill my father and take us to slave for them across the Rio."

Lanham stared hard at the girl, wanting to believe it. It wasn't a new story, exactly. For years the bandits from the other side had harassed much of the Mexican population here almost as much as they harassed the *gringos*. To them you could be only one of two ways: for them or against them. If you were not for them, and you happened to be Mexican, that compounded your sin, for it meant that besides whatever else you had done or not done, you had betrayed your own.

Bad enough to be a *gringo*. Worse yet to be a traitor.

"You must believe me," the girl insisted. "I tell you the truth."

Lanham looked hard at the still form of Galindo. He was almost certain the *ranchero* had been mavericking Daingerfield cattle. Whether he was one of the organized bandits or not, he was a thief. The country would be well rid of him.

The girl pleaded, "Please, do not kill him. We will give you anything we have."

Lanham's gaze swung back to her. Her eyes were begging him. He jerked his thumb at the burned-out *jacal*. "I don't see that you have anything to give."

The girl was silent a moment, staring gravely at her father. Finally she raised her eyes. In the firelight,

Lanham could see the tears. "If you will spare him, I have something to give."

Lanham guessed later that he was too tired and too hungry, for what she said didn't soak in. "What do you mean?"

Trembling, she began to show anger. "You know. Must you make me shame myself before my mother and my father?"

Lanham leaned back in the saddle, taken by surprise. For a moment no words came to him. "I won't kill him," he said finally. "You can keep your virtue." He peered out into the darkness, where he could hear the children whimpering. "Those *muchachos* had anything to eat?"

The girl shook her head. Everything in the shack had been destroyed. Lanham slipped one of the hindquarters from the saddlehorn. "Their father has fed them plenty of Daingerfield beef before. The flavor won't come as any surprise to them."

He rode off into the night, somehow feeling as if he had been taken to a losing in a bottom-of-the-deck poker game. Least he could have done would have been to stay there and make them fix him some beef off of that hindquarter. But suddenly he had wanted to leave more than he wanted to eat.

The girl's tears stayed with him. They bothered him a lot worse than the sight of Galindo lying there wounded. Galindo had more than earned anything that had happened to him. The more Lanham thought about it, the less he figured Galindo deserved a daughter who would offer herself to save him.

The moon came up, finally, and it was welcome, though Lanham could have found the ranch in the dark. All he had to do was strike a trail he knew and stay with it. The horse would have gotten him there anyway, for horses have a keen instinct about going home.

It was eerily quiet and dark. Lanham rode up close and stopped awhile to listen. Times like these, it didn't pay to ride blindly into a place. He heard nothing. He thought of Zoe, and he knew what he had realized from the beginning, that he shouldn't have left her here by herself. But there had been no one to leave with her, and she would not go to town. It had been unthinkable to take her along when he and Vincente rode after the bandits. It would have been equally unthinkable for them to have stayed and not attempted any pursuit. He doubted that anyone could have slipped up on Zoe. She would have been hard to surprise, and once in the brush even harder to find.

He heard nothing to make him suspicious, so he touched spurs gently to the horse's ribs and started out of the brush toward the dim glow that had been the main house.

A chilling metallic click made him haul up on the reins and drop low in the saddle. "Zoe?" he spoke quickly.

"Lanham? Is that you?"

His heartbeat had quickened, and he found his breath unexpectedly short. "It's me, Zoe. Don't you pull that trigger."

"You ought to've sung out."

"I thought of it. But I also got to thinkin' what might happen if I found the wrong people here."

"I came within an inch of shooting you. I wouldn't have missed." She stepped out of the brush and into the moonlight, where he could see her. She stood in her riding outfit—the only clothes she owned now, since the fire—the rifle slack in her hands. She looked behind Lanham, into the brush. "Where's Vincente?"

"He didn't come back."

"They didn't . . ."

"No, they didn't kill him."

"Did you catch up to them?"

"They got across the river ahead of us, Zoe. All but one."

"And him?"

"He's crossed his last river."

She nodded grimly. "I'm glad. I just wish it could've been a dozen of them." She looked at the beef hanging from his saddlehorn. "What's that you got there?"

"A quarter off of one of your steers. You hungry?"

She blinked, seeming surprised. "I hadn't thought about it, but I guess I am."

"I'm as lank as a whippoorwill. We'll stir us up a fire and start a little *barbacoa*." He looked across the vacant yard. It seemed strange, no building left intact, not even a brush *jacal*. He could see the skeleton of the big house, the charred remains of two walls standing like dark ribs against the rising moon. "Nobody showed up yet?"

She shook her head. "Long ways to town. I expect it'll be daylight or better before Bonifacio gets back with help, even if they ride all night."

He gathered dry brush and started a fresh fire, well away from the burned house, well away from the arbor where the bodies lay. He turned his back, trying not to think of them. He cut green mesquite limbs for spits to cook strips of steak. He seated himself on the ground, gazing silently into the fire. Zoe sat beside him. She had never been this close to him before, and he wished the circumstances could have been different. He had wanted her like this for a long time. But there had always been old Griffin.

"You feelin' all right, Zoe?" he asked at length. "I mean, it's closer to the Bailey ranch, over west, than it is to town on the east. I could take you to Bailey's."

"No, Lanham. This is my place now. I won't leave it."

"I don't mean for good. Just for a few days . . . just to get away from here till things settle down."

"Things won't settle down, not till somebody's paid in blood for what happened today. I've made up my mind to that."

"You're a woman, Zoe. Ain't much a woman can do about it."

"I can ride. I can shoot. I can protect what belongs to me. And believe me. Lanham, I'll sure as hell do it."

Angry talk, he figured. Sure, Griffin had brought her up tougher than the average girl. He had tried to make a cowboy of her. But basically she was still a woman, with the natural instincts of one. Violence, he had always thought, just wasn't a natural part of a woman's makeup. Or maybe there were some things he didn't know.

Zoe said, "I don't understand about Vincente. I can't see how he could go without even comin' back to bury his wife."

Lanham studied a while. He didn't want everybody to know, but he decided it wouldn't hurt for Zoe to hear. "She's dead, Zoe. Nothin' he could do would bring her back. So he crossed the river. He went over to hunt down bandits and send them after her, one at a time."

Her shoulder was against him, and he felt her shiver. But when he looked, she was smiling grimly. "I hope he gets them. Every last one of them."

"The odds are against that."

"You said you-all got one today."

"Vincente did, really. And your old daddy. This one had been wounded, and the others had left him." He started to tell her all of it, but he decided to leave out the part about Galindo. The mood she was in, not much telling what she might take it into her head to do. "He was hidin' in a pear patch. Vincente got him."

The beef wasn't really done when he took it off of the spits, but the outside was cooked, and in the moonlight they couldn't see the rare blood red of the inside. What they didn't see couldn't make them sick, Lanham figured. Hungry as he was, it tasted fine. They ate their fill and then sat side by side, watching the fire die away to coals.

"It's a hard country, Lanham."

"I wonder if it's worth what it costs."

"Land has always had to be bought with blood, Dad said. There's been too much blood invested here now for me to do anything but stay." She mused. "How long do you think we'll have to put up with border wars and bandits? With havin' to look over our shoulders like frightened deer everywhere we go?"

"Right now I don't know who's big enough to stop it."

"We got us a sheriff."

"He's been in office since before the big war. Maybe he's gettin' a little tired. Anyway, there's more territory than he can cover, him and a few deputies."

"There's the United States army at Fort Brown."

"Yellow-leg Yankee officers that don't understand the country and don't care if they never do. They're just waitin' for a transfer to somethin' better. And mostly they got Negro troops that come from all over the South and are like a fish out of water in a place like this. They joined the army because they was hungry—most of them—not because they wanted to be soldiers. Every time a patrol goes out to scout the river, the word moves ahead of them. The bandits know where they're goin', how long it'll take them to get there, and how long they'll be gettin' back. All they got to do is cross over behind the troops, raid till they've had a bellyful, and cross back."

"Dad heard a rumor McNelly is fixin' to bring the Rangers."

Lanham snorted. "McNelly!"

"Did you ever see him?"

"No, but I seen a-plenty of them carpetbag State Police, before the people got their vote back and throwed them out. I got no confidence in any man who was ever connected with that outfit."

"He might be different."

"Why? And even if he wasn't counterfeit, he'll still be hamstrung by the same laws that hold the sheriff down, and the army. Anybody they catch, they got to take to town. The bandits get out on bail, and they high-tail it across the river. Or they leave what they stole and nobody can prove they had it. Not one of them ever gets hung. Not one of them ever stays in jail long enough to get tired of the cookin'."

Zoe pondered darkly. "Then it's up to us, isn't it?"

"How do you mean?"

"If the bandits can spit on the law, then we'll have to say to hell with the law, too. We'll have to do what they do, make our own law." She leaned against him. Her hand sought and found his hand. "You'll help me, won't you, Lanham? You'll stay with me?"

He couldn't have said no if he had wanted to. "I'll stay, Zoe."

She leaned against him harder, her forehead against

his cheek. Surprised, he put his arms around Zoe and held her. She was a strong woman, but not so much so that she didn't need the comfort of a man's strength. She was a woman suddenly alone, in grief and shock. It occurred to Lanham that she was in an emotional mood now that he could take advantage of, if he were that way inclined. He had a strong feeling she would offer little resistance to anything he might want to do.

Many a night he had lain on his bedroll and wished for her. Now he had her. But the time was wrong, the situation was wrong. Old Griffin Daingerfield still lay yonder unburied.

Some things a man just didn't do.

6

A while after daylight, a Bailey ranch *vaquero* came by, and Lanham gave the startled rider a message to take to his *patrón*. Well after that, they heard many horses. Lanham grabbed his rifle and signaled Zoe to run for the chaparral. He followed her, looking back. They knelt in the brush and watched cautiously. Lanham knew it was probably help arriving, but he didn't care to stake his life on it. He kept his eyes on the heavy-set rider who spurred out in the lead. He thought he knew, but he waited until certain recognition came.

"It's all right, Zoe. That's Bonifacio."

They stood up together and walked out into the ranch yard. The graying sheriff reined up in front of them. He took a long, grim look at the ruins about him and finally eased his tired body to the ground, stretching his legs. It had been a long night, and he wasn't a young man anymore. He held his hat in his hand. "You all right, Miss Daingerfield?"

"I'll *be* all right, Sheriff. Glad you came."

Sheriff Brown went through the amenities, expressing his regret for the death of Griffin Daingerfield. While he talked, Lanham shook hands with Bonifacio and looked over the faces of the twenty or so men who had come with the sheriff. Most were strangers to him. The majority were Anglos, but a handful were Mexican. The struggle along the border was not altogether on racial lines.

The sheriff said, "I've got a wagon on the way. We can take your father to town."

Zoe replied, "He's not going to town. I want to bury him here."

She received no argument from the sheriff, but she went on, "This was his ranch. He lived for it; he died for it. Here is where he stays."

"And the others, the Mexicans?"

"They were part of this place, too. They died with my father."

The sheriff shrugged. "Your choice, ma'am. We'll put a burial crew to work." He looked around somberly. "I thought we'd need the wagon to help you carry your things to town. But it don't look like they left you anything to carry."

"I'm not goin' to town, Sheriff."

The lawman's voice firmed. "Young lady, I expect *I've* got something to say about that."

Lanham saw Zoe's jaw take a hard set. She wasn't just Zoe anymore; she was a part of old Griffin Daingerfield. "This land belongs to the Daingerfields. It belonged to my mother and father. She died, and then it belonged to my father. He died, and I'm the only Daingerfield left. It belongs to me. Now, damn them, the only way they're goin' to get me off of this land is to put me *under* it."

The sheriff tried argument, but it was like running up against an adobe wall four feet thick. His face darkened, and he turned away to pace up and down the yard. He came back to try again, and the wall still stood.

"I'm stayin'," Zoe said.

The sheriff's jaw chewed, though he had nothing to chew on. "Well, we got other things to do right now. We'll talk about it some more."

"*You* talk about it, Sheriff," Zoe said. "I've had my say."

Brown gave up trying to reason with Zoe. He set in to questioning Lanham. He said he knew it was useless to try to trail the cattle now. It always was by the time a posse could get to the scene.

Lanham said, "They crossed before dark yesterday. We was there just afterward, me and Vincente de Zavala."

The sheriff's eyes narrowed. "This Vincente . . . I haven't seen him. Where's he at?"

Lanham frowned. "He's not here."

"That's his wife they killed, isn't it? He's got to be here."

"He's not."

"Where did he go?"

Lanham's face twisted. He had told Zoe, but he didn't think he should tell anybody else. News had a way of traveling across that river like it had been sent by telegraph. "He killed a man yesterday. He was afraid to come back."

"Who did he kill?"

"We caught up to one *bandido*. He was wounded. Vincente . . . well, you can imagine the way he felt about his wife. The bandit shot at me, and Vincente was defendin' me the first couple of shots. After that . . . he kept shootin' that *hombre* till . . ." Lanham grimaced. "It wasn't a pretty sight. He got scared then. Lit out."

"I don't see what he had to be scared about. If it was up to me, I'd give him a medal."

"Wasn't you he was worried about, Sheriff. Them boys across the river, they got a short fuse and a long memory. Remember old Jesus Sandoval? Bandits killed his wife and daughter, and then he killed some of *them*. He's been sleepin' in the brush ever since, on the dodge. Can't even go to his own place without company, or they'd get him. Vincente figured it'd be that way with him, too, so he lit out north, toward San Antone."

The story sounded plausible enough. If he hadn't known it to be a lie, he would have believed it himself. It satisfied the sheriff.

One of the possemen carried a Bible in his saddlebags, just over his rifle. He was a drifting minister of sorts, working in the fields and on the ranges for sustenance, preaching wherever the faithful would pause to listen. He told of the man Griffin Daingerfield and the mighty rock he had been. He extolled the faithfulness of Hilario Gomez and the tender innocence of the young wife Maria, cruelly taken from this life before she could deliver her first-born into the world to insure her immortality here. He held the Bible open but did not look at it. He quoted it from memory, his eyes closed, and finished with a prayer that was half supplication, half anger: "Oh, Lord, please receive these good people to Thy bosom and show them of Thy mercy, and deliver into our hands those heathen ones who have put them here, and we shall show them no mercy whatever. Amen."

Lanham led Zoe away from the burying. Her

shoulders quivered a little, but no audible sound escaped her. The more he looked at her, the more he saw of Griffin Daingerfield in her eyes, her strong mouth. "It'll be all right, Zoe. Maybe you ought to listen to the sheriff and go to Brownsville with him. I'll stay here and watch after things."

"Don't make me have to fight you, too, Lanham."

He had no intention of doing that. He knew that if she didn't want to go, the only way they could take her would be to put the handcuffs on and drag her. And they would have to fight *him* first.

He heard horses' hoofs drumming in the brush. Turning, he saw dust rising in the west. Half a dozen riders burst into the clearing and trotted their horses across the yard. Andrew Bailey, a neighbor, swung down from a big sorrel and handed the reins to one of his *vaqueros*. He swept his hat from his head in a grand gesture and bowed in a manner that went back far beyond the Confederacy. "Zoe, I got here as soon as I could. I wish I'd known sooner. I wish I'd been here when it happened. It might not have ended this way."

He extended his hands, and Zoe took them. Lanham watched the ranchman narrow-eyed. It wasn't that he had any reason to distrust him; it was just that it had seemed to him that Bailey used to come over here more often than simple neighborliness called for. After all, he had a good-sized ranch of his own, and it had seemed to Lanham that a man with that much country to see after wouldn't have time to go calling so regularly. He had a wife, too. A Mexican wife. Rumor was that he had married her some years ago because she had inherited some land he wanted. Be that as it may, she was his wife. The fact that he was married was probably why old Griffin never regarded

Bailey as one of Zoe's suitors, and why he never ran him off the way he did the others who came to campaign for his daughter. An old sinner in some respects, Griffin had never strayed from *his* wife and wouldn't have thought of it. Probably he never thought it likely that a man of Andrew Bailey's stature would do it, either.

That was one of Griffin's notions Lanham Neal had never shared.

Bailey was a large man of about forty or so, with a square, sun-browned face that Lanham conceded probably would look handsome to a woman; he wouldn't argue that point one way or the other. Bailey was beginning to show a touch of frost at the temples, but anyone who took that for a sign of weakness just wasn't paying attention. Bailey had been tough enough to make a go of the cow business in a country where the weak couldn't stay. He had fought outlaws off of his place more than once, sending them high-tailing it for the river. No one denied his strength or his nerve.

"Zoe," Bailey said, "anything I have that you need, just ask for it. You can come and stay with us for as long as you want to."

"Thank you, Andrew, but I've already fought that out with Lanham and the sheriff. I'm stayin' right here."

"Anything you need, then . . . food, clothes, some men to help you rebuild your house."

"Some food, some clothes . . . I'd appreciate that, Andrew. As for a house, it takes money to buy and haul lumber. What little money I have, I'll need to fight with. If you can send some men to help us build three or four *jacales,* I'll be much obliged."

"Zoe, you're a white woman. You can't live in a *jacal* like some Mexican."

"I did once, when I was little. It was good enough for my mother. I think I can be as tough as she was. I'm holdin' onto the land first. There'll be time enough someday for a house."

Bailey's big hands crushed his hatbrim, and his eyes were dark with concern. "I'll not argue the point with you, Zoe, if you've done made up your mind. But I ought to point out a few facts. You're awful close to the river here. A dozen men wouldn't be protection enough if the *Cortinistas* came again in strength. Beyond that, you're a woman, a good-lookin' *young* woman. You belong in Brownsville, with a good house and pretty clothes and the comforts of town . . . not out here in a mud-and-brush shack with dirt in your hair and watchin' all the time for Cheno Cortina's men."

"Andrew . . ."

"Hear me out, Zoe. You could go to Brownsville. I could run this place for you and split the profit. If there was fightin' to be done, you wouldn't be in no danger. The ranch could pay you and you could live the way a woman like you is intended to."

Lanham still frowned. He knew where *he* would be if Bailey took over. Out. It struck him, too, that Bailey would have to go to town every so often to report to Zoe. Lanham doubted he would take his wife along. Bailey hadn't brought her here the last couple or three years, not since Zoe had blossomed out.

The sheriff listened hopefully. "Andrew's talkin' sense, Miss Daingerfield. You sure ought to listen to him."

Even Lanham would admit it was a logical answer,

except for the part about Bailey going to town so often.

But Zoe turned it down, as Lanham had known she would. "Thank you, Andrew. I appreciate you bein' so concerned. It's good to have friends. But I already told you how it's goin' to be."

Bailey said, "Runnin' a ranch ain't for a woman. You'll need help."

Lanham put in firmly, "She's got help."

Bailey stared at him, and Lanham didn't see any good will. *Probably wishing I was the one had the Mexican wife.*

The wagon came, finally. As it had turned out, its trip was largely wasted. Not entirely, however, for someone had thoughtfully put blankets in it, expecting to haul back Zoe Daingerfield, and perhaps her father. The blankets would come in handy. They had also put in tin cups and a pot and some home-parched coffee. The possemen made good use of that while they rested for the long ride back to Brownsville.

Bonifacio sadly poked through the ruins in a vain search for anything useful he could salvage. He came trudging back empty-handed and slump-shouldered.

Lanham peered at him across a coffee cup. "Bonifacio, I'll need to find some extra help for Zoe. You'll stay, won't you?"

Bonifacio shook his head. "This is a bad place now. The saints will forever shrink from it."

"We're not saints, Bonifacio."

"Those *ladrones* will be back. They will keep coming so long as there are *gringo* cattle to take and *gringo* blood to spill. I do not want them to spill any of mine."

Disappointed, Lanham accepted Bonifacio's decision. "We'll miss you, *amigo*."

"You should leave, too, *caporál.* You should leave and take *la patrona* with you. That Cheno, he has eyes watching all the time. He will know you have stayed. He will know how many are here, and where they are when he wants to strike. Like they knew yesterday."

Suspicion touched Lanham. "You're tryin' to say somethin', Bonifacio. Put it into words."

"I have a family in Matamoros. Cortina, he will send someone to slit their throats. . . ."

Andrew Bailey took a long step forward. "If you're holding something back, *hombre,* I'll slit *yours.*"

Lanham moved between Bailey and Bonifacio. "He won't. But then, *I* might. Out with it, *amigo.*" Bonifacio stared at the ground, trembling. Lanham said, "We been friends. As your friend, I'm askin' you to tell if there's somethin' we ought to know."

Eyes afraid, the chubby *vaquero* shrugged. "Tomorrow I will wish I had not spoken. But I will tell you. Yesterday, when I rode for the sheriff, my horse was tired. I thought to myself, 'I will stop at the *rancho* of my friend Ezequiel Archuleta and borrow a fresh horse.' So I stopped, and I started to tell Ezequiel and his brother Rodrigo what had happened. But they already knew. They told me they were glad I was not here to share what happened to the *gringo patrón.* I asked them how they knew this, and they said they were here. They watched us ride out to hunt for the cattle. The *bandidos* were waiting, hiding. The Archuletas, they went and told them the *patrón* was alone, just him and the old man and Vincente's woman. They said they regretted about the woman. That was not part of the plan. But some of the men from across the river had been into the *tequila.* . . ."

Lanham's fists were clenched so tightly that his

fingernails cut into the flesh. Andrew Bailey's square jaw jutted. Zoe's eyes were half closed, but Lanham could see the hard anger building in them. Lanham's fists loosened, then clenched again. He glanced at the sheriff, and then at the possemen. "Sheriff, I'm fixin' to go pay a call to them Archuletas. Anybody wants to go with me is sure welcome."

The sheriff's worry was plain. "Now, boy, we got to be legal. Let's talk this over a little bit."

"We'll talk it over when we've finished."

Zoe Daingerfield clutched Lanham's arm. "Thank you, Lanham." Her eyes met the sheriff's. "It'll be done by law, Sheriff. Cheno Cortina's law. Let's go, Lanham."

Lanham said, "Not you, Zoe."

But she was already going after her horse. Lanham caught Bailey looking at him with a touch of resentment. Lanham suspected Bailey, too, had been about to propose a ride to Archuleta's. Lanham had beaten him to it. Bailey said, "Better stop her. She's got no business there."

"You'd have to chain her to a mesquite to stop her if she really intends to go. And it looks like she does."

7

The possemen grabbed their horses and swung into the saddle. The sheriff tried to get up ahead of them, to gain control. Lanham spurred into the lead and held it. Andrew Bailey was just behind him, the possemen stringing out. The sheriff made his way up, finally, but Lanham could sense that the posse was following him and Zoe, not Sheriff Brown.

It was ten miles across cactus and mesquite and chaparral to the small cattle and corn-patch place that belonged to the Archuletas. The possemen were tired, for it had been a long night, but they pushed, keeping close to the stolid Lanham Neal and the girl with proud shoulders and angry chin.

Spotted, longhorned cows trotted away at the riders' approach. By habit, Lanham looked for brands or earmarks, for perhaps the confident Archuletas had drifted some of the Slash D cattle over here onto their country, figuring the death of Griffin made it open season on Daingerfield stock.

The last three miles it seemed to Lanham they

ought to come in sight of the Archuleta *jacales* past every draw, every prickly pear patch. It was typical of these brush-country *ranchos,* whether *gringo*-owned or Mexican . . . you never had much sign that you were approaching one. You rode through a thicket and all of a sudden it would lie there in front of you. The Mexican places, especially, looked almost like part of the land, for they were made of materials found close at hand . . . the long, savage spines of ocotillo lined up and tied in tight rows to serve as corrals that not even a *javalina* hog would poke its snout through, the houses themselves made of brush and mud. These places invariably seemed to have risen up out of the ground. They would sink right back into it, soon leaving no trace, if they were ever long abandoned, for there was little or nothing about them alien to the land. For perhaps a couple of hundred years now, Mexicans had roamed up and down this river country between the Nueces and the Bravo, living a while here, a while there. When they left, the hot sun and the warm wind out of Mexico would combine with the infrequent rains to work on what little remained behind, so that in a few years no man would see any sign that anyone had ever been here. Always the land reverted to the lizards and the snakes and the armadillos, the jackrabbits and the *paisano* birds the Anglos called roadrunners.

Zoe Daingerfield's eyes were perhaps sharpened by her hatred. She pointed and gave a shout. "Yonder they are."

Two horsemen had ridden out of an opening in the brush and reined up in surprise at sight of the posse. Lanham glanced at Bonifacio. Reluctantly the *vaquero* nodded. "Ezequiel and Rodrigo."

The Mexicans' faces were hidden in shadow beneath the brims of peaked sombreros, but Lanham had no doubt that Bonifacio was right. In brush country a man often caught no more than a quick glimpse of a rider. He learned to recognize people by the way they sat in their saddles, the shape they made a-horseback. The Archuletas waited uncertainly, reins drawn tight in their hands, ready to ride forward or whip back in an instant.

Somebody fired a long shot that kicked up dust in front of them. The pair whirled their horses back into the brush.

Lanham raised his voice. "Let's git 'em!"

The sheriff hadn't spoken. He never got to. Lanham's arm came up and over in an arc, and he reached down for his rifle. Spurs jingled and horses grunted with the sudden effort of moving into a lope. Saddle guns slapped against leather as they came up out of long scabbards. Somebody gave a Rebel yell, and the posse hit the brush full tilt. Branches whipped and snapped, and men cursed against the painful grab of thorns, but no one pulled on the reins. Horses instinctively sought the easiest way through and riders gave them their heads, for brush country horses handled this best when left alone. Riders trained to the country ducked, stretched, twisted sideways, avoiding the clutching, tearing spines the best they could. In moments they were in the clear and had a good view of the fugitives just ahead of them, spurring desperately. A posseman fired and missed. From somewhere the Archuletas' horses seemed to reach down and pull up more speed. Across the open flat they ran, stretching their legs in long, land-eating strides.

Lanham glanced back once more and saw that Zoe was keeping up with the main body of men, her face flushed. Some of the possemen yelped and shouted like cowboys out to rope a pair of wolves. Now and then one of them fired, though shots from a running horse could as well be fired by a blind man for all the chance they had of finding their target.

The posse horses were far from fresh, but they gained steadily, most of them. The Archuleta horses, probably fresher, were nevertheless the small Mexican kind. They had an endurance that could carry a man across the river and halfway to Saltillo, but not in a hurry. Speed was not their long suit.

Andrew Bailey drew first blood. He pulled his horse to a stop, jumped off, dropped to one knee, took deliberate aim down the barrel of his rifle and fired. One of the Mexican mounts fell. The rider rolled in the grass and jumped up limping, looking back in desperation. The older brother stopped, whirled about and reached down for him. The downed Mexican swung himself behind the cantle, and the two men were running again.

Lanham saw Andrew Bailey look at Zoe with a grim smile of satisfaction. *He scored that one on me.*

Two men on a horse. *They can't get far now.* Lanham rode full speed, the warm wind whipping his face. Behind him he could hear the sheriff trying to give orders. He couldn't hear the words, and he doubted many others could. They were following Lanham, and they would follow him till the hands had all been dealt.

The gap was narrow. The Mexican behind the saddle held onto his brother with one arm and twisted around with a pistol. He fired several times. His aim was as hopeless as that of the posse, but it gave Lanham a sick feeling every time he saw the pistol flash. There was always a million-to-one chance Archuleta might score a hit. It might get Lanham. Or it might get Zoe.

More brush lay ahead. Lanham knew it was important they stop the Archuletas before they get that far. He decided to do what Bailey had done. He slid his horse to a stop, jumped down, brought the rifle into line and fired.

The Mexican behind the saddle stiffened and began to slip off. The brother tried vainly to hold him. Swinging back onto his horse, Lanham saw the brother grab at the wounded one's shirt, but it tore in his hands. The wounded man bobbed a moment, half on and half off. The brother was looking around in panic.

To the left ran a gully, a deep scar washed in the soft earth by runoff from the rains. He turned the horse to it. The shirt split, and the wounded man fell to the ground. The brother pulled a rifle from a scabbard, jumped out of the saddle and let the horse go. He grabbed the wounded man's arm and pulled him toward the gully. Bullets kicked up dirt around him, but he didn't cut and run. He kept dragging.

Lanham held his fire, letting others do the useless shooting. He brought the rifle up and spurred headlong for the Mexicans like the lead hound closing on a fox. The man on his feet saw Lanham coming and swung his rifle around. Lanham saw the flash and felt the sting of the bullet across his cheek. Almost point-blank, Lanham fired and swept past, giving his attention to the reins to keep from riding full speed off into the gully.

The Mexican staggered, hard hit. He tried to bring up the rifle again, but a bullet from Bailey's rifle struck him, and then someone else's. A dozen shots seemed to be fired all at the same time. The Mexican fell, his body jerking from the impact of bullets, dust flying from his dirty cotton shirt.

Lanham brought his horse around and came back. The possemen were circling the downed Archuletas. One of the pair moved an arm, and half a dozen guns blasted him.

Lanham rubbed a hand across his burning cheek and brought it away bloody. With his fingertips he traced the line the bullet had creased. Not deep enough to amount to anything, but it could leave a faint scar he would be explaining the rest of his life.

Zoe Daingerfield sat on her horse, looking down at the two dead men, her cheeks red, her eyes wide and wild. Her mouth cut into a grim smile.

Lanham felt a sudden dismay, for he didn't like what he saw in her face. The sight of the crumpled Archuletas was enough to make a man a little sick to his stomach. In fact, Lanham was. But if Zoe felt any revulsion, it didn't show. On the contrary, she seemed to be glorying in it.

She raised her eyes to Lanham, finally, and gasped. "Lanham, you're shot." He shook his head quickly. "A scratch, that's all."

She rode to him and leaned forward, putting her hand to his face, anxiously checking the shallow wound. Andrew Bailey watched them, frustration in his eyes. *Probably wishing it had been him that got the scratch instead of me,* Lanham thought. *And I'd as soon it was.*

Zoe said, "I'm sorry, Lanham. I didn't mean for you to be hurt on my account."

A sober thought ran through his mind. *I think maybe she's hurt a lot worse than I am.*

The sheriff looked down at the Archuletas, his face

creased with regret. Andrew Bailey told him, "The boys done a real good job. Here's the best two Mexicans you'll see all day."

The sheriff grimaced. "I'd sooner have taken them alive."

"What for? So their friends could get them out of jail?"

"I was thinkin' they might've told us some things if you-all hadn't been so quick-triggered." He glanced accusingly at Lanham, then back at Bailey.

Bailey said, "They'd have told you a bunch of lies, is all. Now we don't have to worry whether the bail is high enough, or the jail is strong enough, or the judge is strict enough. With these two, the jury has already come in. And there's no appeal."

Bonifacio Holguin had held back, loping along behind the possemen, staying in sight but taking no part in the chase. Now he came up hesitantly, his eyes betraying his fear. Lanham thought he knew what was working on the *vaquero*. Bonifacio was certain he was in bad grace for having tried to withhold information. Beyond that, he was a Mexican, and right now almost any Mexican was apt to be suspect.

Zoe Daingerfield's voice was sharp. "Bonifacio!"

The *vaquero* turned his eyes from the dead men. "*Sí, patrona.*"

She beckoned him to one side, where no one would hear except Lanham. "You're not leavin' me, Bonifacio. You'll keep right on workin' for me." Her voice was commanding. "You know this country on both sides of the river. You know the people. You'll tell everybody you've quit me, but you'll go down there and keep your eyes and ears open and let me know who-all is mixed up in these raids, you understand? You're goin' to let me know who they are if they're on this side and when they're comin' back if they're on the other. Savvy?"

Bonifacio's eyes pleaded. "*Patrona . . .*"

"I'll pay you."

"It is not the pay . . ."

"You'll do it, Bonifacio. You'll do it because you were always hound-dog scared of my old daddy, and now you're fixin' to be even scarder of *me*. You'll do it because you know if you don't I'll somehow, someday, get my hands on you. You know that if I live long enough I'll take you out to a handy tree and present you with six feet of rope." Her eyes were narrow and dangerous. "And if I die first, I'll come back in the spirit and put a curse on you and dog your steps till you'll beg the devil himself to take you."

Superstition and fear of bad spirits was strong in many of the border people. Zoe knew it. Bonifacio wept silently, his eyes filling with tears. "*Sí, patrona,* whatever you tell me, I will do it."

Kneeling, the sheriff went through the pockets of the dead men while a couple of his possemen picked up their weapons. The sheriff pushed to his feet. From his hand, a pocket watch dangled on a chain. "You'll want this, Miss Daingerfield."

Lanham leaned forward. He recognized the watch. There was no counting the times he had seen Griffin Daingerfield take it from his pocket and glance at it confidently, then look up as if he were checking on the accuracy of the sun.

Zoe clasped the watch so hard her knuckles went white.

Bonifacio had gone to Brownsville with the sheriff and the posse. Andrew Bailey had returned to his ranch with his *vaqueros,* promising to find Zoe some trustworthy help and send it as quickly as he could. He had left regretfully, for when he was gone there had been only Zoe and Lanham left at the ruins of the Daingerfield place . . . the two of them, alone.

The sheriff's wagon had left the coffee and the pot behind, and the blankets. Lanham cut some more beef off the hindquarter and set it to broil on the mesquite-limb spits while coffee simmered in the pot. Zoe sat across the fire from him, withdrawn into herself. She hadn't spoken since Bailey had left. Her face was still flushed. Her eyes had a faraway involvement with whatever images were running through her mind. She wasn't here with Lanham, not in spirit, anyway.

He was sure the excitement of the chase still ran high in her. The sight of blood had affected her like whisky, and she was still a little drunk on it.

She ate the beef and drank her coffee, staring silently at him. *Maybe she's finally coming back,* he thought.

Darkness fell as they finished eating. He glanced at the blankets. "Zoe, I been thinkin' about what Bonifacio said. If the Archuletas were spyin' on us for Cortina's men, somebody else might be, too. It'd be easy for them to slip in here during the night and get us both. I think maybe we better not stay here, not till we've got some help."

She spoke the first words she had said in a couple of hours. "What do you think we ought to do?"

"After it gets dark we ought to slip off somewhere, out into the brush where they can't find us."

She nodded. "All right."

With darkness he quietly saddled the horses, tied the blankets on behind the saddles and gave Zoe a boost up. They rode in silence a couple of miles. He dismounted and helped her to the ground, then took the saddles off and staked the horses.

"They'd have to bring dogs to find us now," he said.

He spread a couple of blankets beneath a mesquite. "This is for you." He turned away, another blanket under his arm, to find a place for himself.

Zoe caught his hand and turned him around. "Lanham . . ." Her eyes were warm. Her blood was still up. "Lanham, I want to thank you for what you did today . . . for me . . . for my father."

"Zoe, you don't have to . . ."

Her fingers touched his cheek. It was sore now, and the fingers brought pain, but he did not pull away or flinch. "Lanham, I'll never forget that you got this fighting for me."

Her fingers moved on past his cheek and around to the back of his neck, pulling his head down. She raised up on her toes to meet his mouth with her own. He was surprised at the warmth of her face, like she had a fever or something. Her other hand went around him and pulled him against her with an insistence he had never dared wish for. She kissed the wounded cheek, then kissed his mouth again, her breathing warm and rapid.

"Lanham, I want you to stay with me. I don't want you to leave me, not for a minute."

Last night had been the wrong time and the wrong place, and he had told himself there were some things a man just didn't do. Now he couldn't think of any reasons. He could only think of Zoe, of the need she had for him, and he had for her. He kissed her hungrily, the way he had wanted to since the first time he had ridden up to the Daingerfield place and had seen her standing on the gallery of the big house, her full skirt billowing, her long hair flowing in the wind. He dropped the blanket from under his arm and sank with her to the one beneath his feet.

She ran her fingers through his hair. There was something wild and violent in her eyes that might have scared him had he been calm enough to see it as it really was. "Promise me you'll stay with me, Lanham. Promise me you'll help me hunt them down and kill them—every last one of them—the way we did those two today."

He crushed her in his arms, ready to promise her anything. "I will, Zoe. You know I will."

8

Two bodies dangled from heavy limbs of a huge old live-oak tree. They twisted slowly, the Gulf breeze catching the tatters of their poor clothing and fluttering them like forlorn flags. Mexicans, both.

Captain McNelly stared awhile in silence, his jaw set hard, his beard seeming to bristle. "Sergeant, I see some people sitting yonder in the edge of that thicket."

"Families, sir. They've been afraid to cut these men down."

"Families? Then these men didn't come from Mexico. They're natives." McNelly's gaze turned to a local man who had come along with the Rangers as a guide.

The man twisted in his saddle, nervous. "Not all the bandits come from across the river, Captain. Sometimes they have help on this side."

"It wasn't bandits who hung these men. It was one of these local posses, wasn't it?"

The guide looked at the ground. "I wasn't here, Captain. I can't tell you none of the details."

"Then tell me what you *do* know."

"Well, sir, them *bandidos*, they hit Jim Sm . . . they hit one of the ranches here day before yesterday; run off with some mighty good horses. Some of the boys got together and went lookin' for them."

"And when they didn't catch up with the renegades, they chose to hang some local Mexicans instead."

The guide shrugged. "With Mexicans, it's hard to tell who's your friend and who ain't."

"So when in doubt, you just string them up."

"Like I say, Captain, I didn't do it. I wasn't here."

"You know those men hanging there?"

"Yes, sir. They're a couple Mexicans been givin' old . . . one of the ranchers some trouble over a piece of land they claim is theirs. *Claimed*."

The big sergeant nodded darkly. "It's a good thing for some folks that there's a bandit raid every now and again. Gives them an excuse to get rid of a few people they don't like."

The captain eased to the ground, overtaken by a sudden fit of coughing. It racked him mercilessly. Some of the new recruits watched in dismay, but the older Rangers found interests elsewhere and acted as if they didn't see it happen. When the coughing was over, the captain glanced at his handkerchief, grimaced and wadded it back into his pocket so no one could see it. He leaned against his horse, gathering his strength. "Sergeant, I want you to detail a couple of men to cut those bodies down. You ride over and tell those people in the thicket to come and claim their kin."

Hesitantly the guide cleared his throat. "Captain, some of the local boys ain't goin' to cotton to that much. When they hang a man, they want him to dangle there. Lesson to the others. That's why those people yonder been afraid to come and cut the bodies down theirselves."

The captain's quiet voice crackled like fire running through dry saltgrass. "I don't give a tinker's damn what the local boys don't like. I wasn't sent down here to be popular; I was sent to bring law and order to the Nueces Strip. I was sent to bring peace, and I'll bring it if I have to personally shoot, hang or club to death half the male population—Mexican *and gringo*. At least when I leave here the rest of them will be ready for a spell of quiet."

The man shrugged. "Suits me, Captain. I never had any particular stomach for this kind of business myself. But some think it's necessary."

"It isn't. I'm going to stop it."

"Hope you do, Captain. And if you do, you're a bigger man than you look like."

A rain had drifted across this strip of country, and the ground was soft. The chuckwagon mired now and again. Dad Smith, the cook, was down regularly raking huge gobs of mud off of the light wheels. To save the horses—the going was slow anyway because of the wagon—the captain dismounted, loosened his cinch and started walking, leading. The other men followed his example in military order. The guide muttered something about how he wasn't being paid to ride, much less to walk, but he gave up being the lone holdout after a while and walked with the rest.

Hours later one of the scouts came trotting back. "Big bunch of horsemen comin' our way, Captain. Movin' up from the south."

"Look like bandits?"

"No way to tell, sir. They saw us. Way they're ridin', doesn't look like they intend to try and avoid us."

The captain didn't waste motions, nor did he rush. He tightened the cinch, strapped on the pistol belt he had preferred to loop across his saddlehorn rather than carry, and swung up onto his horse. He didn't have to give an order. The older Rangers watched his example and did whatever he did. The newer Rangers, in turn, went by what they saw. The captain laid his rifle across his saddle, not with any threatening gesture but just so it would be seen and appreciated.

Captain McNelly was not given to unnecessary talk. Most of the time his men watched his face—particularly his eyes—and read there what they really needed to know. For the rest of what they *wanted* to know, they usually did without. The captain was a man who kept his own counsel and did not often bother to explain his reasons. Of his men he expected obedience, not understanding.

"They don't appear to be Mexicans, Sergeant."

"No, sir. There's twenty-five, maybe thirty of them. If they was bandits, they wouldn't ride bold as brass right up to an outfit like this."

The captain chewed his unlighted cigar. "Not *Mexican* bandits, anyway." He ordered the Rangers spread out in a skirmish line. He glanced at the local man. "Know them?"

"Yes, sir. The one in the lead, that's Jim Smith. He's one of them that got up a bunch of men after the raid."

Captain's narrowed eyes focused on the leader, a tall, tired-looking man with a week's growth of whiskers and a slump that told of hard days in the saddle. As he came within hailing distance of the Rangers, Smith raised his hand to signal his men to slow from a trot to a walk. He edged up a length or two ahead of his lieutenants. He made a half-military salute that indicated he had seen service. "Howdy, Cap. I expect you'd be McNelly?" He had a deep Southern accent. Georgia, maybe.

The captain's tone was icy. "And what makes you expect that?"

"Word's been out that you was a-comin' soon's you could get you enough men recruited. Nobody knowed just when." He turned in the saddle and swept his arm back to show off his men. "This is our vigilance committee. We're all mighty glad you made it, Cap. We're ready to throw in and help you. Just tell us what to do."

Captain chewed on the cold cigar, his eyes still narrow as he slowly assessed the caliber of the posse. The assessment done, he scowled. "What you'll do is go home."

"Home?" The posse leader pushed himself back in the saddle. "Cap, I don't think you understand how things are down thisaway."

"I understand how things are, and you'd better understand how they're *going* to be. I said you'll go home; I *meant* you'll go home. What's more, you'll stay there!"

Smith colored. "Now looky here, McNelly . . ."

"No, *you* look. In the first place, I'm not *Cap,* and I'm not McNelly. I'm *Captain* McNelly. You'll do well to remember that. In the second place, I want this committee disbanded, and I want you men to go to your homes. There'll be no more of these freelance posses out. If you're the leader of this bunch, you'll give your men that order."

Smith shifted his weight in the saddle. He was a tall man on a big horse, and for that reason he looked down on McNelly a little. He was plainly one who didn't take kindly to orders from anyone he had to look down upon. "I don't know as they'd want to do that."

"It's of no concern to me what any of you want. You disband them or I will."

"You got no authority . . ."

"I *do* have the authority, given me by the governor of the state of Texas to stop all armed and lawless bands of men. That means Mexicans . . . it means Americans . . . it means anybody who goes out in armed groups unless they're under my command. It means you, Smith."

Smith stared sullenly, measuring this little man with his eyes, still unconvinced.

McNelly added, "I have full authority to kill. In fact, I was *ordered* to kill anyone who resists. If you know anything about me, Smith, you know I follow orders. If you *don't* know anything about me, then you may be just about to find out. I'm giving your band ten minutes to break up and go your separate ways. After ten minutes, you'll all be considered a mob, and these Rangers have my orders to shoot." He paused. "If you don't think Rangers will follow orders, then you don't know much about them, either."

Captain raised his rifle a little. Behind him, leather squeaked as Rangers brought pistols and rifles to the ready.

Smith's eyes widened, following the flurry of movement. His gaze cut back to McNelly, and for a few moments he tried to stare the captain down. But McNelly's eyes were steady as a rock, and as hard. The guide nervously began edging away from what might become the line of fire. Smith's chin dropped. He cut his eyes away, cursing softly beneath his breath. He turned his horse around.

One of Smith's lieutenants rode up to McNelly and hesitantly extended his pistol, holding it by the barrel. "You want to take our guns, Captain?"

McNelly might have relaxed then, but he didn't. "No, keep them. You may need them for defense. But *only* for defense. There'll be no more of this useless hanging or shooting of men just because you don't happen to like them. From now on any such act will be considered murder. I've already told you what my orders are. You'd better make up your minds that I'll carry them out."

The rider said, "Captain, I'll never doubt anything I ever hear about you."

McNelly sat in the saddle and watched as the possemen rode by him. A few peeled off and headed east or west or south. Most lived to the north, and they rode that way. But they didn't ride as a group. They made it a point to break up into pairs or threes. Smith was the last to go. He watched in sullen silence. As he started to leave, McNelly called to him once more. "Smith, you'd better remember. If there's any killing to be done, I'll do it. Don't make me come hunting for you."

Smith didn't even look at him. He just touched spurs to his horse and rode off.

Slowly the Rangers reholstered their pistols and slipped their rifles back into the scabbards beneath their legs. McNelly gave no orders. He simply started riding again, south.

The guide reined in beside the sergeant. His hands still trembled a little as he looked ahead toward the captain. "Sergeant, if it had come to a showdown, would he have really done it?"

The sergeant's eyes gleamed. "What do *you* think?"

9

Lanham Neal had an idea Andrew Bailey was just making big talk to impress Zoe, promising so much help. He was wrong. The day after the Archuleta shooting, Bailey brought a wagon, its bed filled with supplies. He wasted hardly a look at Lanham. He swept his hat from his gray-templed head and bowed toward Zoe Daingerfield.

"Zoe, this wagon is yours as long as you need it. I hope you'll use it to carry you to Brownsville, where it's safe."

Zoe Daingerfield came near smiling. "We . . . I appreciate you bein' so generous, Andrew. And I *will* use it to go to Brownsville. But not to stay . . . to bring back more things we'll need."

Bailey's eyes cut to Lanham. "Neal, don't you talk her into any foolish notions."

"Not me. I figure like you . . . she ought to go to Brownsville and stay there. But she's a grown woman."

Bailey frowned, looking back at Zoe. "Yes, that she

is. She surely is." He studied her, and the look in his eyes was not entirely solicitude. "Then, Zoe, if you won't accept my advice, at least accept my help. Anything I have, all you got to do is ask for it."

Zoe took the offer in good grace. "I'll remember that. But now I'll only ask for the loan of the wagon and team. Tomorrow Lanham and I will go into Brownsville and buy whatever we'll need to get this place halfway back onto its feet. And try to hire some help."

"Be careful who you bring back here," Bailey warned. "Lots of people these days you can't trust." He looked straight at Lanham.

Lanham said evenly, "We'll keep an eye out."

Bailey left them reluctantly, looking over his shoulder.

Suspicious, Lanham thought. *But what business is she of his? He's already got a wife, Mexican or not. He's tied up tight.*

As before, they slept in the brush away from headquarters, then set out before daylight along the trail to Brownsville. Zoe leaned against him on the wagonseat, but her mind was far away. "Lanham," she said after a while, "besides some help, we've got to build us some kind of a shelter. I was thinkin' . . . there's a Mexican squatter lives down yonderway. Galindo, I think his name is. He'd know how to build a *jacal*, and likely he'd appreciate a few days of paid work. They're always hungry, his kind."

Lanham swallowed, glad she wasn't looking at him. He had made up his mind she shouldn't know about Galindo, for she would probably want to kill him. "Not him, Zoe. You don't want him."

"Why not? He's close by and handy."

"Vincente told me he's got a reputation as a sneak

thief. You couldn't afford to take your eyes off of him."

"We got awful little he could steal."

"Just the same, we'd be better off to find us somebody else. We got trouble enough."

Lanham didn't have a coin to his name, but he drew five dollars against Zoe's account at the hotel to get himself a shave, a bath and a clean shirt, and to be able to buy a few drinks for prospective cowboys or *vaqueros*. He ate supper with Zoe and said goodnight to her in the hotel lobby where everybody could observe his leavetaking. "See you in the mornin', Zoe. Maybe by that time I'll have us some help."

She wore new but plain clothes she had bought. She was ill at ease, for she had never spent much time in town. "I wish you would stay here with me."

"You know why I can't. Get a good night's sleep on a good, clean bed. You may not have another for a long time."

He bowed the way Andrew Bailey would and backed away from her, hat in hand. Glancing back as he walked out into the night, he saw her watching him until he passed beyond the lamplight.

Lanham knew the saloons where out-of-work cowboys usually sat around waiting for somebody to come along hiring. He had spent time there. He went to these one by one and announced his need. But the word had come to town with the sheriff and his posse. Everybody knew what had happened out at the Daingerfield place.

One cowboy said, "Sure, I need a job, but not that bad. I hear tell them *bandidos* lost a man or two. They don't like that. They're apt to go back one of these days and really sweep out. If you was hirin' twenty or thirty, where a man'd stand a chance, that'd be different. But four or five . . . we'd be like bait on a hook."

It was the same story everywhere, with variations. Lanham went to the Anglo cowboys first, for he figured they were less likely to have any tie with Cortina. When he ran out of prospects among that crowd, he started on the Mexican *vaqueros*, knowing there was always a chance he would pick up a *Cortinista*. After all, a man couldn't tell by looking.

By midnight, when he gave up, he'd found one *hombre*. This man had said he would bring his brother. Next morning they were waiting patiently at the wagonyard when he opened his eyes and blinked at the rising sun.

"Zoe," he told her at breakfast, "all the luck I've had was bad, pretty near. All I could find was two *hombres*."

"Can we trust them?"

"Can we trust anybody?"

"I guess not."

"Just because we use them don't mean we can't keep an eye on them. Unless we want to stay out there by ourselves, we got to take the chance."

She nodded. "All right. Andrew said he would try to find some help for us, too."

Lanham frowned into his coffee.

He went with Zoe to the bank and stood while she made arrangements for cash and to hold what she could of her father's thin line of credit. The bank, Lanham noted, pulled in considerably when they found out Daingerfield's daughter would be running things. But they couldn't back out altogether; they already had too much invested with the old man. The banker gave Zoe many admonitions with which she readily agreed and with which she would dispense the moment she got out of town.

They loaded the wagon and started down the street to meet the two *vaqueros*. Half a dozen Mexican horsemen came toward them, pulling aside as they neared the wagon. Zoe said, "Look, Lanham, one of them is Bonifacio."

Lanham squinted. "Sure enough, it is. Don't speak to him or stare at him. Don't let on like you know him." He said regretfully, "These days, it can be worth a Mexican's life to have friends among the *gringos*." Lanham got cold glances from all the riders as they passed by . . . all but Bonifacio. Plain enough where their sympathies lay. Cortina had them convinced.

Bonifacio didn't speak or give any sign of recognition. "Well," Lanham said, "he done what you told him. He fell right in with the crowd. Now let's see if he finds out anything."

The moon was up when they reached the ranch. Lanham rode in alone, using one of the *vaqueros'* horses. After a cautious look around, he brought Zoe. He hadn't felt secure about leaving her with the two strangers, but it would be even riskier to take her into the ranch without a careful reconnaissance.

The first few days, the *vaqueros* did more work afoot than a-horseback, clearing wreckage and building *jacales*. Lanham and the Reyna brothers took pains with the one for Zoe. At best it wouldn't be pretty, but it would keep the rain off. They built a second for Lanham, not far from Zoe's. A third went up for the men, nearer the corrals.

Lanham was careful always to keep either the two men or Zoe in his sight. On the one hand he appreciated the brothers coming out when no one else would. On the other hand he could not help but be a little uneasy about their motives. They turned out to be a genial pair and good help, Reynaldo and Jacinto Reyna. He found himself enjoying their company and feeling guilty about his lingering suspicions.

Damn a country where a man can't even trust the people who help him.

But he never felt so guilty that he let up watching. Nights, he slept uneasily, coming awake at any sound or movement, real or imagined. And he found himself imagining quite a few.

Often when he awakened, he found Zoe lying beside him silent, her eyes wide open.

"What's the matter?" he would ask. "Can't you sleep?"

She would shake her head. "I keep thinkin' of those men across the river, and of my father. I don't think I'll ever sleep right until they're all where *he* is."

In moods like that she turned to Lanham for comfort. His rough cowboy upbringing had not prepared him to give her real tenderness, but he tried. He found little tenderness in Zoe. Always just beneath the surface he sensed violence, a bitterness fighting constantly for release.

He hadn't told the Reyna brothers about Bonifacio Holguin, for if they were spies it could mean Bonifacio's life. So when Bonifacio came in the darkness of night, Lanham had to fling his blanket aside and run hard to keep one of the quick-triggered *vaqueros* from shooting him. The incident, when it was over, eased his mind on one thing. He needn't worry anymore about the loyalty of the Reynas. Bonifacio had narrowly missed having the fourth grave out in the chaparral.

Trembling, Bonifacio said, "I have come to speak to *la patrona*. She is here, *caporál?*"

"She is here."

"Would you wake her?"

"She's awake." He led the wary Mexican to the mud shack. Bonifacio stopped at the door and turned half around, nervously looking back toward the *vaquero* who had come so near to shooting him. "It is safe to talk here?"

Zoe came to the door, a blanket wrapped around her. "It is safe. Come in, Bonifacio."

There were no chairs, except a crude one Jacinto had fashioned of mesquite limbs and green rawhide. Zoe seated herself, carefully keeping her body covered with the blanket. "You have news?"

Bonifacio sat on the dirt floor, sombrero gripped in both big hands. "*Sí patrona.* As you told me, I have traveled much and listened much. But it is very dangerous. They are suspicious, those *ladrones.*"

"The news," she said impatiently. "What is it?"

"I know of a raid. Not on this *rancho,* but on some other. Do you know a man named Gaspar Montoya?"

Lanham did. "Small *ranchero.* Got a place west of Bailey's."

"*Sí.* This Montoya, he spies for the bandits. They will cross tomorrow night for certain. And if not tomorrow night, the next night without fail. They will meet this Montoya at his place and he will lead them to a ranch where they expect to take many horses. Perhaps the Bailey ranch; I do not know."

"How many men?"

Bonifacio shrugged. "Who can say? However many feel like it when the time comes to swim the river. Maybe ten, maybe twenty, maybe half a hundred. The word is out for the patriots who want to go."

Zoe trembled with excitement. "Lanham, let's go to Andrew's, now. We'll set a trap at Montoya's. This time they'll pay real good."

Her eagerness troubled him. This wasn't the way a woman was expected to act, not according to Lanham's upbringing. "Easy, Zoe. Tomorrow'll be time enough. We best wait for daylight." He looked at Bonifacio. "You won't be goin' with us. We can't risk havin' you seen."

Bonifacio sighed in relief. "It is better so." He wiped sweat from his face, though the night was cool. "I should go now, and be far from here at daylight. If I could have some coffee . . ."

"Sure, *amigo*. Come on down to my shack and I'll boil us both some. Zoe, you better get you some sleep."

But he figured she wouldn't sleep anymore tonight. She would lie awake and alone in her blankets on the dirt floor, planning revenge.

Andrew Bailey paced the floor of his parlor like a caged cougar. "How did you come by this information, Zoe?"

She glanced at Lanham, and Lanham answered for her. "Can't tell you. We'd risk a man's life if the word got out."

"Who would *I* tell?" Bailey demanded. "Some damned Mexican?" His Mexican wife sat quietly knitting. Lanham saw her flinch, her lips drawing a little tight. When he saw that Lanham wasn't going to tell him more, Bailey seemed to accept the story he had been brought. He stomped back and forth across the floor, cursing. "Gaspar Montoya! That lousy, pepper-bellied Judas! When the chips are down, you just can't trust a damned Mexican!" He ignored the fact that his wife was listening. She was a plump, olive-skinned woman seated properly in a corner, keeping her place as Mexican women had been taught to do for uncounted generations, being seen discreetly and heard almost never. Lanham figured she might have been a handsome woman once, ten or fifteen years ago, but dark sadness was graven into her face now. He guessed from her form that she took more pleasure in her table than in her husband anymore. She must know better than anyone that to Bailey she was little more than a piece of property, like his horses or his cattle. She bore with Indian-like stoicism the tragedy of rejection and neglect, but the shadows of it lay deep in her eyes.

It was a tragedy shared by many a Mexican woman, married by an Anglo for her property or for her youthful fire and beauty at a time when few Anglo women were available, then set aside like worn-out merchandise in later years as conditions changed . . . treated as a liability, hidden from the world as a symbol of some youthful folly long since regretted, long since renounced.

She ought to take a sharp knife to him, Lanham thought, *but she won't. She'll endure it however long it lasts, and when he's gone she'll weep over his grave. Provided she outlives him.*

Bailey rambled on in anger. "After all I've done for Montoya. Hired him when he needed wages . . . bought land off of him at a price no Mexican would've paid him."

Bet you didn't hurt yourself none, Lanham thought. *You don't give nothing away. When you give, you figure on getting more in return. Even from Zoe.* He reflected a moment. *Especially from Zoe.*

Bailey said, "We'll hang him so high the buzzards'll have to climb."

Blustery talk always got under Lanham's skin. He hated anything false. "You know you can't do that," he put in irritably. "You'd flush them bandits like they was quail. We got to leave Montoya for bait."

Bailey knew it. He was just talking, giving vent to his anger. But he resented being reminded of it by a cowhand. "Neal, I was in this part of the country when you was in short britches."

Lanham couldn't resist an oblique reference to Bailey's age. "I'd forgot about that. You've known Zoe ever since she was a little bitty girl."

Bailey's jaw worked, but no words came. He went back to the subject at hand. "I promise you this: Montoya's as good as dead. When we've sprung the trap and we don't need him anymore, he's dead."

"*When* we've sprung it," Lanham said. "What you do then won't matter."

Zoe said bitterly, "But I want to be there."

The Reyna brothers knelt on either side of Lanham, peering through the pale light of the half moon at the brush shack in which Montoya lived. Lanham had told them he wouldn't order them to make this ride . . . that he would hold no hard feelings if they didn't. But they had elected to come.

On either side of Lanham, half a dozen of Bailey's cowboys squatted in the short grass, watching the dim glow of a candle through an open door and window. More Bailey men, principally his Mexican *vaqueros,* waited in the brush with the horses. They would come running on signal, or at the sound of trouble.

Crouching, Andrew Bailey made his way cautiously to Lanham. "One of my boys thinks he hears horses comin'. You hear anything?"

Time like this, he can afford to recognize me, Lanham thought resentfully. "All I hear is your boots in that dry grass. If you'd get still . . ." He couldn't see the anger in Bailey's eyes, but he could feel it. *Damn good thing he didn't talk Zoe into letting him run her ranch. He'd of fired me before I could've said I quit.*

He heard horses, moving in a slow walk from south of the shack. The riders paused periodically, perhaps listening and looking. Tensing, Lanham brought his saddle gun into position. Gradually he discerned movement deep in murky shadows. A pair of vague forms emerged cautiously from the heavy chaparral. As they approached the shack, a Spanish voice said something sharp and quick in hardly more than a conversational level.

The candlelight went out. A man came out and walked slowly past the corner of the shack. *"Aqui,"* he answered. Two horsemen moved up.

Bailey whispered, "That ain't no dozen men."

Lanham shrugged. "Couple of scouts, comin' in to make sure everything is *bueno*. The rest are back yonder in that brush."

The low mutter of the men's conversation was barely audible. Their horses stirred restlessly. Suddenly one raised its head and nickered. From behind Lanham and Bailey, from out in the brush where the *vaqueros* waited, came an answering nicker.

It was as if a bomb had gone off at the shack. Montoya shouted. The two riders dropped low in their saddles and wheeled around. Montoya cried out for them to wait for him.

Bailey roared, "Shoot! Don't let a man get away!"

Rifle and pistol fire erupted. Montoya fell gasping. One of the Mexican horses plunged to earth, screaming. Its rider rolled, got up and fell again. The other rider spurred for life.

We spilled it! Lanham angrily pushed to his feet and levered another cartridge into the hot breech of his saddle gun. *Damn it to hell, we spilled it!*

He ran across the yard, pausing once to fire at the fleeing rider. He knew he had thrown the shot away, for he couldn't even see his front sight.

The fallen rider turned over on his side and fired a pistol. Bailey's cowboys and one of the Reynas riddled him. Montoya was bent over on the ground, groaning in pain and gripping a bleeding leg. Lanham saw no sign of a gun around him.

The *vaqueros* brought up the horses. Lanham grabbed his and swung into the saddle. In the moonlight he glimpsed Zoe Daingerfield's excited face. "Damn it, Zoe, I told you to stay back!"

He had as well have tried to tell it to her horse. She spurred after him into the heavy growth of brush.

They ran a mile or so, smelling the dust stirred by the unseen horses ahead of them. Branches slapped his face. Thorns clutched at him, and he felt his shirtsleeves rip from shoulder to cuff. Around him, behind him, he could hear the pounding of hoofs as his pursuing party spurred. He realized it was a lost cause. The way their own group was scattered now, it would be lucky if they didn't start shooting each other in the dim moonlight. He looked around for Bailey but didn't see him.

"Hold it up now, boys," he shouted. "Let's stop right here."

Gradually he saw the men responding to his call and reining in. The riders circled around him. Zoe Daingerfield came up breathing heavily, her blouse rent by some grasping mesquite limb.

"How come we've stopped?" she demanded.

"Because we can't see a damned thing. We could've passed them for all we know. Next thing we'll be pot-shottin' each other. When my time comes to die, I don't want it to be no accident." He still didn't see Bailey. "Zoe, you sure you're all right?"

She nodded. "I didn't want to give up the chase."

"What chase? They just melted in the dark."

Flames licked above the brush. Somebody had set Montoya's shack afire. In the edge of the crazy, dancing light, Lanham saw Bailey standing, hands on his hips. Bailey said, "Did you get any more of them?"

"Never even seen any," Lanham replied. "What happened to you?"

"Damn fool *vaquero* let my horse get loose before I could grab the reins. Left me afoot. So I finished up things around here, me and Rafael." He jerked his head toward a blocky, dark-faced Mexican who always rode half a pace behind him, wherever Bailey went.

Off to the side of the blazing shack, the dancing firelight played on a pair of sandal-clad feet, suspended far above the ground. Lanham couldn't see the rest of Montoya. He didn't have to.

Zoe took a long look, then turned her face away. "It's no more than he had comin'." But she looked as though she might turn sick.

In a way, Lanham hoped she would. A woman

wasn't supposed to take pleasure in a thing like this; it wasn't true to nature. He put his arm around her shoulder and led her toward her horse. "Come on, Zoe. This is a hell of a sight for you to look at."

She said, "It was my place to be here." He knew she hadn't softened, not yet.

Zoe was a long time saying anything more as they rode back toward Bailey's. Lanham noticed that once or twice she lifted her hand to her shoulder, and for the first time he saw a dark splotch on the torn blouse. Even in the poor light, he knew it was blood. He went cold. "Zoe, did you get hit by a bullet?"

"No, I ran into a limb. I guess I must have a bad thorn."

She reined up. They had dropped behind Bailey and the other riders. Lanham pulled aside a part of the ripped blouse and bent over close. "Still in there. Get down, and I'll take it out before it gets any worse than it already is."

She dismounted and pulled off the blouse. Shaken a little, he took out his pocketknife and probed as gently as he could. She caught her breath short and held it.

Lanham heard horses coming back. The two Reyna brothers rode out of the brush. Zoe quickly held the blouse in front of her. Reynaldo Reyna pretended not to see. "Something wrong, *caporál?*"

"Thorn in her shoulder. Nothin' I can't take care of. We'll catch up directly."

Reynaldo nodded, understanding. "*Sí, caporál.* If the Bailey he asks, we will say you are just behind us."

The thorn was big. With Zoe's shaking hand holding matches, he brought it out with the point of the blade. Then he put his mouth to the soft flesh of her shoulder. He sucked the wound clean and spat away the salty blood. Zoe trembled, her head against his chest.

"Now, Zoe, it didn't hurt that much."

"Nothin' hurts. Just hold me, Lanham. Hold me tight as you can."

He felt it then in the warmth of her face, the insistent grip of her hands—the same blood excitement that had come over her as a reaction after the run at the Archuletas', the wild, wounded spirit not yet sated on violence. She clung to him fiercely. She spoke no more, but she seemed to be crying out for help. For a fleeting moment she was a helpless girl, floundering, clutching for any straw she could hold to. He felt a tenderness toward her that he had never known and a wish that he could bring her out of this dizzying vertigo of hatred.

The moment passed and the tenderness was gone and she was no longer a girl; she was a woman, a woman who wanted him as desperately as he wanted her, a woman whose turbulence could be quelled only by another form of violence, one that passed for love. Through the fire that took possession of him, one thought intruded, then was quickly lost in the flame:

I was supposed to help her. But how can I help her if I'm lost myself?

After a long time they were close enough to see the shadowy forms of horsemen ahead. Lanham could recognize the Reyna brothers, bringing up the rear.

Zoe broke the silence. "I'm glad I went. I'm glad I saw. I want to be there when we get the next one. I want to be there when we get them all."

"Maybe what happened tonight'll scare them off awhile. There may not be any more."

"There'll be more. Bonifacio told us about Montoya. He'll find out about the others."

Lanham frowned. He wished he knew what to do. He couldn't beat the hatred out of her, and he couldn't love it out of her.

God help us all, he thought, *if Bonifacio ever makes a mistake.*

10

As they unsaddled in Andrew Bailey's dusty corral, amid tired ponies that pulled away in relief and rolled sweaty bodies in the sand, Lanham could sense a dark suspicion in the way the ranchman peered at him. Lanham took care of Zoe's saddle, then his own.

Bailey said, "You sure Zoe's all right?"

"Like I told you, just a bad thorn in her shoulder."

"She could've gotten shot. You ought to've stopped her."

"She don't ask no questions or look back. Zoe wants to do somethin', she just naturally does it."

He let Bailey make of that what he would. The girl stood fifty feet away by the corral gate, waiting. Bailey looked at her, then back to Lanham. Lanham yielded to a sardonic smile, for he knew Bailey burned with a wish to know but would not bluntly ask.

And I wouldn't tell you if you did.

Bailey said, "I'll take her up to the house to spend

the night with me and the woman." He didn't ask a question; he made a statement. "You'll be all right down here with the rest of the cowboys."

Lanham nodded. "Best part of the night is already over." He watched Bailey stride away stiffly. *He wonders, but he's afraid to find out. He's wished after her for a long time.* Lanham spat. *The hell with him. Let him sweat.*

Bailey would not hear of the idea of letting Zoe go back to her ranch with just Lanham Neal and the two *hombres*. After breakfast he insisted, "I'm sendin' three of my own *vaqueros*." Zoe protested that this would leave him short-handed, but Bailey waved off the objection. "Don't argue. I laid awake thinkin' about it, and I've made up my mind. You need more watching-out-for. These men are dependable . . . as dependable as a Mexican ever gets."

Just how dependable, Lanham found out that night.

He lay on his blanket in his dark *jacal*, smoking a cigarette that tasted like horsehair, his mind running over his many problems—the Slash D cattle, the horses, the *bandidos* . . . and most of all, Zoe. What was he going to do about her? What *could* he do about her? This thing between them, it was getting plumb out of hand. Not in his most shameless dreams when he was working as a cowboy for her father had he ever pictured the situation taking this kind of turn. Sure, he had thought sometimes how fine it would be to marry her, to come home to the warmth of her arms at night, to give love and to receive it in the seemly manner that custom prescribed. But this way was all wrong. A casual dalliance with some saloon girl in a lamplighted back room wasn't considered a mark against a man, for she was *that* kind of woman, and no damage was done. But a man was expected to stand back from a woman of family, a woman of good name, to look at her with his hat in his hand and never touch her—never even *think* about touching her—until they had spoken their vows before a preacher and sanctified the relationship in the eyes of God and the state of Texas.

He hadn't intended it any other way with Zoe; he had no intention of taking advantage of her. But somehow, spontaneously, they had slipped into this alliance with such a surprising ease that he was entrapped before he realized it. Several times he had told himself the honest thing would be to leave before they reached the point of no return. But maybe they already had.

He couldn't just abandon her, the country overrun by bandits the way it was. If Andrew Bailey were a different sort, Lanham could take Zoe to his place and leave her whether she liked it or not. But he had no illusions about Bailey and what he would do. The thought lay thinly veiled in the ranchman's eyes every time he looked at Zoe.

Better me than him, Lanham thought.

He could marry Zoe. He used to think about that sometimes, when Griffin was alive. But there had always been a worry that people would think he had done it to get ahold of this ranch, the way Bailey had married that Mexican woman. Lanham had too much pride to be branded a Daingerfield-in-law.

Anyway, what if he asked her and she turned him down? Times, the way she clung to him, he was sure she loved him. Other times he had a strong feeling that what drove her wasn't love but hate, that she was using him rather than he using her . . . that through him she found release for built-up bitterness. Times it seemed less of love than of contest.

For his own part, he couldn't tell for sure if he was in love with Zoe or if it was just the female magnetism she had. He had never had much time or opportunity to be in love with a woman before, even halfway. He had nothing to compare this experience, no perspective.

Anyway, it was a waste of time trying to analyze the situation. There was no clear way out, no good answer. Wherever introspection ended, he still thought about her . . . still wanted her.

The camp had been quiet an hour or two, and he figured everyone was asleep. He pushed to his feet and started across to Zoe's shack. She would be expecting him. She always did.

A dark figure loomed up out of the shadow. "*Quién es?*"

Lanham could see a rifle. Instinctively he reached for his pistol but found he had left it in the shack. Anyway, he recognized the voice . . . one of Bailey's *vaqueros.*

Irritably he said, "It's me, the *caporál.*"

"In the dark it is hard to tell."

"Well, it's me anyway, damn it. What're you doin' here?"

"*El patrón . . . el Señor* Bailey . . . he said for us to watch all the time over the *señorita.* He said it would be our ears if anything happened to her. So nothing happens, *señor. Entiende?*"

"*Entiendo.* But there's nobody here that means her any harm. Now you can go back down to your own end of the yard. I'll do the watchin'-out up here."

"*El patrón,* he said . . ."

"Your *patrón* can run *his* ranch any way he wants to. *I'm* runnin' this one."

The *vaquero* shrugged, resolute. "I work for *Señor* Bailey. I do as he says."

"Stand there, then, till you get moonstroke." Lanham strode back to his own *jacal.* He was coldly certain now that protection from bandits hadn't been Bailey's only consideration in sending these men. Whatever happened here, a full report would get back to Andrew Bailey in short order.

Well, so be it. I don't see why I give a damn. I don't belong to him, and neither does she.

He lay on his blanket alone, but he didn't sleep much.

In the fringe of brush, Lanham stared a long time at the Galindo place, working up nerve to ride in. He had scrupulously avoided this *ranchito* since the night Galindo had fallen before Vincente's rifle. He ought not to be here now. He told himself he didn't know why he had come.

But he knew. He was troubled by the memory of that angry-eyed girl. He realized the notion was probably crazy, but for a while he had hoped he could settle a question in his own mind. He had been badgered by a suspicion that the feelings which Zoe aroused in him might be stirred by any good-looking girl, that it was simply man-and-woman and not Zoe herself. He had thought that if he could look upon Galindo's daughter and not experience the same wanting, he might be more confident that what he felt for Zoe was gold coin and not Confederate paper.

A pair of playing children saw him ride out of the chaparral and ran shouting to a new *jacal*, built upon the ashes of the earlier one. Lanham tensed. He didn't really expect trouble, but he couldn't be sure. Galindo or one of the women could ram a rifle barrel through one of the openings that passed for a window and blast him out of the saddle. In their eyes they had the right.

Señora Galindo hurried to the door and shouted excited Spanish at her scattered children. From the shack all the way down to the field, he saw them high-tailing it for the brush to hide. Lanham raised his hand as a sign of peace, but he doubted the Galindos gave it much credit. In their situation he wouldn't.

The girl stood in the doorway, a battered old Mexican *escopeta* in her hands. If she fired it, the recoil would drive her against the back wall. She said in Spanish, "That is far enough. We want no trouble."

"I didn't bring any. Put that weapon down before it kills us both."

She held it rigidly. With considerable discomfort, Lanham acknowledged that it was pointed somewhere around his belt buckle. "Don't play around with that trigger."

Cautiously he unbuckled his gunbelt. He drifted his horse to the brush arbor and hung the belt on an ax-cut limb that stuck out. The girl lowered the *escopeta* a little, but she could still blow his foot off.

She said, "You are not welcome here. Who is hiding in the brush?"

"Nobody. I'm here by myself."

"What for?" Her tone was sharp, and now he was close enough to see hostility crackle in her dark eyes. She seemed prettier than he had thought. Anger had a strange undefinable quality that improved a woman's looks, whether it be the flash of her eyes or the dark flush of her cheeks.

He said, "I came to see if your father has recovered."

She glanced down the path toward the field. Turning his head, he saw Galindo coming up toward the *jacal* as if he anticipated a hanging. One arm was still bound. He was thinner; the wound had drawn him down. He stopped twenty feet from Lanham, his face fearful.

"We have done nothing. I swear it."

Lanham shook his head. "No trouble. I wanted to find out if you had done what I suggested . . . if you had moved away."

"We are still here, *señor.*"

"I see that. I thought you was smarter."

"The women . . ." Galindo apologized, turning his good hand palm upward. "I said to them, 'It would be wise to do as the Daingerfield *caporál* says.' And they said, 'This is our land; we stay.' What can one do when his women are both stubborn and foolish?"

The girl broke in, "If you have come to run us off, you have wasted your ride."

Lanham frowned. He wondered which she would do if he told her why he had *really* come . . . shoot him or laugh in his face? "I'll give you the same advice I gave you before: get away. But I won't try to force you."

In general, the Mexican male ruled the family. He might receive a certain amount of grumbling from his womenfolk, but with it he usually got obedience. Lanham could tell it wasn't that way with Galindo; his women controlled the household. Galindo trembled in Lanham's presence. *Señora* Galindo looked frightened but determined. The girl showed no fright at all; she showed only that *escopeta* and a pair of dark, resolute eyes.

"I am thirsty," Lanham said. "Could I have water?"

"Is there not water on the vastness of the *rancho* Daingerfield?"

"It is a long way. Anyhow, I am here. A drink of water is not much . . . not nearly so much as what you once offered."

Her cheeks flamed. "Whatever I have promised, I would still give. But I do not think either of us would enjoy it."

"Just the water, that's all I need." He moved closer to her. "I don't even know what your name is, *señorita.*"

Defiantly she replied, "You can call me *señorita.*"

"Your name would sound better."

"*Adiós* sounds better yet."

Her angry courage reached him, but not in the way Zoe did. Whatever feeling he had toward this girl was more of admiration for spirit than of desire after the flesh. Sure, if he found her thataway inclined, he knew he could accept payment on what she owed him and take pleasure in it. But it wouldn't be with the hungry, helpless compulsion he felt toward Zoe.

He had decided he had found out what he had come for. And he wasn't really thirsty. He touched fingers to the brim of his hat. "Then, *adiós, señorita.*"

11

Jacinto Reyna poked dry sticks under a coffee pot suspended over the fire. His brother Reynaldo lay sprawled on the bare ground, watching Lanham Neal pace thoughtfully in the darkness. At length Reynaldo said, "It is none of my business, *caporál*. But if it were me I would do one of two things."

Lanham stopped pacing. "What're you talkin' about?"

"Those men of Bailey's, who stand guard by the *patrona* and her *jacal*. I would dig a tunnel under, or I would walk over them. I do not like to dig."

"You talk too much."

"A family weakness. But you can trust us, *caporál*, not to talk when we should be quiet. You cannot trust *them*." He pointed in the direction of the three Bailey *vaqueros*, who sat at another fire, playing monte. They hadn't started their guard duty yet for the night. They wouldn't until Lanham went to bed.

Lanham sat on his heels and watched the pot, waiting for it to come to a boil. "I didn't trust you two boys at first, not till I had a few days to watch you. One thing I don't understand is why you came here with me and Zoe. It's not the pay."

Reynaldo's face twisted a little. "You needed help, we needed a job. And you were fighting the *Cortinistas.*"

"You're Mexican. What you got against the *Cortinistas?*"

Firelight flickered in Reynaldo's face, the shadows dark. "You know only two of us. Once there were three."

The coffee boiled. Jacinto poured in a cup of cold water to settle the grounds. Reynaldo suggested matter-of-factly, "*La patrona,* she might enjoy a cup of this coffee."

Lanham pushed slowly to his feet. "Good idea. I'll go find out."

He carried two cups past the Bailey *vaqueros.* They glanced at each other, no man wanting to arise and start the watch. One stood up to follow, shrugged and settled back to his game, for he was winning.

Sitting in the rawhide-and-mesquite chair, Zoe stared at Lanham in surprise. "First time you've been in this *jacal* in two or three days." Her voice carried a little of resentment.

"Bailey's watchdogs. They been like a grass burr I couldn't shake loose of." He handed her the coffee. "Don't burn yourself."

She frowned. "I thought you'd decided you didn't want to burn *yourself.* You've avoided me, Lanham."

"Bailey didn't send them *vaqueros* over here to protect you from bandits. He sent them to protect you from me."

"I don't need that kind of protection."

"He figures you do."

"Andrew Bailey has his own life. We have ours."

She was too naive to realize Bailey's feelings about her, Lanham decided. She had grown up sheltered out here a long way from town. There was much she didn't know. He said, "You don't want wild stories gettin' out. They can hurt you."

"How? *Outlaws* can hurt me. *Drought* can hurt me. But I don't see why idle stories ought to worry me any."

"Zoe, you got no real idea how the world works." He sipped the coffee, wondering how and if he could explain it. She knew little of what lay beyond the chaparral, of the many differences between the things the world *said* and the things it *did*. Her mother had died before she could teach Zoe the lessons a mother is supposed to pass on to a maturing daughter. Zoe had only a vague idea about the contradictory codes which dictated that natural feelings were wicked and shameful and to be suppressed. If she had been a boy old Griffin Daingerfield would have known better how to explain the markings on the moral pathways. As it was, though, he had only been able to tell her that "this you do, and that you don't do." He hadn't been able to tell her why. That was the reason he had chased off every cowboy who came hopefully looking for a smile from her. Now Griffin was gone.

"Zoe, the time has come for you to find out the way the *gringo* world thinks. People are goin' to force their ways on you whether you want them to or not."

She said stubbornly, "I don't care what people say."

"Not now, maybe, but sometime you will. And then you won't think kindly of me."

"Why? What can anybody do to me?"

"Zoe, you carry the Daingerfield name. It meant a heap to your old daddy, but it won't mean much to anybody else if bad talk puts a stain on it."

Her voice tightened. "You're ashamed of me."

"You know better than that." He touched her hand. "Zoe, I'm tryin' to tell you what other people may think. It'll hurt you someday, more than you have any idea."

"The only thing that hurts me now is when you turn your back on me."

"If I was turnin' my back, I'd of already left."

Her hands moved up his arms and around his shoulders. "I don't know what I'd do if you rode away from me. Don't even *talk* about it."

He knew he wouldn't have the will, even if he made the attempt. He pulled her close. "It's the last thing on my mind."

Reynaldo Reyna called from the darkness. "*Caporál*, a visitor."

Lanham recognized the voice. "*Caporál,* it is me, Bonifacio."

"Come ahead," said Lanham. "We'll light the lantern."

Bonifacio paused in the doorway, nervously turning his sombrero in his big hands. He looked back in worry toward the *vaqueros* of Andrew Bailey. "Are they to be trusted? They know me."

Lanham said, "In your case, they're all right."

Reynaldo brought the coffee pot and an extra cup for Bonifacio, who took it eagerly. His hands trembled so that he spilled much of the coffee. His beard was long and black. In the lantern light, his eyes looked sunken and afraid.

Zoe pressed impatiently. "What's the news? What've you heard?"

Bonifacio looked at the dirt floor. If Lanham had smelled tequila, he would have considered Bonifacio drunk. "I have been everywhere. I have heard much." He paused, until Zoe pressed him to go on. Slowly, unwillingly, he continued, "The Captain McNelly, he has come with all his *rinches*." That was a word the border Mexicans used for "Ranger," often as not with a strong dislike. "He and his men, they have been riding everywhere. They try to keep it a secret, but I know where they have a camp in the brush not ten miles from here."

Lanham blinked. He had no idea they were so close. "I don't know that they'll help much," he said, "especially if they operate like the carpetbag State Police. And why shouldn't they? It's McNelly's old outfit. What can they do that the other law couldn't?"

Bonifacio shrugged. "They are the *rinches*." He said it as if the word carried some black witchcraft, some mysterious invincibility.

"Sheriff's been tryin' a long time. We still got bandits."

Bonifacio commented, "It is said the sheriff is not happy. He has no kindness for McNelly, and no help."

Lanham grunted. He was not surprised, for there was enough ill feeling in this country to go around for everybody, including lawmen. If McNelly were to succeed where local law had not, it might not bode well for the sheriff's future, because his office was elective. But, of course, there was another side to the coin. If McNelly's tactics proved too strong for the average voter's blood—even if he succeeded in suppressing the bandits—there might be a substantial advantage in having opposed him from the beginning. Lanham remembered old Griffin Daingerfield remarking once that a man's biggest interests were women, money and politics, and that the older he got, the smaller his interest in women, the greater his involvement in politics.

The sheriff was not a young man.

Zoe said, "We made good use of the information you brought us last time, Bonifacio. We got Montoya."

Hands shaking, Bonifacio reached for the pot. "I heard."

"You have more news for us now?"

"They plan another raid."

Lanham said, "I hoped they'd think twice about comin' back."

"You killed one of their men, and you killed Montoya. That burns in their blood like yellow mescal. The call is out for tomorrow night." Lanham saw pleasure in Zoe's widening eyes. It was not a cheerful sight. "Tomorrow?" she gasped. "Where?"

"Same country, *mas o menos.*" His mouth turned down gravely. "It would be good, *patrona,* if you left this place. Go to Brownsville."

"This is my land, Bonifacio."

"They will have it before they are through. No one can stop them. And if they take you, what they do to you will be terrible."

"If I take them, they won't like it either. And I'll take them. With you for my eyes and ears, and Lanham for my fist, I'll have them all."

Bonifacio's eyes held a sadness Lanham had never seen. "You are *la patrona.* I can only tell you what I think."

"I'm stayin' right here on this ranch."

Bonifacio shrugged, giving up. "Tomorrow, then.

That is their plan. I can say no more." He pushed to his feet. "It is better I go now. *Caporál,* you will walk with me?"

"Sure." Lanham followed to where the Mexican's horse stood.

Bonifacio untied the reins and paused, reflecting darkly. "I am a simple man, *caporál,* a *vaquero*. I am not a hero. It is a bad thing, this being a spy."

"I reckon it's not pleasant."

"Some of these people deserve to die, *verdad,* because they are *hombres muy malos*. But there are others. It is bad for a man's soul to help kill another man who thinks he is doing good for his country. I look at their faces and I feel like Judas Iscariot."

"You could just ride away from here and never come back."

Bonifacio looked helpless. "You heard *la patrona*. She said she would put a curse on me."

"She is no *bruja,* no witch. And she's not in league with any."

"Strange things happen along the river."

"Bonifacio, there's no such . . ." He broke off, for he knew he was wasting his breath. The *vaquero* believed.

"The worst of it is that I might have to betray a friend."

"A friend?"

"*Caporál,* you said Vincente de Zavala went to San Antonio. He did not."

Lanham feigned surprise. "What do you mean?"

"I saw him below the river. We came upon each other by accident. He rode by as if he did not know me." Bonifacio's eyes met Lanham's. "It is unthinkable that he would join the *bandidos*. But there he was. What else can we believe?"

Lanham figured the less Bonifacio knew, the better. It was not inconceivable that sooner or later the bandits might put the *vaquero* to a test beyond his endurance. What he did not know, he could not tell. "You're mistaken."

"No, *caporál*, it was not a mistake. So steel yourself. The day may come that you must kill Vincente."

The melancholy Bonifacio disappeared into the darkness of the mesquite. Lanham could sympathize with his guilty feelings about being a spy. Lanham felt the same guilt, sending this hapless, frightened little man back.

12

Lanham watched Bailey's *vaqueros* gesturing as they reported to their *patrón*. Bailey looked straight at him, and Lanham could smell his hatred the way he could have smelled bad whisky.

So now he knows for sure. Well, to hell with him.

It amazed Lanham how the Reyna brothers sensed things. Reynaldo sidled up to Lanham and pretended to work on his stirrup. "*Caporál*, you had better worry as much about the Bailey as about the *bandidos*."

"I'll watch him," Lanham said. He had for a good while.

Bailey's ranch was spread out broadly from east to west, most of the way down to the river. There was no way of knowing where *Cortinistas* might move into it. Well before dark, Bailey gathered all the men and struck out in a long trot, taking the lead. He had made one half-hearted attempt to persuade Zoe to stay at the house with his Mexican wife, Josefa, but it did no good. Lanham had known it wouldn't. Bailey's manner with Zoe now lacked some of the careful respect he had always shown her. But Lanham saw no real change in the man's eyes as he looked at Zoe. Bailey still wanted her . . . perhaps even more now that he knew someone else had her.

One by one, Bailey dropped off the men in positions to stand watch. "Now, you all know where I'll be waitin'. Don't any of you get into a mix with them. Don't let them see you. Once you see whichaway they're headed, come to me. We'll hit them all in a bunch, not one at a time."

Bailey didn't look at Lanham as he picked the spot for him to drop off. He hadn't spoken to Lanham all day, or even acknowledged his presence. "Here, Neal," was all he said.

Zoe said, "I'll stay with Lanham."

Resentfully Bailey nodded and rode on without argument. It was dusk before he came back. Ignoring Lanham, he asked Zoe, "Everything all right?"

"It won't be all right till we get those bandits."

"We'll get them. We're fixin' to square a bunch of things." Bailey glanced at Lanham, and Lanham felt a chill.

They watched so long as there was light, and when there was no longer light, they listened. Lanham loosened the cinches and sat on the sparse grass beside Zoe. She touched his hand, then drew back. A poor time to be thinking of love, it seemed to Lanham. Then he decided he had misjudged, for she sat with her head back, listening intently.

The night was quiet except for the occasional chatter of birds quarreling in the mesquite, and now and then the bawl of a longhorned cow whose calf had strayed off. Lanham settled back for a long wait.

It was a longer wait than he expected. Pale streaks began rising in the east. Sleepy-eyed, Lanham watched daylight reach up over the brush and push back the darkness. He glanced at Zoe stretched out in the grass, her head on her arm, eyes closed, breasts rising and falling with the even tempo of her breathing. She had stayed awake most of the night, but she had finally nodded away a couple of hours ago. She would be angry that he had let her sleep.

Well after daylight, Andrew Bailey reined his fidgeting bay to an abrupt halt, yanking against the bits in a manner he would have fired an employee for. He took a long, hard look at Lanham, then at the sleepy girl just coming awake. "You-all hear anything? Anything atall?"

"Quiet as a Mexican graveyard," Lanham said.

"Maybe you was too occupied to pay attention."

Lanham's fists knotted. "You're tryin' to say somethin', Bailey. I reckon you better not."

Bailey waved him off with an impatient motion of his hand. "Never mind. You sure your information was good, about that raid?"

"Good enough. Maybe they decided to do it *mañana*. That's an old Mexican custom."

After riding on down the line to see after the rest of his men, Bailey came back, his horse foaming at the bit. Bailey was foaming a little, too. "Not a sign, not a damned thing, anywheres down the line. Your man was drinkin' tequila, that's what I think."

Lanham doubted that, but he had no inclination to argue with Bailey. Nothing was likely to alter the man's ideas anyway, so why sweat? Lanham didn't think enough of him to care whether he changed Bailey's mind or not.

Bailey said, "Of course there's always a chance they'll still come, even in the daylight. Mexicans, they don't get in no hurry without there's a posse on their tails. We'll leave some men to keep scoutin' while the rest of us go in and eat. You stay, Neal."

Lanham glanced at Zoe. He didn't figure Bailey would try anything with her so long as he had other men along. "Zoe, you better go."

She didn't argue with him. He figured she was hungry.

Lanham half expected that someone eventually would bring grub to him or relieve him so he could go in. After a few hours he decided he should have known Bailey better than that. He hitched his belt tighter, talked to himself a little and stayed. It wasn't the first time he had gone without when his belly said "eat.".

The sun had passed its midday peak when one of the Bailey *vaqueros* loped up excitedly. "*Señor,* I go for the *patrón. Allá* . . ." he pointed west ". . . they are taking horses south, toward the river."

Lanham began tightening his cinch. "Somebody watchin' them?"

"*Sí,* two men. Will you go and help them if there is trouble?"

"I'll go." Lanham felt his spirits rise, and his faith in Bonifacio. "If we have to, we'll hold them at the river till you get back with Bailey and some more guns. *Ándele, amigo.*"

Presently he cut across fresh horse tracks. The way the horses were strung out, he could only guess at the number. Forty or fifty, maybe. Hard to guess how many riders. *I'll find that out soon enough,* he thought soberly, *and I probably won't like it.* He trailed the horses, moving in a long trot. He began to smell fresh dust which hadn't had time to settle.

He spotted the two Bailey riders trailing after the horses at a discreet distance, keeping watch on the men ahead of them. They evidently gave no thought to the possibility of someone coming up behind them. If he had been an outlaw, Lanham could have shot both of them at close range with a pistol before they even knew he was around.

"It's just me," he spoke. "Don't anybody get excited."

They almost fell out of their saddles, trying to shift position to get the drop on him. They recognized him and let their pistols slide back into their holsters. "*Bandidos* just ahead of us, *señor,*" one of them spoke quickly. Lanham nodded. The *vaquero* went on, "It was me who saw them first. They were just riding along as if they were on their way to church, driving all those horses."

"How many?"

"About forty horses . . . maybe forty-five."

"I mean how many men? The horses ain't likely to shoot at us."

"Five men, *señor.* It will be easy, when the Bailey gets here. They suspect nothing. They are laughing, singing. They think they will get away with the Bailey his horses."

Lanham shrugged. It made sense, as far as it went. The only thing that bothered him was how the bandits had gotten onto Bailey's country from the river in the first place. They hadn't left any tracks doing it. They could have been playing the game safe, of course. They could have come up somewhat to the west, then cut across to minimize the exposure.

He rode along with the *vaqueros,* well behind the horse herd. *Five men.* Looked like there ought to have been more willing patriots than that to come over here and give the *gringo* Bailey a taste of *Cortinista* revenge. But patriotism was always a variable commodity. Sometimes it talked loudly in a border *cantina* but spoke softly in the gray light of dawn. It was that way on either side of the river.

Bailey finally rode up with the men he had gathered along the way. His face was flushed with excitement. Lanham noted with displeasure that Zoe was with him. *Damn it, she ought to've stayed at the ranch.* A rifle rested across her lap. *Hell-bent for vengeance. If she don't burn it out of her system, it'll get her killed.*

Stiffly Lanham said, "Well, Bailey, I sure hope you enjoyed your dinner."

Bailey's look was one of hatred. "How many men they got?"

"Five."

"Five?" Bailey sounded disappointed. "We could as easily have taken care of ten."

"We ain't done nothin' about the *five* yet. We just been sittin' here talkin'."

Bailey's face reddened. He motioned with his arm and set his horse into a long trot. The men fanned out on either side of him in a skirmish line. They began overtaking the other riders rapidly.

Lanham suggested, "Just to be safe, Bailey, reckon we ought to be real sure them are your horses?"

"They're on my country. Who else's would they be? If they scare you, Neal, stay back."

It was not so much a battle as a rout, a bloody running fight that lasted perhaps three minutes. For Lanham Neal, it was over in fifteen or twenty seconds.

The men driving the horses were taken by surprise. They never looked back until Bailey fired the first shot. They milled in confusion, abandoning the horse herd and broke into headlong flight.

Lanham never fired. At the distance he figured it would be a wasted shot. Bailey and his *vaqueros* kept shooting anyway. The fleeing horsemen fired back, more in desperation than in hope.

Lanham's horse had just started to jump a low bush when the bullet caught it in the head. Lanham saw the spatter of blood just as the horse's feet left the ground. He felt the animal jerk and go limp. It is a shattering sensation to have a running horse die beneath you. Lanham had time only to kick his feet free of the stirrups and throw an arm up over his face. There was time, too, for one quick thought: *That shot came from behind me, not from in front.* The ground slammed against him, and the horse's legs struck his shoulder as the animal came over. Lanham lay stunned, mouth half full of dirt, lightning flashing in his eyes. Horsemen rushed by him, and he tensed, waiting for another bullet that didn't come.

That Bailey! That damned Bailey! Wonder how much he paid a vaquero to do it?

He felt Zoe's hands on his shoulders and heard her frightened voice. "Lanham! Lanham!"

That damned Bailey! Bet he's riding off laughing up his sleeve, thinking he's got me killed . . . thinking she's as good as his.

He pushed painfully to his knees, spitting sand, trying to blink the flashing out of his eyes. Zoe attempted to help him to his feet, but he couldn't make it.

"Lanham," she cried, "are you shot?"

He didn't have breath for an answer. All he could do was shake his head and gasp for air. Through burning eyes he could see Bailey and his *vaqueros* fading through the dust, and he could hear the shooting. Lanham rubbed a hand carefully over his shoulder. Pain jabbed like a knife. But he was sure he hadn't been struck by a bullet. When he could speak, he said, "Just the fall jarred me. It was the horse that got shot."

It was hard to tell whether Zoe was more angry or scared. "They might've killed you. I hope Bailey gets every last one of them!"

He could have told her it wasn't horse thieves who had shot his horse. But he decided she wasn't ready to believe anything bad about Bailey . . . not yet.

Zoe looked anxiously after the hard-running horses, and Lanham could tell she was eager to go. He caught her hand. "Stay here, Zoe. You got no business in a thing like that."

"If I don't go now, I can't catch up."

"You don't need to. It's Bailey's ranch, not yours. There's men dyin' up yonder. You got no call to watch."

She gave up, for by now she couldn't have overtaken them anyway. Lanham tried to push to his feet, but he couldn't steady himself. Zoe holding him, he sank back to his knees and stayed there, struggling to regain his breath. He rubbed his shoulder again, wondering if the impact had dislocated it.

Zoe knelt, tears in her eyes. "How bad is it, Lanham?"

"No bones busted, far as I can find. I'll just be sore as hell."

She began wiping dirt from his face with a handkerchief. Done with that, she kissed him sympathetically. "I didn't want you hurt, Lanham. I wouldn't never want you hurt."

He caught her hands with what strength he had. "It hurts me every time I see you come on a ride like this. It ain't noways right, Zoe. You're a woman. I want you to promise me that from now on if there's fightin' to be done, you'll leave it to the men."

"If you didn't love me, Lanham, you wouldn't worry about me. I'm glad for that. But I can't make you a promise. You know why."

"At first I *thought* I knew why. Now I don't think that's reason enough. You're a woman. You ought to act like one."

"I've been a woman with *you,* Lanham. Don't ask me for more than that."

"It'd please me better if you'd just go to Brownsville and get out of this bloody mess."

The shooting was a long way off now and trailing into sporadic firing. The shots finally stopped altogether. Lanham shuddered, for he knew what that meant. Zoe looked toward the source of the sound, though the action was out of sight beyond the brush. "They got them, Lanham."

He sensed satisfaction in her voice. "We had them outnumbered. It couldn't have turned out any other way."

"You don't sound pleased over it."

In the back of his mind lingered a strong suspicion that many of the raiders were not so much outlaws as misguided Mexican patriots, defrauded into believing they were doing all this for the glory of Mother Mexico, when the main thing they were doing was putting gold and silver into the ample pockets of red-bearded Juan Cortina. But he didn't say that, for he knew it was not a thought shared by Zoe, and nothing he could say would change the ugly memory of her father lying dead amid the horsetracks left by *Cortinistas* on a cruel foray. He said only, "I'm just glad it's over with."

And I wish it was the last time.

With Zoe's help he finally got to his feet. He staggered over for a look at his horse and saw that it was dead, a fact he had not doubted. He thought about taking his saddle off, but he would need help. He hunted around for his pistol, which he had dropped in his fall.

Zoe said, "They're comin' back."

That made Lanham hunt a little harder, for though he doubted they would do it with Zoe and her own riders present, he couldn't completely dismiss the chance that Bailey or one of his men—probably that evil-eyed Rafael—might try to finish the job they had done on him. He found the half-buried pistol and tried to blow the dirt out of it.

Lanham saw disappointment in Bailey's eyes. "I seen you go down, Neal. Thought sure them bandits had done for you."

Dryly Lanham replied, "Better luck next time."

"Won't be no next time for these," Bailey declared, turning his attention to Zoe. "They've reformed. Permanent."

"All of them?"

"All but one. There was one got away in the brush."

Lanham gritted his teeth, partly in pain and partly in anger. More than one bandit had gone free. One of them was talking to Zoe. But accusing Bailey would be like roping at the moon. What could Lanham prove?

The Reyna brothers struggled to recover Lanham's saddle. The Bailey men rounded up the scattered horses. Lanham limped around gripping his stiffened left shoulder. The way his face burned, he knew he must look like a peeled rabbit. He started examining the animals the *vaqueros* brought in. "Bailey! Them ain't your horses. I don't see a one of them that's got your brand."

Bailey cursed. "You got sand in your eyes." But he began to look for himself, and he showed surprise. A *vaquero* came around the horse herd and said, "*Patrón,* we have saved the horses of the *Señor* Tompkins."

That appeared to be so. Every brand Lanham saw was a T.

Herb Tompkins was a contemporary of old Griffin Daingerfield, a crusty cowman of hardy Texan heritage who never asked for anything and never apologized for anything, either. His main ranch lay north of Bailey's, but Lanham remembered that another part of the T ranch lay south, somewhere down on the river.

Bailey rubbed his hand over his face. Lanham got the impression he was disappointed it wasn't his own horses being stolen. Bailey turned to Zoe Daingerfield. "I been wantin' a long time to get that contrary old reprobate in my debt. He's too damned independent to suit me."

"Right now," said Zoe, "I'm a lot more worried about Lanham. He took a bad fall. We need to get him back to your place to rest."

Bailey made no show of sympathy. "Never seen the cowboy yet that you could kill with a hickory club. But I reckon one of them T horses is good enough for him. Rafael, rope out that Roman-nosed gray for Neal."

Bailey knew horses; Lanham would grant him that. He had glanced into the *remuda* and picked out the meanest-looking animal in it.

Reynaldo Reyna saddled him for Lanham and

asked quietly, "You want me to try him first? You look in no condition to ride broncs."

Lanham gritted, "I'll ride *this* one if it kills me." It almost did. The gray pitched a few jumps. Any other time, Lanham could have ridden him without missing a puff on his cigarette. The horse jolted him hard, but Lanham stayed. Afterward, they started for Bailey's.

He lay on the hard plank floor of the front gallery most of the afternoon. Periodically Zoe applied a cool, wet cloth to his skinned face. It helped his feelings, if nothing else.

Late in the afternoon he heard horses and sat up. Bailey walked out onto the gallery, squinting against the sun. A bearded old brush-country cowman rode up, flanked by half a dozen grim *vaqueros*. This was Tompkins.

"Bailey," Tompkins called, "I got trouble. Raiders. They killed some of my men and took a lot of my horses."

Bailey stepped confidently down from the gallery to meet him. "You must've missed the man I sent to tell you. We got your horses back. I got them penned yonder in my big corral."

The old cowman's bearded jaw dropped in surprise. For a moment a grin broke over his face. Suddenly it was gone, and the gray color of his beard seemed to spread over his cheeks. "How'd you get them?"

"We jumped the raiders over west of here. We killed four of them. One got away."

Something in the old man's face brought Lanham to his feet. Instinct told him something was badly wrong.

Tompkins' voice was cold as cemetery clay. He pointed to one of his riders. "Here's the one that got away. He's one of my own. This mornin' I sent five men south with horses, bound for my river ranch." His stubby finger jabbed straight at Bailey. "You miserable, stupid, bloodlovin' son of . . . You killed four of my Mexican cowboys!"

13

It had been a long, sad ride home. Zoe sat weeping in her *jacal*. Lanham paced the yard in the dusk, the shoulder hurting him every step. The Reyna brothers hunched beside their fire, sipping black coffee in silence. None of the Bailey *vaqueros* had returned with them.

In his mind Lanham kept hearing the faraway sound of the Tompkins riders, singing as they drove the horses. It was a Mexican song he had known for years, one he would never forget if he lived to be a hundred. He walked to the fire and tried some of the coffee out of the Reynas' pot. Usually they made fair coffee, but tonight it wasn't fit to drink. Or maybe Lanham just wasn't fit to drink it. He sipped a little and turned the cup upside down. Reynaldo glanced at him, then looked away, nursing his own sorrow. The Reynas had been in on the chase all the way. Lanham didn't dare ask them if they had shot anybody.

He looked toward Zoe's shack. She hadn't been out since they had reached home. "I'll go try and talk to her again." He spoke more to himself than to the Reynas. "Not that it'll do any good."

He found her sitting in the rawhide chair, staring at the dirt floor. He lighted the lamp, and he could see the redness of her eyes. "Come on out, Zoe, and get you some air. You ought to eat you some supper, too."

She shook her head, not answering.

"Wasn't your mistake; it was Bailey's."

"It was everybody's mistake. We were all in on it."

"Well, it's done." He couldn't dismiss it the way Bailey had tried to, telling everybody within earshot that it didn't matter much anyway, that they were just Mexicans. It was a wonder to Lanham that Bailey managed to keep any Mexican *vaqueros,* much less his wife. "Zoe, nothin' you or anybody can do will change what's already happened. Main thing is to be sure nothin' like it ever happens again."

"How can we be sure of that?"

"For one thing, if any more shootin's to be done, we'll leave it to McNelly and his Rangers. That's what they come for."

Zoe's tears still trailed down her cheeks. "Why didn't those bandits come, Lanham? If they'd come like they was supposed to, this wouldn't have happened."

"We can't blame this on the bandits. We done it ourselves."

"At least you have one consolation, Lanham. You didn't kill anybody."

"I might have, though, if one of Bailey's *vaqueros* hadn't shot the horse out from under me."

"One of Bailey's . . . What do you mean?"

He hadn't meant to say it. The words had slipped out. Now he'd have to go on with it. "Wasn't the

Tompkins cowboys who killed my horse. That bullet came from behind me."

"You sure?"

"Sure's I'm standin' here."

She puzzled. "Must've been an accident."

"You bet it was. He figured on killin' me."

Zoe stared, not believing. "Not Bailey. Why would he?"

"Next time you're around him, Zoe, watch the way he looks at you. He wants you bad enough to kill whoever stands in his way. And I'm standin' in his way."

"Lanham, you're wrong."

He shrugged. "You just watch him, that's all."

At least she wasn't crying anymore. He had gotten her mind off of that, for the moment. She held her silence a long time. Finally she took his hand. "Lanham, what'll we do?"

"We'll stop worryin' about killin' bandits, that's one thing. If Bonifacio brings any more reports, we'll send him to the Rangers. We'll be busy enough just takin' care of this ranch."

"The men who killed my father . . . they're still down there somewhere."

"They'll get caught up with, sooner or later. A man pulls a knife often enough, somebody'll eventually cut his throat for him. Let God take care of them, Zoe."

She shook her head. "His vengeance goes awful slow, sometimes."

"But He gets the last crack at them. Some day they all got to stand there in front of that gate and let Him pass judgment. So *let* Him pass judgment. We got a ranch to run."

She didn't reply.

* * *

Into that brooding camp, Bonifacio came back. Lanham could tell by the set of the *vaquero*'s shoulders that he hadn't heard. Bonifacio looked almost cheerful in comparison to his last visit here. He swung down from the saddle and walked straight to the Reynas' fire. "How about some coffee?" When the Reynas just sat and looked at him blankly, he said again, "It's been a long ride, and I'm dry. How about some coffee? What's the matter with you *hombres* . . . you *borracho* or something?"

Lanham strode out with his hands shoved deep into his pockets. "No, Bonifacio, they're not drunk. Get you a cup."

Bonifacio looked at him in the firelight, puzzling. He poured the coffee. "Thought I should come and tell you, *caporál* . . ."

"Tell me what?"

"Tell you the *bandidos* didn't cross the river after all."

"We found that out."

"Is that why you all look so *triste*? You didn't kill any bandits."

"No, no bandits."

"It is just as well. You don't have to carry any of them on your conscience. And neither do I."

Lanham couldn't return Bonifacio's gaze as the Mexican squatted on his heels by the fire. He looked into the glowing coals, flexing his hands. "How come they didn't ride across?"

"A strange thing, *caporál,* a thing to make your blood run cold. They had it planned to come, and then the thing happened. Three of the men who would lead it, they died."

"Died?"

"All the same night, but not together. Each one in a different place, but each the same way, his throat slit from one ear across to the other. It would have been a horrible sight, except . . ."

"Except?"

"Except every one of them had been on the raid here, the one that killed the *patrón* Daingerfield. A thing to make a man wonder, no?" Bonifacio shuddered. "It is as if the *patrón* his angry spirit had come to take revenge. Perhaps he is here with us now, in this dark."

A chill ran down Lanham's back. He knew what vengeful spirit had been on the prowl. Vincente de Zavala! The irony of it cut him deep. Vincente had killed three of the guilty. But because of that, four innocents had died.

Bonifacio said, "They are saying it is the evil eye. Another bandit was hit by the *susto,* the great fright. A *curandero* broke an egg under his bed and passed the shell over him, and the egg went cloudy. It is a sure mark of the evil eye. Do you think it could be the *patrón* himself?"

Lanham didn't try to answer the question. "We made a mistake today, Bonifacio. We was out huntin' those bandits you said was comin'. We killed four men. Turned out they wasn't bandits. But they're dead, just the same."

The cup sagged in Bonifacio's hands, and most of the coffee spilled on his boots. He did not notice it. He stared at Lanham, and slowly he seemed to draw into an agonized knot. "Four men?"

"Four men."

Bonifacio slowly turned his hands, looking at them. "It is there, then, the blood. I can feel it, cold as death."

"You're not responsible. The rest of us, but not you."

"Who was killed?"

"*Vaqueros* from the Tompkins ranch."

Bonifacio slumped, his sorrow beyond measuring. "I had friends there."

"You didn't shoot anybody."

"Judas Iscariot did not nail Jesus to the cross."

Zoe came out of her *jacal.* "Did I hear Bonifacio?"

The Mexican didn't answer. Lanham replied, "Yes, Zoe. I just told him."

She came to the fire and saw the Mexican's distress. "Don't accuse yourself, Bonifacio. It was those bandits' fault. They'll pay for it."

Lanham looked up, half inclined to argue the point. But what was to be gained?

Zoe asked Bonifacio why the bandits hadn't come, and he told her. She nodded grimly at Lanham. "Vincente."

Lanham wished she hadn't said it, but he replied, "I reckon."

Bonifacio didn't comprehend. "What is this about Vincente?"

Lanham frowned. The subject shouldn't have come up, but there it was. "I lied to you about Vincente. He didn't go north; he went south. He went for blood."

Zoe said with satisfaction, "And he got it."

Bonifacio blinked. Things were starting to add up for him. But he had one puzzle. "Tonight I rode by the Galindo place. I found him crippling around, and he told me Vincente had shot him. Why would Vincente shoot Galindo if he was only after outlaws? You didn't tell me about that, *caporál.*"

Zoe's eyes sharpened. "You didn't tell *me,* either."

Defensively Lanham said, "Vincente made a mistake, that's all. You had any supper, Bonifacio? We'll fix you somethin'."

"I ate at Galindo's." Bonifacio was not about to be sidetracked. "Vincente is not one to shoot a man without reason."

Zoe began pressing, too. "He's right, Lanham. Vincente wouldn't shoot a man unless he had cause for it. And you wouldn't lie to me without cause. Now, how come you did?"

"I didn't lie to you."

"You didn't tell me the whole story. That's the same thing." Anger was rising in her voice.

Trapped, Lanham ground his teeth together. Well, hell, it all had to come out sometime. "The day it all happened, nobody was in a mood to reason. It was a plain-out mistake, and I figured the less said the better. But all right: when Vincente found his wife and old Griffin dead, he started lookin' for somebody to kill. He took a notion Galindo had throwed in with the bandits, so he put a bullet in him. That's all; he just jumped off the deep end."

"He must've thought he had a good reason."

"We found a wounded bandit hidin' in the brush close to Galindo's. I told you about him. He's the one Vincente killed."

"You told us about the bandit; you didn't tell us about Galindo."

Lanham was sweating. "I didn't see any real evidence against him. And I figured if I said anything, somebody'd ride over there and shoot him like a dog."

Zoe's voice was sharp. "Like a *mad* dog!" She turned on him. "You had no right to keep this from me, Lanham . . . no right."

"If you could see yourself now, you'd know why I done it. You got killin' in your eyes, Zoe."

"And why not? That Galindo, he's fed his family off of Daingerfield beef for years. My daddy could have hung him a dozen times, and *should* have. Vincente knew, if *you* didn't. The only thing I can't understand is why he didn't finish the job and kill him."

"I stopped him, that's why. I figured he was wrong."

Her eyes were narrowed. "I think I'd rather trust Vincente's judgment in this than yours. He knows these people, he's one of them."

"You don't shoot a man on suspicion."

"Don't you?" In the flicker of firelight, the deep shadows made her face look a little like old Griffin Daingerfield's. And she sounded like him. "I'll decide that for myself. We're ridin' over there, Lanham."

Reluctantly he said, "I'll take you in the mornin'."

"Not in the mornin'. Now!"

"This time of the night? Don't talk like a crazy woman. It's waited all these weeks. It'll wait till mornin'."

"I'm goin' tonight, Lanham, with you or without you. And if I decide Galindo has had a hand in this, I'll kill him."

She wasn't bluffing, he realized with a chill. She was old Griffin's daughter. "That's why you're not goin', Zoe. You're goin' to go back to your *jacal* and get yourself some sleep, and then we'll thrash this thing out tomorrow. You'll see things clearer in the daylight."

"I'll see to shoot that Galindo. I can do that in the dark." She turned. "Reynaldo, catch me a horse. Catch one for you and your brother, too. I'll want you-all to go with me."

Reynaldo looked at Lanham. Lanham shook his head. "No, Reynaldo. Just stay right where you're at."

She turned on Lanham in fury. "*I* own this place, not you. *I'll* give the orders."

"Not this order."

"You're fired, Lanham Neal. Get off of my place."

"I'm stayin' right here. Somebody's got to keep you from makin' a mistake, Zoe. I'm stayin', and so are you."

She turned sharply and moved toward the *jacal*. She stopped then, looking angrily back over her shoulder. "If you won't help me, I'll bet Andrew Bailey will."

Before anyone could stop her, she trotted to Bonifacio's tied horse, shoved a foot into the stirrup and swung up, her skirts flaring out and riding high up her legs. She shouted at the horse and broke him into a run. Lanham lunged at the reins but missed. The horse struck him with its shoulder and sent him stumbling. The pain of today's fall pounded through him again. On hands and knees, breathing the dust left by the horse's hoofs, he stared in dismay at the darkness which had swallowed her up.

Reynaldo came running. "Maybe we can catch her, *caporál*."

Lanham pushed to his feet. Futility had a taste like lye soap. "Time we got our horses caught and saddled, she'd be too far off in that dark. We never would find her." He gripped his shoulder, for the pain was considerable. "Bonifacio, you said you know where the Rangers are camped at. Reckon you could find the place tonight?"

"I could get close. With daylight, I could find it in a hurry."

"That's what you better do, then. Go fetch that carpetbagger and as many Rangers as he can spare. Get them over to Galindo's as quick as you can. It may take them all to stop a shootin'." He turned to

Reynaldo and Jacinto Reyna. "I'm goin' to go see what I can do to get Galindo the hell out of the way."

"We'll go with you," said Reynaldo.

"It'll mean your jobs."

The brothers looked at each other and made their decision in a hurry. "Today we helped kill four men," Reynaldo replied. "Perhaps the saints will like us better if now we help you save one."

"Thanks, *amigos*. We better be gettin' after it."

14

Galindo was not so crippled as Lanham had thought. Fear grabbed the *ranchero,* and he took little time rolling up a blanket with a few supplies in it, catching a horse and striking out for the river in a lope. He left his family behind with no more than a hasty *adiós.*

If they caught him, they wouldn't have much, Lanham thought disgustedly, looking off into the early-morning darkness, listening to the fading hoofbeats. He turned to *Señora* Galindo, somehow apologetic even though he knew he had no reason to be. If Galindo had no more pride than to abandon his family, it wasn't any fault of Lanham's. "I see you have an oxcart," he said in Spanish. "Pick out what you want to take, and we'll load it for you. We'll have you on your way by daylight."

"On our way to where?" The chunky Mexican woman frowned. "We have nowhere to go. This is home."

"Not for long. They won't let you live here anymore."

"Our name is on the papers in the house of the law in Brownsville."

"It's a long way to Brownsville. Besides, they have your husband's name on *another* list. We'd better get you started."

Señora Galindo just stood there. The daughter spoke sternly, "My mother is trying to tell you, we are not going. Here we are; and here we stay. With Papa or without him."

Lanham turned to the Reynas. Reynaldo made a gesture which said in essence that if a foolish woman has made up her mind, there is little use in a man making a fool of himself also by arguing with her.

"When those people get here," Lanham warned, "their inclination will be to burn this place down around your ears, the way Vincente did."

The girl said, "You can stop them."

He did not share her confidence. "Even if we managed to talk them out of it—which I doubt—your father is gone. You'd have to work this place without his help."

Her eyes said what her lips could not, for it would be disrespectful: *we always did.*

Lanham tried to think of other arguments, but nothing came to mind that he thought would sway these women. He shrugged, finally. So be it. All he could do now was wait. "You have any coffee? I'd sure like to fix some."

He built a fire in the outdoor pit and boiled coffee in a bucket. It didn't taste very good, but it gave him strength, and it gave him something to do with his hands while he waited for daylight. He wondered where Bonifacio was, and if he really knew how to find the Ranger camp or if he had just been bragging.

The children had stirred out of their sleep briefly when their father left, but they had returned to their blankets. The mother and the oldest daughter didn't go back to bed. They sat in front of the house near Lanham and the Reynas, waiting in passive silence. Lanham looked at first one of them, then the other. He spent a lot more time studying the girl than her mother. It seemed to him she could be a surpassingly pretty girl in her own way if she had some American-woman clothes and fixed herself up American-woman style. But he knew that was just prejudice; he ought to accept her by her own standards. To the Mexican people she probably looked fine just the way she was. The longer Lanham stared at her, the better she looked to him. He decided it was unfair to judge her by any measure other than her own. She was young; that was the main thing. To him, most young girls looked pretty unless they ate too much and got fat. There probably had never been enough food around here anyway. She had pleasant features. Beyond that she had a spirit that must have come from her mother's side of the family, for Galindo hadn't shown any.

Good thing for Galindo he's got strong women, or he wouldn't even own a pair of britches, Lanham thought.

The cup gradually went cold in his hands. He nodded off to sleep. After a while Reynaldo Reyna awakened him with a gentle nudge. Lanham looked up startled, into the sunrise.

"Horses, *caporál*."

Lanham heard them. He pushed to his feet. "Sure do hope it's those Rangers." But he had a strong feeling he wouldn't be that lucky. He got his rifle and motioned for the Reyna brothers to split up, one on each side of him. He motioned for the women to go into the *jacal.*

Andrew Bailey and Zoe Daingerfield broke out of the brush, followed by half a dozen of Bailey's riders. Lanham raised his rifle to the ready but avoided pointing it at anyone. The Reynas were not so particular. They pointed theirs at a couple of the Bailey men who had spent so much time at the Daingerfield place, watching Zoe and Lanham.

Bailey and Zoe came up close and stopped. Zoe's eyes angry. "We came for Galindo."

"Too late. He's already *por allá,* across the river."

"I saw the women run for the shack. He wouldn't go off and leave his family."

"The hell he wouldn't."

Zoe looked at him hard, until she evidently made up her mind he wasn't lying. "All right then, he's gone. But we'll make sure he don't have anything to come back to." She pointed at the remains of the fire where the coffee bucket sat. "Let's burn it, Andrew."

Lanham said, "Let's not."

Zoe blinked. Bailey said, "You won't stop us, cowboy." He swung down from the saddle and took a step toward the fire. He stopped abruptly, looking down the muzzle of Lanham's rifle.

"I'll stop *you,*" Lanham told him.

Bailey's mouth dropped open. "You won't kill me."

"Why not? You tried to kill *me.* Difference is, I'm a heap sight closer to the target."

Lanham allowed himself a cautious glance at the *vaqueros* and saw that the Reynas had them under control. The only one Lanham had to worry about was Bailey. And, perhaps, Zoe.

In a minute he knew he didn't have to worry about

Bailey, not unless he turned his back on him. Bailey tried to show defiance, but fear seeped into his eyes. *I got him,* Lanham thought. *Get the drop on him and he's like a dog—all bark and no teeth.* "Climb back up on that horse, Bailey."

Bailey tried to stare him down, but Lanham thrust the rifle barrel forward. Bailey backed off, putting his left hand up on his horse's mane, the right on the saddlehorn.

Zoe's voice was bitter. "How come you're doin' this, Lanham?"

"Because what you're fixin' to do is wrong. Shootin' people, burnin' them out . . . that ain't your true nature, Zoe. One of these days this sickness is goin' to leave you, and you'll hate what you've done. We can't undo what we did yesterday, but we can stop before we do any more. Let me take you home."

Anger mottled her face. "When I finish what I came to do, I'll go home. You won't be goin' with me."

She wasn't through yet; he could tell that. *Where the hell is Bonifacio at with them Rangers? What if he got lost in the dark? What if they moved their camp?*

Lanham made up his mind to stall her as long as he could. Maybe if he kept her talking, the anger would boil out of her and she'd start thinking on a straight line again. Maybe she would get out of the notion, though offhand he couldn't remember any notion he'd ever seen her get out of if she had once made up her mind about it.

Zoe hadn't come here to argue. She swung her leg over the man's saddle she was riding and dropped to the ground, skirts flaring. Resolutely she moved toward Lanham. He backed away, trying to maintain the distance between them. She leaned over and took a burning stick out of the fire.

"Call them women and tell them to get out of that shack. I'm fixin' to touch it off."

"There's kids in there, Zoe. You burn that *jacal,* they got no place to live."

"Tell them, Lanham."

"No, Zoe. You're not going to burn that shack."

He heard a commotion behind him but didn't dare look back. He could tell that the women and the children were coming out, scared.

Zoe watched them. Most of all she watched the girl. "Now maybe I see why you were so interested in protectin' these people, Lanham. I didn't know they had a girl like that."

"I never touched, her, Zoe. Never intended to."

She didn't believe him. She started toward the shack, holding the blazing brand in front of her. Lanham said, "Stop, Zoe."

She kept moving, her eyes on him. He raised the rifle to his shoulder. She paused in doubt, regained her confidence and started again. Lanham aimed the rifle. When she didn't stop, he took a half breath and squeezed the trigger. The brand leaped from her hand, showering her with sparks and splinters. With a startled cry she jumped backward, her eyes hurt and bewildered. Bailey reached for his pistol but caught himself and raised his hands again as the muzzle of Lanham's rifle jerked toward him, smoking.

The surprise drained from Zoe's eyes, and her jaw set hard. "That proved it, Lanham. You won't shoot me." Leaning down, she picked up the bullet-shattered stick. A blaze still clung stubbornly to it. She started toward the shack again. Lanham backed slowly, keeping in front of her.

"Zoe . . ."

She kept walking.

When she was two paces from the shack, he knew there was only one way to stop her. He brought the rifle to his shoulder again. "Zoe, stop!"

Glaring, she took another step. Cold sweat broke across his face. "God help me," he whispered, and he fired.

She screamed. The stick dropped to her feet. She staggered backward, clutching at her arm.

Bailey stood like stone, gray with fear. The *vaqueros* froze in their saddles. Zoe slowly went to one knee. Blood ran between her fingers. Her face was white as milk.

Lanham dropped the rifle and ran to her. He grabbed her to keep her from sagging to the ground. "Zoe, I didn't want to do it."

Tears ran down Zoe's cheeks. She turned her head to look at the wound. Lanham ripped the sleeve away and saw his aim had been good. The bullet had not bitten deeply enough to strike bone. "I'm sorry, Zoe. You made me do it."

Zoe jerked away from him, her eyes bitter. The Galindo women took over. They stanched the flow of blood. *Señora* Galindo brought fresh goat's milk and cleansed the wound while Zoe sat in resentful silence, wincing. She wouldn't look at Lanham, but she stared at the girl, hating her.

One shot had taken the fight out of Bailey and his men.

"Zoe," Lanham said, "you're goin' to get a whole lot sicker before you get any better. Send Bailey and his bunch on back. I'll take you home when you're able to go."

Her gaze swung slowly to him, her eyes clouded. "You won't take me anywhere, Lanham Neal. If ever you set foot on my place again, you'll be shot. If I can do it, I'll shoot you myself." She looked around for Bailey. "Andrew, take me home."

Bailey stepped forward, arms outstretched to take her. He helped her onto her horse, then swung into his own saddle. He paused for a last word. "Takes a lot of guts, Neal, to shoot a woman."

Lanham made no reply. *It took more than anybody will ever know,* he thought, suddenly shivering. He stood and watched until they disappeared into the brush, and he listened until they faded beyond hearing. He turned finally to the Reynas. "We're out of a job . . . all of us."

Reynaldo shrugged. Jacinto said, "We have been out of a job before."

"I didn't want to shoot her. I hope you know that."

"We know. If you had to do it again, you would have to do the same."

Lanham looked down at the stick of wood Zoe had dropped. Some of her blood still spotted the ground. "I don't know. I doubt I could."

The Galindo girl brought a basket-covered jug from the shack and held it out to Lanham. "You need this."

He took out the corncob stopper and tipped the jug three times before he passed it on to the Reynas. The girl stared at him a long while, her eyes grateful. She said, "Words aren't enough."

The tequila churned in him. "Words'll do. I didn't ask you for anything; I don't expect anything."

She was a desirable girl, but he didn't want to think about that. He wanted to think about Zoe. "Better go see after your mother. I think this whole thing has left her a little sick."

Reynaldo watched the girl go. Philosophically he

said, "It is not all bad, *caporál.* You have lost one woman, but you have gained another."

The Rangers came, finally. Lanham muttered under his breath and pushed to his feet, waiting while they rode across the clearing. He looked a moment at Bonifacio, silently cursing him for being so slow. Then his gaze went to the slight, bearded man who led the riders. This must be McNelly. Lanham was not much impressed by the looks of him. From the stories he had heard, McNelly should have stood seven feet tall.

Bonifacio spurred out in front, relief washing across his face as he saw that the place was still intact. "I was afraid, *caporál.* But I see we got here in time."

"In time, hell; you're too late."

"I see no damage done."

Lanham pointed to the blood on the ground. "It was done. *La patrona* was shot."

Bonifacio slumped, till Lanham told him the wound was not serious. "Go to her, Bonifacio. She'll need help. You're the only old hand she has left."

Lanham went back to the coffee bucket. By now the coffee had boiled black and vile, but it went with the way he felt.

McNelly came to him presently. "Mind if I have a cup of this?" There was a pallor to his skin. He looked as if he needed something more medicinal than coffee. Lanham said, "Help yourself. You'll regret it."

"Those *vaqueros* of yours, they told me what happened. Today and yesterday. I can imagine how you feel."

"Can you?"

"As I understand it, this Galindo is a thief, possibly even in league with the river bandits."

"Could be. We don't know that for a fact."

"This Galindo girl . . . something between you and her?"

Lanham cut the captain a sharp, angry glance. "You ask a hell of a lot of questions. No, I never even seen her but once or twice in my life. Never was within three foot of her."

"That's what I figured. So what you did today, you did because you knew it was right, and not for personal reasons."

"I had a personal reason. I had to stop Zoe before she . . . before *we* . . . went any farther than we already had. I stopped her because she was wrong." He clenched his teeth. "Always did seem like I brought hard luck to everybody I was ever around. I sure didn't do *her* no good."

"She means a great deal to you, doesn't she?"

"Like I said, you ask too damn many questions."

"I've had to do things I didn't like, Neal, things I regretted and *will* regret to the last day I live. But they were duty. Duty comes first, if a man thinks anything of himself."

"I wasn't thinkin' about duty. Last time I worried about duty, some damn Yankee shot me in the hip."

"Maybe you didn't figure it as duty, but that's what was beneath it." McNelly's face twisted at the taste of the coffee, and he spat it out. A show of judgment, Lanham thought.

McNelly said, "I take it you're out of a job."

"I'm a fair-to-middlin' cowboy. I'll find work."

"Some of my recruits quit when they found out how things really are down here. Maybe I could use you."

"I bring bad luck to everything I touch."

"That's a foolish notion."

Lanham's face creased. He saw no reason he ought to like this man. "Folks say you're a carpetbagger."

McNelly shrugged. "I've heard that."

"I was a Confederate soldier."

"So was I." McNelly studied Lanham with a keen, steady gaze. "By what you did today, I take it you feel that this border trouble has gone far enough. I came here to put a stop to it. I can use your help, but I won't beg you. I won't even ask you again. You can take it or leave it."

Feisty little booger, Lanham thought, if he was a carpetbagger. Lanham sipped the coffee, his eyes shut. Damn, this stuff *had* gone to the bad. A man who'd drink this would do anything. He finished the cup.

He didn't ask about the pay. He didn't ask what his job would be. He asked only, "When do we start?"

15

Being in McNelly's Rangers reminded Lanham somewhat of service in the Confederate army, and that was not particularly a recommendation. Captain ran it like a military organization. They rode in columns, and they moved on strict command. The thought of Ranger service had never entered Lanham's mind, so he had nourished no preconceived notions. If he had, he wouldn't have pictured it like this.

McNelly had no place for the Reynas, so they bade Lanham *adiós* and went on the drift. It didn't seem to bother them. As native Mexicans they eyed the Anglo *rinches* with a certain natural doubt and wouldn't have joined the outfit if they had been asked. Though being out of something to do had always bothered Lanham, he had observed that the Mexican people didn't fret over it much. They accepted it passively, the same way they took other ill fortune. They went hungry sometimes, but they had faith they would never starve to death.

Captain had spoken with Lanham perhaps five

minutes at the Galindo place. Once he enlisted him, he didn't talk to him again. He assigned him to a "dab" and turned his back. From then on, it was as if McNelly had never met him. The captain rode at the head of the column, brooding and withdrawn. Even with a company of Rangers behind him, he seemed somehow a man alone.

What the Rangers called a "dab" was more or less what Lanham remembered from army days as a squad, groups of about eight men each, if each dab was up to strength. Not all of them were. In charge of Lanham's dab was a tall, bestubbled sergeant who wore a Mexican-style sombrero and heavy Mexican spurs. An old border man, Lanham judged him. At least he had probably seen service down this way before. "*Ben acá,*" the sergeant beckoned to Lanham when they reached camp. The words were an Anglo corruption of a colloquial Mexican summons. Lanham followed him to the headquarters tent. There the sergeant dug out a duty book, made an entry and had Lanham sign it.

"I want the terms understood right now, so there won't be no questions asked later or no misunderstandin' with Captain," the sergeant said. "The pay is thirty-three dollars a month in state scrip. Maybe you can get it cashed and maybe you can't. The state'll feed you, when you get fed atall. You furnish your own horse. If he gets killed in line of duty, the state'll pay for him . . . in scrip. You furnish your own pistol; the state'll furnish shells. It don't want them wasted. When you shoot at somethin', hit it." He paused, waiting to see how it was soaking in on Lanham. "We come into some luck in Corpus. Storekeeper set us up to a bunch of Sharps rifles. Here's yours."

He handed Lanham one. Lanham thought it probably was the heaviest weapon he'd ever hefted. He broke it open and looked. Fifty caliber. Buffalo gun, was what it was.

"This thing," he said, "would blow a man half in two if you was to hit him with it."

"If you shoot at a man, you *better* hit him," the sergeant warned. "Captain don't want nobody in his outfit who goes around missin'."

Lanham frowned, running his hand over the piece. It wasn't something a man would carry lightly, or use without doing some tall thinking about it.

The sergeant handed him five cartridges. They weighed like a pouchful of rocks. "If them won't fit your cartridge belt, carry them in your pocket. When you've shot five bandits, you'll get five more cartridges."

Lanham nodded. "When do we ride again?"

"When Captain tells us to."

"He's bound to have a plan laid out."

"Captain's always got a plan, but nobody asks questions; they just do like he tells them, *when* he tells them."

"You mean all these men go along blind, like the tail on a dog, lettin' him send them into God knows what?"

"He don't send you, he *leads* you. You want to scratch your name off the roster and give back that rifle?"

Lanham looked toward the cook's wagon. "I come this far; I'll stay awhile. Besides, looks like pretty soon it'll be time to eat."

Red beans, hardtack and a little sidemeat made up the menu. There were extra plates in the wagon but no cups, and Lanham didn't have one of his own, so he had to pass up the coffee. A couple of young Rangers came over and squatted beside him, setting their plates down. One extended his hand. "Name's Joe Benson." He didn't look as if he had ever shaved and still didn't really need to. "This here is Cebe Smith." Lanham shook hands with both of them. Benson said, "You can drink out of my cup with me till you find you somethin'. How's the dinner?"

Lanham answered with a shrug, for if he answered that he liked it, he would be lying, and that was no example to set for the young. Smith said, "It ain't always like this. Sometimes we ain't got sidemeat."

Benson laughed, "Don't let him scare you. Most of the time we got beef. Usually always some rancher gives us a critter to butcher. But when we run short and there's no rancher, we're out of luck. Captain won't let us kill a beef without it's given to us or we buy it."

He held out his coffee cup, handle forward. Lanham took it gratefully. Eating, he let his gaze run over the Rangers. They were a varied lot, most of them younger than himself. A few he judged probably were war veterans, but most had been too young to serve. *Boys,* was his first thought. *What the hell they doing here? They ought to be home helping their daddies chop cotton.* But a closer study told him they looked able enough for it. Young or not, they all had one thing in common: a determined, self-confident look in their eyes. Dusty and worn, perhaps, but every one of them appeared fit enough to saddle up and make thirty miles before dark.

Joe Benson and Cebe Smith each wore a pistol and a gunbelt. Looking around, Lanham saw the rest of them did, too. He got a strong feeling they all knew how to use these pistols, and they would do it when the occasion came. On the Texas frontier, a boy didn't remain a boy long. Hardship made him into a man, or it buried him.

He stared at Joe Benson. "How come you here, boy? Your daddy know where you're at?"

"My daddy's been dead two years," Benson replied. "Since then I been up the trail twice with a cow outfit, all the way to the Kansas railroad."

Smith said, "Show him your arrow wound, Joe."

Benson put down his plate and rolled up his sleeve to reveal a ragged scar. Lanham nodded soberly. "You're old enough. Glad you boys are in my dab."

Of all the men in the outfit, the captain himself looked the least fit. He sat to one side, picking at his food, his mind far away. He coughed occasionally, and his face paled. The nighttime ride to the Galindos', and then the return, had worn him to the bone.

Man like that, Lanham thought, *ought to be home in bed. Trouble comes, he won't be able to meet it.*

That, Lanham would find, was about as wrong as he had ever been.

Conversation with the young Rangers revealed that they had been sending out patrols for days, quietly searching the draws and valleys, the heavy brush and the scattered mottes for sign. "Captain's got him a spy system," Joe Benson confided. "Figures if the bandits work thataway, he can do it, too. One of them brought him a tip the other day. A bunch of us made a forced ride to the Rio Grande after a string of stolen stock and a passel of them bandits. We got there just as they rode out on the other bank. They hoorawed us a little and fired a few shots at us, but wasn't nothin' we could do. They got clean away, with the cattle, too."

"They were still in rifle range, wasn't they?"

"Law says we can't shoot across the river. Them, they don't bother about the law. They can do it and we can't. Odd thing, the way the law always seems to work out in favor of the lawbreaker and against the officer. Someday maybe they'll fix that."

During the next few days, because he had a better knowledge of the country than most of the Rangers, Lanham found himself being sent on patrol almost constantly. They would start before daylight and usually get in about dark. Whoever was in charge of each patrol would report to the captain that they hadn't come upon anything in particular. Yet all along, the captain knew raiding parties were working. Lanham could see the frustration building in him, and a sullen anger.

One day, off duty, Lanham saw a Mexican riding into camp on a gaunted horse. He was a lank, hunched figure of a man with straggly hair that hung down almost to his shoulders and a ragged beard that hadn't felt a comb. His eyes lit on Lanham a moment, and it was almost like being touched by a hot poker. Lanham felt his hair seem to rise on his neck. He'd never seen the man before, but instinctively he knew him. Old Sandoval. Jesus Sandoval, whose bony brown hands carried the stain of blood from more bandits than any man would ever know.

It was McNelly's rule that no one except members of the company rode into camp armed. Lanham figured Sandoval was going contrary to the rule, but he made no move to stop him. Something about the old Mexican made ice form in his veins.

He had heard the stories. Likely as not they weren't altogether true, but behind any smoke had to be some fire. Way the stories went, Sandoval once owned a small *rancho* on the Texas side of the river. Bandits from *el otro lado* raided his place and left his wife and daughter dead. Sandoval silently crossed the river carrying nothing but a gun, a knife and a heart twisted in hatred. By the time his identity was discovered and he was forced to retreat to the Texas side, he had sought out and butchered a majority of the men responsible. Now he hated all border jumpers. He lived only to spill the blood of bandits.

Odd, the name. *Jesús.* It was a common name in Mexico, for the people seemed to feel that only good could come for a child who carried the name of the Son of God. An ill-fitting name, though, for a man whose soul boiled with hate.

Lanham heard someone call, "Captain, here comes Casoose." In English, following the Mexican border pronunciation, that was how the name sounded. Sandoval disappeared into the tent with the captain. Directly someone went to fetch coffee. It wasn't any of Lanham's business, but curiosity plagued him, and he watched the tent. The captain and Sandoval hunched over a map in animated conversation. He could see the dab leaders gathered close, anticipating orders but not breaching discipline by asking questions.

Presently the captain came out and called the men to order. He picked a detail, including Lanham. McNelly caught his favorite horse, a big King Ranch bay named Segal. Sandoval roped a fresh mount, a paint. Captain ordered extra cartridges for the Sharps rifles, to be placed in each man's saddlebags. On signal, Sandoval and a local scout named Rock led out, the captain behind them. The Rangers followed in a military column.

They rode hard that afternoon, pushing the horses

almost to the limit of their endurance. Lanham could tell they were swinging toward Brownsville. After a long time the captain slowed, putting out two patrols, one on either side. The column moved slower then, and watchfully.

A while before dark, one of the patrols came back. Riding with them, sombrero brim flopping, was a Mexican prisoner. Lanham glanced at Sandoval. He saw the old *ranchero* straighten, his eyes on the prisoner the way a cat watches a mouse trapped in its paws.

One of the corporals saluted the captain, then jerked his thumb toward the captive. "Captain, we raised this 'un out yonder aways. Couldn't give a good account of himself. One of them bandits, we figure."

The captain had been lying down to rest. Lanham hadn't understood how a man in his frail condition could stand up to the ride he had made. Yet the captain did not look fatigued now. His stern eyes studied the captive. With a jerk of his head, he signaled for Sandoval.

"Ask him who he is. Ask him what he's doing here."

A number of the Rangers including Lanham could have questioned the prisoner in competent Spanish, but none of them could do it in the chilling manner of Sandoval. The prisoner recoiled from him instinctively, fearing him on sight. The old *ranchero* asked a few questions, to which the captive gave ready but stammered answers.

"He lies, *capitán*," Sandoval said. "He says he is a rancher. He says he has a place over there." He pointed. "But I know all the people. He does not belong."

"Ask him where the bandits are, with the cattle they've stolen."

That was the first Lanham knew about their mission, though he had suspected it had to be something like this.

Sandoval translated the question. The way McNelly listened, Lanham figured the captain understood most of what was being said. But Sandoval was more than just an interpreter. The captive persisted in his story that he owned a small place *por allá*, and a few head of livestock, and that he knew nothing of bandits.

McNelly's eyes narrowed. "You still do not believe him, Casoose?"

Sandoval's long hair caught the wind as he shook his head. "He lies, *capitán*."

McNelly's eyes went hard. "Then reason with him. Your own way." McNelly walked back to the place where he had lain resting. Sandoval went to his paint horse and took his rope down. Lanham could see sweat break on the prisoner's face as Sandoval led him toward a tree, helped by one of the corporals. The old Mexican fitted his loop around the man's neck, tossed the end of it over a heavy limb, then pulled. Blood rose in the prisoner's face as his feet slowly cleared the ground. Sandoval held him there a moment, then let him down.

At the distance, Lanham could not hear the questions, but he could tell Sandoval was talking, and the choking prisoner was answering him. Again the rope tightened, and the man's feet slowly cleared the ground. Sandoval held him a little longer this time.

The third time, the man was almost purple when Sandoval let him down. He crumpled, gasping, the words pouring out of him like a torrent as his breath began to come back. Sandoval and the corporal caught his arms and half supported him as they brought him back to the captain.

"His memory is better now, *capitán.*"

Lanham's nerves tingled from watching. He turned to the sergeant. "I thought it was illegal to do a prisoner thataway."

"Old Casoose is the one who done it, and he never read a lawbook in his life. As for the rest of us, I didn't see a thing. Did you?"

"I reckon not, but it's a hard way to treat a man."

"It takes extreme measures, sometimes, to fit an extreme situation."

Almost eagerly now, the prisoner spilled all he knew. Lanham listened as the man described the raid the bandits had made, the cattle they had picked up, the route they were taking back to the river. With a stubby brown finger he pointed to places on McNelly's map. Among other things, he admitted he was a forward scout, making sure the way was clear.

"I knew it," the corporal muttered. "I could smell it soon's we saw him."

The captain made the prisoner go back over the story a second time, and then a third. He pressed for details, trying to trip him up. Finally he seemed satisfied. He had written down the names of the other raiders as the prisoner had given them to him. If they weren't caught today, they would go on the list for whatever time in the future they might fall into Ranger hands.

The prisoner looked relieved now that he had unburdened himself. He rubbed his neck, where Sandoval's rope had burned him. But there seemed a sense of security about him. The Brownsville jail never held the border bandits for long. They were always out on writ before the arresting officer could unsaddle his horse.

McNelly said, "Casoose, you know where to take this *hombre?*"

Sandoval nodded. *"Sí, capitán."* His jaw set hard, he motioned for the prisoner to mount his horse. At gunpoint, he took him away.

He'll be half the night getting the bandit to Brownsville and back, Lanham thought. But he didn't concern himself much. He lay down and stretched on the ground. He had already figured out that when a man rode with McNelly, he took his rest when and where the opportunity showed itself.

To his surprise, Sandoval rode back in about thirty minutes.

Alone.

Lanham glanced at the sergeant. "He couldn't of got to Brownsville in that time. He couldn't of . . ."

The thought stopped abruptly. He saw that much of Sandoval's rope was missing. Frayed ends showed where it had been freshly cut with a knife.

The sergeant said, "Captain couldn't afford to waste a man goin' to Brownsville. We couldn't be burdened with a prisoner on our hands on a forced ride. And we sure couldn't just turn him loose."

"Ain't there no other way?"

"You think of one?"

Lanham couldn't. But his stomach turned over.

16

No fires, no coffee. Men rode better on a lean stomach, McNelly said. Long before sunup, the Rangers were in the saddle, riding steadily but not pushing the horses hard as they moved across the salt flats and the hardpan, through the marsh grass and around the mottes of scrub oak. In the beginning ground fog gradually burned away. Rock, up front, drew rein and rode in a tight circle, leaning out of the saddle as he studied the ground. He had found the trail.

"Pushed them through the night," he told the captain, "figurin' on hittin' the river as soon as they can."

The captain was tense. "How far ahead of us?"

"Not far enough. We'll catch them."

"Lead out, then."

The scout struck a lope. Captain ordered the Rangers into double file and followed. Nobody talked. Lanham had been wishing for coffee, but now he forgot about it. He felt excitement building in him and could see it in the faces of the men around him as he turned in the saddle to look back. For a little bit, suspecting a battle lay ahead, he wondered what the hell he had let Captain talk him into joining this outfit for. But he decided he couldn't blame McNelly for it. The captain hadn't begged him.

Caught me in a weak moment, Lanham thought. *Looks more like a preacher than a fighter, and I always did have a weakness for a sermon.*

He saw Rock rein to a stop on a ground swell. The scout made a circular motion with his upraised hand, then dropped it and pointed. He had seen the bandits. Captain McNelly spurred up to the scout and took a spy glass from his saddlebags. Lanham didn't need the glass. He could see a herd of cattle far ahead, on the open prairie.

To the sergeant, Lanham said, "This is the Palo Alto Prairie. Oldtimers say the Mexican War started here, back in '45."

The sergeant's eyes were on McNelly. "There's fixin' to be another one now in just a little bit."

Across the open prairie, unhidden except for a scattering of salt cedar and Spanish dagger, the bandits milled excitedly.

"They're figurin' now," the sergeant said. "They're askin' themselves if they can make the river before we can get to them. But they can't."

"So they'll leave the cattle and run," Lanham speculated.

"Don't you bet on it. They're takin' count of us. Right now they probably figure we're Yankee troops out of Fort Brown, and up to now the troopers've been no match."

Lanham tried to count the riders, but the distance was too great. He guessed it was twenty or so. The bandits were pushing the cattle again. They had decided to bluff. And if the bluff failed, they probably figured on making a fight of it with Yankee troopers.

They had a surprise coming.

The captain motioned for the Rangers to ride in close. His voice was not strong, but his eyes were like the muzzle end of a double-barreled shotgun. "Boys, you all know what we came down here to do. So far, we've misfired on every shot. But today we're going to find out who runs the Nueces Strip—law or outlaw. Watch me for signals. I'll be easy for you to see; I'll be out front. Hold your fire. Don't shoot till I do. Don't scatter or get out of line. Fire straight ahead, or you'll shoot each other. Pick your man and don't let him go till he's dead. Any questions?"

There weren't any. When Captain spoke, there never were. He started the big bay down off the swell toward the Palo Alto Prairie, spurring Segal into a run. Heart quickening, Lanham leaned forward in the saddle and held his place in the column. The horses moved across the hardpan flat in a lope, hoofs shattering the crusted surface. Lanham dodged pieces of crust flung up by the horses in front of him.

Ahead lay an old riverbed of a type the Mexicans called a *resaca*. Left isolated when the river changed its course in some ancient time, it held a half-stagnant collection of rain and seep water. Seeing that a fight was coming, the bandits left the cattle and gathered in a fringe of brush at the far side of the *resaca*, waiting in confidence to repulse these brash *yanqui* soldiers who so foolishly challenged their right to other men's property.

Nearing the *resaca,* the captain slowed. He motioned for the Rangers to spread in a skirmish line. They moved out, right and left, spacing themselves about five paces apart. To the right lay a stretch of timber. McNelly signaled a lieutenant to take a few men and cut off any retreat in that direction. Then he rode out into the water.

Ahead, in the thin brush at the other side of the *resaca,* the bandits began to mill. Lanham decided they had probably figured out by now that these were not regular troopers. Sporadically the bandits began dropping a few shots at the Rangers. These plinked into the water, most of them short of the target. Lanham reached down for the rifle, remembered the captain's order and stopped his hand. His horse shied as a bullet kicked up a spray of water right in front of it.

Bandits or not, in a minute one of them is going to get lucky. Lanham brought the rifle up, wishing to hell the captain would fire that first shot. But McNelly sat straight in the saddle, eyes trained dead ahead, the horse wading.

Bandit fire became heavier as the outlaws realized this bunch of determined-looking men wouldn't turn around and go back. A horse screamed and went down thrashing. Its rider jerked his rifle from the scabbard, kicked his feet out of the stirrups and kept advancing afoot, the water up to his knees.

Sure as hell he'll start shooting now!

But the captain looked back only long enough to be sure the man was all right. He kept riding, still holding fire. Bullets kicked up water around the horses. Another mount went under, its rider cursing.

Suddenly one of the bandits broke and ran for his horse. Some of the others followed. But some stayed in the brush, firing. Lanham was sure he felt the hot kiss of a bullet as it went by his ear. His blood was racing now, his mouth so dry he couldn't have said a word. In his mind, though, he was shouting: *Captain, for God's sake . . .*

And finally McNelly raised his pistol and fired. He was so close to the outlaws now he could have chunked a rock into them. In the brush, a man cried out.

That was what the Rangers had waited for. Every outlaw who moved found himself a target, and the fire was deadly. Straight ahead of him, Lanham saw a man in a brown sombrero crouching in a clump of tall marsh grass. Lanham pulled the horse to a stop, raised the heavy Sharps and drew a bead. The recoil shoved him roughly backward, and the sound was like a cannon going off. He saw the man pitch forward across the grass, his bloodied sombrero rolling into the water.

Guns boomed on both sides of Lanham. He saw the flash of guns inside the brush and held his breath, expecting the smashing impact of a bullet.

Those bandits still on their feet after the first crackle of Ranger gunfire began retreating, running for their horses. The captain had one pinned down in front of him. McNelly called, "Somebody come help me. I'm out of shells."

At that the bandit jumped up and charged at him afoot, shouting in hatred at the *rinches apestozos*. It had been a ruse on Captain's part. He calmly leveled his pistol and shot the outlaw through the mouth.

A wounded bandit rose up out of the heavy grass almost directly in front of Lanham. In astonishment, Lanham looked at the beardless face of a Mexican boy who couldn't have been more than sixteen or so. He watched the boy raise a pistol, holding it with both hands because blood streamed from his right arm. He brought it to bear on Lanham. Lanham held the Sharps, but it had just as well have been a chunk of stovewood. He couldn't bring himself to fire.

Beside him, the sergeant's rifle boomed. The boy jerked backward, cut half in two.

"Your gun jam, Neal?" the sergeant asked quietly.

"No, *I* jammed."

The Rangers hit the brush. A sudden blast of gunfire ended the fighting there, though beyond the brush the escaping bandits spurred across the prairie in a disorderly rout.

Lanham found himself face to face with Captain McNelly. McNelly's eyes were narrowed and stern. "You had an outlaw in front of you, Neal. The sergeant had to shoot him for you. Why?"

"He was just a boy."

"He had a pistol on you. Boy or man, he was fixing to kill you. This is war. Next time, don't hesitate. Kill a man!"

The captain turned away. Lanham stared after him, his jaw set in anger. To the sergeant, he said, "That's the most cold-blooded son of a bitch that I ever saw."

The sergeant gave him a hard look. "It's a cold-blooded situation."

Somebody called, "Captain, I got one dyin' over here. He's callin' for a priest."

McNelly walked to the dying *bandido.* Solemnly he put away his pistol and took a Testament from his pocket. He removed his hat and read from the Book until the man's breathing stopped.

Lanham watched in surprise. The incongruity was too much for him. The sergeant said triumphantly, "Didn't know it all, did you, Neal? Didn't know Captain trained for the ministry, did you? War come along, or he'd of been behind some pulpit today, savin' souls in old Virginia."

Captain put his Testament away. He pointed south.

"Some of them are trying to escape. Let's don't let them."

Enough outlaw horses were left in the ticket that the Rangers whose own mounts had taken wounds were able to find something to ride. They sprang into the big-horned, open-treed Mexican saddles and spurred across that broad expanse of hardpan. Fleeing outlaws with flagging horses found little to hide them. The straggling bandits jabbed big-roweled spurs into horses that had driven cattle all day yesterday and all last night. One by one, the Rangers overtook them. One by one, Ranger gunfire emptied the saddles. Some of the bandits lay on the ground and kept firing until they were literally shot to pieces. As each one was dispatched, the McNelly men spurred on again, after the others.

The long, running fight stretched over mile after mile of prairie. The sun was high when the final bandit rolled on the hardpan and went limp with one arm under him, legs doubled, eyes staring sightlessly into the sun. Almost before the dust settled, flies had found him.

McNelly signaled one of the Rangers to stop the runaway horse and bring it back. Lanham noticed a King Ranch Running W brand on it. That was one thing that gave the bandits an advantage all along: they were mounted on the best of stolen horseflesh.

McNelly leaned forward in the saddle and fell into a coughing spell. Lanham eyed him narrowly. *Damn wonder he's even here, a man no healthier than he is. By rights he ought to be lying back yonder with them bandits, dead of exhaustion.*

McNelly straightened his shoulders presently as if to show he could make another run if he had to. But his voice was weak. "Boys, you've done finely. Did any of them get away?"

The sergeant answered, "Not as I seen, Captain. Looks like we got them to the last man."

Lanham found himself strangely compelled to look at the corpse, against his will. "An ugly sight."

McNelly replied, "But long overdue. This is the first real blood drawn against Cortina's bandits. I intended it to be a total disaster."

Lanham watched the captain, wondering what held him up. He could see a flush in McNelly's normally pale face, a fire in his eyes. He knew then that excitement itself could act as a tonic. It could raise a man's blood like whisky, driving him beyond himself, beyond the limits of ordinary endurance. This same excitement had impelled Lanham. Now, the long chase over, a nauseous reaction began to set in upon him. The sick-sweet smell of blood brought him suddenly to a grave realization of what had happened here. He hadn't had time to comprehend fully that at least one man back yonder had died by Lanham's own hand—a living, breathing man, his brain smashed by a Sharps bullet as big as Lanham's thumb. The thought was instantly sobering.

Lanham's nervous fingers found a bullethole in his brush jacket. He stared, wondering when he had gotten it.

The exuberance of victory played high in the Rangers' young faces. They were brave, they were tough, they would do to ride the river with. They were too young to realize fully what they had done. And, maybe, thought Lanham, that was a blessing.

This kind of thing, he knew, could get in a man's blood like whisky. One finger still exploring the bullethole, he made up his mind it wasn't going to get in *his* blood. He'd stick with McNelly through whatever it took to see this thing to a finish; and then, by George, he was going to *quit*.

The shooting had drawn a couple of Mexican *rancheros* whose *adobes* lay at the edge of the prairie. They ventured out cautiously, taking their time. Sandoval rode over to investigate, found he knew them and brought them to McNelly.

"A su servicio, capitán," said one, taking off his hat and bowing in the saddle. "Those were bad men. You did well."

The other said timidly, "I think perhaps some cattle of my brand were in the herd they stole. Would it be permissible, captain, for me to look?"

"After a while," the captain told them, using Sandoval as interpreter. "First we need a cart or wagon to haul the bodies."

"Sí, capitán," said the one who had asked about the cattle. "I shall go and bring it."

While the *ranchero* rode away, Sandoval and the other Mexican set to work bringing the bodies up into a straight line for the wagon. Lanham saw them tie a rope around a bandit's booted feet and drag him across the hardpan like timber being hauled to a campfire.

He turned quickly away. *Damn it, boys, I can't watch this.*

The Rangers fell into double file and moved at an easy trot back across the prairie toward the *resaca* where the shooting had started. Along the way they gathered the bandit's horses. A couple stood spraddle-legged, slowly bleeding to death from wounds. One was down. These the Rangers unsaddled, then shot, salvaging the gear.

After a while Lanham became aware of sporadic shooting, somewhere ahead. The captain reined up, listening, then swept his arm forward and moved into an easy, swinging lope. They came at length to a rush-filled, brackish pond. A Ranger stood shirtless beside a wounded sorrel horse. He had wrapped his shirt around the horse's neck to protect the wound from flies. As the riders approached, the Ranger pointed toward the pond and gave a signal for caution.

"Captain," he said, "we got a dead Ranger over yonder, and a bandit hemmed up in them rushes."

McNelly stiffened. "What Ranger?"

"Cebe Smith, sir. He's just a boy; he didn't know better. He got too close, and the bandit shot him."

Lanham shut his eyes. He heard Joe Benson cry out, for they had been friends.

Smith. A kid, that's all he was, a kid. But that's all most of them were. Wild, brave, gallant, foolish boys.

The Ranger said, "That snake is wounded, Captain. But he can still shoot."

Grimly the captain detailed the Rangers to surround the pond, being careful not to get opposite one another. On signal, several of them fired into the rushes. Lanham saw the tops of the rushes began to move as the bandit, in panic, sought safer ground. Rifles boomed. A groan came from the rushes, then a moment of thrashing, then quiet.

"All right, Casoose," the captain said, his eyes terrible, "you can fetch him out."

17

They rode double-file into Brownsville, Captain beside old Sandoval, leading them in. Word of the battle had preceded them. People stood almost shoulder-to-shoulder on both sides of the street. Some looked in awe, some cheered, some watched in silent curiosity. In many eyes Lanham saw stark hostility. Many here were openly sympathetic to the red-beard Cortina and his lusty bravos, for those were *hombres valientes* who dared twist the tail of the yanqui ox, dared spit in the *gringo*'s eye. The Texas Mexican people were divided on the subject of Cortina's raiders. Many Mexicans had suffered as much or more than the *gringos*, many had died at their hands. Yet many others had not been victimized. To these this was a holy struggle, race against race. To these people of the old blood, there was no Texas south of the Nueces River. All this was still morally part of Mexico, in spite of the lies on the *gringo* maps. Two wars had not changed their minds. And if it took bandits to fling the extranjeros back across the Nueces, then God go with the bandits.

Captain McNelly was keenly aware of the hostility. He dispatched a lieutenant to round up all patrols and bring them into town. They might be needed here more than in the brush.

An army officer rode toward the Rangers at the head of a small detachment of Negro troops. He brought his hand up in a sharp salute. "I'm Major Alexander, of Fort Brown. You, I take it, are McNelly?"

The captain returned the salute with only a nod, reserving himself till he knew how the wind blew. "I'm McNelly."

The major's stern expression gave way to a smile. "Congratulations, Captain. You've done what the army has wanted for months to do. Can I be of service?"

The captain relaxed a little. "Thank you, Major. I'd be pleased if you could send an ambulance out to Palo Alto Prairie and pick up a load of reformed bandits we left there. They gave us a little difficulty. They'll give you none."

"As good as done. Anything else?"

"I've got a couple of men with wounds. Nothing serious, but I'd appreciate it if your post surgeon could attend to them."

"I heard you suffered one fatality."

Captain nodded. "We'll want to bury him here."

"In the post cemetery. We'll give him full military honors."

Captain studied the major with a little of surprise. Evidently he hadn't expected much cooperation.

The major saw. "Captain, these border outlaws have spilled soldier blood. They enjoy shooting one of our Negro troopers almost as much as they like killing a *gringo* rancher. These men at the fort will stand behind anything you want to do."

"Enough to give my men a good feed? They've had nothing."

"Bring them on, Captain. They won't go hungry."

The post physician bound up the few wounds, and an ageless Negro cook fed the half-starved Rangers in a military mess hall. Lanham ate heartily and washed it down with enough coffee to drown a mule.

The army ambulance came in with its grim load. Major Alexander rode out with the captain and the Rangers to meet it. "They're your bandits, Captain," the major said. "What do you want to do with them?"

McNelly's eyes were like flint. "The town square. I want to haul them to the town square."

A sullen crowd followed the ambulance afoot. Lanham eyed them with uneasiness. They gestured angrily, shouting insults after the Rangers. To them, the men in the wagon were martyrs, slaughtered at the hands of Godless men who had stolen part of Mother Mexico.

It seemed to Lanham that McNelly deliberately set a slow pace as he pointed the way for the ambulance. At length he reined up on the plaza and pointed. "Right here. Stack them!"

The major blinked. "Stack them?"

"Right here: I want everybody to see. I want everybody to count them." His eyes held sparks as he looked at the gathering, threatening crowd. "I want them to get a good look and a good smell, and to know that these are just the first."

Grim-faced, young Joe Benson stepped down from his saddle. Other youthful Rangers pitched in to help him with the task. Lanham held back and let them, for this was a dirty job not to his liking. He felt a tug at the pit of his stomach as he watched them fling out the man he had killed in the brush at the edge of the *resaca*. The man had died with his eyes open, and those eyes seemed to look at Lanham.

He hadn't consciously kept a count, but as the last body hit the ground he found himself saying, "Sixteen."

Sandoval—who had enemies in the crowd and bluntly defied them by his presence—brought up a couple of acquaintances who began naming off the bandits whose bodies they could recognize.

"Camillo Lerma. *Coyote* Jiminez. Tellesforo Diaz. Guadalupe Espinosa. The *gringo* Ellis . . ." Sandoval grinned in perverse satisfaction. "*El Cheno,* he will be most unhappy, *Capitán*. These are some of his favorite *bravos,* some of the best thieves and throat-cutters in his command."

"Good," said McNelly. He turned to Sergeant Armstrong. "Put an eight-man guard on this plaza. Let the people come and look all they want to, but shoot any man who tries to move a body before I give the order. I want to be damned sure Cortina gets the word. I want to be sure everybody does."

Lanham was chosen for first guard. It was just as well. He couldn't have slept anyway, knowing what must be going on across the river in Matamoros, stronghold of Cortina and his violent band. He could imagine the fury that must be raging in the *cantinas,* fed now by tequila and mescal, and an inborn hatred of the *diablos Tejanos*.

Down on the Rio, the military had tied off the ferry to stop across-the-river traffic. Soldiers stood their posts up and down the bank, their worried eyes looking south toward the candlelit windows of Matamoros.

Joe Benson dropped down beside Lanham. He still

seemed stunned by the loss of his friend. "You reckon they're a-hatchin' somethin' across yonder, Lanham?"

"It's a big town, damn sight bigger than Brownsville. They're strong enough to do just about anything they make up their minds to. Cortina came and took over this town once, back in '59. Folks say he raised a lot of hell before the Mexican army talked him into goin' home."

Even off duty, Lanham rested little. He sat watching the plaza, half expecting a howling mob to burst into the street, rescuing the bodies of the fallen raiders and spilling *rinche* blood in these sands. They could do it if they decided to; he had no doubt of that.

"I hope they come," said Joe Benson. "I'd love to get a few of them for Cebe Smith."

"We already got them," Lanham pointed out. "Sixteen of them."

Joe was grim because of his loss, but Lanham perceived exhilaration in the other young Rangers. They met this situation with a boyish sense of high adventure and patriotism, and a boundless faith in the captain. Lanham knew that to most of them, as to many of the Mexican people on the opposing side, this was primarily a battle of race against race . . . that to them the enemy here was as old as the Alamo.

It wasn't that way with McNelly. Whatever misgivings Lanham had about him otherwise, he was convinced the captain didn't take this as a war of white man against brown. He had more perception than that. To McNelly, as to Lanham, this was a contest of law against outlaw, of order against disorder, right against wrong. If he was merciless in pursuit of justice, it was not out of racial motivations. He would be merciless anywhere in enforcing what he considered to be the right.

Sitting there through the long night, Lanham let his sleepless mind drift. Much of the time he thought of Zoe. The memories brought him pain, and he would force himself to think of the Galindo girl. But Zoe kept coming back. It would have brought Zoe a savage satisfaction if she could have seen this plaza, the outlaws lying dead in the sand. Lanham was glad she couldn't.

Dawn came, and Lanham met it with burning eyes red-tinged from lack of sleep. The captain came after daylight to relieve the guard. "Anything to report?" he asked Sergeant Armstrong.

"No, sir," the sergeant said, glad the long watch was over. "None of them bandits tried to get away."

"I think the message has been made clear now," McNelly said. "We'll leave the disposition of the bodies to Sheriff Brown. Mount up, boys. You'll have breakfast at the fort. Then we've got a Ranger to bury."

Word from across the river was that Cheno Cortina had paced his floor in a black fury all night, swearing vengeance with every breath. Rumor had it he wouldn't allow the Ranger to be buried in the ground he considered still a part of Mexico.

Major Alexander suggested, "Maybe it would hold down trouble if we got the funeral done quietly, and early, before anyone knows."

Captain McNelly's thin frame stood straight as a ramrod. "I *want* them to know. That boy died defying Cortina and his bandits. He'll not be buried like a coward."

So Private Cebe Smith defied Cortina to the edge of the grave. His flag-covered coffin was placed in a hearse. The Rangers lined up in double file behind the captain. Two full companies of U.S. regulars marched after the Rangers through the long streets of Brownsville, a tacit declaration that the troops at Fort Brown were in full support of McNelly. Every man was armed, for the river was no barrier if Cortina decided to send an army.

But the muddy Rio Grande ran quietly, undisturbed. At the military cemetery, men stood with heads bared as a bugle sent up a message that was part grief, part defiance. Across the river, Cortina must have heard it clearly.

But he had heard McNelly's message clearly, too.

18

It was one thing for Cortina to pace and rant in the luxury of his quarters, vowing revenge against McNelly. It was another for him to persuade hungry, *huarache*-shod volunteers to swim the river and do the job. Those sixteen bodies gathering flies in the Brownsville plaza had made an impression that no number of official government protests and diplomatic notes could ever do. The border simmered in suspense and hatred, but few men dared make an opening move on the *jefe*'s behalf. However intense their feeling against McNelly, they respected him as a strong man on horseback. Where raiding bands previously had often numbered in the dozens of men, *el Cheno* found it difficult now to get more than a few men to take the trail at a time. They grabbed whatever they could find in a hurry and fogged it for the river as if that *diablo* McNelly and his fearsome *rinches* were right on their tails.

On both sides of the Rio, the story began to spread that McNelly was something more than human, that he had strange powers, perhaps given him by the Devil himself in some Mephistophelian rite. Among those given to superstition, McNelly became a dread symbol of the omnipotent powers of Darkness.

He was not omnipotent; he was merely shrewd. Once before, McNelly had been on the river, carrying a special commission to study the border bandit problem and make a detailed report for the United States government . . . a report it filed away and did nothing about. The acquaintances he had made then stood him in good stead now. He began setting up a spy system, seeking out—through emissaries such as old Sandoval—those bandits whose loyalty to money was stronger than their loyalty to their chief. There were many of them. There always are. He located, too, honest citizens of both Mexico and Texas who were in a position to bring information and did so from a sense of right. Many who had hated the bandits had feared them too much to bear witness against them. Now, since Palo Alto, their courage began to rise.

If the situation on the border showed improvement, McNelly himself did not. The rigors of the campaign had fallen upon him with all their weight. He took a room at a hotel in Brownsville. He tried to ride out to the Ranger camp daily for inspection and to give orders, but he was gaunt and pale, and gradually his trips became less and less frequent. There was talk that the hotel people wanted him out, though they didn't have the nerve to tell him so. Plainly, Captain McNelly was a consumptive. No hotel man wanted a consumptive in his place; it scared other guests away.

McNelly would have scared them regardless.

His brain kept working, though his body was weak. His spy system continued to grow. And as it did, the wandering patrols had better and better luck cutting off bandit forays, for even from his sickbed McNelly was sending them where he knew the action would be.

The post physician checked on him regularly. Alarmed, he tried to persuade the Ranger officers to send for Mrs. McNelly, but none of them had the nerve to act without McNelly's orders, and they knew he wouldn't approve. So the doctor sent for her himself, asking no permission. He said: "I'm not in your command, McNelly. I can do what I damn well please."

They found an empty adobe house at the edge of town and moved the captain there. In the country, with his wife's cooking, he would have a better chance to recover . . . if recovery was in the cards.

Looking at him, Lanham Neal wondered. But he offered no comment. The captain lay on a cot in the shade of a huge cottonwood, watching his young son Rebel wrestling with a balky Mexican burro. Lanham said, "I believe you sent for me, Captain."

"Yes, Neal, I did. Sit down."

There was nothing to sit on but his heels, so Lanham squatted, careful not to let his big-roweled spurs gouge his rump. The captain asked him various questions about the scouts he had been on, the reports he was hearing. Lanham answered him matter-of-factly, sensing that wasn't what he had come for.

Presently Captain said, "I have a man here. I want you to identify him." He glanced toward the adobe house. "Casoose!"

Old Sandoval walked out from around the corner, flanked by a tall young Mexican. Lanham pushed quickly to his feet. "Vincente!"

Vincente de Zavala smiled and grasped Lanham's arms in an *abrazo*. "*Caporál!*"

Lanham stood off at arm's length and gave Vincente a careful look-over. The *vaquero* was leaner than when Lanham had last seen him. He bore a fresh knife scar on his cheek. But mostly what Lanham saw were his eyes. They seemed to have sunk back a little, and they carried the burned-in pain Lanham had become accustomed to in Sandoval's. "You've ridden some hard trails, *compadre*."

Vincente shrugged. "From what I hear, so have you."

Lanham turned to McNelly. "Whatever Vincente tells you, Captain, you can bet your money on. I'm tickled that he's back on this side of the river."

Vincente said, "I am not staying here, *caporál*. When it is dark, I will go back over. But now I work for you and *el capitán*, not just for me." He touched a hand to the Bowie knife on his belt. "They know the *capitán*. They do not know me."

A chill ran up Lanham's spine. They might not know Vincente, but they already knew of that blade.

The captain nodded in satisfaction. "That's all I needed you for, Neal. He came to me through Casoose. Said he had ridden with you. I just had to be sure."

"What if I hadn't identified him, Captain?"

McNelly's pale face did not change expression. "I'd have turned him over to Casoose."

Captain's orders had been for the men to stay out of trouble in Brownsville, but one night a few of them heard fiddle music in a Mexican danceroom and decided to take part in the *baile*. Words were exchanged, knives flashed and blood spilled on the floor. It added to the Rangers' reputation as fighters, which was perhaps a gain in some respects, but it ran against the captain's principles. When his men fought, he wanted it to be for something more substantial than dancing with a winsome *señorita.*

Captain McNelly got back on his feet. He put his wife and boy on the stagecoach for their home near Burton, saddled the big bay Segal and rode to the Ranger camp with a new set of orders. He was moving the company to Las Rucias, away from Brownsville's easy temptation to the Rangers and to those who hated them.

Some said hopefully that Captain was cured. Lanham could tell at a glance that he wasn't. McNelly was riding the river on borrowed time, and probably he knew it better than anybody.

At the new headquarters in Las Rucias cow camp, the McNelly spy system began paying dividends. Here his informants could be bolder. They could take a chance and ride straight into camp without worrying that they would be seen and reported by townspeople whose loyalty remained with Cortina. And the Rangers could move with more freedom from surveillance. More and more, the scouting parties were catching up with raiders on the Texas side instead of tracking them to the edge of the river and looking helplessly at them encamped on the opposite bank. After Palo Alto Prairie, those scattered small parties of bandits no longer tried to bluff it out to keep a stolen herd of cattle or a *remuda* of horses. At first sign of pressure, they abandoned their booty and spurred for the river. Sometimes they made it. Occasionally other Rangers waited there in ambush.

Cortina was feeling the pinch. Ships waited at the port of Brazos Santiago, past Matamoros, their holds ready for beef. Cortina had beef orders in his hands that would have meant a fortune, and these orders were going unfilled.

* * *

One day Lanham rode in with a scout detail after a long search upriver. It hadn't been a good scout. They hadn't seen anything but tracks. Lieutenant Robinson met Lanham at the corral.

"Neal, Captain wants to see you. You can eat later."

The urgency in his voice made Lanham forget that his stomach had growled at him the last thirty miles. He went straight to McNelly's tent. The captain lay on his cot, failing again. He shouldn't have sent Mrs. McNelly home. "Neal, I believe you're acquainted with a rancher by the name of Bailey? Andrew Bailey?"

Lanham's mouth hardened. "Yes, sir. I know him."

"We just got word there was trouble on his ranch. Bandits took a shot at him. Killed a woman instead."

It was as if McNelly had hit him on the head with the flat side of an ax. "A woman, sir?" He reached out for a chair and leaned on it to steady himself. "What woman?"

"Message didn't say." Compassion showed in the captain's eyes. "The girl you wounded at that Mexican place . . . would she likely have been with this Bailey?"

Lanham's voice dropped to a whisper. "I wouldn't be surprised."

The captain sat up, trying to keep pain from showing in his thin face. "Not much a person can do when his time comes . . . or *hers*. The Book says the day and the hour and the manner of our passing are written down at the moment we're born. So a man lives, and he tries to do his best, and he fights like hell when he's called upon because they can't kill him till his time comes. But when it comes, he'll die even if he tries to run.

"You better go to Bailey's, Neal. It's your place to do it. Take young Benson with you."

Lanham drank a cup of black coffee, stuffed some hardtack in his pockets and rode off on a fresh horse. It was all he could do to keep from running his horse to death . . . and Joe Benson's with it.

The boy protested after a while. "Lanham, you're spurrin' that horse like you hated him. Who you mad at?"

That brought Lanham back to earth. He realized the lad knew nothing about Zoe. He simply said, "I'm mad at *me.*"

Zoe . . . Zoe . . . if it's Zoe, I'll . . . He clenched his teeth, knowing there was nothing he could do. *I oughtn't to've left her. I ought to've hog-tied her and taken her to Brownsville whether she liked it or not, instead of leaving her there with that land-hungry, woman-hungry Bailey.*

They hit Bailey's place at midafternoon. Lanham recognized a Mexican *vaquero* in the corral as one of those Bailey had sent to watch him and Zoe. *"Dónde está el patrón Bailey?"* he demanded.

The vaquero's eyes were wide in astonishment. He pointed toward the house. *"A casa.* Why do you come here *senor? El patrón* will kill you."

"He can kill me," Lanham said, "just after he gets back from the moon." He reined the horse directly up to the house and swung to the ground. "Bailey!"

The wooden door moved inward. Bailey stepped out across the gallery, a rifle in his hand, pointed vaguely in Lanham's direction. He stared in surprise. "You remember what I told you I'd do, Neal, if ever you was to cross my sights?"

Lanham calculated his chances of drawing his pistol before Bailey could finish bringing that rifle into line. They were somewhat short. "You sent for Rangers."

Bailey blinked. "You're a Ranger? I don't see no badge."

"They never issued any. But you swing that rifle any farther around and I'll sure as hell prove it to you."

Bailey dropped the muzzle of the rifle. "I thought all you ever shot was women."

Lanham flinched, hating Bailey. "What about Zoe? We heard there was a woman killed."

"You never cared none for Zoe. You shot her yourself, remember?"

"I did my best not to; you know that. Now, damn you, tell me about Zoe before I ram that rifle down your throat."

A woman's voice came from inside the door. "What do you want to know?"

Lanham jerked his head around and saw her. "Zoe! You're all right?"

"Not altogether. I've still got a stiff arm. You'd know about that."

"We heard a woman was killed. I thought . . ."

Bailey said solemnly, "A woman *was* killed. My wife."

It took Lanham a minute to recover his wits. He stared first at Zoe, then at Bailey, feeling foolish. Finally he brought out, "Sorry. I know she was a good woman. I expect she was a real loss to you."

"A terrible loss," said Bailey. His voice betrayed him. Lanham could tell he didn't mean it. Suspicion already touching him, Lanham said, "Maybe you better tell us what happened."

Bailey laid the rifle against the wall and motioned for the two Rangers to come up onto the gallery and sit on a bench. His brow furrowed in pain that he obviously didn't feel. "Josefa'd been sick some lately. Zoe came here with me and my *vaqueros* after you shot her. I intended to have Josefa take care of her, but Zoe was takin' care of Josefa more than the other way around. She had one of them Mexican *curanderas* comin' over regular; thought somebody had cast a spell on her. You know all that stuff these people believe in. I tried to tell her it wasn't doin' no good. Yesterday I decided I'd just have to haul her into Brownsville to see a real white-man doctor. Four or five miles from the ranchhouse here, somebody took a shot at us from out of the brush. At *me*, I figure. They hit her instead. Killed her right off."

Lanham gazed intently into Bailey's face, looking for any sign that might betray the man as a liar. "Who did it?"

"Bandits. They got cause enough to want to kill me."

So have a lot of us, Lanham thought, glancing at Zoe. "See anybody?"

"No. I just wheeled the buckboard around and whipped the horses all the way home. Went back later with the *vaqueros,* but we couldn't find much of anything."

Lanham frowned. "I reckon we better look at the body."

Bailey said callously, "You'll need a shovel. She's under six foot of earth."

"You buried her without waitin' for an investigation?"

"Weather's hot, Ranger. You know that."

"Then you better show us the place where it happened."

Bailey shrugged. "Want to go, Zoe?"

Zoe looked at the floor. "No, I saw Josefa. I don't want to see where she died."

Bailey stepped down off the gallery. "I'll gather a few of the boys." Lanham watched him stride toward the barn, then brought his gaze to Zoe. He found her still looking at the floor. He wished he knew some proper words to say. "I been thinkin' about you an awful lot."

"I think about you, too . . . every time my arm starts to hurt."

Lanham bit his lip. "I been hopin' you'd realize there wasn't nothin' else I could do. I wouldn't of hurt you for the world."

"Not even for that dark-eyed Mexican girl?"

Lanham shook his head. "You still goin' to stay here now that Bailey's wife is gone?"

"Why not? He'll need somebody."

"People will talk."

"I stayed with *you* once, remember? We just let them talk."

Whipped, Lanham walked down to his horse. Joe Benson followed, boiling with questions he knew better than to ask.

Bailey headed them out the wagon road. After a while he reined up and pointed. "Right there. That's where we was. And yonder . . . yonder in the brush is where the shot come from."

The brush didn't appear very thick to Lanham. "Looks like to me you could've seen a man in there."

"With a dead woman and two boogered horses on my hands? I didn't do much lookin'. Not till later, when I come back with the boys."

"Find tracks?"

"You always find tracks in this country. All the

tracks you want. Trouble is, they don't tell you much."

They can tell you if you want to know, Lanham thought. He rode over to the place where Bailey said the shot came from. He found it hopeless. Bailey's *vaqueros* had ridden around here so much that if there had been any tracks, they were lost in a tangled maze.

Bailey sat with legs braced in the stirrups, hands pushing against the pommel of the saddle, stretching himself. He did not look bereaved. "Well, Neal, what do you think?"

Lanham saw no reason to dodge it. "I think you're a damned liar. I think you're a murderer. I think you went and killed her yourself."

Color surged into Bailey's face. He instinctively reached for his pistol but caught himself.

Lanham went on, "You already had all you wanted from your wife . . . her land. Now there was another woman with good looks, and land, too . . . Zoe. You took advantage of the bandit trouble to get rid of the old one. She didn't have anything more to give you anyway. You rigged the whole thing."

"No, Neal. I had to take her to a doctor. She was sick . . ."

"Sick with seein' and knowin' what was goin' on in your mind. You think a Mexican woman's not just as smart as any other? She saw through you better than Zoe did. She knew you didn't have Zoe here just to protect her. She knew you wanted Zoe and that sooner or later you'd have her. No wonder that poor woman was sick. No wonder she had a *curandera* tryin' to break a spell. You're the one put the spell on her, like you're puttin' it on Zoe."

"You're crazy, Neal." Bailey glanced at Joe Benson. "Can't you tell he's crazy?"

Lanham said, "I may have some of the details wrong, but I'd bet everything I own—which ain't much—that I got most of it pegged."

"Is that what you're goin' to tell your Captain McNelly?"

"You bet you."

"Even if it was true, you couldn't prove it."

"No, Bailey, that's the hell of the thing. I can't prove it."

Bailey went a little easier. "What you figure on tellin' Zoe?"

"Nothin'. She wouldn't believe me if I did."

Bailey gained confidence. "You're right. If you was to tell her the sun would come up tomorrow out of the east, she'd look for it in the west. She hates you, Neal. Same as I do. If you wasn't a Ranger, and if I didn't know that crazy captain you've got would come and wipe us out to the last man, I'd kill you right where you're at."

Lanham felt a fury rising that would go out of his control if he didn't get away from here. "I won't always be a Ranger, Bailey."

"When you're not, come back. Then I'll kill you."

"Maybe you'll *try*." Lanham jerked his head at Joe Benson. "Come on, button. Let's get out of here."

He found himself riding a familiar trail, going back. He didn't take the direct route he had used coming out. Joe rode alongside him patiently, his eyes asking questions. Lanham didn't volunteer him any answers until they rode into a ranch yard.

Joe said, "Looks deserted. What place is this?"

"Belongs to Zoe Daingerfield, the woman at Bailey's."

What Joe didn't know, he guessed at. He said simply, "Oh."

Lanham didn't dismount. He sat there, gaze slowly covering the yard, holding a bit on the empty *jacal* he and the *vaqueros* had built for Zoe.

Joe finally said, "My old daddy told me that a sore never heals if you keep pickin' at it."

Lanham scowled but let it pass. "Come on, we're wastin' time."

He knew another trail, and he took it, too. Joe said, "I thought camp was yonderway."

"It is. But we're goin' thisaway."

He rode out of the brush and into the clearing where the Galindo *rancho* lay. Relief came as he saw that the shack still stood, just as he had last seen it. He had half thought Bailey or Zoe might have come back and burned it.

Captain's orders about such things seemed to have taken hold.

Galindo children scattered like chickens, until they recognized Lanham and knew it was all right. They edged back cautiously. *Señora* Galindo came out, saw who it was and broke into a broad smile. But Lanham didn't see it, particularly. He was looking for the girl. In a moment she stepped out the door, trying to straighten her hair.

"*Señor* Neal," she smiled. "We are blessed by your presence."

Joe Benson stared, open-mouthed. "What's that she said, Lanham? What's that she said?"

Lanham translated for him. He told the girl, "I have been wondering if you were all right. Have you been bothered by anyone?"

"We are fine, *señor.* No one has come to bother us. We are grateful to you for that."

Joe had to know what she was saying. Lanham told him, then added, "You ought to learn to speak Mexican."

Joe nodded. "I believe I will."

Señora Galindo asked them to stay and she would see what she could find for the Rangers to eat. Joe was for it, but Lanham told him in English so the women couldn't understand, "You can see they got very little. Anything we eat is that much taken away from the kids."

He lied that they had already eaten. Lanham looked at the girl, measuring her against Zoe, wishing this girl could make him stop thinking about the woman he had lost. She got prettier every time he saw her, seemed like. Maybe that was because he was hungry. If he played his hand halfway right, he figured he could have her.

But he knew, looking at her, that it wouldn't work. She was still a girl, and a girl wasn't enough, not after Zoe. Zoe was a *woman*.

He took off his hat and said his *hasta luegos* and rode away, knowing there was no use in coming this way anymore.

Joe Benson kept looking back. "By George, Lanham, I do believe that's the prettiest Mexican girl I ever seen. Maybe the prettiest girl of any kind I ever seen. You got a claim on her?"

"No claim."

"Would it be all right with you if—sayin' my duties was to bring me thisaway again—if I was to stop off and visit with her some? Now, I don't mean for any bad purpose, nothin' like that. Not with that kind of a girl. I mean just to talk with her."

"You'd have to learn Mexican."

"I'd learn it. I'm tellin' you, Lanham, I'd sure learn it."

Lanham came very near to smiling, for a minute. "I'd have no objection atall. I think it'd be a dandy idea."

19

Captain McNelly was dubious. "You have a lot of reason to dislike Bailey. Maybe you're letting that color your opinion."

"My opinion is worse than I could tell you, Captain."

"You still couldn't prove anything."

"No, sir."

"Sooner or later, fate always overtakes a man like that. He'll make a mistake one day. Right now we have border bandits to worry about."

Word from spies across the river indicated that Cortina was getting desperate to meet those lucrative beef contracts. He had stepped up his encouragement to his followers. After all, those *gringos* were on land stolen from your fathers and grandfathers, he argued, and those are grandmother's cattle. Who has a better right? Cortina upped his paying price for stolen beef to twelve dollars a head. That was enough to start some hesitant *bravos* trying their luck again. The Rangers stopped some, but with 150 or 200 miles of the Rio Grande to cover, the thirty-man McNelly force couldn't hope to catch them all.

Despite sporadic Ranger successes, Lanham could tell the captain was becoming more and more restless over the many bandits they never even saw, the ones they knew about only by the tracks on the muddy banks of the river, and by the reports of murdered *vaqueros* and stolen livestock that drifted down from the north.

The gray of his sickness was coming over Captain again. Lanham knew someone ought to send for Mrs. McNelly, but the army doctor wasn't here now. Any Ranger who dared could toss his commission in the river.

Ailing, the captain still didn't divulge his plans. But times when he felt like it, he began talking to the men. Times, he allowed himself to get closer to them than he ever had before.

He knows his days are numbered, Lanham thought.

Captain would talk of his guerrilla days in Confederate service in Louisiana, or he would talk of religion, a subject on which he was exceptionally well versed. Lanham had seen brutality in the man, but he remembered there had been brutality in the Bible, by men favored of God. Like these, perhaps, McNelly was convinced he worked in a righteous cause.

Once, while Lanham was resting between scouts, he heard the captain give his appraisal of what it would take to clean up the border for good and all. "War!" McNelly said. "A war would put a stop to the raiding. I'm afraid nothing else will. The soldiers, they try, but they're tied down by red tape and foolish rules. That bunch in Washington is afraid they'll hurt Mexico's feelings, so they won't let a soldier cross the river, even in hot pursuit. Cortina knows this, and he takes advantage of it.

"Down in Mexico City, they've got too many troubles of their own. They've got revolutions on their hands. They can't be worried about one tin-pot border politician. They could put a stop to Cortina in a hurry if they put their minds to it. And war with this country would *put* their minds to it, you can bet. Let our government move troops into Mexico and the *politicos* in Mexico City would come awake in a minute. They don't want to fight the United States."

Lieutenant Robinson, late of Virginia, said, "But the United States doesn't want to fight them, either, Captain. So it's just not going to happen."

"You never can tell, Lieutenant." McNelly had a scheming look in his eyes. "You never can tell."

Summer gave way to fall, and raids continued, though still not on the scale they had been before Palo Alto Prairie. Captain rode when he could. More often, he had to lie in camp. Two or three times Lanham found Vincente de Zavala there, delivering information. Usually when Vincente brought word, bandits died.

With spies, there was always the risk that sooner or later one would light both ends of the candle. In the end it was not a Mexican who betrayed McNelly . . . it was a *gringo* renegade he had come to trust. This spy parleyed a long time. When the captain came out of his tent, he told the men to get ready to move. On McNelly's orders, the camp cook fed them hardtack, beans and coffee.

Lanham knew what that meant: a long, hard ride. They rode east, which surprised him, because most of the raids had been to the west. After a long time they angled north. Captain knew where he was going, but he didn't confide. He just kept riding, right into the teeth of a Texas norther. Without food—without so much as coffee—they pulled up at last in a large thicket and sat down to wait for what the *gringo* spy had told the captain was coming.

Nothing happened the first day. Captain sent scouts out to patrol, but they found nothing. The company waited wet and cold, bellies empty. The captain himself finally rode out for a *pasear,* though he looked too sick to do it. He came back empty-handed.

Four days they waited in ambush. The raiders never appeared. And at last old Casoose, out on a one-man circle, came in with a galling report. It had been a ruse. The captain's spy had taken a payoff to lure the Rangers out of the way. Then raiders by the dozens had crossed the Rio Grande from an upriver stronghold, Rancho Las Cuevas. They had looted and burned ranchhouses and stores, slaughtered *vaqueros* where they found them, gathered uncounted horses and perhaps eight hundred cattle.

Lying cold in his wet blankets, Captain had been sick even before Sandoval came back. Now, as he listened, his thin face was almost blue. The spirit seemed gone from him. He had taken a licking, the worst licking of his life. It was obvious he would die if he stayed here this way. Sick at heart as well as of lung, McNelly turned the command over to Lieutenant Robinson and rode north to seek recuperation in the warmth of his own house, the good air of his farm, the tender care of a loving wife.

Along the border the word quickly spread that McNelly was gone. His enemies said he had been whipped and had run out like a dog, tail between his legs. Others said he was dying, that he would never come back.

When Lanham Neal watched Captain ride off on Segal, thin shoulders hunched against the cold, he had a strong feeling he would never see McNelly again. His throat tightened, and his eyes burned. Smoke from that damned fire, he thought.

Sure, McNelly had some things about him that were hard to accept. He could be ruthless when there was a need for it. Turning prisoners over to Casoose was the thing that stuck most in Lanham's craw. But what Casoose did to the bandits was no worse than what the bandits did to those *gringo* cowboys or Mexican *vaqueros* or store clerks who fell into their hands, and particularly any comely young women who might strike a border jumper's fancy. Hell, it was a war whether they chose to call it one or not.

One thing always in McNelly's favor was the blanket order he had given his Rangers from the first, "Leave the law-abiding citizens alone. Don't kill a beef, don't even kill a chicken, unless a man gives it to you, or unless you pay him for it. Go hungry if you have to, but leave the honest man's stock alone. Go into a house only if a man invites you to. Sit down only when he says so. Whether he be *gringo* or Mexican—black, brown or white—if he's done no wrong, molest him in no way. We're after outlaws, nothing else."

Well, Lanham thought, *he's been whipped. But it wasn't Cortina that did it; it was lung fever.* No *man alive is big enough to bring the captain down.*

The Rangers tried after the captain left, but it just wasn't the same. The officers were less certain of what to do. Emboldened, the *Cortinistas* returned to raiding on their old scale, and this brought fear back to many of the people who had cooperated with McNelly. The spy system disintegrated. Palo Alto Prairie had been a flash in the pan, some were saying. Pure luck, and nothing else. The captain had been a failure, and the Rangers were a farce.

It was an unhappy camp at Las Rucias. Lanham Neal was glad to be out on scout as much as he could, not that being on scout meant much in the way of results. Sure, they killed an outlaw now and again, but it didn't seem to discourage anybody. What was a man when beef had jumped to eighteen dollars a head?

One cold day Lanham rode in from a wasted scout and found a chunky, sad-faced Mexican *vaquero* hunched at the campfire, disconsolately waiting. "Bonifacio, *como le va?*"

Bonifacio stood up. "*Caporál,* it is good to see you."

"If it's good, why don't you smile a little bit? You look like you'd been to a funeral."

Bonifacio shrugged. "I have come to talk to you about *la patrona*."

"Zoe?" Lanham frowned. "What happened to her?"

"Nothing. Not yet. But perhaps soon."

"What's *goin'* to happen to her?"

"The Bailey, he says he will marry with her."

Lanham turned away so Bonifacio couldn't see his face. "His wife's not hardly even cold in her grave." He grimaced. "What does Zoe say?"

"She says nothing, *caporál*."

"She look happy?"

"She has not looked happy in all this time."

"She send you to fetch me?"

Bonifacio shook his head. "She does not know I am here."

"She made any sign she don't want to get married to Bailey?"

"No sign. It is something I feel. I think you should come to see about her, *caporál*."

Lanham got a cup of coffee and sat beside Bonifacio, staring into the fire, pondering a long time. "Never did seem like I could bring her any luck. If I was to ride over there now, I'd probably kill Bailey, or he'd kill me. Either way, she'd suffer for it."

"You don't help her?"

"If I knew a way. But like you said, she didn't send for me. She ain't said she don't want to marry Bailey. She's a grown woman, Bonifacio. I got no claim."

"That Bailey is *un mal hombre,* mean as a Comanche. It is said among the *vaqueros* that he killed his wife."

"Is there any proof?"

"Nobody saw. But they whisper it, when he cannot hear."

"If there's no proof, there's not a thing we can do."

"*Amigo* . . ." Bonifacio paused. "If he has killed one wife, might he not someday also kill another?"

Lanham let the cup sag. The coffee spilled. "Bonifacio, quick as you get the chance, ask her if she wants me to come and get her. If she says yes, come tell me and I'll be there faster than a man ever rode. If you don't come back, I'll figure she said no."

"She will not ask for you. She is a woman of pride."

"But a *woman* . . . old enough to make up her own mind."

Bonifacio rode away as discouraged as when he came. Lanham watched for him the next day, and the day after that. When the fourth day passed, he knew the *vaquero* was not coming. Somehow Lanham had known he wouldn't. But somehow, also, he was bitterly disappointed.

20

November came, and cold winds drove down from the northern prairies across the hill country of Central Texas and on to the coastal plains and the desert lands below the Nueces. Without McNelly, the little company of Rangers stayed encamped at Las Rucias, making half-hearted scouts up and down the river, occasionally running into *Cortinistas* but most often just finding where they had been. When they took a prisoner, the Rangers would send an escort with him to Brownsville. Usually the man was out on bond before the Rangers finished scribbling their report in the sheriff's office.

It suited the sheriff's jealous staff. "You Rangers been too high and mighty," a deputy snarled at Lanham. "I'm glad to see you bulldogs wearin' a muzzle."

The Rangers wouldn't turn any prisoners over to Casoose, not since the day he had tied two of them to a tree by their necks and to a saddle horse by their feet and had whipped the horse away. Even fanatic old Sandoval wouldn't have done a stunt like that if

McNelly had been there. McNelly believed summary execution had its place, but cat-and-mouse games did not.

Discouraged, half expecting disbandment orders from Austin any day, afraid the captain would die without ever coming back, some of the Rangers began talking about going home. Some talked of hunting cowboy jobs in the Nueces Strip, but winter was a bad time to be out of work, for not many ranches would be hiring now till spring. With the Rangers there was the promise of regular pay, at least until Austin decided the McNelly company was no longer of service. It wouldn't bother the legislature to leave a bunch of men stranded down on the river in the middle of winter. They weren't running a charity ward.

Lanham Neal had about made up his mind to strike out for the Texas Panhandle and new country. Folks were saying McKenzie and the army had corraled the Comanches, and now cattle herds were venturing into that vast tableland. Maybe there'd be work up there for a cowboy. If he couldn't find a job, perhaps he could hunt buffalo the rest of the winter. One thing sure, he didn't want to stay down here in the Strip anymore, once he left the Rangers. Bonifacio had brought him the news when Zoe Daingerfield married Andrew Bailey. Well, that was a door slammed for good. Nothing here to hold Lanham anymore. Sooner he wiped the river mud off of his boots, the better.

He particularly wanted to leave after the appalling day Vincente de Zavala and Casoose led a patrol toward a thin column of dark smoke. They found a small Mexican *ranchito* lying in black ruins, the *ranchero* hanging in his own brush arbor, his wife dying of bullet wounds, several small children crying in terror.

"*Mi hija,*" the woman gasped. "They took my daughter."

The Rangers spurred out, following the tracks of the *ranchero*'s pitifully small herd. They hauled up at the bank of the river, too late as usual. Lanham's heart sagged as he saw a tiny figure lying silent and still, like a crumpled rag doll. Dismounting, he gently turned the girl over. He recoiled at the sight of the knife plunged into her breast.

Joe Benson cursed softly. "Why couldn't they have let her go? Why'd they have to kill her?"

Lanham shook his head. "She might've done this herself." He looked across the river, gritting his teeth. "Patriots!"

Old Casoose Sandoval knelt by the girl, the tears flowing unashamedly down his leathery brown cheeks and into the tattered beard. He began a cry that was half a moan, half a curse. He was remembering another time, another girl.

In bitter frustration Lanham said, "Nothin' more we can do here. Nothin' but take her home."

Old Sandoval grasped the knife and pulled it out. He wiped what blood he could onto the girl's torn dress. From his pocket he took a whetstone and began to work on the blade. Madness was in his eyes. "*Amigos,*" he said, "tell the lieutenant I will be back in my own time. I go across the river."

Lanham had no inclination to stop him. "Go ahead, Casoose."

Vincente de Zavala put his hand on the scout's thin shoulder. A little of the madness was in his eyes, too. "I go with you, old man."

Riding away, the Rangers carried the girl across

Joe Benson's saddle, and Joe rode behind Lanham. Joe kept looking back toward the luckless girl. "Lord, Lanham, I wisht the captain was back."

Lanham shook his head. "Forget it, Joe. I doubt we'll ever see him again."

He was wrong. One afternoon a soldier from the United States cavalry detail at Edinburg galloped into Las Rucias camp with a telegraph message just received over military lines. Lieutenant Robinson gave a whoop. "It's Captain! He's at Ringgold Barracks!" The Rangers cheered.

Ringgold! Lanham had never been there, but he knew it was upriver at Rio Grande City.

"Says for us to get the hell down there as fast as we can ride. He'll meet us at Las Cuevas crossing. We're goin' after bandits!"

Old Casoose led the way, ducking and dodging through the tangles of brush, setting a hard pace, licking his cracked lips in anticipation. A wild new enthusiasm fired the young Rangers now. Gone was the black discouragement of the last long weeks. Captain was waiting at Las Cuevas! A new deck of cards was about to be dealt.

It was one of the fastest forced rides in the history of the Texas Rangers—fifty-five miles in something like five hours. Shortly after dark, the entire company reined up at the bank of the Rio Grande, horses lathered and winded, so tired they trembled and let their heads sag. It was a wonder half of them hadn't died.

There stood Captain, his face thin and colorless but his clothes fresh, his beard trimmed, his eyes a-flash with the fire of old. Like a dying candle, Captain would flare brightly before life snuffed out.

Behind him waited a young army officer and a sizable company of U.S. troops. Captain shook hands with his own officers, glowing in pleasure. "Boys, it's good to see you; mighty good. How've things been?"

Lieutenant Robinson answered obliquely. "They'll be better, Captain, now that you're back. Just tell us what you want us to do."

Not that Captain wouldn't. McNelly took the black cigar from his mouth and used it to point at the river. "Boys, they're testing us. Word from our spies is that Cortina has got an order for up to eighteen thousand head of beef. To get that many he'll have to amass a small army and make a sweep over the whole Nueces Strip. They've just finished a raid of sorts, feeling us out, seeing if they can get away with it. And they *did* get away with it, up to now. You can see their trail." He pointed to a mass of cattle and horse tracks, spread like a muddy blanket over the river bank, disappearing in the murky water.

"Boys, across yonder, back from the river aways, lies Rancho Las Cuevas. You've heard of it. It's the biggest den of border bandits west of Matamoros. It's the stronghold of old Juan Flores Salinas, and he's one of the biggest chieftains Cortina has. A few hours ago, those Cuevian bandits crossed something like 250 Texas cattle right here. A Mexican lookout got word to the army, but by the time the troops could get here it was too late. The *Cortinistas* had the cattle across the river. They fired some shots. They knew the soldiers wouldn't fire back. Outlaws can ignore international law. Soldiers can't . . . at least, they don't.

"Boys, that river has stopped us once too often. If they get away with this one—and they think they already have—they'll be back here in force for the biggest raid since Santa Anna. A lot of good people in

Texas will die . . . *gringos* . . . Mexicans . . . all kinds. Now, they've got those stolen cattle in corrals over yonder. One of our spies has already looked."

He pointed, and Lanham Neal recognized a grim Vincente de Zavala.

"I'm going over there," Captain said matter-of-factly. "I'm going to get those cattle and bring them back. I'd like all the help I can get, but I'll not order a man to go. Every man who crosses the river with me will be a volunteer."

The men looked at each other, weighing the danger. Captain said, "I can't guarantee you'll come back. I can't guarantee you anything but a damned good fight. Any of you who want to go, step up."

Lanham waited to see how many others would go. He didn't intend to swim across there with nobody but the captain. One of the reasons for McNelly's recklessness was his firm belief in predestination—that a man couldn't be killed until it came his appointed time to die. Lanham did not share the comfort of that belief. One after another, the Rangers stepped forward. Lanham went with them.

The captain nodded, pleased. "Good. We'll take time to fix some supper, then. We've got an old rowboat tied up here on the bank. It's leaky, but it'll make it across. We'll start putting you over after midnight, when the *Cortinistas* have given us up and gone to sleep."

While they waited, more troopers arrived. The soldiers had tied into the military wire that followed the river from Ringgold Barracks to Fort Brown. An operator was tapping out messages for McNelly as well as for the army officers. Word came that Major Alexander was on his way from Fort Brown with a Gatling gun.

Lanham could tell by the stars when it was midnight. He hadn't slept. Captain moved to rouse his Rangers, but he found them already waiting. He asked one of the army lieutenants, "You coming with us?"

"I want to," the officer said, "but I have to wait for the wire to bring me orders."

Vincente de Zavala stood ready. Captain shook his head. "I can't let you go, *amigo*. My Rangers all know old Casoose. Most of them don't know you as well. In the dark they might make a mistake."

Vincente seemed inclined to argue, but nobody argued long with Captain. Vincente stepped back and faced Lanham Neal. "*Caporál,* you know what is across that river?"

Lanham said, "Never been there."

"Three hundred, maybe four hundred *bandidos* and Rancho Las Cuevas. How many *rinches* does our captain have?"

Lanham swallowed. "Not near enough."

Sergeant Armstrong overheard. "Ten to one ain't no odds for Captain. Anybody ever tell you about the time Captain took forty men and captured eight hundred federals over by New Orleans? Trotted his men out in sight time and again, here one time, yonder the next . . . convinced the Yankees they was surrounded by a force twice their size. They just laid down and give up."

"You think he can do it again here?"

The sergeant shrugged. "I just let Captain do the worryin'."

Lanham thought, *I expect I'll help him worry a little.*

Captain went over on the boat's first trip, taking the lead as always. Presently the boat was back for three more. Lanham had to sit and wait, and the waiting was not good. It gave him too much time to wonder if the captain really had a plan or if the fever had robbed him of reason. *Ten to one*. Lanham figured it six ways from Sunday, and it still came out impossible.

Casoose and four others tried swimming their horses across. On his next return, the boatman brought an order from the captain that no more horses be brought. They had all but gone down in treacherous quicksand on the far bank. This operation would be carried out afoot. In Lanham's view this only lengthened the odds. But he wasn't the captain.

Early-morning fog had settled in wet and heavy by the time the last Rangers made it to the Mexico side. Captain asked one of the men anxiously, "Any word from the military?"

"They're still waitin' for orders, Captain."

"They'll wait till hell freezes over, then," Captain said in frustration. "If they haven't been given orders by now, they never will be. We'll do it by ourselves." He pointed to a cattle trail that led up the bank and into the dense fog. "The horsemen will lead out."

Casoose was more or less familiar with the land, so he rode in front, walking his horse. The trail through the mesquite and willows and sacahuiste was too narrow for a double file. The men strung out.

Lanham was a cowboy and not used to walking. His feet ached before he had traveled far. They ached a lot more before the Rangers finally hauled up at a fence which had wooden bars for a gate. Ground fog still clung thick and heavy, so that at times, even in the spreading light of dawn, the Rangers had not been able to see each other all the way from the head of the line to the rear. Captain ordered the men up close.

"Boys, we're at Rancho Las Cuevas. You all know what we're up against, but we've got surprise in our favor, and the fog. We'll hit them hard and fast. Kill everybody you see except women and children. They're all *Cortinistas*, gathering to raid Texas. I'm counting on them not knowing how many of us there really are. If we hit them hard enough, they'll figure it's an army. Don't hesitate. When you see a man, shoot. All right, Casoose, let down the bars."

The Rangers passed through the gate and immediately spread out into a skirmish line. Lanham saw the broad form of sheds and other out-buildings. Ahead, he could hear the sound of axes, chopping firewood for breakfast.

A man shouted, *"Quién vive?"* He fired one shot. A Ranger rifle roared, and the sentry went down. At that, Casoose gave a wild yell that made Lanham's hair stand on end, and he spurred his horse forward. The Rangers broke into a trot, shouting.

Woodchoppers started throwing their axes aside and running for their guns. One stood foolishly staring, bewildered. He went down as if struck by his own ax. Ranger rifles and pistols cracked in the dawn. One after another, the sentries and woodcutters fell. Out of a long building, men came running, fumbling sleepily with their buttons, peering through the fog. A few fired wildly, but most never lived long enough to trigger a shot.

In moments the shooting was over. Across the broad yard Lanham saw bodies crumpled, many of them not dressed. Not one was a Ranger.

The Texans paused for breath, watching for more men to pour out of these buildings.

Lanham felt a stab of misgiving. Vincente had said

three or four hundred men. There wasn't room for that many. He had seen a dozen or so at most. Something was terribly wrong.

Casoose knew the answer. "*Capitán!* In this fog, we have made a mistake. This is not the Rancho Las Cuevas. This is Las Cachuttas. It is an outpost, only."

Captain stood stiff, dismayed. "Where is Rancho Las Cuevas?"

Casoose pointed, "*Poco mas allá.* Maybeso half a mile."

Captain was not a cursing man, but had he been, he would have scourged the heavens. "They're bound to have heard the shooting. They'll be ready for us now. But maybe they'll be cautious about meeting us. They don't know how many we are. Boys, we're going on."

They made the half mile in a hard trot, Lanham's feet still hurting. The fog was thinning some but still provided cover. The sand caused heavy running, and the brush was thick and clutching. Any moment Lanham expected a whole Mexican army to come bursting through that fog, guns blazing. The Rangers wouldn't last long enough to unshuck a *tamali.*

Up front, Casoose topped a rise and signaled. Captain immediately ordered the men to fan out. Lanham moved forward cautiously, not in any hurry to look.

Ahead of them and down a little, the *rancho* lay like a small village in a dish-like opening, its sides enclosed by a stockade fence of upright poles. Down in the corrals, Lanham could see a flurry of activity. The *Cortinistas* were saddling their horses, some already done and shouting for the others to hurry. Many seemed to be fumbling along. Lanham realized they must have celebrated last night, enjoying the success of their raid across the river, anticipating greater glory to come. Mescal must have flowed abundantly. The Rangers had caught them in a drunken sleep.

Corral gates opened, and horsemen charged out. They couldn't see the Rangers hidden in the brush and the fog. They rode straight into the Ranger guns. The Texans waited for Captain to give the signal. He raised his rifle to his shoulder. In a moment it belched flame, and a rider pitched from his saddle, directly under the hoofs of the other horses. Flame lanced in a ragged pattern from points all up and down the brushline. Horses plunged to the ground, screaming. Men shouted in pain and anger and fright. Some men lay still. A few tried crawling away but were quickly picked off.

Those riders not hit in the first savage volley wheeled their horses around and spurred desperately back toward the stockade. Ranger rifles kept firing, and more *Cortinistas* fell.

In the moments of lull that followed, the Rangers hurriedly strengthened their positions. Lanham moved from his exposed location and threw himself belly-down in a small depression behind a bush. At the stockade, he could see the *Cortinistas* milling in confusion and anger. They came boiling out, charging again without leadership, without purpose. It occurred to Lanham that they still couldn't see the Rangers hidden in the brush. The bandits expected to see mounted men. They rode headlong into the Ranger position.

A second time they met a blistering volley. They were too close to haul around and go back. Those who survived the first shots came spurring, trying to overrun the line. Most of them didn't make it. A few sped past the Rangers, seeing them too late. These, caught behind the line, never had a chance. The Rangers could not afford to let them get away, for they had seen how few the invaders really were.

The lull was longer after the second charge. Down in the corral Lanham saw that more men and more horses were ready. Now he could see the bandits rallying around one man who sat astride a fine horse.

Captain looked through his spyglass. "It's the old man . . . Juan Flores Salinas. They've got a leader now, boys. This time they'll draw blood." From the direction of Camargo, other men were galloping in, drawn to the aid of Las Cuevas by the thunder of the guns.

"Boys," said the captain, "when we lost the surprise, we lost it all. They'll cut us off if we stay here. Let's break for the river. Don't shoot unless you have to."

That was the best suggestion Lanham had heard since supper. He joined the irregular line of running men. Captain stayed back with the five horsemen as a rear guard, giving his Rangers the best of it.

Somehow, though Lanham ran and stumbled and fell and pushed to his feet and ran some more through the sand and brush and angry grabbing of thorns, he didn't tire. His feet didn't hurt anymore. Maybe the direction made the difference. Somewhere ahead of them, hidden by the patchy fog, lay the Rio Grande. With three or four hundred aroused Cuevian bandits behind them, Texas was going to look mighty good . . . if they made it.

He wouldn't have bet much on their getting there. It seemed inevitable that Salinas would send flankers loping around to cut them off, then surround them and begin a systematic annihilation.

But he didn't. Captain's strategy was still working.

The bandits had no idea how many invaders had hit them. Surely they must have thought it was several times the actual number, for only lunatics would have attacked a strong position and challenged a force ten times their size. The Mexicans knew by now, of course, that the Rangers were falling back. But they didn't know how far they had gone. The logical supposition was that they had moved only far enough to set up a trap.

The first two charges so terribly lacerated the Cuevians that old Salinas was cautious about riding into a trap and losing more of his force. On horseback, he moved forward no faster than the Rangers were moving backward. No Ranger had fired a shot during the retreat, and no *Cortinista* had as yet actually seen a Ranger in the fog.

The Rangers passed Las Cuchattas, where they had made that mistaken assault. The dead still lay unmoved. At the sight of the Rangers, a few women retreated quickly into their *jacales*. It was as if the whole camp was dead.

Nearing the river, the bandits became bolder, for they realized now they faced a retreating force, not a trap. Captain, in the rear guard, fired a shot and brought down a horseman. Sporadic firing started. The Rangers slowed their retreat, looking back over their shoulders for targets. Reaching the riverbank, they dropped down behind a shallow ledge and faced around, rifles and pistols ready, providing cover for the rear guard. The fog was lifting, burning off under the heat of the morning sun.

The Cuevians spotted the Ranger position. The old *jefe* rallied his men to charge.

Across the river, the U.S. troopers now could see what was going on. The Gatling gun had arrived.

A nervous soldier set the gun to firing. The bullets passed over the Rangers' heads, into the ranks of the bandits. Several fell. Salinas signaled a charge, to get down into the lower ground where the Gatling gun couldn't be used for fear of hitting the Rangers.

Lanham watched the heavy line of horsemen thundering toward him through mesquite and willow. His mouth was dry. His heart seemed to be in his throat. His hands were slick with cold sweat as he brought the rifle into line. Across the river, the Gatling gun still chattered. At that distance it did little damage, but it was a comforting sound.

Ranger guns blazed in another volley. The old *jefe* was one of the first to fall, plunging headlong from his silver-studded, big-horned Mexico saddle. The first line of Cuevian horsemen was cut down like a stand of wheat struck by the whispering blade of a scythe. Some of the horses plunged over the bank, around the Rangers. One went straight down into quicksand, screaming as it disappeared. The others cut back. So did the surviving horsemen. They spurred away, the charge broken.

Captain stood up and looked. The fallen chieftain hadn't stirred. The *jefe* of Cortina's western division lay dead in the sand.

"Boys," said Captain, "dig in. I imagine we've stopped them awhile."

Lanham knew then that Captain had no intention of going back across the river. He had come for cattle.

In the long lull, an army officer crossed with two men in a boat. Other troopers shucked their clothes and swam over to reinforce the McNelly position. Beaching his tiny craft, the officer hurried to McNelly. "When we first heard the shooting, we thought you were all dead."

McNelly smiled grimly. "There are lots of dead, but none of them are ours. We haven't lost a man." He paused, looking wishfully across toward the Gatling gun. "When are the rest of them coming over?"

The officer said soberly, "Except for a few volunteers, I doubt they ever will. Face it, McNelly. The wires are saying you've invaded a sovereign land. The army isn't going to back you."

McNelly frowned. "*You're* backing me."

The officer removed his shoulder straps. "Unofficially, that's all."

The Cuevian force had pulled back out of sight. The Rangers and the underwear-clad soldiers who had come to aid them took advantage of the quiet period to dig holes in the bank and pile up fortifications in front of them. Lanham dug grimly, knowing his life might depend upon it, wondering how long before the bandits nerved themselves for another assault.

The Cuevians didn't make a move. The Rangers finished their digging and settled down to rest. Rest was fine, but it had one disadvantage: it gave them too much time to think. Their situation here was not one Lanham enjoyed thinking about.

After a time, Major Alexander came across in a rowboat. McNelly met him at the bank. "You come to help us?"

Alexander shook his head. "Orders, Captain. I have a telegram here for you from Colonel Potter at Fort Brown. He advises you to retreat at once to the Texas side."

McNelly read the telegram, his eyes narrowing. "He's ordering you to give me no assistance."

"That's right, Captain."

"But I thought . . ."

"So did I. But he's under pressure. Orders are orders, Captain. What answer shall I give him?"

McNelly held silent a moment, chewing his black cigar. Lanham watched intently, for that was a sign the devil was in him. McNelly said, "Tell him no."

"The colonel is already catching hell. He won't be pleased."

"Just the same, tell him no."

Alexander accepted the decision without rancor. "I'll tell him." He started for his boat, then paused. "When did your men last eat?" Told they hadn't eaten since supper, the major said, "I'll send some food over. I don't guess that is the same as military support."

Seeming not to see the soldiers who had scattered among the Rangers, he went back across the river.

During the long afternoon, the Cuevians made sporadic probes at the Ranger lines. Each time, fire from the McNelly men and the soldiers drove them back.

Across the river, the military telegraph was all but smoking. In the early-morning excitement that followed the first sound of gunfire, the young telegraph operator had assumed the worst and reported that McNelly's command was wiped out. Fort Brown had set up a relay system with eastern points and had delivered a report into Washington. Queries and orders began crackling back down the line until they came out at the key beneath the rough telegraph pole where an army signalman had spliced into the border wire. Off and on during the afternoon, an officer would punt the boat across to keep McNelly posted on latest developments. One thing became clear: government officials from Texas to Washington were in a stew about McNelly's position.

So were the Mexicans. From Fort Brown, telegraph

communications were sent to the American embassy in Matamoros, and the messages were relayed to the American official in Mexican Camargo, opposite Rio Grande City, instructing him to oversee McNelly's surrender to proper Mexican authority.

McNelly's reaction was to chew his black cigar ever more vigorously. "Surrender, hell!"

Major Alexander came across in the boat and regretfully gave orders for all remaining troopers to return to the Texas bank. He handed McNelly another telegraph message. "This one," he said, "comes from the top. It's from Belknap himself, the Secretary of War."

McNelly almost bit the cigar in two as he read. "He demands that we retreat at once to Texas. He doesn't ask. He *demands*."

"What answer do you want me to give him?"

McNelly's thin frame was straight and stiff. He dug a piece of brown wrapping paper from his pocket and found a stub pencil. "I'll write him the answer myself. I'll tell him he can take his United States army and go to hell!"

Alone now, the Rangers held their vigil on the quiet bank, listening and watching. At one point a small party came under a flag of truce and picked up the Cuevian dead. There was no sign of assault.

Lieutenant Robinson asked, "Captain, you think they'll try us again?"

Captain nodded. "Probably. They've got to do *something*. They can't just let us stay here."

"How long do you think we can keep standin' them off?"

Captain pondered. "Long enough." He pointed his cigar toward the river. "Those soldiers over yonder, they're on our side, orders or not. They've already come to our aid once. If they see we're about to be wiped out, they'll come again. They'll come in force, despite anything the Secretary of War or anybody else has to say. That will mean an official unit of the United States army has invaded Mexican soil. And that, Lieutenant, is an act of war."

The lieutenant's jaw dropped. "Captain, are you tryin' to start a war with Mexico?"

Captain smiled grimly. "The Mexican government has gone to sleep and let Cortina take complete control on the border because they've got bigger things on their mind to worry about. They know he's bloodthirsty; they know he's corrupt. Still, he's just a little problem compared to all the others they've got. But give them the threat of war with the United States and all of a sudden Cortina is a problem—the biggest one they have. They'll have to move quick. If we can get the United States army over here, we can force the Mexican government itself to stop Cortina."

The lieutenant stared in awe. "Captain, this is too audacious even for *you*. With thirty men, you're tryin' to force the hands of two governments."

"Thirty *good* men," McNelly pointed out. "And well-placed."

"Cortina may be corrupt, but he's also intelligent. Think he won't realize the spot you've placed him in?"

McNelly shrugged. "If he does, so much the better. He'll have more respect for us from now on. A lot more respect. He'll know that what we've done once, we can do again."

Lanham Neal silently shook his head and looked down at his shaking hand. If he lived to be a hundred and six, he would always believe Captain had had this whole thing planned before he ever crossed the river.

21

Captain McNelly had taken the boat to the Texas side to send messages on the military wire when the flag of truce showed up. Five horsemen rode out into the open. Four were Mexicans, one a *gringo*.

Lieutenant Robinson had been left in charge. He watched distrustfully until the riders brought their white flag out well into a clearing that lay between the riverbank and the heavy brush beyond. "Sergeant Hall, you hustle over and notify Captain. I'll take four men, and we'll parley till Captain gets here."

He picked four nearby Rangers. Lanham Neal was one. They moved out, rifles carried at the ready. Walking, Lanham warily eyed the *gringo*. "Lieutenant, do you know him?"

Robinson nodded. "Doc Headly. He's on Captain's 'wanted' list if ever he steps over to the Texas side. He's a *Cortinista*."

The horsemen stopped and waited. Lanham could see that the *gringo* carried a carbine. A piece of paper was clamped in its hammer. The *gringo's* eyes were suspicious. "I've got a message here for the commanding officer."

"I am the commanding officer," said the lieutenant.

"You're not McNelly. I want to see McNelly."

"McNelly's across the river. I'm in command till he gets back."

Headly nodded. "Then I reckon while we wait for him, we'd just as well stand easy." He reached into a nosebag tied to his saddle and fetched out a bottle of mescal. "How about a little smile?"

Robinson said, "I never drink while I'm on duty."

"A pity." The renegade doctor offered the bottle to the other Rangers, who turned him down, then tilted it for a long, long swallow. He passed it on to the Mexicans who flanked him. "Man never knows when the next drink is coming. He ought never to turn one down."

By the time McNelly came, the bottle was almost drained and a flush had risen in the *gringo*'s face. "McNelly," he said arrogantly, "do you know who I am?"

"I do," the captain replied evenly. "Your name is known to every peace officer from Austin to the river."

Headly's eyes showed a beginning of anger. "Do you realize what you've done? You've unlawfully invaded a peace-loving sovereign nation, and you've killed honest, peaceful citizens. One of them was the *alcalde* himself, the beloved Juan Flores Salinas. Have you any idea how many good citizens of Mexico you've killed today?"

McNelly said he didn't. The *gringo* said, "Close to eighty."

McNelly frowned. "Is that all? I hoped it was more."

"This is a grave situation. Your action is unexcusable. It has put relations in a very precarious position between the United States and the Republic of Mexico."

"I didn't come all the way out here to listen to a harangue. You've got a letter under that hammer. If it's for me, let me have it. If it's not, I suggest you get the hell away from here."

Headly extended the carbine to McNelly, butt first, so the captain could take the letter. "It is from the chief justice himself, representing the state of Tamaulipas."

Lanham watched the captain's face, and he could guess what the letter said. He figured that a man who would tell the United States Secretary of War to go to hell would have even choicer words for the chief justice of a robber pueblo.

"What's your answer?" Headly demanded.

"I came to get those Texas cattle. I'll stay till we have them."

"I may as well tell you. Three full regiments of Mexican troops are on their way here from Monterrey and from Matamoros to drive you out of Mexico."

"You'll need them all," said McNelly.

Headly's eyes narrowed. "You're foolish, Captain. How many men do you have with you?"

Listening, Lanham realized the bandits still had no idea how many Rangers lay waiting beyond that bank. They were fishing for information.

"Enough," the captain said, "to march to Mexico City!"

Lanham heard a voice and turned. A Ranger came running, rifle in hand. "Captain! Captain, there's men yonder a-horseback, fannin' out around you. They don't aim to let you get back to the bank."

Lanham's breath stopped momentarily. He could sense rather than see the movement, obscured by the brush.

Tightly the captain barked, "All right, boys, each of you draw a bead. If any one of those bandits fires a shot, all five men on this truce team are to die. And Headly is mine!"

Looking down the muzzle of McNelly's pistol, the *gringo* swallowed. His flushed face went almost purple. To one of the Mexicans he said in Spanish, "Tell them to back away. Tell them under no circumstances is any man to shoot."

The Mexican seemed extremely happy to go and deliver the message, away from point-blank range of the Texan guns. The Cuevians pulled off.

"Now," said the captain, letting the pistol sag a little—but not too far—"you came out here to treat with me. You're going to treat. I want those cattle back. Every single head. Not one of us is leaving here till we've come to an agreement. Not you, and not me."

Headly blustered and fumed. Captain reminded him the Rangers had come prepared for war and would press it as far as was necessary. Moreover, the United States army waited just across the river. The bandits already had had a taste of their Gatling gun. Would they like a sample closer at hand? Would they like a full-scale war with all the power of the United States to press it?

In the end Headly took a long swig from what little was left of the mescal. "The cattle are penned at Camargo."

"I don't care where they're penned. I want them in Texas. If you want to leave here without a war, you'll write out an order now and sign it. Otherwise, we'll attack within the hour!"

Headly's hands shook so much he couldn't write. McNelly wrote the order for him, on his own terms. "This specifies," he pointed out, "that the cattle are to be delivered to the Texas side of the river tomorrow morning opposite Camargo. No excuses, no exceptions. All the cattle!"

The *gringo* signed the order in a wobbly hand. He finished the bottle and turned away like a whipped dog.

Captain said, "Tomorrow morning. If the cattle aren't there, we'll be back."

The truce party rode away.

McNelly walked to the riverbank, elated. "Boys, we've done it. We've met them on their own ground and whipped them down. Let's go back to our own side of the river."

Relief and jubilation was the mood of the Rangers as they set their boots victoriously back on the Texas side to the cheers of waiting soldiers and a considerable gathering of *gringo* and Mexican civilians, drawn by word of the fighting. They ate a hearty supper of beef, brought by a nearby *ranchero* who still had a few cattle left the bandits hadn't stolen. Then they saddled and rode to a point opposite Camargo, near Rio Grande City.

The longer Lanham Neal thought about the situation, the less sure he was. They were on the north bank again and the Cuevians still had the cattle on the south bank. An agreement with bandits was worth only whatever the bandits considered it to be worth. Lanham lay on his blanket, looking across at the flickering candlelight that marked Camargo. He didn't sleep much.

He had lost track of time, but somebody told him next morning that it was Sunday. He could see the cattle pens, well beyond the bank across the river. A mile, maybe, but it could as well have been a hundred, if the Cuevians didn't choose to deliver. The armed riders around the pole corrals were not a hopeful sign.

After breakfast, Captain McNelly walked down to the ferry landing with a note to Diego Garcia, who would be in command now that Salinas was dead. It asked for early delivery of the cattle as specified in the agreement signed by Headly. Presently a Mexican messenger was back with a reply. It seemed, he said, everyone had overlooked the fact that this was Sunday. No business could be conducted on the Sabbath.

Captain began chewing the cigar. "The business was conducted yesterday," he said. "Now I want those cattle."

Negotiations were carried back and forth through the morning by way of emissaries with no sign of success. After treating his Rangers to a dinner of coffee and *pan dukes*, Captain took them all back down to the river and counted off ten men closest to hand. It was Lanham's dubious fortune to be standing there in front.

"We're going over," he said, "and wind up the negotiations."

The ferry ride was slow. Lanham looked into the muddy water, bleakly wondering why the hell he had ever given in to the moment of weakness that had made a Ranger of him. The first trip across that river had been risk enough. A second trip looked like suicide.

His feelings were shared. He heard one of the Rangers murmur, "I'd as soon not be a part of this Death Squad."

The captain was calmly talking to the old ferryman, asking him if he had been to church.

I wish I'd gone to church this morning, Lanham thought. In San Antonio or someplace.

The least Captain could have done was to bring the whole company, he worried. *Thirty men can put up a lot more fight than ten.*

But as the ferry neared the Mexico bank, he began to see the captain's reason. Sight of all those Rangers would have alarmed the Cuevians and brought reinforcements on the run. The ten created no stir. Only a handful of customs officials and Rurales waited at the ferry landing.

Captain stepped off first and hitched the ferry's rope to a post. He walked serenely toward the waiting officers. They wore uniforms of the Mexican government, but they were Cortina's men. Their allegiance was to him, not to Mexico City. Captain picked out the one who appeared to be in charge. "I have come for the cattle."

The officer seemed annoyed. "Has it not been made plain to you? This is Sunday. It is not proper to do work on the Sabbath."

The gate of the corral was open, and the cattle were being driven out. They were being pointed south, not north toward the river. Before this Sabbath was over, they would be far away.

Captain said: "I have a paper duly signed by an officer, and I took it he was a gentleman. He agreed the cattle would be delivered today. No word was said about the Sabbath."

"I am in charge here, not he," the official said stiffly. "It is impossible to deliver the cattle today. Even if it were not the Sabbath, no duty has been paid on these cattle. Duty must be paid before they can cross into Texas."

"No duty was paid when they crossed into Mexico *from* Texas," McNelly pointed out, "and by the Eternal none will be paid now."

The captain moved with the quickness of a panther. He threw the customs officer to the ground and shoved his knee into the man's belly, jamming the muzzle of a pistol against his head. The Rangers, startled, swung their weapons to cover the Rurales and the other customs men.

"Now, you mealy-mouthed son of a bitch," the captain gritted, "you'll honor that agreement or die!"

The officer sputtered in surprise and panic. "Take the cattle! Take the cattle!"

"No, we're not going to take them. The agreement was that they would be delivered. You're going to lie here with my pistol against your head till they're across that river. One bad move from anybody and I'll scatter your brains in the sand. What's more, we'll kill every scoundrel here."

One officer was allowed to ride out to the herd and give the order. The Rangers held their ground, watching as the Cuevian *vaqueros* stripped off their clothes, herded the cattle into the Rio Grande and swam them across. Not until they saw the herd shaking off the muddy water on the Texas bank did McNelly release his hold on the customs officer and motion for his men to return to the ferry.

In the slow calm of the crossing, Lanham Neal found himself trembling, a reaction to the tension that had ended. He gazed at the serene little captain, who stood on the forward end of the ferry. Captain was dog-tired, face colorless, but his teeth were clamped jubilantly on a cigar that was pointed straight up in victory.

Cortina doesn't rule the border anymore, Lanham thought. McNelly does. When Cortina is gone and forgotten, they'll still remember McNelly.

On the Texas bank, a throng of people waited—Rangers, soldiers, civilians, cheering wildly. In all the years of the border raiding, this was the first herd of stolen cattle that had ever come out of Mexico back into Texas. This was a whipping from which the border bandits would never recover.

Far away in his Matamoros stronghold, Cortina probably didn't realize it yet, but this was the day that had broken his back.

Just before the ferry touched the bank, McNelly turned to his men. "Meet them proudly, boys. We went over there with our heads and our backs up. We've returned the same way."

22

On the riverbank, Lanham Neal found Vincente de Zavala and Bonifacio Holguin waiting for him. Bonifacio rushed forward and gave him the *abrazo*. "*Caporál*, I heard you were killed."

Lanham tried to smile, but it wasn't in him. "I'm still here."

"They said at the *rancho* . . ." Bonifacio broke off and turned his face away to avoid the shame of tears.

Vincente looked grave. "Bonifacio has brought news, *caporál*. About *la patrona*. It is not good."

"What about Zoe? Somethin' happened to her?"

Bonifacio faced around slowly, his gaze on Lanham's boots. "It is the new *patrón*, the Bailey, her husband. He is crazy with jealousy, *caporál*. A traveler brought news from Las Cuevas crossing that all the Rangers had been killed. *La patrona*, she cried much, for she knew you were with them. The Bailey, he was much angry over her crying. He beat her. Now, *caporál*, it is good for a man to beat his wife a little bit once in a while, for this keeps her happy with him and shows he loves her. But the Bailey, he beat *la patrona* much more than a little. She fought him, and he beat her until she was almost dead.

"It is whispered among the *vaqueros* that it was Bailey himself who killed his first wife. It is whispered that he will kill *la patrona* also, if he beats her again. He has her land. He knows now that he cannot ever have her love. Her love is for you. It always has been."

"She married *him,*" Lanham said.

"At a time of foolish pride. She is her father's daughter, and the Daingerfield, he was always a stubborn man. She is much woman. Once you had much love for her. I think you have it yet, from your face."

"Bailey's her husband. I got no right."

Vincente de Zavala put in a contribution. "If he killed her, *caporál,* you would then kill him, *no es verdad?"*

Lanham nodded soberly. "I reckon I would."

"Then stop him now, *before* he kills her. You will save yourself much trouble."

When it was put that way, Lanham could see enough logic in it to justify himself. He had known from the first that he wasn't going to stand by and do nothing. He went to McNelly.

"Captain, I got to ask you for leave. There's somethin' I got to do. Somethin' personal."

McNelly was not that lax. He had to have particulars, and Lanham was obliged to give him the whole story. McNelly rubbed his beard, troubled. "Neal, I can respect your concern, but this is something between a man and his wife. It's not something in which the Rangers have any right to intrude."

"I wouldn't be goin' as a Ranger, sir. I'd be goin' as Lanham Neal."

"You'd have to resign. I couldn't allow the Rangers

to become entangled in a family problem, much as I might want to."

Lanham said regretfully, "Then, sir, I reckon I better turn in my resignation. I'll be leavin' directly." He paused. "Sir, before I go, there's one thing I just got to say."

"What's that, Neal?"

"Captain, you're no carpetbagger!"

Riding up to the ranch headquarters, flanked by Vincente and Bonifacio, Lanham Neal watched the Bailey barns and main house carefully. He had no particular plan. He meant to go directly to the house and see about Zoe. Whatever Bailey decided to do, Lanham would meet that problem as it arose.

The dark Rafael and another *vaquero* were shoeing a horse in a corral. Lanham was close enough to recognize the animal. One of Griffin Daingerfield's. It hadn't taken Bailey long to exercise his property rights. The *vaqueros* straightened and watched as Lanham and his *compadres* rode to the house. One of them dropped a hammer and trotted into the barn.

Lanham swung down from the saddle. "Remember, boys, anything that happens between me and Bailey is our fight, not yours. All I want you to do is keep his *vaqueros* off of me."

"He may kill you, *caporál*," Vincente said.

"If he does, then do what you want to." Lanham paused on the front gallery and lifted his pistol halfway out of the holster, then let it slip back. He wanted to be sure it would draw easy if he needed it. "Zoe!" he called. "It's me, Lanham. I'm comin' in!"

He stepped through the door, blinking in the dim light. He heard a woman's startled cry before he saw her. Zoe stood in a bedroom doorway, a pistol in her hand. She let it sag.

"Lanham? Lanham?" She cried out as she stumbled toward him. He saw the ugly bruises and the swollen eye before she fell into his arms. "They told me you were dead," she sobbed.

"I'm here, Zoe. I come to help you."

"Lanham, I tried my best to hate you, but I couldn't. I still loved you, even when I was bein' a fool."

"I come to take you away from here, if you want to go."

"Yes, I want to go. I want to go home. Take me before I kill him, or he kills me."

"Home's not far enough. He'll come after you."

"He'll wish he hadn't. I've made up my mind that he won't ever touch me again. Me, or anything that belongs to me."

"We could go to the Panhandle or someplace, far off, where he couldn't reach you."

Zoe was still a Daingerfield. "That land is mine," she said stubbornly. "I'd rather die than leave it for him. Take me home, Lanham."

She hadn't changed, and suddenly he realized he never wanted her to. He drew her fiercely into his arms, still wanting her as desperately as ever. "Throw some things together, Zoe. We'll get out of here."

He heard heavy boots strike the wooden gallery, and he knew Bailey must have been at the barn. "Neal!" Bailey roared. "Neal, I know you're in there. You come out here, right now."

Lanham pushed Zoe aside. All the way over here, he had vacillated between a hope that Bailey would be gone and they would miss him, and one that he would be here with his back up so Lanham could give him everything he had coming to him. The first wish had won out in the final test of judgment.

Lanham looked out the front window. He couldn't see Bailey, but he could see that Vincente and Bonifacio were holding Rafael and half a dozen *vaqueros* off to a neutral distance. The fight would be between Lanham and Bailey . . . them alone.

Lanham had a strong conviction that if he stepped to that door, Bailey would blow a hole in him. Looking around for another way out, he saw a second door in the far end of the parlor. It opened onto the gallery but just around the corner.

"Bailey," Lanham called, "I come to take Zoe away from here."

"She belongs to me. You can't touch her. She's mine like the land is mine, and the cattle, and the horses. Touch her and I got a husband's right to kill you. The law can't lift a finger."

"You beat her, Bailey. Law don't give you a right to do that."

"What I done is between me and her. The Rangers fixin' to step in between a man and his wife?"

"I'm not here as a Ranger. I quit. I'm here as a friend to get her out of your reach."

"Or just to get her, maybe? She's damaged goods, Neal. Somebody else besides you has had her now. Even if you was to have her again, you couldn't forget that."

Zoe stood in the bedroom doorway, face stricken in fear. "Maybe he's right, Lanham. Maybe you couldn't forget that."

"And then again," said Lanham, "maybe I could." He weighed the distance to the door at the other end of the room. He picked up a lamp from a table and hefted it, getting the feel of its weight and balance. "Bailey," he shouted, "I'm comin' out. Let's talk it over."

"Come on," said Bailey.

Lanham hurled the lamp at the facing of the front door and turned on his heel, sprinting for the other door. He was halfway there when the lamp shattered. He heard the boom of Bailey's pistol, like a cannon the way it echoed in the room. He had been right; Bailey was poised to shoot him the moment he stepped into view.

But Lanham was out the side door as Bailey fired a second shot in reflex. Lanham had his own pistol in his hand. He hove around the corner. Bailey saw him from the tail of his eye and swung, pistol coming up for another shot.

Lanham didn't hesitate. McNelly had taught him better. He squeezed the trigger once and then again. Bailey slammed back against the gallery railing, eyes big in surprise. Steadying himself, he began bringing the pistol up again. He moved slowly, agonizingly.

Those two were for Zoe, Lanham thought coldly. *This one is for your other wife.* He fired once more, and Bailey went over the railing.

Bailey's *vaqueros* made no hostile move. They were still under the guns of Vincente and Bonifacio.

Lanham walked across the gallery to look down at Bailey. He became aware of a crackling noise and jerked around. One of Bailey's shots must have struck sparks off of something. The kerosene from the shattered lamp was going into flame. Lanham rushed into the house and looked around urgently for something to beat out the fire.

Zoe stopped him. "It's a miserable house. All it's ever known was pain and fear. Let it burn."

Lanham shrugged. “I reckon it's yours to do with as you want to. He's dead.”

Zoe had time to gather a few belongings before the flames reached the point of danger. She carried them onto the gallery on the side away from the fire. Outside, in the daylight, Lanham saw more plainly how she had been beaten. He hadn't had time yet to regret killing Bailey. Now he was sure he never would.

The Bailey *vaqueros* were getting nervous, wanting to do something about the fire. Lanham raised his hand. “She is *la patrona*. She says let it burn.”

Rafael and another *vaquero* grabbed Bailey by the legs and dragged him clear of the flames. By the casual way they did it, Lanham knew they had been attached to him only by wages, not by any regard. Lanham had nothing to fear from them now.

“Vincente, Bonifacio, you can put your guns up. Let's get away from this heat.”

In minutes the house was swallowed in flames. Zoe buried her face against Lanham's chest. “I don't want to look. I don't ever want to see it again. I just want to get away from here.”

“You're his widow. The place belongs to you now.”

“Not by rights. In a way, he stole it from Josefa's family, marryin' her just to get it. They can have it back. I never want to set foot on it again.”

“You're givin' away a lot.”

“I still got a place of my own.” She looked up at him and corrected herself. “We have a place of *our* own, Lanham. Whatever belongs to me belongs to you.” When Lanham didn't say anything, she went on anxiously, “Maybe you don't want that place anymore. You said we might go to the Panhandle. All right, we could do that. We could sell the ranch and go fresh. We could leave this border country and never look back, if that's what you want to do. Only, take me with you, Lanham. Don't leave me here by myself."

He still didn't answer. She cried out, "Lanham, say something. Say you want me, or say you don't want me. Say *something* so I'll know you've heard me."

He nodded soberly and held her tighter. "I heard you, Zoe; I was just thinkin'. I was thinkin' that a lot of blood has been spilled on this Nueces Strip for us to run away and leave it now. Your daddy's . . . lots of people's. And Captain . . . he's just about broke what health he had left. He's got death in his face now; I doubt he'll live out the winter. If we was to leave now, it'd be like sayin' that was all for nothin', like it didn't mean nothin' to us. But it *does* mean somethin', Zoe. It means I'm stayin'. *You're* stayin'. There's been too high a price paid for us to leave."

"We don't have a lot to start on, Lanham. A piece of land, a couple of mud shacks and what few cattle the bandits didn't steal."

"There's somethin' else . . . my Ranger wages I've saved up. I got over a hundred dollars I didn't spend."

"A hundred dollars!" He could feel her tears soaking through his shirt and touching warm against his skin. "With all that to start on, nobody can stop us. We're rich!"

KELTON ON KELTON

I was born at a place called Horse Camp on the Scharbauer Cattle Company's Five Wells Ranch in Andrews County, Texas, in 1926. My father was a cowboy there, and my grandfather was the ranch foreman. My great-grandfather had come out from East Texas about 1876 with a wagon and a string of horses to become a ranchman, but he died young, leaving four small boys to grow up as cowpunchers and bronc breakers. With all that heritage I should have become a good cowboy myself, but somehow I never did, so I decided if I could not do it I would write about it.

I studied journalism at the University of Texas and became a livestock and farm reporter in San Angelo, Texas, writing fiction as a sideline to newspaper work. I have maintained the two careers in parallel for forty-two years. My fiction has been mostly about Texas, about areas whose history and people I know from long study and long personal acquaintance. I have always believed we can learn much about ourselves by studying our history, for we are the products of all that has gone before us. All history is relevant today, because the way we live—the values we believe in—are a result of molds prepared for us by our forebears a long time ago.

I was an infantryman in World War II and married an Austrian girl, Anna, I met there shortly after the war. We raised three children, all grown now and independent, proud of their mixed heritage of the Old World on one hand and the Texas frontier on the other.

THE DAY THE COWBOYS QUIT

Dedicated
to those fine chroniclers of the West Texas cowboy:

J. EVETTS HALEY
BOB BEVERLY
LAURA V. HAMNER
PAUL PATTERSON

1

In later years people often asked Hugh Hitchcock about the Canadian River cowboy strike of 1883. If they were strangers he looked them over carefully before he answered, and sometimes he did not answer at all; he figured there was no way of explaining it to anyone who did not understand the nature of the old-time cowboy.

It irritated him like a prickly pear thorn imbedded under his hide that some people seemed to think cowboys spent their time loping around aimlessly on horseback and firing their pistols. Many of the men he had known in the Texas Panhandle never owned a pistol, and probably half the cowboys between the Canadian and the Pecos could not have shot themselves in the foot if they had tried. What they did most in those days was work, from before they could see in the morning until they could no longer see in the evening.

Those days, Hitch always said, a man proved himself with horsemanship. A rider a cut above average was looked up to, even by the sourest wagon cook. If a man's saddle did not have a shine to it, they knew nothing good would come of him.

Next to his way with a horse, a cowboy was proudest of his independence. He worked for other men, but they owned nothing of him except his time. He was a free soul. He could ride from the Rio Grande to the Powder River and seldom see a fence. He could start that ride with five dollars in his pocket and have three left when he finished, if that was the way he wanted to travel. Money did not rule him.

The Canadian River region of Texas then was less than ten years settled, the sandy-bottomed river cutting a deep, rough gash across the heart of that uplifted tableland known to the Spanish as *Llano Estacado*, the Staked Plains. It was a grand plateau, larger than some Eastern states, a vast treeless ocean of grass often flat to the eye but gently rolling when a man tested it in a wagon, finding himself alternately easing downward or putting forth extra effort to climb. A decade before, this prairie had teemed with grazing buffalo, fleet white-rumped antelope and the roving packs of gray wolves which lived among them, pulling down the halt and the lame. Across this unmapped sunny land had roamed the Comanche and the Kiowa, brothers to the wolf. They had known its hidden watering places, its changing seasons, its hunger, its bounty, its angry storms, and its quiet peace.

Now the buffalo were gone, and with them the Indian. White men's cattle by the hundreds of thousands had plodded and bawled up the long trails from South Texas, and down through Raton Pass from Colorado, spreading out over these seemingly infinite miles of open grasslands, finding water in occasional creeks and streams fringed with cottonwood and hackberry and black walnut, almost the only timber from the eastern caprock to the New Mexico breaks. Out in open country, wood was so rare that men gathered dry buffalo and cow chips for fuel wherever they found them, hoarding them in sagging cowhides lashed loosely beneath their wagonboxes.

Now most of the plains grass was claimed by right of occupancy, and already the more observant cowboys could see that it grew less tall. Dust stirred easier now, a sign of overgrazing because these great herds of longhorned cattle did not migrate with the rains and the changing seasons as had their wild and shaggy predecessors. Already men in their eagerness for gain foreshadowed their own defeat by demanding more from the land than it could produce. And those in a position to hire demanded more of other men.

Hugh Hitchcock always said cowboy independence triggered the cowboy strike. There came a time that some men decided independence was too costly when the wrong people had it, so they tried to mold others to a pattern of their own cutting. And when you crowd a man too far, he may do something in self defense that is not sensible either.

Old cowboys in later years argued no end over the causes of the strike, and the starting of it. To each it began in a different place and a different way. To Hugh Hitchcock, looking back, it started the day Rascal McGinty and the Figure 4 rep went to their guns over ownership of a roan cow.

He always remembered the kind of day it was—the sun bright over the gentle roll of the open plains, the sky blue as a pretty woman's eyes, the brown winter grass starting to show tinges of springtime green, the first prairie flowers bursting scarlet and yellow and white. He remembered Rascal McGinty and that red face of his and red hair and a temper to match them both. Rascal was riding Sweetheart, an ill-named mustang bay he had traded for, a long-tailed pony ugly as a mud fence but able to stay with a man to the last crossing—an honest horse that would work his heart out, but only after he had done his damnedest to bust the rider first. That bay was a lot like Rascal.

Hitch always recalled that Dayton Brumley was riding a Figure 4 sorrel called Blaze for the crooked streak that ran from forelock down to a snip nose. Blaze had fox ears and three stocking feet and an R Slash branded on his left hip, and moved with as smooth a saddle gait as Hitch ever saw.

He forgot in later years just what Dayton Brumley looked like. After all that time a man couldn't be expected to remember details.

She wasn't much of a cow; she had seen too many hard winters, and the scrubby calf punching its long nose futilely at her near-dry udder showed she had been less than choosy in the bull she associated with. But to a syndicate outfit like the Figure 4, its bookkeepers dreading each encounter with the Kansas City board of directors, every calf branded meant dollars of capital gain on the ledger. To a wage-working cowboy like Rascal McGinty or his brother Law, trying to build a shirttail herd for themselves, even a crippled cow or a blind one was of value so long as she could yet conceive and deliver. When Dayton Brumley rode into the "stray" herd and called the cow's brand a Figure 4, Rascal stood straight up in his stirrups. His voice carried halfway across the gather.

"The hell you say! That cow's an LR, sure as ever was."

Hugh Hitchcock heard, and the voice was a warning flag. Hitch was wagon boss on the W's "river division," that part of the ranch which lay nearest the Canadian, and the McGinty brothers worked under him. He knew Rascal's emotions lay always near the surface, the volatile cowboy quick to laugh or quick to explode like the Sharps Big Fifty that had cleared these plains and river breaks of buffalo. No one could ever judge which direction Rascal would jump.

A cowboy came spurring. "Hitch, you better git over yonder. There's apt to be trouble." Instinctively they always looked to Hugh Hitchcock; that was why he was wagon boss.

Dayton Brumley ignored Rascal and again called the pair as property of the Figure 4. On open range before barbed wire cut all of Texas into pastures, cattle of many brands mixed together. Boundary lines were an invisible thing; the cattle drifted wherever they found the grass green and the water good. At roundup time the big ranches sent their chuckwagons and teams of men to the various divisions, and they sent cowboy representatives to neighboring outfits' wagons, each to watch out for the interests of the brand that paid him. The calves were branded according to the marks of ownership on their mothers, and when a calf became weaned and still had no brand, it was by custom considered a maverick, belonging to the man on whose range it was found. In practice it more often belonged to the man whose loop caught it first. One purpose of the roundup, then, was to leave as few mavericks as possible for the quick-loop men.

Identification of the cow was usually easy, for a cowboy who couldn't read his own name soon learned the brands of the ranches around him. But sometimes a brand healed poorly or haired over heavily. That was a time for negotiation, and failing agreement it was a time when someone must arbitrarily play the role of judge and declare ownership by reasoning, instinct or favor.

Rascal McGinty's nose was slightly flattened. He always claimed the damage had been done by a horse, but Hugh Hitchcock had long suspected it happened in a fistfight.

"Go slow, Rascal," Hitch said quietly as he pushed his gray horse between the two men. A young W rider named Joe Sands had a rope around the calf's neck and was waiting for Hitchcock's judgment before he dragged the animal out to the men afoot by the branding fire. The roan cow was bawling and making as much fuss over her offspring as if it had been blue-blooded Durham stock brought down from the east.

Hitch expected to find Rascal crackling in anger; instead the unpredictable cowboy was grinning like a possum. "The Figure 4s need to buy ol' Dayton a set of eyeglasses, Hitch." Nobody ever called Hitchcock *Hugh* except his mother. "I know that old cow," Rascal claimed. "I can recollect the color of every calf she's given to me and Law."

Hitch's natural inclination was to accept Rascal's word because they had been friends so long, but he knew that was not the right and proper way. "Let's have a look at her." He rode slowly around the cow, frowning at the earmarks. She had more than one. He leaned from the saddle for a close look at the brand. "Somebody done a bad job with the iron. Way it's haired over, she could be either one or neither one. I been tellin' you, Rascal, your LR brand is too much like the Figure 4."

"Tell *them*," Rascal grinned. "Me and Law, we had our brand first. Let the Figure 4 change theirs." The thought pleased him because the Figure 4 outfit was reputed to own forty or fifty thousand head.

Dayton Brumley, crowding forty, was an employee too far removed from policy-making to comment. Stubbornly he said, "I call her a Figure 4."

Another cowboy trotted up on a nervous-eyed dun. Law McGinty, four or five years younger than Rascal, demanded, "What is it, Rascal? That rich damn-yankee outfit tryin' to steal our cow?"

Brumley colored. At least Rascal hadn't accused him of stealing. "Boy . . ." he said threateningly.

Rascal made a placating gesture to his brother. "Don't bust your cinch, button. Hitch is fixin' to set things straight."

Hitch had an uncomfortable feeling Rascal was taking advantage of friendship, putting Hitch in a position where he must stand up for a preconceived judgment. He said, "We'll stretch her and take a good look." He dropped his loop over her horns and took up the slack, then motioned for Law to catch her hind feet. They laid her down helpless on the ground, and Hitch dismounted. He depended on the gray, Walking Jack, to keep the rope taut. He purposely had put Law on the heels because that obliged the cowboy to stay in his saddle and out of trouble; if Law allowed any slack on the heels, the cow could kick loose from the rope and get up. She would not be in good humor.

On his knees Hitch carefully ran his fingers over the brand, trying to feel through the hair any scar that didn't show to the eye. This was complicated by the fact that he was missing the tip of one finger, pinched off between a rope and a saddlehorn a long time ago. A missing finger or a gimpy leg were marks of a working cowboy. He shook his head. "Still can't tell."

Rascal stepped from his saddle, fishing in his shirt pocket. "I said I know that old cow, and I'll prove it." He brought out a pair of tweezers and began plucking hair.

Hitch came near smiling despite the potential seriousness of the matter. Probably not another man on the roundup was so certain of argument that he would carry tweezers. Though Rascal was a W cowhand, he was also an owner of sorts whose nature called for him to protect his interests with whatever degree of belligerence seemed appropriate.

It bothered Hitch, assuming responsibility for a dispute like this. No court could consider him completely neutral. He and Rascal and Law McGinty had known each other before they had come to the Panhandle. They had helped Charlie Waide bring his W herd up here from cattle-poor South Texas brush country in the late '70s. At thirty, Hitch was a little younger than Rascal, older than Law. Rascal was as good a roper as Hitch and unquestionably a better bronc rider. Yet Rascal had evidenced no hard feelings when Charlie Waide set Hitch up as second in command only to himself. Rascal had seemed to accept it as proper, for there was an indefinable character in Hugh Hitchcock that caused cowboys—even better ones—instinctively to follow him. Law McGinty, then a kid of eighteen or so, had taken a sour view of Rascal's being passed by and temporarily fell out with Hitch over it, but Rascal had told him flatly, "Charlie knows what he's doin'."

Dayton Brumley hunched over Rascal, critically watching his work with the tweezers. If he saved them a hundred such cows the Figure 4 would not raise his wages a dollar, but he had an old-time cowboy loyalty: when you worked for a ranch and accepted its pay, you stood up for it to the turn of the final card. If you couldn't be loyal to an outfit, you called for your time and rode away.

Rascal's tweezers caused a definite outline to begin showing through the hair. "Like I told you, Hitch, she's comin' up an LR, plain as the tobacco in ol' Dayton's *mus*-tache."

Brumley grunted angrily. "Because *he*'s got the tweezers."

Hitch could tell the thing was still dangerous. "Settle down, boys. One cow ain't worth a fight."

In his saddle, Law McGinty said, "Not to an outfit that's got fifty thousand like her. But to a little man grindin' himself to the bone for thirty dollars a month she's worth a fight. You ought to know."

Hitch knew; he had a brand too. Many of the cowboys who had first come north onto these plains had established small herds of their own to run on the free grass with those of the men they worked for. Charlie Waide had been so nearly broke when he came here that he had been able to keep only those men willing to take pay in calves instead of cash. Hitch had owned two shirts and one pair of ragged britches then; he hadn't even had enough money to get a blacksmith to make a branding iron for him. So he had taken Charlie's W iron, branded it, then turned it upside down and stamped it again to make a combination he called the Two Diamonds. Now he had a little one-section claim over on a creek where he had built a dugout he almost never used. He had a hundred and thirty or forty Two Diamond cows and their calves grazing the red clay breaks and the shortgrass prairies. Most of it was still state land, the grass belonging to the man whose cow happened to eat it.

Hitch decided Rascal had picked long enough. He

ran his fingers over the brand and was seventy-five percent sure. "Dayton, it looks like an LR to me."

He saw triumph in the McGinty brothers' faces. But Brumley was adamant. "It looked like a Figure 4 till he took the tweezers to it. If I'd of had the tweezers it'd still be a Figure 4."

Rascal's hands knotted into fists. "You callin' me a cheat?" Brumley didn't say so out loud, but the answer lay plain in his eyes. Rascal took a step toward him, and Law swung a leg over the cantle.

Hitch moved quickly. "Law, you stay up there and keep that rope tight. Rascal, you and Dayton go cool off. In opposite directions. We got work to do here."

Rascal gave no ground. "Whichaway you callin' that calf?"

Hitch thought he had made it plain enough. He saw a heavyish man riding around the herd toward them, and he felt relief. "Yonder comes Charlie. We'll have him confirm it, then we'll hear no more about this cow."

Solemn-faced, Charlie Waide climbed down from the saddle. He took his time as if he were older even than his late fifties. He was careful in bringing his left hand from the saddlehorn, for his arm had been stiff since a Yankee saber had slashed it in the war. There hadn't been a day in eighteen years that it hadn't brought him pain. "I come in after ridin' twenty miles from the eastern division and find somebody pawin' sand," he said irritably. "What in hell's the matter here?"

"No trouble, Charlie." Hitch wanted to spare him worry; Charlie had enough of that. "Just been a little question come up over the brand of this cow."

Charlie Waide glanced impatiently at Rascal and

Brumley, then knelt and ran his fingers over the brand. "I'd call her an LR."

The red-haired cowboy laughed. Rascal could afford to, now that the judgment had gone his way. But Hitch took no chances. "Rascal, I'll see that the calf is branded for you. I want you to go to the wagon and find out how much Trump lacks havin' dinner ready."

It was a useless errand, for Trump Tatum always had dinner ready at straight-up noon and would be cussing if he didn't see cowboys on the way. But Rascal took the order without question. He rode off, his back straight, his hat cocked a little to one side, a picture of justice triumphant.

Dissatisfied, Brumley said, "Charlie, I'll have to talk to the company about this."

Waide's eyes narrowed. He had been boss too long to be crossed. "You do that."

"It ain't the cow, Charlie, it's the principle." Brumley rode into the herd to seek out Figure 4 cattle that had strayed into W country. Waide stared after him balefully, running a big rough hand through hair that had turned gray years too early. "One damned cow," he grumbled. "The Figure 4s will lose more than that between the barn and the haylot."

"He could get himself killed someday," Hitch said. "Reckon they know it?"

Waide shook his head. "He's just a name on the payroll."

Hitch nodded at the cowboy who still held the calf on the far end of the rope. "Tell them to put an LR on him, Joe." Hitch waited for Charlie to get to his horse, then he took the rope off the cow's horns. She would come up looking for a fight, and he didn't want Charlie caught on the ground. Hitch's own father had not come home from the war. Charlie was as near a father as he had had since.

Law McGinty gave slack on the rope, and the cow shook her heels loose. She got up rump first, slinging her head and trying to choose between several targets. But her calf blatted in fear as it was dragged unceremoniously toward the branding fire, and her motherly instincts sent her trotting and bawling in its dusty wake.

Charlie paid no attention to the cow. He still watched Brumley.

Hitch said, "He'll cool off; so'll Rascal."

Charlie's bewildered face was furrowed. "Ain't nothin' like it was, Hitch. This was a cowman's country once. A cowman gave his word and another cowman took it. Now it's a different breed . . . syndicates, Yankee bankers, English money and all that. Ain't enough anymore just to know the cow."

Charlie Waide knew the cow. But he found himself ill at ease among a new kind of ranchers who knew cows as figures on a ledger rather than flesh and blood creatures of leg and long horn; who thought of a herd of cattle as a large sum written in black at the bottom of a page rather than as a teeming mass of bawling beasts, strung majestically across a mile or more of God's green grass, the brown dust rising and swirling above them like some living thing, the air sharp with the bite of hoof-flung dirt and the mingled smells of trampled green grass and calves' milky breath and fresh manure.

Hitch had accompanied Charlie last year on a trip to Kansas City to try to float a loan. Charlie had been in a cold sweat the whole time, going from bank to bank with a new white hat crushed awkwardly in his big hands, trying to talk the language of men he couldn't understand, men measuring him for what he owned and not for what he knew or what he was. Charlie had finally obtained an expansion loan, smaller than he wanted, and he had to sign over everything but his own blood to get it.

Charlie Waide had always been strict about liquor; he didn't allow the cowboys to drink on the place. But he stayed drunk all the way home, downing whisky as a purgative to cleanse away the stain of humiliation. He told Hitch at the time, "I felt like a crippled horse penned up amongst a pack of gray lobo wolves. I was fishin' in deep waters against that crew." Hitch had felt that Charlie's time in Kansas City had scarred him deeper than his encounter with the Yankee saber. The Yankees at least had been an enemy he could see and understand and shoot at. To Charlie Waide—at heart basically still a cowboy—the world of finance was the Tower of Babel. But he was in it to the gray tips of his mustache. To remain a cowman of major proportions these days, a man had to be.

The roan cow was the only one that day whose ownership caused any dispute. Most cows in the gather clearly showed the W brand. A few carried small-owner brands like the Two Diamonds of Hugh Hitchcock, or the LR of Rascal and Law McGinty. Some carried the syndicate's Figure 4. When one appeared questionable, Dayton Brumley took a careful look for the benefit of the company he worked for, but earmarks or a quick clipping of hair were enough to establish ownership. Hitch made it a main-order of business to be sure the McGinty brothers and Brumley were kept far apart. He hoped by dark they would be too tired to do anything more about their grudge.

Late in the afternoon Law McGinty asked Hitch if it would be all right for him to drop out and ride over into the breaks to see his wife. "I'd be much obliged, Hitch. I'll be back by daylight. Her bein' in a family way and all, I like to look in on her pretty regular."

That suited Hitch fine, for, it got Law out of the way awhile. "I wisht you'd take Rascal with you."

Law made a weak smile. He had never been open and easy with Hitch the way Rascal was. "If you was married, Hitch, you'd know not to ask a man a thing like that."

Law rode away without supper. Kate McGinty would cook him a better meal than he would get at the chuckwagon. Watching, Hitch pictured the loving reception Law would receive from his handsome young bride, and the thought brought him an empty feeling of something missed. Kate McGinty was a farm girl happy to live in a rude dugout on the small claim her husband and brother-in-law had made, for never in her life had she known anything better. On the contrary, this might be the best home she had ever had.

If ever I have a woman of my own, I'd want to give her something better than that, Hitch thought. His chance of having such a woman was slim; they were scarce. This was a man's country.

Trump Tatum's chin was fuzzy, but he had more hair on one joint of his index finger than on all of his head. He had been Charlie Waide's wagon cook fifteen years or so. Before that he had cowboyed while Charlie was struggling to rebuild a South Texas ranch that had gone to ruin during the time they were all off trying to save the South for Jefferson Davis. Bad horses had forced Trump to hang up his saddle in favor of the pots and Dutch ovens. Except for broken bones that precipitated the change, it wasn't necessarily a bad thing; a wagon cook drew a better wage than a working cowboy; and he ruled his tiny domain with an autocracy that not even a ranch owner often challenged. Trump Tatum had his rules, and the cowboys either knew them or learned them damned quick. A minor infraction could spark sarcasm bitter as gypwater, and a major breach could send Trump into a glorious case of the "rings" that would spoil coffee for three or four days.

At the same time, he had a protective feeling for the cowboys whose digestion he was slowly ruining. He seemed to sense the tension resulting over the roan cow, and a benevolent gleam shone in his wrinkle-edged eyes like the welcome glow of a lantern to a man lost at night on the open prairie. "Boys," he said, "I figured this evenin' would be a good time to use up that dried fruit Miz Waide brung to the wagon. I fixed you-all a nice cobbler for supper."

Cobbler pie was an infrequent treat in a plains cowcamp, for there wasn't a decently bearing fruit tree in perhaps two hundred miles. Beef and beans were the mainstays, and it was little wonder that now and again the average cowboy developed a painful case of boils. In such events it was usually Trump Tatum who lanced them, which was only proper because his cooking had helped create them in the first place. His chuckbox was a combination commissary and medicine chest, carrying some remedy for everything from hemorrhoids to snake-bite.

Trump grinned at Rascal. "I know how partial you are to cobbler."

Suspiciously Rascal said, "If you're tryin' to sweet-do me into draggin' you up some firewood . . ."

"You know I never had no such notion."

"The hell you didn't." Rascal was pleased as he looked at the cobbler in the deep Dutch oven.

Why shouldn't he be pleased? Hitch asked himself. Rascal had won his dispute. Hitch felt almost a resentment against his friend, for he harbored a nagging suspicion he had been used. He disliked having to feel even a twinge of guilt toward Dayton Brumley and the Figure 4, for he had no particular respect for the outfit. But that, he supposed, was what a man put up with to earn the extra twenty dollars a month as wagon boss instead of being a straight cowboy. Sometimes he wished he had stayed where he used to be, for it had been more fun and no worry. Sometimes responsibility had an uncomfortable fit, like a right boot on a left foot. But men delegated responsibility to Hitch whether he wanted it or not.

Dayton Brumley still brooded over the roan cow. As rep for the Figure 4 he enjoyed the privileges—such as they were—of the regular W cowboys, as did reps for the other brands. But tonight he kept to himself, taking a long time unsaddling his horse. He waited until the W men and the other company reps had all filled their plates before he went to the chuckbox and got one for himself. Spooning into it quietly, he strode out to his bedroll and squatted down alone.

Trump Tatum leaned his thin old frame against the wagonwheel, his uneasy gaze touching Brumley first, then Rascal. In contrast to Brumley's somber mien, Rascal was laughing and talking as if no roan cow had ever been born. Rascal had always loved to talk.

It was not customary for a wagon cook to carry food to anybody; a man came to the fire and helped himself or by God did without. But when the rest of the men were through, Trump took the Dutch oven to Brumley. "Wouldn't want it said the W wagon didn't feed its neighbors."

"The Ws is all right," Brumley said. "It's just one or two of them that works for it who bother me some."

Rascal was too busy talking to hear.

Supper done, Trump began rattling the tin plates and cups in his washtub, then dropping them into a second tub of scalding hot water. A kid horse jingler—low man of the outfit—fished them out gingerly with his fingers and dried them to put them back into the chuckbox. He caught some caustic comment from Trump when he let a hot one drop to the sand at his feet.

Charlie Waide walked away from the wagon, out where the night horses had been staked. He stood a long time staring into the starlight, his hand reaching up and rubbing his bad left arm. Hitch finished his coffee and joined him. "Arm hurtin' you tonight, Charlie?"

"Arm hurts me every night. Nothin' new about that."

"You got somethin' else on your mind, then."

"There's always worries enough to go around. That damned roan cow is apt to bring trouble to camp even yet; been better if she'd died last winter. Then, I owe enough to break two Kansas City banks. And finally, there's ugly talk goin' around some of the wagons."

"Talk?"

"Discontent. I can't find out enough to get to the guts of it. Heard any talk around this wagon, Hitch?"

"Only about horses and cattle and women."

Charlie Waide frowned. "I hope it stays that way."

For an hour or two before they crawled into their blankets, the cowboys usually sat near the campfire, feeding it just enough to keep it from dying. By turns they told yarns, sometimes of things which had happened on drive that day, more often of things from other years, other outfits. Times they talked of badmen like Billy the Kid, who had stolen cows up and down this Canadian River country and was hardly more than a year in his grave. Times they talked of other cowboys they had known, or of women encountered in the cowtowns and at the railheads. Most often the conversation centered around horses, for to the cowboy the horse was more than a tool of the trade, he was a friend; a servant, yet something of a god; an occasional tormentor, yet a creature deserving admiration that bordered on deification. The cowboy was prone to invest the horse with a super intelligence it never really had, and a code of honor invented in the mind of the rider. Small wonder, then, that a man was judged more on his horsemanship than on whatever personal vices or virtues he might possess. The most notorious cow thief in the Panhandle since passing of the Kid was a man named Cato Bramlett. In speaking of him the cowboys gave less attention to his being a rogue than to the fact that he handled a horse unusually well.

Charlie Waide drifted to the fire, listening, and finally he seated himself in the circle. It was not an accustomed place to him anymore, for in the pressure of the times he seemed to have lost the gift of laughter. The younger men who had not known Charlie in an olden day stood a little in awe of him, and perhaps a little afraid. But for a while then Charlie was not an owner, he was another cowboy reaching back into memory. For a while the hunch seemed gone from his shoulders, and he was as young as any man here.

It pleasured Hitch to see this rare transformation

in Charlie Waide, to see him for a little while the way he had been in another time when he wasn't big and struggling to become bigger, when he ran two hundred cows instead of twenty thousand. It seemed a pity, in a way, that he had ever changed. Charlie began telling fondly about a bay horse he once had traded from a Mexican and had ridden off to war, only to lose him in battle. "Many's the good horse I've ridden before and after," he said wistfully, "but never one I thought more of than that bay. When the war was over I went lookin' for the Mexican, thinkin' he might have some more horses of the same blood. But he'd got himself killed in some war down in Mexico, so I reckon the blood was scattered and lost. They sure had good horses in them days, the likes we'll never see again."

Rascal McGinty fidgeted to talk, and the moment Charlie finished, Rascal grabbed his chance. He told about a horse he had gotten once from a Mexican. Stolen; no, *stolen* wasn't the word for it because down in that Rio Grande country in those days you didn't steal when you took from a Mexican, you only exacted vengeance for the Alamo and other atrocities. So, for that matter, did the Mexican when he stole from you. Thieving took on the aura of patriotism. The way Rascal told it, that horse could do almost anything except count cattle. Upshot of the story was that the Mexican was a lowdown scoundrel who came one night in the dark of the moon and stole the horse back. "We'd of hung that thief if we could've caught him," Rascal laughed, "but the horse was so fast that nothin' we had could get close enough to give us the smell of his dust."

From the distance came the sound of a horse-drawn vehicle bouncing across the tufted prairie grass. Trump Tatum lifted the lantern from the chuckbox lid up onto the top, so it might better serve as a guide. Hitch pushed to his feet and dropped extra wood on the fire so it would blaze up. The cowboys had to move away from its heat. He heard the driver curse this God-forsaken country as a wheel dropped into a hole, and he knew the voice. He frowned at Rascal, then at Dayton Brumley. The general manager and major stockholder of the Figure 4 was coming; Hitch could have done without him very well.

He had no inclination to walk out and meet the man, but Charlie Waide arose stiffly, grunting a complaint against arthritis, and stepped forward to extend the hand of hospitality from one owner to another. Brumley went too, for this man was his boss.

Prosper Selkirk was not by birth or training a range man, but he had been in cow country long enough that he knew better than to ride up into the wagon cook's domain and raise dust. He stopped at the edge of the firelight. A saddled horse was tied to the rear of the buckboard. Charlie Waide stuck out his hand. "You're travelin' late, Prosper. But Trump's still got some supper left."

Selkirk nodded, leaving any thank-yous implied rather than spoken, and perhaps none were even thought of. He jerked a thumb toward three sleek greyhounds tied in the back of the buckboard. "Take care of the hounds, Brumley." He did no more than glance at the man, the way he might glance at a company horse. To Charlie he said, "The dogs ran themselves down chasing loboes, and dark caught us. I'm just making a visit to all the neighbors' wagons in the interest of the Figure 4."

Charlie Waide was never at ease in the company of Prosper Selkirk, for he considered him one of the Kansas City crowd. But he made a show of hospitality. "Everybody gets treated fair and square at the Ws." He motioned toward Hitch. "You know my wagon boss, Hugh Hitchcock."

Selkirk said simply, "Nice to see you again, Hitchcock."

Hitch felt a nudge of resentment. Selkirk didn't offer to shake hands. He knew Hitch well enough to address him as Hugh or Hitch if he had chosen, and he hadn't enough respect to call him Mister Hitchcock. So, it was just Hitchcock. Hitch thought, *The hell with him.*

If this had been some luckless cowboy stumbling in late, Trump Tatum would have chewed him up and spit him out, but he deferred to Selkirk. "Biscuits is cold, Mister Selkirk, and the steak is apt to be a little greasy now."

Selkirk's offhand reply was made without thought to the way it might sound to Tatum. "I never count on much around these chuck-wagons. I'll survive until I get home to something better."

Tatum had fetched a plate and utensils out of wooden drawers for him, but now he left them sitting on the chuckbox lid and jerked his thumb toward the wagon. "Cups is in yonder," he said and turned his back.

Selkirk hit him with another unconscious insult. "I suppose the leftovers would be good enough for the dogs?"

Tatum neither turned nor tried to answer. He stalked off toward his bedroll in angry silence. It wasn't enough having to take this treatment from Selkirk; he would catch hell for the next week from the cowboys, for they would hurrah him until he crowned somebody with a skillet or starved them into submission.

Selkirk was in his late forties, basically an indoor

man whose aptitude at figures in a banking institution had earned him the confidence of men owning substantial fortunes and wanting more. Selkirk knew how to make money for them, and incidentally for himself as well. The Figure 4 to him was a beef factory, little different from a shoe factory or a plant for the manufacture of farm implements. The Figure 4 was basically a set of ledgers that must always show a comfortable figure in black at the bottom of every page. Under his direction it usually did. The neighboring ranches were regarded as competitors for the beef buyers' dollar, and the cowboys were names on a payroll book that seemed always to show too much money paid out for the services rendered.

Hitch knew Dayton Brumley was still fretting over that roan cow. He watched Brumley talking as Selkirk ate the cold supper without enthusiasm. In the muffled conversation he heard his own name and stood up, glancing at Charlie and finding Charlie watching him. Charlie motioned for Hitch to join him beside Selkirk.

Charlie told the Figure 4 manager, "You know Hitch is a good man with cattle. He called that brand an LR and so did I."

Selkirk stopped chewing and frowned at Hitch, measuring him. "Charles, if you say she was an LR, I'll accept that as the word of one gentleman to another."

Charlie seemed to want to settle it beyond any question. "She belonged to Rascal and Law McGinty; they been cowboyin' for me a long time. They're as honest as the day is long."

Selkirk put down his plate and took a long sip of black coffee, face creasing in the dislike of it. "Never seems civilized to take it without cream," he remarked. "Pity with all these cattle there is never any milk." He seemed inclined to throw the coffee out but didn't. "Charles, that brings up a point I've wanted to talk to you about, that you let some of your men run cattle of their own."

"I always have."

"It's a bad practice. We don't allow it at the Figure 4."

"So I've heard."

"Have you ever thought what such a practice can lead to?"

"It leads to me bein' able to keep good men here when some outfits have to scratch to find men that know which end of the cow eats grass."

"There are always men looking for jobs. We can hire all the cowhands we ever need at twenty-five dollars a month and turn others away. We don't have to grant special favors."

Charlie said, "There was a time I couldn't pay twenty-five dollars. I gave my men cattle."

"An expedient of the time. When times change, a business enterprise should change with them. Has it ever occurred to you, Charles, how easy it would be for some of your men to brand your cattle with their own irons? And when one of them finds an unbranded maverick out on your range, how do you know he puts your brand on it and not his own? You can't watch them everywhere they go."

"I hire men I can trust."

"No man can be trusted if the stakes are high enough. I've heard rumors, Charles, even about your men."

Charlie Waide began to anger. "If rumors was cattle, this whole country would be overstocked and the grass grazed down to the roots." He didn't look at Selkirk, nor did he glance at Hitch.

Hitch had sat still as long as he could. "Charlie's right, Mister Selkirk. Treat a man fair and you can trust him."

Selkirk had not asked for Hitch's opinion. "You have some cattle in a brand of your own, don't you, Hitchcock?"

Hitch's teeth ground together. He didn't know whether the man was implying anything or not; Selkirk had an unfortunate habit of saying a thing in its worst possible way. "Charlie Waide has personally watched me brand most every cow I own."

"I wasn't singling you out, Hitchcock. I was only pointing out that your position might prevent your being altogether the best judge of what I consider to be a bad practice." He switched his attention to Charlie. "I've been in conference with some other major owners. Most of us agree it would be a healthy thing on this range if we made a blanket order that no man employed for wages be allowed to own cattle."

By now every cowboy was listening. Even Trump Tatum had come back from his bedroll, barefoot and in his underwear.

Charlie Waide said, "Some of these men stuck with me through cruel hard times, and they been years buildin' up a shirttail outfit of their own. What kind of a man would take that away from them?"

"I'm not suggesting you take anything away, Charles. Nobody advocates cheating any man out of his rightful due. We would all agree to buy such cattle at a fair market price and vent the brands to our own. Then, after a specified date no man on a ranch payroll would be allowed to own cattle. That would take away the incentive for brand changing and maverick chasing and all these other evils that stand in the way of sound business practices on these ranches."

Charlie Waide stood up and rubbed his bad arm where the night air had brought the ache again. "You do as you please on the Figure 4s. This here is the Ws."

"You're not alone on this range. You owe the rest of us something, too."

Charlie scowled. "I don't know how you figure that. Was you here helpin' me when my herd was dyin' of the Texas fever? No, you wasn't. Was you here when the Indians kept comin' back off the reservations and cuttin' across this country, takin' cattle, shootin' at whoever got in their way? No, you wasn't. But there's men here that was, like Hitch and the McGintys and some of the others. I don't take nothin' away from them and they won't take nothin' away from me."

Selkirk retreated a little. "Perhaps you're right; perhaps no one in your employ would take cattle from you. But they might not be so scrupulous in respecting the property rights of the rest of us. How do you know, for instance, that they would not take Figure 4 cattle if the opportunity presented itself? And on a range as large as this one, there is always opportunity."

Dayton Brumley took a stick and began to sketch in the sand. "Like that cow this mornin', Charlie. You and Hitch called her an LR, and maybe you was right. But can you say for sure she was *always* an LR?" Brumley drew a Figure 4 brand in the sand. It was open-topped for easy healing.

4

"Now looky here," he said. "All a man has to do is add a little at the top and bottom. He's got an LR."

4R

Rascal McGinty came around the fire in a rush. Before Brumley could get to his feet, Rascal hit him. Brumley staggered and fell on his back. Cursing, Rascal grabbed him and tried to pull him to his feet. Hitch threw his arms around McGinty and wrenched him loose. "Rascal . . ."

Rascal fought free. "Ain't no boot-lickin' Figure 4 puncher goin' to call me a thief!" His eyes wide, he ran for the chuckbox.

Trump Tatum said hoarsely, "I got a pistol in there!"

Dayton Brumley scurried desperately for his bedroll and rammed his hand down into his canvas war bag. Hitch knew he kept a .45. Hitch ran for Rascal. As Rascal fished the cook's pistol out of the chuckbox, Hitch grabbed his arm. "Rascal, let go of it!"

"He called me a thief."

"I want that gun, Rascal, before somebody gets killed."

They struggled for possession. Hitch lunged forward, jamming Rascal against the wagonwheel and trying to bend him backward over it. He had a tight grip on Rascal's wrist and tried to slam it against the corner of the chuckbox. The cowboys scattered like quail. Resisting, Rascal pulled the trigger. The pistol went off with a roar like a cannon. Glass shattered from the lantern atop the chuckbox. The lantern tumbled to the ground, spilling coal oil into the sand and setting it ablaze. Rascal tried to step away from the flames at his feet, and as he did, Hitch wrenched the pistol from his hand. Turning quickly, he saw Dayton Brumley crouched by his bedroll, pistol ready.

Prosper Selkirk's voice was crisp with authority. "Put it back, Brumley. There'll be no fight."

Brumley seemed not to hear until Selkirk spoke again, sharper. Seeing that Hitch had the other pistol, Brumley slowly let his own sag and finally placed it back into the canvas sack. He was on hands and knees.

Most of the cowboys had hit the ground on their bellies. Now some pushed to their feet, but others lay still. The kid horse jingler called querulously, "Is it all over, Hitch?"

"It's over," Hitch said, shaking a little. "You can get up." He moved partway to Brumley. "Dayton, you owe Rascal an apology."

Brumley was in no mood to apologize. Hitch thought it probable the man couldn't even speak. Selkirk spoke for him. "He apologizes. It wasn't meant the way your man took it; it was only meant to show what *could* happen."

Hitch knew better. Brumley *had* meant it, but it would be foolish to say so in this atmosphere.

Charlie Waide found his voice. "And you, Prosper, you've seen what can happen, too. Better go slow in makin' implications against a man."

Selkirk turned to his rep. "Brumley, it's best you leave this wagon tonight . . . *now*. Gather your things and go over to our east wagon; send Estep to rep for us here."

The cowboys went quietly to their blankets, though nobody would sleep much. Rascal sat by himself on the wagon tongue, trembling in delayed reaction. Old Trump Tatum scratched himself through the long underwear. "Hitch, maybe we ought to go talk to him."

"And say what? Best thing is to leave him alone."

Trump picked up the shattered lantern. It was beyond repair. He stepped gingerly, trying to avoid broken glass with his bare feet. "Hell of a note, is all I can say. I'm glad it's over with."

Is it over? Hitch asked himself.

Prosper Selkirk stood beside Charlie Waide. "If this doesn't change your mind, Charles, I'll find something that will. You've got to be with us; we won't have you against us."

Charlie gave Selkirk a long, harsh frown. "Goodnight, Prosper."

As the Figure 4 manager moved toward his buckboard and the bedroll he carried there, Charlie Waide walked stiffly to Trump's chuckbox. He reached deep into it and came out with a bottle Tatum kept for medicinal purposes. He walked around to the wagon tongue, nudged Rascal and without saying anything handed him the bottle. Rascal looked up at him, blinking in surprise. He uncorked the bottle and took a long double swallow, draining much of the whisky.

Charlie retrieved the bottle, took a swig that finished it, then growled, "Go to bed now, Rascal. Go to bed before I haul off and kick your butt!"

2

Hitch slept little. When Trump Tatum got up grumbling to start breakfast, Hitch got up too. He hunkered on the far side of Trump's stingy little wood-saving fire to nurse the coffeepot along, and Trump fussed about his being in the way.

Trump always kept two lanterns, one over his pots and one over the chuckbox. Because Rascal had shot up one of them, Trump had to make do by carrying the other back and forth. He complained so much that Hitch promised to find him another the first chance he got. Hitch could always predict Trump Tatum's mood because it was almost always the same: irritable.

Hitch worried, "That thing last night could've turned out a lot worse. I keep wonderin' if there was somethin' I ought to've done different."

Trump said, "You done your job the way you seen it; you wasn't partial to no man. Don't fret over what you can't change. Take things as they come and stay cheerful, I always say."

By the time the water boiled, Rascal was up. He

came silently to the fire, nodding at Trump and Hitch and glancing to see if the coffee was ready yet. His sleepy eyes showed he hadn't slept. Rascal furtively rubbed his right hand.

"Hurt?" Hitch asked.

"A little. You gave it a right smart of a wrench."

"Had to."

Rascal nodded soberly. "I know." He squatted on his heels and stared into the flames. "A man ought to have better control of himself. I might've killed Dayton Brumley if you hadn't stopped me."

"Or he might've killed you."

"We're a pair of damn fools, him and me. The hell of it is, I know I'd do the same thing again."

Hitch frowned, knowing that was true. "Well, he's gone."

"But his boss ain't. Dayton only said out loud what Selkirk was thinkin'."

The cowboys began getting up from their soogans before Tatum ever called "Chuck!" Law McGinty rode in about the time the horse jingler brought the remuda for the men to catch their morning mounts. Law turned his horse loose among them and went to the wagon for a plate. He knew nothing of what had happened here last night, and Hitch had as soon somebody else told him. He was mostly concerned that Law was late getting his breakfast. The other cowboys were ready for their horses.

Law said, "I'll be there, Hitch, before they get mounted."

Hitch nodded. "How was Kate?"

Law blinked. "Kate? Oh, she's fine. Gettin' along fine." He wolfed down a biscuit and some steak while Trump Tatum watched sourly. Trump hated to see his cooking taken for granted.

Hitch said, "She oughtn't to stay there by herself much longer. You ought to send her someplace, or get somebody to go stay with her."

"It ain't that time yet. Kate'll do fine."

Prosper Selkirk was up and out of his bedroll, finally. The Figure 4 manager was not given to such early hours. Even Hitch wondered sometimes why everybody got up so early in a cowcamp. Often he would ride many miles, then sit idly and smoke cigarettes waiting for the morning to turn light enough that he could see what he was supposed to do. Custom, he guessed. It was considered slothful of a man to let sunrise catch him in bed.

Selkirk's greyhounds had been tied to the buckboard wheels all night. Now he turned them loose to allow them to stray out of camp and attend to the pressures of nature. The thin-bodied dogs moved cautiously around the remuda, watchful of the hoofs. Most of the horses were unacquainted with dogs but knew the wolf; they watched with ears pointed warily forward.

The cowboys formed a circle around the horses in the thin light of approaching dawn, stationing themselves twenty feet apart and holding ropes up between them to fashion an improvised corral. It would not have held any horse determined to get away, but the horses had been conditioned by training to respect the rope. It was as impenetrable to them as if it had been ten feet high and of solid oak.

It would be chaotic for so many cowboys to try to rope out their own horses. Custom had delegated this responsibility to two or three individuals, Hugh Hitchcock chief among them.

"Catch me ol' Quanah," Rascal told him. Hitch, afoot inside the loosely held rope corral, shook out a large loop and spotted Rascal's horse about three deep in the milling bunch. He brought the loop up, gave it a backhand twist and sent it sailing forward into the horses. It fell over the head and neck he had aimed for. The horse dropped its head, hoping to shake off the loop, but Hitch pulled up the slack. Once caught, Quanah came out of the remuda without resistance. He had learned through hard experience that it was useless to fight the rope.

In a few minutes horses were caught for very man. The rope corral fell, each man recoiling his own part of it. The remaining horses were turned back to the jingler to be loose-herded on grass until needed for another change when the morning's drive was finished and the day's gather brought into a single herd for working. The cowboys saddled their horses. Each moved hurriedly to be able to watch the show, for in every man's string were some green broncs, and on any given morning one or more were sure to buck.

It would not have been much of a show had it not been for Selkirk's greyhounds. One black horse crowhopped, and that was all of it until Selkirk realized his dogs were out of sight and became uneasy. He whistled. They came in a run, too close to a wild-eyed bronc whose back was still humped under Joe Sands. The bronc bawled in fright and went straight up. When he came down from the third jump he fell hard on his side. The horse struggled to its feet, but Joe Sands didn't get up. He lay grinding his teeth and writhing, trying not to cry out in pain.

Hitch hit the ground and flipped his reins back for Law McGinty to catch. Sands tried to pull up and couldn't. He cursed fervently. "My leg, Hitch. I think that Goddamned crowbait busted my leg."

As other cowboys gathered around, Hitch felt of

the leg. Sands cried out. Hitch found Charlie Waide standing there, his face grave. "It's sure as hell broke, Charlie. We better get him to town."

Waide nodded. "You take him, Hitch. We'll throw the stuff out of the hoodlum wagon."

Hitch looked around for Selkirk. "Prosper Selkirk has got his buckboard here. It'd be faster and easier."

Waide turned to the Figure 4 manager. "If it wouldn't be no imposition . . ." The way he put it made it a statement of expectation.

Selkirk was momentarily taken aback. "I had planned . . ." He bit off the words. The cowboys plainly held him responsible. "I suppose it's the least I can do."

Rascal McGinty put in, "Hitch, me and Law got a light spring wagon over at our claim. Wouldn't be out of your way none to haul Joe by there. Then you could take our wagon and let Mister Selkirk go on about his business." Rascal's resentment was plain.

Selkirk said, "Anything you want." He seemed relieved that he might get away from here with no more responsibility than that.

The cowboys put Selkirk's team to the buckboard and brought it around. They fetched Joe Sands's blankets and tarp, spreading them in the bed of the vehicle. Carefully they lifted the groaning man and covered him with a blanket Trump Tatum spared.

The bedroll took up most of the room. Selkirk looked back worriedly. "Where'll I put the dogs?"

Hitch had a quick answer but didn't use it. "They got four legs," he said curtly. He clucked the team into movement, Selkirk's saddle-horse tied behind. Selkirk hadn't had time for breakfast, and Hitch didn't give a damn.

They rode in silence, Hitch devoting his attention

to finding the smoothest ground and bouncing Sands as little as possible. He looked ahead, too, borrowing all the problems he might encounter down the road. Foremost would be to find a team that could pull the McGinty wagon. The McGintys had a pair of horses, but they might be grazing miles from the unfenced camp. Hitch made up his mind that if he didn't find them close by, he would keep Selkirk's. Selkirk could either go to town with him or stay at the McGinty camp.

Selkirk finally decided to talk. "Where is this place we're going?"

"The McGinty's claim. Law McGinty's wife lives there in a dugout."

"A dugout?" Selkirk showed disapproval. "I can imagine what kind of woman she must be to tolerate that. Probably looks like some hard-used scullery maid."

"She's a good woman, Mister Selkirk, and pretty as a spring day."

Selkirk grunted in disbelief and changed the subject. "You tell the doctor that whatever the cost is, I'll pay it. Since my dogs precipitated the incident, I think it is only proper."

Hitch hadn't expected that. The man came up a notch in his estimation, but only a notch. "What if it turns out the leg won't heal straight? What if Joe winds up crippled? You goin' to guarantee him a job the rest of his life?"

"I couldn't promise a thing like that."

"Charlie Waide would. Trump Tatum'd still be cowboyin', likely, if one of Charlie's horses hadn't boogered him up. Charlie'll see to it that Trump's never hungry the rest of his life."

"No man can expect to be insulated from all risk. If I invest my entire fortune in a bad venture and lose it, nobody guarantees to take care of me the rest of my life. When a man gets on one of those bad horses he knows the risks; he implies his willingness to accept that risk when he agrees to the job."

"He accepts the job because he's partial to eatin'."

"The same reason I take a risk and invest capital."

"There's a difference between a man's limbs and his money."

"Not basically. Your cowboy offers his skill in the marketplace; he sells the service of his hands, his arms, his legs. That is his equivalent of capital. I sell my capital and the service of my brain. We all sell something; we all risk whatever we sell. We're all at the mercy of chance."

"Looks to me like you got more chance, though, than Joe has."

Hitch decided it was fruitless to argue viewpoints with Prosper Selkirk; they were the products of two different types of world. Neither would understand the other and perhaps they were never meant to. Anyway, understanding the other man made it more difficult to reject his ideas, and Hitch did not feel like putting up with any such complications. In his view Selkirk was wrong, so why talk about it and cloud up a clear picture?

They dropped into the rough country that broke away to the river. Hitch pointed. "Yonder's the place."

Selkirk had to look hard before he was able to find the dugout, set into a hillside and almost hidden unless a person knew what to look for. The earthen roof and the sod front made it blend into the ground from which it came. The pole corrals were easier to see, cut from the cedar and hackberry and other small timber native to these breaks and the riverbottom. To his relief Hitch saw a couple of horses grazing down the draw . . . the McGinty team.

A woman stood by the well, drawing up a bucket of water on the windlass. Her plain gray dress fluttered in the breeze as she heard the buckboard and turned to look, raising her hand to shade her eyes.

Selkirk said, disappointed, "I thought you told me she was pretty."

"She is."

Selkirk shook his head. "I suppose it depends on what one is accustomed to. I never could reconcile myself to these rawboned, sunburned country women down here, living in a hovel like that."

"A hovel?" Hitch had never regarded it that way. True, it wasn't fancy, but hundreds of hardy women were living in the same type of dwelling all over the Texas Panhandle, raising kids, standing by their men while they either made their fortunes or lost the little they had. Hitch said, "The house you live in don't matter so much; it's your feelin's that count. Kate, now, she thinks that cowboy hung the moon. Fixin' to bear him a child pretty soon. She come from a farmin' family that scratched the hard earth for every bite they ate and every stitch of clothes they wore. She wouldn't call this a hovel."

"When you burrow into a hillside like a badger, I'd call that a hovel."

Like most settlers, the McGintys had a dog. It came bouncing out barking to meet the buckboard. Selkirk had to call back his hounds. Kate McGinty stepped away from the well, her hand still over her eyes. She was by nature a slender woman, though anyone with eyes to see would know she was carrying.

Hitch saw apprehension in her face and said, "No, it ain't Law."

As the buckboard came up even with her she looked anxiously at the hurt cowboy. "Joe Sands. What happened to him?"

Hitch told her. "I need the borrow of your wagon, Kate."

She nodded quickly and told him what he had already seen, that the horses were grazing in the draw. Her eyes glistened with sympathy. "Anything I can do for him, Hitch?"

He had always been drawn to this girl; she had compassion. She had known hardship all her life, so anyone else's trouble was her trouble too. He said, "Joe's pained considerable. If Law's got a bottle stashed someplace . . ."

"In the house," she said, and hurried down the hewn-log steps to floor level of the dugout.

Selkirk exclaimed in surprise, "She called that a *house*."

"You judge a person by his heart, not by his house. Kate has a heart as big as a door."

Selkirk observed the canvas flap through which Kate disappeared. "She hasn't even *got* a door."

Hitch pulled the Selkirk buckboard up beside the spring wagon that belonged to the McGintys. Selkirk had to speak roughly to the dogs to keep them away from the shaggy black one of Kate's. The two men carefully got their arms beneath the blankets and lifted Joe Sands from one vehicle across to the other. Selkirk was stronger than Hitch had thought, looking at him. Joe sucked breath between his teeth, and when they set him down he cursed vigorously. Then he said, "I hope Kate didn't hear that."

Hitch shook his head. "She'd of understood." He

turned to Selkirk. "I'll borrow your horse and go fetch that team. You can wait here or in the dugout. Maybe Kate has got some coffee."

Selkirk eyed the dugout disapprovingly. "I'll go fetch the team. She's a friend of yours; you visit with her."

As Selkirk swung into the saddle, Kate came out with a whisky bottle. Selkirk touched a hand to his hatbrim in deference to her, which Hitch noted with satisfaction. If Selkirk did not particularly respect cowboys, at least he respected their women. Or perhaps pitied them.

Hitch held up the whisky bottle. "Bourbon?"

Kate shook her head. "Land sakes, I wouldn't know one kind from the other."

"No matter. Anything'll help." He took the cork out and raised Joe's head so the cowboy could drink. Joe accepted the whisky almost desperately. "Thanks, Miss Kate. Thanks."

"You're welcome. It helps my conscience anyway."

"How's that?" Hitch asked.

"For a minute there I was glad it was Joe instead of Law. I'm ashamed of the thought."

Joe said, "We're even. I wish it was Law instead of me."

Hitch watched Selkirk move down the draw and hoped the man knew enough about horses to bring them back rather than run them off. He turned to the woman. "You're lookin' fine, Kate, real fine."

"Thank you, Hitch. In all my life I've never felt this good." She touched a hand to her stomach. "It's movin' now; it's alive." She colored. "I don't reckon a man would understand."

Hitch could only imagine that he did. He didn't

know what else to say, so he repeated, "You're sure lookin' fine."

He remembered when Kate's father had moved his family here from some failure down in Central Texas. He had picked a level piece of ground to squat on and had violated the virgin prairie with his plow. All the old man seemed able to raise was kids, and those half hungry much of the time. He was of a hard-luck breed Hitch had seen everywhere he went, the kind who always sought new places and started new projects but never carried them quite to completion, always stopping shy of success and turning away in failure, leaving what he had begun for someone else to pick up and turn into prosperity. The old man had worked himself into his grave, leaving the family to scatter like brown leaves in a winter wind. Hitch had seen Kate when she was fourteen or fifteen, a skinny freckled-nosed kid whose large blue eyes sparkled with life and promise. He had seen her at eighteen and had been much taken by her, for then she was a woman grown, a gentle but enduring woman who could take the worst punishment this raw land could give her. But Hugh Hitchcock had made the mistake of admiring in silence, while Law McGinty had moved in fast and claimed her.

Hitch said, "I was tellin' Law he ought to get somebody to stay with you, or maybe you ought to go to your mother. She still in town?"

"She washes for people and does cookin' for the *ho*-tel when they need it. I got no business in town, Hitch. This is home."

"You'll be needin' help."

"I'll have it when the time comes. There's a few other women up and down the river. There'll be somebody come." He could tell she wasn't worried.

Her mother had borne many a child, one or two of them alone. She said, "I sure wish Law could come home once in a while, though."

Surprised, he asked, "You haven't seen him?"

"Not in maybe three weeks. He's all right, isn't he?"

"He's fine," Hitch said looking away to hide the suspicion in his face. "He's real fine." He had been on the verge of telling her Law had left the wagon to come here last night. Obviously, wherever Law had gone, it hadn't been home. Hitch fished for words. "Kate, you and Law are gettin' along all right, aren't you?"

"Sure, Hitch, why wouldn't we?"

He forced away his frown. "No reason. He's a good boy, that Law. I'll give him a couple days off soon and make sure he gets home."

She gripped his arm in gratitude, and the unexpected touch of her fingers startled him. "Thanks, Hitch," she said. "You're a friend." She waved her arm toward the dugout. "Law says after the baby is big enough, we'll expand the house, build another room. Says it won't be much longer till we'll have enough cattle so he can quit workin' for the other man; he can come home and stay here with me. We'll live like the rich folks in town do. That'll sure be fine, won't it?"

"It'll be real fine." Hitch turned to look for Selkirk and the team. He could see them coming up out of the draw. But his mind was on Law McGinty. Where had Law gone last night?

The thought that came was an ugly one. He never had pictured Law as unfaithful, but maybe in her condition Kate was less attractive to him and he was seeking companionship elsewhere. Like Kate had said, other women lived up and down the river. Perhaps somewhere Law had found one young and pretty, and not pregnant.

Hitch pulled the gate shut as Selkirk brought the horses into the corral. The horses turned to eye him balefully. They hadn't been used in a while, and they liked it that way. Hitch figured he would have to keep a firm hand on the reins the first few miles till they settled down to the notion of working for a living. He made a point of catching them without a rope, though that took longer, for he didn't want to spoil them. Kate would need to catch them herself occasionally, and it was unlikely she was good with a loop; few women were.

Selkirk helped put the team to the McGinty wagon. "I meant what I said, Hitchcock." Hitch glanced at him. "About what?"

"About paying this man's doctor bills. I'm not as cold and conscienceless as you think."

"I never said nothin' against you, Mister Selkirk."

"You don't like me, though."

"I just don't understand you, is all."

"I've watched you, Hitchcock. You're sure of yourself; you have an easy way of leading men. I think I understand you better than you understand me. If ever you get tired of working for Charles Waide, come to see me."

Hitch doubted he would tire of Charlie; if he did, it was unlikely he would willingly turn in Selkirk's direction.

Selkirk said, "It would be strictly business. You don't have to like a man to do business with him."

It damn sure helps, Hitch thought, though he didn't say so. He glanced at Kate. "I'll let you know how things go with Joe Sands." He flipped the reins, and the fresh team highstepped out of the yard.

He had to fight the horses a while till they settled down. He heard Joe say, "Hitch?"

"Hurtin' you bad, Joe?"

Joe Sands took a draw on the bottle. "It ain't that. I was thinkin'. I heard what Kate said about not seein' Law. You reckon he's cheatin' on that girl?"

"I wouldn't know, Joe."

"I'll stomp on him, is what I'll do."

Hitch smiled. "It'll be a long time before you stomp anybody."

3

By the time he had helped the doctor set Joe's leg, all the black coffee Hitch had downed was turning over and trying to come up. The doctor assured him that the leg would heal properly, for cowboys were a tough lot. But Hitch knew from experience that cowboys were not usually as tough as they looked to a man in town. They were flesh, blood and bone like everybody else, and subject to a great deal more breakage than most.

"You don't reckon this'll leave him crippled?" Hitch fretted.

"If whisky'll cure him, he's a cinch."

"Joe don't normally drink thisaway. Charlie don't allow it at the ranch. I bet Joe ain't been drunk three times in his whole life."

Hitch was defending not only Joe Sands but all the cowboys, for the face the townspeople saw when the hands got their rare trips to town was not the one they wore the other twenty-nine days of the month. The doctor said, "Maybe not, but when he wakes up it'll be hard to tell which hurts him the most . . . his leg or his head." He paused thoughtfully. "You need to leave him here in town where I can look in on him."

"I'd figured on it. I'll go now and hunt him a place to stay."

He walked from the small frame house, grateful to be outside. He looked up and down the dusty street past flat-topped adobes and picket shacks and square-fronted clapboard houses like the doctor's. A dry smile came as he mused that these were the people Kate McGinty considered rich. When the winter blue northers howled down off Canada's snowfields and lashed across these wide-open plains, there probably wasn't a house in town half as snug and warm as the dugout she lived in. Yet he knew there was not a woman on the Staked Plains who had not rather freeze to death in an unsealed twelve-by-twelve box cabin than spend the winter cozy in a soddy or a dugout. It was a matter of vanity, of prestige.

Well, it wasn't winter now, and he had to find Joe Sands a bed. But even more pressing for the moment was his own need for a drink to blunt the ordeal of setting Joe's leg. He brought the wagon about, walking the team down into that section locally known as Hogtown, where dwelled those people who took it as their mission in life to make the working cowboy feel like a king, until he ran out of funds and had to abdicate. Hitch stopped before a brown adobe structure of questionable architecture whose vertical sign over the front door said COWBOY BAR.

Fant Gossett made sure his place lived up to its name. He catered to the cowboys and small shirt-tail ranchers who scratched for a living up and down the river. A man like Prosper Selkirk or even Charlie Waide was unlikely to let his shadow fall across Fant's door, and that suited Fant just as well. He knew which end of the wick burned for him. He said loudly and often that he had rather have ten fun-seeking cowpunchers spend a dollar apiece over his bar than for one demanding rich man to spend ten. Fant Gossett had never earned a dollar in his life punching cows himself, but folks who ought to know said he had built a small fortune catering to the riders who did.

He greeted the W wagon boss at the wide-open door as if Hitch was a long-lost brother come home from out west, though Hitch suspected that Fant had to fish a minute to remember his name. "How do, Hitch? Come in this house!" Fant swung his heavy arms open in a big gesture of welcome, displaying in rotund grandeur a broad middle that two gold watchchains couldn't reach across. He had the whitest teeth Hitch had ever seen, locked into a perennial grin beneath a black mustache, generous in size. "How's everything out at the Ws? How's that cranky old Charlie Waide?" Gossett demanded as if he had been waiting a month to hear. He didn't give Hitch time to answer, though. He said, "Seen you haulin' somebody to town in a wagon. Got a man hurt?"

Hitch told him about Joe Sands. Gossett's brow creased in studied concern, though Hitch would bet even money Fant couldn't have picked Joe Sands out of a crowd. Downing a shot of bourbon and pouring a second to sip slower, Hitch said, "I got to find Joe a place to lay up. Was wonderin' if you got a spare room with a cot in it, or know where there's one to be had? And I'd need somebody to fetch Joe his meals."

Fant frowned in thought. Hitch added, "Prosper Selkirk's payin' for it."

Fant's interest stirred. "Selkirk? You mean that tight-fisted dude is goin' to turn loose of a little Kansas City money in this town?" Hitch could almost see the man's mind totting up figures. Fant said, "Just so happens I got a little house I been rentin' out, and right now there ain't no girl . . . no renter in it. It'd be a jimdandy place for Joe. My good little ol' wife would be plumb tickled to fix extry at mealtime for a stoveup cowboy."

"Just because Selkirk's payin' for it don't mean I'd want it costin' no more than was fair."

"The farthest thing from my mind! I wouldn't ask no more than was right. A dollar a day . . . no, better say a dollar and a half when you figure how extravagant my wife gets with her cookin' if it's for sick folks. She's got a heart as big as her rump is broad, and that's considerable." His eyes narrowed slyly. "I bet I could find a girl who'd be glad to look in on that cowboy and be sure he don't die from lonesome."

"Remember, Fant, he's got a broken leg."

"A happy spirit helps heal the body."

"Selkirk might frown on payin' for the extras."

"No charge, just a bonus throwed in with the room and the chuck." His smile began to fade. "It'd be only fitten that I get my hands on a little Selkirk money. You know he's made it awful hard against the Figure 4 cowboys drinkin' any liquor at any place and any time. They come to town damned seldom. Figures to starve this little ol' town to death, is the way I see it."

As Hitch saw it, this "little ol' town" had no more than a toenail hold on survival at best, and its passing might solve as many problems as it created. But he wouldn't say so and insult a man in his own place of business.

He heard a scuffling of hoofs in the street and the

squeak of saddle leather as a man swung to the ground, spurs jingling. A cowboy walked through the open door, slapping his dusty clothes with a hat. He had a stubble of whiskers and a ragged brown mustache grayed considerably by a coat of dust. "Rye, Fant," he growled before he reached the bar. He downed the glass in one quick gulp, then coughed as if everything inside him was coming out. "Damn," he rasped, "that stuff clunks when it hits the belly, like a horseshoe dropped into a bucket. Ought to be agin the law to sell whisky that bad."

He tapped the empty glass impatiently against the bar. "More!" Gossett had held the bottle open and tilted as if knowing one drink wouldn't reach all the way. He refilled the glass.

Hunching over the bar, the cowboy demanded, "How much?"

"Fifty cents. Two bits a shot."

"Two bits?" The cowboy stared in protest, his mouth hanging open. "Ain't enough to poison a man, you got to rob him, too. When did it go up?"

"It's always been two bits, Asher. You just forgot."

The cowboy grumbled, "Then it's always been too damned high. Always some son of a bitch tryin' to squeeze a nickel out of a cowboy's sweat and blood."

"You sure came in with a burr under your blanket," the barman said. "Horse step on your foot or somethin'?"

"I quit the Snaketracks, that's what I done. I up and quit. I hope lightnin' strikes the whole damned outfit and kills everything but the lobo wolves and rattlesnakes, and I hope they multiply."

Hitch turned his head to smile. He had worked with Asher Cottingham, and he couldn't remember that anything had ever suited that cowpuncher. Cottingham had been born protesting, and thirty-odd years of experience had only shown him what a great variety of things the world held for him to detest.

Cottingham turned his attention from Gossett. "Hitch, you still nursemaidin' that ol' tightwad Charlie Waide?" He didn't give Hitch a chance to answer. He demanded, "Ol' Charlie given you-all the law yet?"

Hitch didn't know what he was talking about. Cottingham pulled a folded paper from his shirt pocket and slammed it against the bar with the palm of his hand. "This here is what I mean. Read that if you want to see how low and mean an outfit can get." His eyes snapped like the popper on a whip. "They tacked this on our bunkhouse door."

Fant Gossett stared in curiosity as Hitch unfolded the paper and glanced at it, then handed it to him. Fant said, "I been hearin' about these, but this is the first I seen."

Hitch had recognized it. The Nine Bars had posted the same set of rules a while back. A Nine Bar rep had brought a copy to the W wagon, and the cowboys passed it around to snicker over. They burned it to keep Charlie from seeing it and getting ideas. The majority were commonsense rules long observed but never formally written. One forbade drinking, card playing or gambling of any sort and required "proper decorum" about camp; forbade use of the rope on cattle except in actual need; forbade abuse of horses. A man couldn't make much quarrel against these.

Many would object, though, to rules which forbade use of a company horse on any private business and forbade the keeping of individually owned horses without the express permission of the manager, which in effect could set the cowboy afoot except when he was working; forbade "tramps and idlers" more than one night's stay in a camp, a sharp departure from traditional range hospitality and a direct move to eliminate the unemployed chuckline riders who if down on their luck could pass the winter free by spending a few days as guests in one camp, a few days in another; forbade employees' owning cattle in their own brand less than two fences away from the ranch where they worked, which in the Panhandle's open range country effectively canceled out their right to own cattle anywhere.

Hitch said, "A little extreme, some of them. But if a man don't like the rules he's free to go and work someplace else."

Asher Cottingham said bitterly, "Pretty soon there won't be noplace to go unless we stop these big outfits before they get any bigger."

"What do you mean, stop them?"

"They're teamin' up against us, Hitch. I'm sayin' it's time the cowboys done a little teamin' up of their own."

"Seems to me like the people that own a place have got a right to run it as they please."

"Not if they're goin' to step on us. Not if we was to call a halt. Ever occur to you, Hitch, that if all the cowboys was to quit at the same time, them ranchers would go to their knees in a week? Their money wouldn't save them; nothin' would move if we didn't do their dirty work. We'd have them by the short hair."

Hitch blinked incredulously. "You're talkin' about a strike!"

"You're damned right. There's a bunch of them been talkin' about it."

Hitch took another drink, a big one. It came to him

now why Charlie Waide had been trying to find out from him about talk around the wagon. "I've heard of factory strikes and miners' strikes, but I never heard of a cowboy strike."

"Nobody ever heard of the United States, either, till George Washington and some of them boys decided to show the Englishmen whichaway the river forked. We're not towheaded schoolboys to be treated like this, we're men, and *white* men at that." His eyes slitted. "There's a sight more cowboys than there is owners, Hitch. We'd have them beggin' us."

Hitch stared into his glass. The liquor had somehow gone sour. This kind of talk made him uneasy; it went against all his tradition of loyalty to the brand a man worked for, made him feel even a little guilty as if by listening to this he was somehow condoning treason. He tried to change the subject. "Been any rain over on the Snaketracks?"

Fant Gossett didn't let the subject shift. "Asher's got a point, Hitch. Them big outfits are out to run this country and ruin this town. Now, you know as well as I do that they control the politics. Half the counties you see on the map ain't organized; the ranchers don't *want* them organized. And them that is, they're under the ranchers' thumbs. The owners make sure the cowboys vote their way, and there ain't enough dissident votes to swing an election agin them. Now they've taken it in their heads they're goin' to squeeze everybody off of the range but themselves. They been meetin' with one another, figurin' how to divide it all up."

Hitch shook his head. "Some of them old boys have fought each other over grass and water till one hates the ground the other walks on. They wouldn't agree to what time it is."

"You been tendin' ol' Charlie's cows and ain't had

time to see it, Hitch. They're tryin' for one thing to fix it so there don't no workin' man run any stock of his own."

Hitch conceded that. "Selkirk tried to push that idea on Charlie. Charlie didn't bite."

"He will when they show him where it touches his pocketbook. Another thing, they been tryin' to buy out or push out all the little outfits they can, especially the Mexican sheepmen. There was Mexicans here with sheep when the Comanches still had this country. Me, I got no particular love for a Mexican, but his money spends as good as anybody's. Selkirk goes up and down the *plazas* with a sackful of money and shoves it at them Mexicans, lettin' them know that if they don't take what he gives them and move, they'll get moved anyway. Soon's he gets their names or their X on the paper, he burns their houses so they can't tarry. Been a bunch of them already trailed their flocks back over into New Mexico. Thing like that hurts this town."

"They got paid."

"Paid ain't enough. Selkirk could offer me fifty dollars for a bottle of cheap rotgut and I wouldn't sell it to him if he didn't treat me white." Fant shook a thick, stubby finger near Hitch's nose. "It was little men that built this town, and without them it'll die. You think them big outfits give a tinker's damn for us? They can buy everything out of Dodge City or Kansas City or someplace that don't even need their money, and they can starve this town to death. They don't want no town here because a town means families, and families means kids, and kids means schools, and that takes taxes. Ever see a big rancher that didn't choke into a conniption fit over the thought of payin' taxes?"

Hitch didn't reply though he kept thinking that what Fant Gossett paid in taxes would probably starve a field mouse. He looked first at Cottingham, then at Fant. "Fellers, you're talkin' crazy. There won't be no strike in this country."

"Why not?"

He tried to think of an answer. "It just ain't done, that's all."

Cottingham glowered. "It'll be done if they don't change their ways."

Hitch had intended to stay and rest awhile in the cool quiet of Gossett's adobe walls, but he disliked the turn of the talk. In his view you didn't accept a man's pay and cuss him; if you couldn't stand up for him you left. Which was just what Cottingham had done, though Hitch would bet a paint pony that Asher had been talking rebellion while still on the payroll. He set his glass on the bar. "Fant, the liquor's good. You get that house ready; I'll have Joe brought over when the doctor says to."

Gossett nodded. He waited until Hitch was almost at the door, then called, "Hitch! It occurs to me that Asher here is out of a job, and you-all at the Ws are short-handed since Joe busted his leg."

Hitch gritted his teeth. If a man wanted a job he ought to ask for it himself. Hitch said, "We're not short enough to hurt us."

Cottingham grunted. "Let the other men work a little harder so ol' Charlie won't be out no extry wages, is that it?"

The pair were beginning to irritate Hitch like gravel in his boots. "Charlie Waide alway treats a man fair."

Cottingham said, "I don't know as I'd want the job noway. How much they payin' at the Ws?"

"Thirty and found. It's as good as there is."

"Thirty dollars a month." Cottingham's mouth turned downward. "Hell of a lot for a poor man riskin' life and limb to make some rich man richer. Keep your job, Hitch. I don't want it."

"I never offered," Hitch said stiffly, knowing he ought to go instead of letting the argument run on. But he had to add, "I wouldn't want you out there agitatin' the men."

Cottingham looked surprised. "Me? I never agitated nobody in my whole life."

4

Asher Cottingham had enjoyed hard luck all his life; people had always conspired against him. When he was about fourteen his father had told him he was old enough to go out and work for wages. Very low wages they had been, too, to hear him tell it. Nothing made him happier than to have somebody listen to all his sad stories. That day must have been one of the happiest of his life.

Cottingham said he intended to go visit some friends at one of the Figure 4 wagons and would like to ride partway with Hitch. Hitch figured what he was after was a few days of free chuck at Selkirk's expense, but that was Selkirk's problem. The cowboy invited himself to tie his horse behind the wagon and climb up into the seat. Hitch was not thrilled by all that company.

"Look at this," Cottingham said, waving his arm, "all this land claimed by the Figure 4s. Ought to be a law against companies like that in the first place. A workin' man ought to be able to stand up face to face with the man he works for, like in the old days. Tryin' to talk to a company is like fightin' your way through a tangle of spider webs; you never can get to the heart of things, if it's even got a heart. I say no man ought to be allowed to own more than he can personally take care of."

"If that was the case," Hitch asked dryly, "who would you work for?"

Cottingham deliberated. "I don't know, but there ought to be a law."

It was a time of grand relief to Hitch when they came finally to a fork in the trail and Asher Cottingham climbed down from the wagon. Hitch had listened to all he could stand; Asher was one of those people always advocating tearing down whatever he disliked but having no idea how to build back something better in its place.

Asher said, "Well, I reckon I'll have to let you make the rest of the trip by yourself."

"I'll miss you."

The solitude afterward gave him time to think, to ponder whether trouble was indeed coming to the Canadian River country and to assure himself that there was no reason it had to involve the W. He didn't know a man in the outfit who was sore at Charlie Waide.

As he came onto W land, Hitch began pulling out of the trail to inspect every grazing bunch of cattle he saw. The cattle would raise their heads warily at the approach of the wagon, and many would hightail it across the prairie. But the vehicle itself was an object of curiosity because the cattle saw few of them, and the horses had no men astride to suggest the trouble which cattle associated with riders. Many cattle would run a little way, then turn to look. This was an area over which the roundup crew had already worked. The calves bore fresh brands just now in the process of healing.

At length Hitch came upon a group of cattle that kept pulling away, maintaining a respectable distance between themselves and the wagon. But they were not so far that he did not find himself staring in disbelief. "Slick-ears," he said aloud, as if the team knew what he was talking about. "I swear, there's slick-eared calves in that bunch."

He tried to maneuver the wagon around the cattle, but they kept edging away from him. Finally he had to unhitch one of the horses, get on it bareback and kick it bareheeled into a trot that took it around the cattle. Bringing them to a halt, he counted twenty cows and fourteen calves.

Slick, all right, he thought, looking at their unmarked ears. *Ain't but two branded calves in the bunch*. Those two were W calves, following W cows. The rest of the cows were Figure 4s plus one Snake-track, and not one of their calves carried a brand.

Can't hardly see how we missed them in the roundup; we worked this strip like a fine-tooth comb.

But there they were. Puzzling, Hitch decided the Figure 4 cows must have drifted over onto this part of the W in a bunch, perhaps pressed by the roundup crews on the Figure 4. Some spooky cattle always had a tendency to keep moving out in front of the roundup, avoiding capture as long as they could. But these cattle, though shy, didn't seem inclined to break and run once he had circled them.

Well, he would tell the Figure 4 rep and let him take them back to the range where they belonged. It would have to be done before long, for once the cows began kicking off these calves and weaning them, the calves would be considered mavericks. Sure would cripple the Figure 4, he thought sarcastically, to lose a dozen calves to a maverick hunter.

In late afternoon he heard the bawling of the day's gather before he reached the roundup ground. The branding crew was sweaty and dirty and moving with the slowness that indicated a day's work was nearly done. Recognizing his own team and wagon, Law McGinty rode out from his position on the perimeter of the herd. "See you got back," the young cowboy said needlessly.

Hitch watched him with suspicion. "Thought about takin' your wagon by your place and leavin' it, then decided you'd rather take it back yourself. Give you a chance to see your wife." He paused, considering whether to say more. "Law, there been trouble between you and Kate?"

Law seemed surprised. "Why?"

"You left here the other night sayin' you was goin' home. Yesterday she told me it'd been a spell since you was there. Now, maybe it's none of my business, but I think you owe Kate better treatment."

Color rose in Law's face. He offered no explanation.

Hitch said, "You take this wagon home tonight and act like a husband. Be back here by daylight."

Law was solemn. "All right, Hitch. Want me to start now?"

"I think that would be a dandy idea."

Law tied his horse behind the wagon so he would have a way to return to camp. Hitch climbed down, carrying a new lantern he had bought for Trump Tatum, and handed the lines to Law. He watched Law turn the team and start across the prairie, skirting the bawling herd. Hitch turned his attention to the cattle a moment, but he was afoot and would be no help at the herd. He could go to the branding fire, but it looked as if they were about done anyway. He walked to the chuckwagon and poured a cup of coffee. Bewhiskered Trump Tatum eyed the lantern with no words of gratitude, as if it were no more than his due. He made some comment to the effect that supper wasn't ready yet and that a boss set a poor example showing up at the wagon ahead of his men, the sun still an hour high. Hitch ignored him, which annoyed Trump even more.

Charlie Waide rode in from the herd directly. This surprised Hitch a little; he expected Charlie to have moved on to another wagon by now. Charlie kept close watch on them all. The rancher fetched coffee and sat down on a bedroll, his shoulders hunched, the bad arm plainly hurting him. He tried to avoid letting Hitch see the pain in his face, but Hitch caught it anyhow. Charlie asked, "How'd you leave Joe Sands?"

"He'll mend."

"Didn't happen to run onto another hand to take his place awhile?"

"I saw Asher Cottingham. I didn't hire him."

"Good. His jaw works like a gate-hinge. Anyway, last I heard he was at the Snaketracks."

"He quit." Hitch considered a moment, then decided to tell him about the Snaketrack posting the new company rules.

Charlie nodded gravely. "Not a bad set of rules, though, the most of them. They make sense."

"You seen them, Charlie?"

"Weeks ago. The owners been passin' them around."

It struck Hitch funny now, remembering that the cowboys had taken pains to burn the rules from the Nine Bar to keep Charlie from seeing them. They should have known he was always a jump or two ahead.

Hitch found his coffee cold. He sloshed it around in the cup, not wanting to drink it but too frugal to throw it out; he could remember times when there hadn't been any. "You wasn't thinkin' about postin' them rules yourself, was you, Charlie?"

"What do you think of them?"

"The good ones are understood without you havin' to write them down on paper and makin' men look like boys that need to be told to wipe their nose. The bad ones . . ." He left the rest unsaid.

"Maybe times change."

"You ain't changed, Charlie; neither have these men. You don't need to post rules like that; these men won't let you down."

Charlie's eyes were tired and worried. "I had company today. Owner of the Nine Bars was by to see me. Said there's some ugly talk amongst cowboys around the country. You hear anything in town?"

"Just Asher Cottingham bellyachin'; nothin' I'd take stock in. I get the notion some of the boys resent the new rules, but that's nothin' to concern yourself about. It's outfits like the Figure 4s and the Snaketracks and the Nine Bars that'll have the trouble if any comes."

"So, it's true, then, about the strike talk?"

"Ain't been none of it around this wagon, and there won't be. I'll guarantee you that."

"Can you, Hitch? Can anybody guarantee anything anymore?"

The roundup progressed methodically the next several days. Charlie Waide left to spend a while at his other wagons. A couple more cows showed up whose brands were impossible to identify definitely as either a Figure 4 or an LR, so Hitch arbitrarily called one for the McGintys, one for Selkirk. He sensed Law was a little sore about it, but Rascal accepted it in good grace. By now a new Figure 4 rep had replaced Dayton Brumley. To Hitch's relief he seemed disinclined to make any fuss. On the contrary, when Hitch called one of the cows a Figure 4, the lanky rep said, "You sure, Hitch? If there's any question I'd rather the McGintys got her. Selkirk and his crowd won't starve to death."

Hitch appreciated harmony in camp, but on the other hand he respected a man who stood up for the outfit that paid him. He made a mental resolution that if this cowboy ever came looking for a place on the W payroll, he wouldn't get it. Hitch's feeling was reinforced that night at supper when he heard the cowboy relating his grudges against the ranch he worked for.

"I sure was glad to come to the W wagon," the man said. "I'd about had me a bellyful of ol' Selkirk and his crowd treatin' us like we was English servants, or like maybe we owed them money. Selkirk seems to think everybody is tryin' to cheat him out of somethin'. Guilty conscience, I'll bet; he's done to other people and he don't want nobody doin' it to him. It'd serve him and the Figure 4s right if some of the New Mexico cow thieves was to come over and sack them out."

Rascal McGinty chimed in, "Boys, them big outfits are tryin' to get a stranglehold on this country and everybody in it."

The trend of the talk irritated Hitch. "What do you know about it, Rascal? Charlie Waide's the only man you've worked for. He ever treat you less than fair?"

"I wasn't pointin' at Charlie."

"Well, be damned sure you don't."

Hitch loosened a little. Maybe he had jumped on Rascal a little too hard. He said, a little more evenly this time, "Rascal, whatever the other outfits do, the Ws has always treated a man right. It always will."

"Always is a long time, Hitch. People been known to change, even people like Charlie."

"The day Charlie Waide ever let us down, you can all get up and leave here, Rascal. I'll be out there in front, leadin' you."

Law McGinty's eyes narrowed. "I'll remember you said that, Hitch. If things ever come to dividin' up the blankets, we'll hold you to it."

Hitch shook his head. "I'll bet all my chips on Charlie."

The day Charlie Waide came back, Prosper Selkirk showed up in his buckboard. He didn't have the greyhounds with him. The Figure 4 rep saw Selkirk's rig when it came over the hill, and Hitch grinned as the cowboy craftily contrived to get busy on the far side of the herd, trying to keep out of his boss's sight and hopefully off of his mind. Charlie Waide walked his horse around the herd and jerked his head at Hitch, indicating he wanted Hitch to ride down to the wagon with him. Hitch said, "You don't need me, Charlie."

"I don't care to talk to him by myself. Anyway, he may want to go over your tallies. Quicker we satisfy him, the quicker he'll get the hell away from here. If he spends the night that rep will stay out with the wild bunch and go hungry."

At the wagon Charlie offered coffee and the other

amenities, while Trump Tatum offered nothing but an acid stare. Selkirk seemed agitated and in no mood to socialize. "Charlie, has there been any talk among your men?"

Charlie asked innocently, "Talk about what?" though Charlie had to know very well what Selkirk meant.

"Rebellion. It's spreading across these ranches like the plague."

Blandly Charlie said, "I've heard no talk, except that some of the boys ain't keen on the rules certain outfits have posted."

Selkirk's voice was critical. "I don't believe you've recognized the seriousness of the problem in which we find ourselves, Charles."

"I ain't got no problem. I ain't posted the rules."

"If it comes to us, it'll come to you. This kind of thing is a contagious disease. We have to cut it off before it becomes worse."

"You figurin' on shootin' a few cowboys?"

"You know better than that. But I do intend to root out the troublemakers and get them off of this range."

"You go right ahead and do what suits you, Prosper. It's no problem of mine."

"It *is*, can't you see that? This problem must be faced by every substantial rancher on the plains, and the only way is to band together, to meet this trouble with our combined strength. It is becoming a contest of wills, Charles. We have far too much invested here to be thwarted by troublemakers and lazy malcontents."

Charlie Waide frowned. "You ever try to just sit down and talk man-to-man with the hands that work for you?"

"How could I do that? From the first I found they

were mocking me. Behind my back they called me a dude, a damnyankee, and worse. No, I don't talk *with* them, I talk to them. That's the only way you can treat men of that type, with authority."

Hitch was surprised to find himself seeing Selkirk's side of it, a little. He doubted Selkirk had ever tried very diligently to communicate with his cowboys on any congenial plane, but he knew that even a good effort might have failed. As a group, cowboys—like the ranchers they worked for—had a tendency to be intolerant of men whose ways and values were different from their own. In particular they resented what Selkirk stood for . . . Yankee money, generally considered to have been squeezed from the flesh and blood of the South. Though the Civil War was long since over and the men who had fought in it were now middle-aged or older, the sectional bitterness was still much alive.

Charlie said, "You-all just don't understand one another."

"They understand me. I won't be bullied or threatened."

"We've got law here," Charlie pointed out. "The ranches control it, and I'd think the county sheriffs can take care of any trouble."

"The law can't stop all this talk, and it can't control a range overrun with all sorts of undesirable people. That is where we can give the law some assistance. I've called several of the owners and managers over to my place tomorrow for a talk."

"War conference, you mean?"

"Call it what you wish. I want you there, Charles."

Charlie was ill at ease. "I don't see where I got any part in this."

Selkirk stood up. Anger hardened the set of his jaw.

"Charles, we are rapidly reaching a point where those who are not with us must be considered to be against us. I have no intention of letting you be against us."

Charlie was on his feet too. "I ain't against nobody, but I intend to run my outfit and let you run yours."

Selkirk stared at him with hard, ungiving eyes. "I hate to hold this over your head, but I will if I have to. You have a large loan on this ranch, and it's with a Kansas City bank, is it not?"

"Why ask me? You seem to know all about it."

"Would you care to guess who is a member of that bank's board of directors?"

Charlie swallowed, stunned.

Selkirk said, "I'll see you tomorrow, Charles." He dropped his cup into Trump Tatum's washtub, climbed into the buckboard and left without looking back.

5

Charlie was ringier than a wagon cook after Selkirk left. He bawled out the kid jingler for herding the remuda too tightly and not giving the horses a chance to graze. Rascal McGinty caught thunder for trying to brand a calf with an iron not hot enough. Charlie raised cain with Trump Tatum because half an oven of biscuits was left over, and that was wasteful of flour. He said if Trump did not learn to be sparing and help keep the costs down, he would find his employer bankrupt and himself working for some Kansas City bank . . . if he was working at all.

Rascal grumbled, “I don’t like Charlie goin’ to that meetin’.”

“He’s got to,” Hitch said.

“Charlie’s fought Indians and he’s fought Yankee soldiers, but he never could stand up to Selkirk’s brand of thimbleriggers.”

“Nobody’ll make Charlie do somethin’ he don’t think is right.”

“They’ll crowd hell out of him. If he was to agree

to that rule against a cowboy ownin' livestock, it'd ruin us, Hitch. Me and Law, we ain't got so many cattle that we could make a decent livin' for us and Law's wife and that youngun comin'."

"I'll guarantee Charlie."

Law McGinty demanded, "How much is that guarantee worth, Hitch?"

"Meanin' what?"

"Meanin' if Charlie was to weaken, what would you do about it?"

Hitch kept arguing for faith in Charlie, but Law relentlessly pressed him for an answer, and Rascal backed his brother. At length Hitch said, "If Charlie ever did turn his back on us, I'd roll up my bed and leave here."

Rascal glanced at Law, then back to Hitch. "And let the rest of us come with you?"

"And let the rest of you come with me."

"That's the kind of guarantee we wanted, Hitch."

"That's how much faith I got in Charlie."

Charlie made no move to join the cowboys around the fire. He kept to himself, which—considering the mood he was in—suited everybody. He called Hitch over. "Hitch, you're goin' with me."

Hitch argued, "Them ranchers don't want me. My little bunch of cows don't make me an owner in their eyes. I'd be like salt in their wounds."

"If it itches them, let them scratch."

"Likely I'd be a hindrance to you."

"Damned if I'm goin' over there by myself. I want somebody with me who talks the same language I do, who can keep that Yankee highbinder from tyin' me in a knot with fast talk."

"I'd sooner get stomped by an outlawed stud."

"So had I. But we're both goin'."

* * *

Hitch had not been to the Figure 4 headquarters since the syndicate had bought its much smaller forerunner from a buffalo hunter who had stayed to traffic in cattle after the heavy guns had killed out the shaggy herds. He saw not a trace of the soddies that had been here before. He saw frame buildings, the management house and the office sitting along one end of a big open yard that lacked only a flagpole and some cavalry to make it look like a military quadrangle. The cookshack and the long bunkhouse sat at the opposite end, the barns and corrals set in almost perfect straight lines, all buildings and fences coming to neat ninety-degree angles. It had the look of having been designed on a drafting table in Kansas City and set down here without an inch of deviation from plan. There was not a hint of decoration anywhere, nothing that did not serve some utilitarian purpose.

"Like an Army post," said Charlie Waide.

"Or a prison," Hitch replied.

Buckboards and wagons and horses stood around the office building. "Guess we're not the first ones here," Hitch said.

Charlie shook his head. "And I don't intend to be the last to leave."

They dismounted in shade at a hitching rack near the office. Hitch loosened the cinch to make the horse easier during what could be a considerable wait. Charlie frowned at the open door, dreading, then squared his shoulders and strode in. Hitch looked back regretfully toward the barn where he could see a few cowboys working, then followed Charlie.

A dozen or fifteen men sat in a cramped room that served as an office. Hitch surmised that the rest of the building was sleeping quarters for a city-raised bookkeeper who wouldn't feel at home in the bunkhouse with the cowboys. He knew most of the faces and names; these men were ranch owners and managers. He noted no representation from the small outfits and nester-type operations. These men counted cattle by the thousands and tens of thousands. It struck him that this was probably the first time so many had ever met in a group. Some had become enemies through competition for land. He saw gray-bearded, hawk-eyed old John Torrington of the Snaketrack and Allie Clay of the Nine Bar, bitter rivals who once had been so near killing each other over a few sections of second-rate grazing land that when one went to town he sent a couple of men ahead to make sure the other was not there. Now they were brought together in an uneasy alliance, but no nearer together than they had to be. Torrington sat in one corner, Clay in another.

Selkirk stood at the front of the room, one hand on a rolltop desk that had dozens of rolled-up papers sticking out of convenient little pigeonholes. A thin and fleeting smile crossed his face as he paused in his talk to acknowledge Charlie.

"I doubt, gentlemen, there is anyone in this room who is not acquainted with Charles Waide. Charles, I'm glad you could come."

Charlie said stiffly, "Don't recall that I was given any option." He took up two or three minutes of Selkirk's time working through the room shaking hands with friends and acquaintances. He was warm to some, coolly businesslike with others. A few were old-line cowboy-ranchers of his own stripe, who had battled their way up despite drouth and flood, fire and storm, Indians and Texas fever. John Torrington, for an example, was one of the fire-eating breed who had fought Mexicans on the border, Indians on the plains; he had been fighting somebody all his life. More of the men, though, were of the newer corporate breed, transplanted from the board room of a bank or a mercantile firm. Many had been easy learners in the ranch business, hiring dependable men who could take care of the cowcamp details while they concentrated on the broader aspects. After all, they did not have to be cowboys; they could hire plenty of men to do the horseback work. Their own task was planning and high-level decisions, and this the majority had learned to do well. That they might not know or at least might not particularly appreciate the traditions which had grown up among cowboys and old shortgrass ranchers was to be expected. Traditions did not produce beef, nor did they retire a loan.

For that matter, many of the old-line ranchers themselves had discarded practices and outlooks that once had been their hallmark. New times called for new ways.

Done with hand-shaking, Charlie turned toward Hitch. "Fellers, I brought my wagon boss; most of you know Hugh Hitchcock."

Some spoke to Hitch, some didn't. Selkirk said, "Nice you could come, Hitchcock. I think you'll find coffee down at the cookshack, and some cowboys to talk to."

Charlie Waide put in, "He can drink coffee at the Ws. I brought him to take part in this thing with me."

Selkirk rubbed his hands uncomfortably. "As you wish, Charles. I thought he might not feel that he fits in."

"Hell," rasped Charlie, "I don't fit in either, but I'm here. Let's get on with it. I want to be back at the wagon tonight."

Whatever Selkirk's line of talk had been, Charlie had thrown him offstride. "Charles, these men here already know, but you probably have not heard. Most of the work force left the Snaketrack yesterday. The Nine Bar has lost two-thirds of its hands, too."

Charlie glanced at Hitch in surprise. Hitch felt a chill. Somehow he hadn't believed when he had listened to the angry talk in Fant Gossett's saloon that it would ever get past the jawing stage.

"You see now," Selkirk continued, "the problem we're up against. It will probably come to the rest of us shortly; a thing of this sort tends to become epidemic. Now, I realize there are some among us who have had differences of opinion in the past—even violent differences. But we have to put that behind us and face this threat united. Struggling along separately we can be hurt like a crippled animal caught by the wolves apart from the herd. But together, with our combined strength, we can snuff out this insurrection with a minimum of damage. And cost." He paused as if to give this latter element its proper emphasis. "Now, as to strategy: I think from the experience of the Snaketrack and the Nine Bar that most of us have some men who will not join the strike, either for fear of losing their jobs, for apathy, or for lack of courage."

Charlie suggested, "They might just be *loyal*."

Selkirk nodded and went on. "The point is that we'll have these men as a crutch until we can hire others. And make no mistake, there *will* be other men we can hire. We do not have to let ourselves be panicked by a few malcontents and their followers.

"We all know this trouble goes deeper than just the hired hands on these ranches. We know some of these men are thieves, and that other men who may not be thieves themselves nevertheless condone them because they hate us for our success. Up and down the river are small squatters and that sort who dignify their position by calling themselves ranchers; in reality they are maverick runners and cattle thieves. Then in these miserable nesterments that pass themselves off as towns are people who agitate against us. In short, gentlemen, we stand against a motley array of ragtag enemies who represent a threat to the growth and security of this entire region. Whatever we do has to be calculated to clear the range once and for all of this obstructionist element. Until we, the substantial owners who have a bonafide investment in the future of this region, can control it and shut out these undesirables, there will be no security for us or for our property."

Bearded old John Torrington of the Snaketrack squinted his flinty eyes and spoke out angrily, "Hell, looks to me like the thing to do is to find out who these troublemakers are and go stretch a little rope. That'll by God put an end to it."

Selkirk seemed embarrassed. "Gentlemen, the idea has some merit, and perhaps a few years ago it would have been the best way. But now the law of Texas will not stand for it. They would have the Rangers on us in a week. We have to accomplish the same thing by more subtle methods and with as little violence or bloodshed as possible. We don't have to choke a man to death with a rope. In the business world we can choke him off financially by refusing him a loan or other support." He looked directly at Charlie. "With these cowboys, all we have to do is refuse them jobs, until they spend whatever they have in their pockets. Then they have no choice but to leave this country."

A murmur of argument began to rise. Torrington declared, "The hell with the state law; it's none of their business. We control the county law around here, and there ain't much anybody can do if we run our own courts. I say let's stretch some rope!"

Selkirk waved his hands, trying to get order back into the meeting. Charlie Waide and John Torrington stood toe to toe, arguing angrily. They had argued before over land Charlie used and Torrington wanted. "Gentlemen!" Selkirk pleaded. "Gentlemen!" In a minute the men had settled enough that Selkirk was able to take the floor again. "I must say I agree with the spirit of John Torrington's argument, though the application of it under today's civilized conditions might bring us more problems than it would solve."

Torrington declared, "Charlie Waide, I know for a certain fact that you once dispatched a thief without the benefit of a judge. No use you turnin' squeamish over it now."

Charlie said, "Not once, John, *twice*. There was a time you didn't even know about. But it was different then; we didn't have law, so we made our own. Now we got law."

"And it's ours," Torrington said. "I say if we help it along with a little summary judgment and save the county the expense of some trials, we'll throw the fear of God into the rest of them maverick chasers and brand burners and strike agitators. It'll clean this country like a grassfire."

Charlie said tightly, "If they was to hang all the maverick runners, John, me and you would be the first to go. You know that neither one of us had a seat in our britches till we'd mavericked us a herd."

"That was a long time ago. Times change."

"Exactly what I'm tryin' to tell you."

Selkirk said, "Gentlemen, we're arguing needlessly over a moot point. There'll be no wholesale hanging, so we're wasting time talking about it. Our immediate problem is this strike."

Charlie Waide said, "I ain't clear in my own mind what set it off. Maybe if we was to just give them boys a little raise in pay . . ."

Selkirk shook his head. "Out of the question. None of us will stand for being blackmailed or bullied. If the situation merited more wages we would have given them without having a pistol put to our heads. Wages, gentlemen, are set the same way cattle prices are set, by supply and demand in the marketplace. We cannot set our own cattle prices; we take what the market will bear. So long as there are men all over the country willing to work for twenty-five dollars a month, it would be folly on our part to pay more." He eyed Charlie levelly. "Charles, since you bring this up, I should comment on one of your practices that has contributed to our problems. Too often a cowboy who does not like what he earns on the Figure 4 has gone to you at the W and received more pay than I was giving him. This creates dissatisfaction among the other men and undermines the position of other ranch operators. We could eliminate this by cooperating closer with one another."

Charlie said, "Cattle are sellin' higher this year. I figure if I can do it, you-all can do it too."

Selkirk argued, "Charles, the only place you can find money to pay more wages is out of your profit margin, and I have reason to know it is as thin as paper already. I say this: that if a man is not willing to work for what an employer is willing to pay him, he ought to go somewhere else."

Charlie said, "I got men who came here with me

from South Texas and went through hell with me. We was like partners then. Without them I'd of gasped and gone under. I figure I owe them."

"How long will you owe them, Charles, the rest of your life? They've eaten your food and taken your wages for years. You've treated them well and paid them all that you ever agreed to. Certainly, we appreciate what these men went through years ago. Many of us went through the great war on one side or the other, but we do not expect to live on the country's gratitude all our lives. A man makes his way on what he does *now*, not on what he once did. We cannot let what happened years ago stand in the way of progress. This is a raw frontier no longer. It is a modern, civilized country, and we are in a position to build it on a sound business basis without false sentimentality and without clinging to outmoded customs and attitudes.

"I have been a banker long enough to know that the one object of anyone in any business venture is to show a profitable return on investment. Without this, the nation would collapse; there would be hunger all over the land. We strive to make this region prosperous and healthy for business, and in doing so we do the entire nation a service. We cannot jeopardize this great purpose by lack of unity or by sentimentality toward a few cowhands long since amply repaid.

"Now, there have been objections to the adoption of the rules we have set up, but they are sensible rules that simply establish an order of conduct. Anyone who objects is probably a misfit anyway. As I see it, we in this room face the same type of pressures as these cowboys do except that ours are multiplied many times over. Each of us has financial backers, partners or whatever, who look at us as coldly and objectively as we must look at our employees. If we fail to perform, we are discarded with no hesitation. I do not see that the workmen who accept our wages are entitled to more consideration than those of us who bear the burden of responsibility."

Worriedly watching Charlie, Hitch thought he could see at least partial acceptance in the old rancher's leathery face. Selkirk made an effective argument for his case, Hitch conceded.

Selkirk evidently thought he was gaining ground, for he pressed the attack, looking directly at Charlie Waide. "The crux of this matter is the allowing of some men on our payrolls to own cattle. Most of us know we are sustaining losses we cannot pinpoint. Some come from outlaw bands raiding out of New Mexico who hit us and run away with cattle when they find the way clear; the death of Billy the Kid did not stop all of it. But far more serious, I believe, is the slow attrition of our herds due to dishonest people on our payrolls and to scurvy pilfering by some so-called ranchers who squat among us on starvation claims. Losses of this size can be compounded into ruin if we stand by and do nothing.

"We cannot afford to subsidize this dishonesty any longer. We must agree together to stop this custom of allowing our people to own cattle. This will remove the incentive for a majority of the stealing. Then if we can find effective means to remove these marginal operators who only survive by robbing us, we will have the way clear to make this region efficient and profitable without the eternal vigilance now required of us."

He paused, watching Charlie Waide. "Charles, the majority of us have agreed to impose the cattle rule. How about you?"

The other ranchers turned their attention to Charlie, who fidgeted and looked at Hitch. Hitch watched him uneasily, feeling the pressure of these other men heavy against him.

Selkirk pressed, "Well, Charles?"

An old rawhide rancher who had come out of the brush country said, "I ain't among them, Charlie. If you say no, you ain't by yourself."

That rancher didn't have any money borrowed from Selkirk's bank. Looking nervously at the others, Charlie got carefully to his feet. "I'll answer you this-away, Prosper." He motioned toward Hitch. "You-all know Hugh Hitchcock," he told the crowd. "He's the caliber of man I got workin' at the Ws. I'd trust Hitch to the moon and back with everything I own. I feel the same way about the rest of my hands. Now, I can see your argument about the cattle rule. If I didn't have men like Hitch I might be easy convinced. But I don't want Hitch to lose his cattle, or the other men like him. If I was to go along with you-all it'd be like tellin' the men I didn't trust them nomore. I won't do that."

Selkirk said narrowly, "You put a lot of trust in men you may not know as well as you think you do."

"I know them."

"But what if you're wrong? What if one day you find some of them *have* betrayed you?"

Blinking, Charlie glanced at Hitch as if wondering whether Selkirk knew something Charlie didn't. "I'd stake all I got on my men."

Selkirk's voice carried a hard threat. "You *are* staking all you've got."

Charlie stared at him, hating the power Selkirk represented, hating Selkirk because he envied him, a damnyankee. "You want to spell that out to me in English?" he demanded.

Selkirk said, "I don't think I have to."

Flushed, Charlie pushed through the men and out the door. Hitch followed, glancing back in concern at the angry Selkirk. Outside, Charlie cursed vigorously a moment. Then he said in misery, "Hitch, the son of a bitch can fair gut me if he takes a notion."

Hitch saw Charlie weakening. Selkirk had hit him where he was vulnerable.

Charlie was so unsettled that he forgot to tighten the cinch before he tried to mount, and Hitch caught him to save him from a fall. Charlie cursed and fought his way free. "Dammit, I can make it myself!"

When Charlie was like that, the best thing was to leave him alone. The older he got, the more true this had become. Hitch silently tightened his own cinch and swung into the saddle. He noticed that when Charlie mounted, he did so slowly. He was wearing out, for it had been a long ride over here. But Hitch didn't mention it, for that would have invited a cussing. Hitch rode in silence, letting Charlie simmer. At length Charlie settled enough to start paying attention to the cattle they passed, and at one point he stopped to look at three horses that watched curiously beside the trail. After a long time Charlie declared, "There's truth in some of what Selkirk says."

"He's wrong about the W cowboys."

"There ain't a man on the Ws would steal from me, is there?"

"You know those men better than that."

"Always thought I did. But times change. Things ain't what they was, and maybe people ain't either."

They rode slowly, sparing horses that already had put in a long day. Once in a while Hitch looked uneasily at Charlie, seeing weariness grind the old rancher down. They hadn't come prepared to camp, but they needed to. Hitch couldn't afford to suggest it directly, for Charlie would ride all the way to the wagon out of pure stubbornness.

Hitch said, "Charlie, I been thinkin' these horses need water, and I could sure stand some coffee. Wouldn't be far out of our way to go by the McGinty place."

"I'm doin' fine," Charlie said pridefully, "and I don't think the horses are sufferin' any. But if you're that weak . . ."

Hitch smiled thinly.

Approaching the McGinty claim, Charlie said, "I ain't seen that girl Kate in a long time. She close to deliverin'?"

"Lookin' at her, I'd say she was."

"And that boy's leavin' her out here all by herself?"

"I've tried to get him to send her to town. She don't want to go."

The sun was low, and Hitch hoped for Charlie's sake that Kate would talk the old man into staying for supper. By that time it would be getting on toward dark and Charlie would probably agree to stay the night. He needed the rest.

A tall, slender woman stood in front of the dugout, peering curiously at them from under the protection of a big slat bonnet. This, Hitch knew at a glance, couldn't be Kate McGinty, but the bonnet hid her face. He finally recognized Kate's mother.

"Howdy, Miz Fallon. Didn't figure to see you here."

The gaunt woman studied him with no great friendliness. She had little use for people so much more fortunate than herself. "Where's that fiddlefooted husband of hers? Why didn't you bring him?"

Concerned, Hitch asked, "Somethin' the matter with Kate?"

"No, she's fine, but it's no credit to him. He ought to be here seein' after her. He ought to know a young woman ain't no heifer to be left to calve by herself."

Charlie Waide leaned forward in the saddle, hunched in his weariness. "I was just fixin' to tell Hitch, we could take and send her up to W headquarters till she's delivered."

"No need," the woman said, "though I reckon it's civil of you to be askin'. I'm here with her now, and I'll stand by her. It pleasures me anyway, gettin' to stay in a place as nice as this." She waved her hand toward the low-slung dugout, and Hitch thought at first she was being bitter. It occurred to him then that she meant it; this was better than most of the places she had ever lived.

Hitch dismounted, stiff from the ride. He walked a little to exercise his legs. "We thought we'd stop and see about Kate, and water the horses. Thought maybe, too, we might be lucky enough to beg us a cup of coffee."

Kate McGinty spoke from the dugout opening. "We'd be tickled, Hitch. You-all come on in." She held the canvas flap open. He stared a moment, distressed by the splotched color in her face. He hadn't been around women much in this stage of the game; he didn't know if this appearance was normal or if possibly something was wrong with her. All he knew was that she didn't look quite right for Kate.

"Charlie," Hitch said, "I'll take and water the horses. Why don't you go set a spell?"

Charlie gave him no argument, a fact which bore witness to his fatigue. Mrs. Fallon went into the dugout ahead of Charlie. Kate stood in the doorway, holding the flap and watching as Hitch swung back into the saddle, leading Charlie's horse. After watering them he turned them loose in a corral to roll and rest.

Kate McGinty walked heavily down to meet him. "There's a little grain in the shed." He thanked her and fed the horses sparingly. "It's late," she said. "You-all ought to spend the night."

"That'd be up to Charlie. Sure it wouldn't put you out none?"

"We'd be tickled." That expression, often repeated, seemed to sum up Kate's attitude toward almost everything. She was so used to adversity that she appeared immune.

He said, "You ought to be in the house, restin' too."

"Exercise is good for a woman in my condition, or don't you know?"

"That kind of experience is out of my line."

"It shouldn't be. You ought to find you a woman, Hitch. She'd be good for you, and I know you'd be good for her."

He couldn't tell her he had long wished he had claimed her before Law McGinty did. And he could not tell her he was waiting until he could provide a woman something better than this, for it would seem he was downgrading what Law had given her. "A cowpuncher like me is always too busy, seems like. I'm in no hurry. The Lord always provides."

"He provides for them that helps theirselves."

It seemed to Hitch that Law McGinty wasn't helping himself much, letting a handsome little woman like this sit alone while he prowled the river looking for something else. Granted, she wasn't at her best right now, but she wouldn't be in this condition much longer. A man ought to be willing to wait. "I sent Law home with the wagon the other night," he said.

"I thank you, Hitch. He should've come on his own."

Hitch felt obliged to make excuses. "Law's a man, Kate, but he's still got a little of the boy left in him. Maybe he don't realize yet the way you feel about him, the way you need him."

"I'm grateful you sent him. Even if it was just for an hour or two, I'm glad you made him come."

An hour or two. Hitch remembered that Law hadn't come back to camp till about daylight.

"It'll be better someday," Kate said hopefully. "When the place is bigger and we got more cattle, he'll have time then to stay."

Hitch turned away to hide the anger that gnawed him. *Damn that Law; somebody ought to take a horsewhip to him.*

By the time Kate and her mother got the coffee made, Charlie had relaxed and was an easy mark for an invitation to stay for supper. By the time supper was done, it was dark outside. Kate asked them to stay; the horses needed a rest anyway, she argued, and there were plenty of blankets in the dugout which Rascal McGinty had built for himself, well apart from this one he had given up for Law and Kate. In his weariness Charlie was not hard to persuade. They sat around in lamplight awhile, talking of all manner of things. By Fallon and McGinty standards, Charlie Waide was a rich man, but he had known these same privations in his earlier years. He didn't seem out of place here.

The men finally said their goodnights. They would be up at three in the morning without awakening the women; they could make the wagon by breakfast. In Rascal's dugout Charlie took the lone bed. Hitch spread a blanket on the hard-packed dirt floor, wrapping it over him. Charlie was quickly snoring, but Hitch lay awake looking up at the low roof, unaccustomed to the musty, earthy smell of the place. He thought back on the meeting at the Figure 4, on the trouble that had come to the river country, wondering if the W would be lucky enough to see it pass by.

They rode sleepy-headed by starlight, stomachs lank. Charlie was hunched. The long ride yesterday had been hard on him, and the short night had not given him enough rest. Maybe today Charlie would have the good judgment to stay at the wagon.

Charlie said, "That's a sweet little woman Law has got. Takes me back a long ways." He lapsed into silence, remembering. "I don't see that bein' short one more man would cripple us. You send Law home to stay with her till she's through her time."

"He needs the money, Charlie."

"Hell, I didn't mean to take him off of the payroll. I'll work his butt off later and make up for the lost time. You send him home, Hitch."

"I'd be tickled."

"And Hitch . . ." Charlie paused until Hitch prompted him with "What?"

"Hitch, if ever you see another little woman like that, don't you stand off next time. You grab her."

6

It was still dark when they came upon the horse jingler and rode into camp with him and the remuda. The jingler was uneasy, remembering how he had been chewed on. He kept edging away from Charlie like a colt shying away from some mean old stud.

The cowboys, gathered around the fire eating their breakfast, did not notice that the jingler brought company. Hitch heard a familiar voice talking loudly.

Charlie rubbed a big hand across his mustache and started to curse. "Asher Cottingham! Get rid of him, Hitch. I'd sooner have smallpox in camp." Charlie turned back toward the remuda.

Hitch walked closer to the fire and stopped to listen. Cottingham was talking small treason and didn't realize Hitch was there. "Like I was tellin' you boys last night, I'm offerin' you a chance to come along and join the strike. I'm goin' on to some more wagons today. Any of you wants to come along, you're welcome." He launched into a tirade against rich old misers and greedy damnyankees getting richer off of other men's hard labor. He declared that all the cowboys had to do was stand together and the ranchers would come begging.

Funny, Hitch thought, oddly detached from it all for a moment, how sometimes both sides of an argument will tend to sound the same. In a way, what Asher Cottingham said was akin to what Prosper Selkirk was saying in the ranchers' meeting except he had the gun pointed the other way. The blind striking out at the blind. What they both needed was a deep blue bruise across the breadth of the butt.

Hitch demanded, "Asher, you about finished your breakfast?"

Cottingham almost dropped his coffee in surprise. "Just about, I reckon."

Hitch clenched his fists. "Then finish it and let's see how fast you can get yourself out of this camp."

"Now looky here, Hitch, this ain't bein' hospitable."

"You got a lot of nerve to talk about hospitality after you come and eat a man's chuck and sleep in his camp and try to turn his friends against him. I've changed my mind; you ain't even finishin' that breakfast. You get yourself up and catch your horse."

Cottingham pushed to his feet, grumbling. "Highhanded damned outfit if you ask me. I ain't done a thing to bother you, Hitch."

"Whatever hurts Charlie Waide hurts the Ws, and whatever hurts the Ws bothers the hell out of me. Clear out, Asher! Don't let me catch you on the Ws again."

Cottingham dropped his plate into Trump Tatum's washtub and stood by the wagonwheel a moment, trying to muster a show of defiance but unable to bring it off. "All right, I'm goin'. Any of you boys got any sense, you'll go with me." He received no response, and he added, "Everybody else is doin' it. If you don't want to work for thirty a month the rest of your lives, you better go with me."

Hitch took a couple of strides toward him. "I said move, Asher. Go while you can still ride a-horseback, else they'll have to come fetch you in a wagon."

With the jingler's help Cottingham caught his horse out of the remuda and rode away from camp. Law McGinty frowned critically at Hitch. "Treated ol' Asher a little rough, didn't you?"

"You want to go with him?" Hitch demanded. Law shook his head.

Charlie Waide walked up to the wagon, cursing softly. "In my own camp! I didn't think it'd come to my own camp."

"Nobody followed him," Hitch pointed out.

He ate breakfast and began to rope out horses for the cowboys. Law McGinty asked for a sorrel named Redfish. Instead Hitch perversely caught him a black. "You ain't rode ol' Stepper in a while; he needs a little work." Hitch's voice was testy as he watched Law bridle the horse, plainly biting back a retort. Hitch said, "Me and Charlie spent the night in Rascal's dugout. Kate's all right; her mother's with her."

That surprised Law.

Hitch said, "You should've known. In fact, you ought to've taken the old lady out there yourself. It's dangerous, Kate bein' alone."

"Wasn't much I could do, us bein' so busy here and all."

"This afternoon when we get through you take your stuff and go stay with her till the baby comes."

Doubt showed in Law's face. Hitch told him, "Don't worry; you'll stay on the payroll."

At the wagon Charlie watched Law top off the black, which seldom failed to pitch in the cool of the morning. He walked out to Hitch. "Thought you was lettin' Law go home."

"This evenin'. We can use him all day and still get him home by dark."

Charlie studied Hitch curiously. "You act like you're mad at him."

Hitch shook his head, not wanting to tell Charlie his suspicions. "Seemed to me like he was spurrin' that horse a little hard, is all."

Charlie seemed to sense that wasn't the real reason. "Have patience. He's young; he don't know how he's supposed to treat a woman."

He's old enough to use her, Hitch thought harshly. *He ought to be old enough to do her right.*

When they got through working cattle that afternoon, Law McGinty caught a horse that belonged to him rather than the company and tied his bedroll behind his saddle. Charlie Waide watched him, a little of a smile lifting his heavy gray mustache. "You take good care of that little woman now, Law."

"You bet I will, Charlie." Law rode away.

Watching him narrowly, Hitch rode to the wagon on his favorite gray horse. "Trump," he said to the bald cook, "you got any cold biscuits you was goin' to throw out, and maybe a can of tomatoes? I got a trip to make. May be a little while comin' back."

Puzzled, Charlie Waide asked, "What's up, Hitch?"

Hitch shrugged, wishing Charlie wasn't there.

"It's somethin' I can't tell you about, Charlie. Maybe there's nothin' to it. You'll just have to trust me."

"I've always trusted you, Hitch. But I think I ought to know."

"When I get back. Please, Charlie, this is one time you got to ask me no questions." Hitch took a quick cup of black coffee, accepted the sack Trump handed him and rode off in the direction Law had taken.

He took his time, not wanting to push too fast and unexpectedly ride up on the cowboy. He would have a hard time explaining himself. It was easy enough to follow Law's horsetracks, and Hitch had to be content with that awhile. It might be that Law would want to go home first to get shed of the bedroll and the other things he had brought. Yet on the other hand if he had come home to stay until the baby arrived, what excuse could he give to ride away almost immediately? No, the more Hitch thought about it the more likely it seemed that Law would go visit his woman friend first. Somewhere down the line Law would change direction. Hitch intended to follow him till he found out who he was dallying with, then walk in and stomp salvation into him.

At dusk he began pushing, knowing that after a while the tracks would be difficult to follow, and he might lose Law. The tracks took a sudden turn to the left. Hitch missed them and had to ride back and hunt. He could tell by their depth that Law had started moving in a slow lope, making up time. Hitch touched spurs to Walking Jack. At length he could see Law in front of him, and he slowed. Law moved in an easy trot now, looking carefully from side to side as if searching for something. That struck Hitch as odd, for Law wouldn't find a woman out here. This was Figure 4 country.

At almost darkness he saw Law move to the left. Hitch swung down from the saddle to avoid being seen. In a few minutes Law moved into an easy lope and disappeared into a wash. He came out three hundred yards farther on, pushing a little bunch of cattle. In the poor light Hitch could not tell, but he guessed Law had fifteen or twenty head. Puzzled, he watched Law bring the cattle to a stop and ride around them gently, looking them over. Law started pushing the cattle back in the direction from which he had come.

He'll see me now if I don't be careful, Hitch thought. Walking, he led the gray down the lee side of a rise and ground-hitched him; the horse was trained to stay as if he had been securely tied. Hitch worked his way up the rise far enough that he could watch. The cowboy had the cattle moving now. Gently he rode in among them to push out one cow and calf, then drove the others away. The cow tried to rejoin the bunch, but Law gave chase in a run, throwing her and the calf so far back that she abandoned the effort.

Hitch remained still a long time, waiting for Law to get well past him. He rode back to look at the cow and calf Law had left behind. The cow wore Charlie Waide's W brand.

In the darkness Hitch could follow within fifty to a hundred yards. That was close enough to smell the dust, to hear the plodding hoofs, the occasional lift of Law's voice as he urged a tired calf into movement. They walked a long time, and gradually Hitch's suspicions began building to conviction, for he remembered the unaccountable unbranded calves he had found days ago. He resisted a growing impulse to confront Law. No, he had come this far; he would see it through.

By the stars he knew they were into the early hours of the morning when Law reined to a stop. The cattle drifted on, not realizing they no longer were being pushed. They were now well within the W lands, in an area over which Hitch's roundup crew had passed several days ago, an area that would not be worked intensively again until fall.

Law slouched in the saddle, leisurely rolling himself a cigarette. He raised his leg and laid it across the saddlehorn, showing he didn't intend to drive the cattle any farther. He sat there smoking, watching the cattle disappear in the moonlight.

Well, Hitch thought, *now is as good a time as any.* He pushed forward. Law didn't hear him until he was almost there. Instantly Law's leg came down from the horn and he whirled around, reaching for a pistol he didn't have. If he had brought it, he had it tied in his warbag.

"Stand easy," Hitch said. "It's me."

"Hitch!" Law said shakily. "What the hell you doin' out here?"

"Same question I was fixin' to ask you."

"I don't suppose you'd believe me if I said I was enjoyin' the night air?"

"I'd say you was enjoyin' the smell of unbranded calves a lot more."

"How long you been behind me, Hitch?"

"Long enough. I've trailed you since you left the wagon."

"And you seen me drivin' a little bunch of cattle that had strayed from home. That's what Charlie pays me for."

"I seen you cut out a W cow and her calf and leave them. I'm guessin' them other cows you brought was wearin' the Figure 4 brand, and maybe others. You wasn't bringin' them home; you was bringin' them off of their own range and onto Charlie's. You're sleeperin' them cattle, Law. You throwed them onto country that has already been worked. You count on them calves bein' weaned by their mammies this summer so they won't be followin' a branded cow. Then you can safely brand them with your LR."

"A maverick's fair game, Hitch."

"Not when you create them yourself."

"You ain't seen me break no law. You didn't see me take them cattle to my own land. You didn't even see what brand them cows carried; for all you know, they're LRs, every one. You didn't see me lay a hand on one, brand anything or alter an earmark, did you?"

"No, I didn't."

"So when you take tally, you didn't see a damned thing, Hitch. Looks to me like the best thing you can do is forget you ever followed me." He stared in curiosity. "Why did you?"

"Suspicious."

"Why?"

"I knew you hadn't been goin' home every time you said you was. I figured you was visitin' some woman."

Law's eyes narrowed. "When I got Kate? You must be crazy."

"I thought you was. I figured I'd catch you with that woman and beat you within an inch of your life."

"Damn you, Hitch, you ought to know I ain't low enough to cheat on Kate."

"Wouldn't you call a man low when he steals off of people who trust him?"

"I've never stole from Charlie, not one time. I've made it a point to never take no W cows. Time or two I've picked up W cows in the dark, and when I seen my mistake I went ahead and put a W on their calves. But I sure ain't got no compunction about puttin' an

LR on the rest of them. Big outfits like the Figure 4s and the Snaketracks, they don't own the land nomore than I do. A lot of them got their start maverickin' cattle; now they don't want nobody else to do it."

"Brandin' an honest maverick is one thing; makin' a maverick out of another man's calf is somethin' else. There's no excuse for what you done, Law. Don't go tryin' to make up one."

"It's no skin off of your nose, Hitch. I don't see you got any call to give a damn."

"There's a lot you don't see, Law. But I think you know that I got to let you go from the Ws."

"Why, Hitch? I'll take a paralyzed oath that I ain't never took from Charlie. For Kate's sake if not for mine, you got to forget tonight."

"Forget what I seen with my own eyes?"

"You know me and Rascal ain't got enough cows yet to make a livin' for Kate, much less for the youngun comin'. Give me a little more time and I'll have enough cows that I don't need the Ws; I won't need *no*-body. But right now I got to have that job."

"You ought to've thought about that before. There's people who would hang you for no more than I've seen tonight. All I'll do is take you off of the payroll."

Law seemed to realize there was no use in pleading; he had too much pride for it anyway. "What you goin' to tell Charlie?"

"What you told me, and what I've seen."

"What'll I tell Kate?"

"Start with the truth."

"If the word gets out, there won't nobody in this country hire me."

"Somethin' else you ought to've thought about."

Resentfully Law said, "I always suspicioned you'd

turn out this-away, Hitch, when the chips was down. Charlie gave you the boss job when by rights it ought to've gone to Rascal, or even to me; we'd been with him longer. You was always a little better than the rest of us, or thought you was. But there was one thing you didn't get."

"What do you mean?"

"You didn't get Kate. I could tell you wanted her, and I made up my mind I'd get *something* that you couldn't have. I got busy and won her."

"You married her out of spite?"

"That's how it started, only the joke was on me, Hitch. I come to love her. Why else you think I been sleeperin' these cattle, tryin' to build us a herd of cows so big that there couldn't nobody touch us or hurt us? It's cows that make a man big in this country, and I aim to have enough that Kate and the baby will have everything they ever need."

Gravely Hitch said, "What she really needs, you can't buy or steal. Go home to her, Law."

Law nodded. Crisply he said, "Don't be comin' around, Hitch. You won't be welcome."

Hitch sat and smoked while he listened to hoofbeats trailing away. Anger had drained, leaving him a heavy sense of sorrow and disappointment. He almost wished he *had* caught Law with another woman. He thought of Kate, and he wondered what Law would tell her. Probably not the truth, not all of it. Whatever Law told her would probably be turned in such a manner as to be unfavorable to Hitch. Well, maybe that was best; she was Law's wife. A little twisting of the story might hurt her less than the unvarnished truth.

He reached the wagon a while before Trump Tatum was due to get up and start breakfast. He flopped on his bedroll, not bothering even to take off his spurs. He lay sleepless, staring at the morning star. When Trump got up, Hitch did too. The cook eyed him suspiciously but seemed to sense it was best to ask no questions. Hitch haunted the coffeepot until it came to a full boil. He poured in cold water to settle the grounds, then dipped out a cup and began to drink it, disregarding its scalding heat.

Pinching off sourdough in biscuit-sized chunks and putting it into a greased Dutch oven, Trump said, "You look ready to challenge a wildcat to barehanded battle."

"I already did."

"Lose?"

"Everybody lost."

Trump ached with curiosity, but Hitch gave him no satisfaction. Presently Charlie Waide got up. He was usually the first to the coffeepot. He looked a moment at Hitch as he dipped his cup into the simmering brew and brought it out brimful. "I see you're back."

Hitch nodded.

"Want to tell me about it?"

"No, but I'll have to sooner or later."

"You trailed after Law, didn't you?"

"Yep."

"Find the woman?"

Hitch glanced at him in surprise, for he had no idea the same suspicion had come to Charlie. Charlie said, "Hell, Hitch, I could read it in your face. A young feller like that, he gets to itchin'. I ain't so old but what I can remember how it was. I hope you kicked him good and proper."

Hitch studied his cup. "We was both wrong, Charlie. It wasn't a woman." Reluctantly, the words coming slowly like a calf dragged out of a herd at the end of a rope, he told what he had found. Charlie's cup sagged and the coffee spilled between his feet, but he was oblivious of it. His face fell; he took it harder even than Hitch had expected. Finally he asked, "What did you do to him?"

"Told him not to come back."

Charlie turned away in painful silence. Hitch waited a little, then said, "He swore he never branded none of your W cattle."

"Do you believe him?"

"I want to believe him."

Charlie rubbed his face. "That boy has worked for me since . . . Hell, I can't hardly remember when he *didn't* work for me. I just can't see what could've got into him . . ." He noticed that his coffee cup was all but empty. Stiffly he walked back to the pot, refilled the cup, then moved out away from the firelight, out into the darkness. Hitch looked down at his boots, wishing he hadn't followed Law, wishing he'd never had to find out.

The jingler came in with the horses, and the cowboys arose for breakfast. Charlie came back into the edge of the firelight but didn't take a plate. He stood silent and depressed, watching the men. When they started toward the remuda he told Hitch, "Don't catch me a horse. Ol' shoulder's hurtin' me some. I think I'll stay at the wagon this mornin' and rest."

Hitch nodded. "Sure, Charlie." He paused once on the way to the remuda and glanced back frowning. He hadn't liked the look in Charlie's face. The old man was not well.

The horses caught and the pitching ones topped off, the cowboys followed Hitch as he led them out on the morning drive. Rascal pulled in beside Hitch.

"Charlie don't look good," he declared. "Somethin's chewin' on him. Meetin' go bad the other day?"

"He sure didn't enjoy it none."

"He didn't give in to them, did he?"

"You know Charlie better than that."

"I know he wants to be as big as the rest of them. I think it kind of gets his goat sometimes that them city-raised dudes are bigger than he is. If he was in enough of a tight, he might throw in with them."

Hitch rode a while trying to think what to say. "It ain't Charlie you better worry about, Rascal; it's Law." He watched Rascal's face for some sign that Rascal might know what he was talking about. He saw only puzzlement.

"What about Law?"

Hitch told him. Rascal's mouth dropped open. "There's bound to be a mistake someplace."

"There is. Law's the one that made it."

With Rascal, there was never any telling how he would react. His first response was an angry, "I ought to whip you!"

Hitch said evenly, "I'd sooner you didn't."

Rascal simmered down a little as the full gravity of the matter soaked in on him. "I didn't know about it, Hitch. I swear I didn't."

"I never thought you did."

"What'll we do now, Hitch? I can't make a livin' for the three of us—four, pretty soon—on the thirty dollars a month I'm gettin' here. You reckon Charlie'd pay a little more?"

"It's Law's mistake. You can't expect to carry the whole burden by yourself."

"Maybe if Charlie paid a little more we could still make it, Law takin' care of the place, me bringin' in money from the outside work."

"Charlie's already payin' as much as anybody in the country."

"But it ain't enough, thirty dollars a month."

"There's more cowboys gettin' twenty-five dollars than there is thirty."

"That don't make it right; it ain't right by a damn sight. Cows worth what they're worth today, we ought to be gettin' more."

"Charlie's always paid as much as the best."

"But them ranchers always work together. They keep the workin' man down."

Rascal was whipping himself into anger because of what had happened to Law and, perhaps without realizing it, was trying to twist the whole thing around to blame Charlie Waide for it. Hitch said, "Rascal, you and me and Charlie have always been friends."

"We was friends when Charlie didn't have nothin'. But when a man starts to get into big money he's apt to let old friendships go. Charlie's gettin' big, Hitch. Sure, I'll grant you that what Law done was wrong. But he done it on account of Kate and that kid. The few cows he might've took from the big outfits didn't hurt them; hell, the wolves will get ten times that many."

"It's still wrong."

"After this thing with Law, Charlie may not want me around nomore either. He may not trust me."

"I trust you. And if I do, then Charlie will."

"I don't know. I don't know nothin' no more."

Rascal pulled back to brood alone, and Hitch decided the best thing was to let him go.

7

When the cowboys brought the day's gather to the roundup grounds at noon and went to the wagon in relays to eat, Charlie Waide stayed out of their way. He sat by himself in the shade of the wagon, his back against the wheel, his head down.

Hitch eyed him uncertainly a while, then finally went to him. "You sick, Charlie?"

Charlie never looked up, but his voice was wicked. "Hell yes, I'm sick. Sick of bein' bothered. Go on and eat your dinner. If I need you, I'll send for you."

Hitch retreated, looking back.

Trump Tatum spoke quietly, taking care to keep his back turned so Charlie wouldn't see his lips moving. "Hitch, if he'd done all the walkin' in a straight line this mornin' instead of around and around that wagon, he'd be halfway back to South Texas. You'd as well of shot Charlie in the gut as to've told him about Law."

Defensively Hitch said, "He had to know."

"Wisht you'd learn that there's times when a little

lie or two is head and shoulders above the truth. I'm glad I ain't cursed with bein' overhonest."

Charlie watched the cowboys, his eyes half closed so nobody could read what was going on behind them. When the hands turned their horses loose at sundown, Charlie was still there, sitting against the wagonwheel. Hitch walked to him, stopped and waited to see if Charlie would speak. Charlie didn't.

Hitch asked, "Want to see the day's tally?"

"Wrote it in the book, didn't you?"

Hitch nodded. Charlie said, "Then I'll see it when I'm damned good and ready." Hitch could tell that was going to be the extent of the conversation. He went to the fire to see if Trump had coffee ready.

Trump rubbed his hands on a sack that he wore for an apron, and he grumbled, "Next time you give him a jolt like that, I hope you take him with you instead of leavin' him on my hands."

"He don't look any better than he did at dinner. Has he talked any?"

"Some."

"About what?"

Trump shrugged. "Ain't my place to say. He'll say it for himself in his own good time, I expect." Hitch didn't like the implication in Trump's eyes. He pressed for more, but the cook limped back to his work at the chuckbox. All Hitch would get out of him would be coffee.

After a while Trump called "Chuck!" The cowboys got their cups and plates and filed by the Dutch ovens and the coffee pot. Hitch waited till Charlie came, then followed the old man. Charlie took his plate and returned to his station by the wagonwheel. He gave Hitch no invitation, so Hitch went to his bedroll and sat there to keep an eye on the rancher. Charlie dabbled at his food a little, then gave it up and set the plate on the ground. He sipped his coffee, head slowly turning from one side to the other, eyes moving from one man to another and another and another.

Hitch suspected he could read Charlie's thought: *Which one next?*

The cowboys were uneasily aware of Charlie's quiet scrutiny, for by now the word had gotten around about Law. One by one they finished and dropped their plates noisily into the tub. When all were through, Charlie pushed to his feet. In an unusual breach of cowcamp etiquette he left his full plate and his cup lying in the boot-flattened grass. "Boys," he said gravely, "I got somethin' to say to you . . . all of you."

Hitch glanced at Trump Tatum. The old cook quickly turned to his chuckbox. With a sense of foreboding, Hitch joined the circle of men around the fire. Charlie was inside the ring, pacing a little and rubbing his shoulder. He kept it up a while after all the men gathered, as if dreading what he was about to say. He stopped, looking into the fire, his hand still on the bad arm. "Boys . . ." He paused to clear his throat. "Boys, durin' the war a Yankee officer damn near cut my arm off with a saber. I'd rather have had him cut off both arms than go on with what I'm about to say, but I'm forced to say it."

In the firelight Hitch could see cold anger in the old rancher's face, and he shivered.

Charlie said, "I always tried to treat every man right and to pay a fair wage. I always told everybody who would listen to me that I had me the best bunch of cowboys in the state of Texas. I said I could trust them to the ends of the earth, and I think I still could, with most of you. But by now you've all heard what happened last night.

"I know every one of you is different. I take it on faith that what Law done, he done by himself. I'll take it on faith that he spoke the truth when he said he never stole from me. But he did steal from neighbors after I promised them they had nothin' to fear from any man on the Ws. In doin' that he betrayed me as much as if he'd stolen my cattle. He compromised my word. You-all know the other ranches have put pressure on me to make me post the same rules they've got. I held off because I didn't think we needed them. Now Law has pushed me into a hole I can't climb out of. You-all know what the rules are. You can consider that from now on they're posted for the Ws!"

Hitch swallowed. "All of them?" He sensed a stir of disbelief among the cowboys, and of displeasure.

"All of them!"

"Not the cattle-ownership rule, Charlie."

"That one most of all. If I'd of had it in the first place, we wouldn't of had this mess." Charlie looked at the men one at a time. "Boys, I didn't think anybody would ever do to me what Law done. I've bent over backwards to let you-all run your own cattle, them of you who wanted to. We've even branded them for you and kept your tallies. But times change, and we all got to change with them." He seemed now to see anger stirring among the men. "There won't no man get hurt. I'll pay fair market. I'll buy your brands right now at a fair figure and accept the book tally for the count. Or if you'd rather, you can go out and get you a bonafide bid from anybody else and I'll give you five dollars a head above his best offer. I want to be fair." He looked at Hitch. "That is a fair way to price them, ain't it?"

"Charlie, most of us look on them cattle as a hedge

against the future. How can a man put a price on his future?"

Half a dozen voices came up in quick and angry agreement. Hitch felt a sudden fear for Charlie's safety and moved protectively toward him, to help him if it came to that.

Rascal McGinty grabbed Hitch's arm. "See there, Hitch, me and Law was tellin' you this was liable to happen. You promised it never would. Now you better see that he changes his mind!"

Hitch said, "Charlie, let's back off and think about this."

"I been thinkin' about it since mornin'. I ain't eaten all day for thinkin' about it. I keep comin' back to this; it's the only way it can be."

"Charlie, there was promises made a long time ago."

"And they been kept, every one, till Law broke his."

Rascal McGinty flared. "We been loyal to you, Charlie. You're forgettin' what some of us went through to put you where you're at today."

"And you had *my* loyalty every month, when I paid you." Charlie's voice was gritty. "No, I ain't forgotten a thing. Maybe that's been the trouble: maybe I've remembered too long." What he said then was an echo of the argument Prosper Selkirk had used against him. "I've paid you a hundred times over for all that, Rascal. Don't keep hangin' it over my head."

Rascal leaned into Charlie's face. "You know we can't stand still for this. You better think on it some more."

"I've done my thinkin' and had my say. Anybody wants to sell me his cattle, I'll buy them. Anybody wants to leave, I'll pay him." Charlie pushed through the cowboys and walked back to the wagon. He fished in the chuckbox but found no whisky. He poured a fresh cup of coffee and carried it out into the darkness.

Hitch stared in numbed disbelief. A door which had stood open for fifteen years had been slammed shut in his face; it might never open again. Rascal grabbed Hitch's arm. "I been tellin' you, Hitch! See what you got us into? What you fixin' to do now?"

Defensively Hitch said, "I didn't get you into nothin'."

"If you'd kept your mouth shut about Law this wouldn't of happened."

"That wouldn't of been right."

"You call this right?"

"Give Charlie time. He's hurt and he's mad. Give him time."

Rascal demanded, "How much time is he givin' *us*? Wouldn't surprise me if he's wanted to do this all along and just waited for an excuse. He wants to be as big as them other ranchers—wants it so bad he can taste it. Think he'd let a bunch of two-bit cowboys stand in his way? Not when it comes down to the tawline he won't. The old Charlie we used to know is dead and buried . . . buried in ten years of cattle tallies."

Hitch trembled in anger. He found Rascal's grip so tight that it hurt his arm. "Turn me loose, Rascal."

Rascal dropped his hand but not his voice. "Asher Cottingham called it right. Them boys that've gone on strike, they're the smart ones."

"That's enough. I won't listen to no more of that talk."

Rascal pointed a finger in Hitch's face. "You *will* listen to it. A few days ago I told you I was afraid

Charlie would sell us out. You said he wouldn't, and if he ever did you'd be the first to leave. I'm holdin' you to that, Hitch."

Hitch all but lost his breath. "You can't mean it."

"You're the one that said it. Now either you change Charlie's mind or you go out of here with us to join them boys on strike."

Hitch looked from Rascal to the other men, trying to assess this as flash anger that would pass. "You-all ain't serious."

Rascal looked around for support. "You see any other way? Be damned if we'll take this lyin' down."

"It'd be a mistake to leave here."

"It'd be a worse one to take this like a whipped dog."

"Give me time to talk to Charlie."

"Do it fast. Him nor nobody else is takin' me and Law's cows."

The angry rise of other voices convinced Hitch that at that moment the cowboys were stirred enough to follow Rascal McGinty into anything he took a notion to do. Maybe if Hitch could hold things together until the air stilled, something could be worked out. Hitch walked past them to the chuckbox and stared uncertainly into the darkness where Charlie had gone. Trump Tatum watched him sorrowfully.

"Hitch, don't you let Rascal stampede you."

Hitch turned to the crippled cook. "Trump, what'm I goin' to do?"

"I don't know. But whatever you do, take it slow."

"Reckon I can talk Charlie out of this?"

Tatum shook his head. "I watched it build all day, watched him whip himself into it. You know Charlie when he's made up his mind; you ain't got the chance of a snowball in hell to change it."

"If I don't, Rascal is fixin' to take the boys out of here."

"Don't you let Rascal rimfire you into somethin' you'll wish you hadn't done."

"I *did* give Rascal my word; I counted on Charlie."

"Makin' a promise for somebody else was one mistake. Don't compound it with another."

"I take it that if the boys went on strike, you'd stay here."

Tatum grimaced. "I'm old and I'm boogered up in the legs. I got no cattle, but I do have a job. If I lose what I got here, I wouldn't have nothin'. Maybe Charlie's wrong, but that don't mean he ain't my friend nomore, and it don't mean the strike would work. Times are changin', Hitch; nothin' stands still. Me and you, we're seein' the sun go down on the old free times for the man on horseback. Nothin'll stop that, not a strike or anything else. The old-time cowboy is goin' the way of the buffalo. The big ranches are marked, too, only they don't know it yet. That's why a strike is useless. Win, lose or draw, we've all had our day. The ranches . . . the cowboy . . . we're all fixin' to go down together under all them planters, and all that wire. I say hang onto what we can and be thankful we was here to see it while it lasted."

"Looks like you've studied on this a right smart, Trump."

"Kneadin' dough and boilin' beans leaves a man lots of time to think. We're comin' into a time when the individual don't count for much, Hitch. You'd just as well get used to the idea."

Hitch grunted. "Stand back and take it like a sheep? No, Trump, even if we lose, we need to fight and kick all the way to the slaughterhouse." He caught sight of Charlie standing alone beyond the wagon. Reluctantly he walked out and stood beside the rancher a long time without speaking. The silence between them was oppressive. Charlie said, "Hitch, I didn't mean to include you in the cattle rule. Bein' my wagon boss . . . my manager, even . . . you're high enough up that I can make an exception for you. Keep your cattle."

"I been with these boys too long to accept a right they couldn't share in."

Charlie said, "Maybe some kind of workin' partnership, then."

"That'd be the same, Charlie. It wouldn't be fair to the others."

"There comes a time when a man has got to take care of himself. You better be doin' it."

Hitch started to say, *Like you, Charlie?* but bit it off unsaid. He tried rolling a smoke and found his hands so nervous he spilled most of the tobacco. "Charlie, you told me you wouldn't ever do this. I believed you. I put so much faith in you that I went and gave the boys my word. I went and promised them that if ever it happened on the Ws, I'd leave here with them."

"You oughtn't to've told them that."

"I gave my word, and I'm stuck with it."

"Tell them you've changed your mind."

Hitch shook his head. "I keep *my* promises, Charlie." Instantly he wished he hadn't said it.

Moonlight revealed hurt in the rancher's deep-furrowed face. "I'm protectin' my ranch. I've done what I had to do. Now, Hitch, I reckon you'll do what you think *you* have to. I'm sorry."

Defeated, Hitch returned to the chuckbox. He got a fresh cup out of the drawer and poured himself more coffee. It was half grounds, but he gave little heed. He sipped it, aware that the cowboys were silently gathering around him. Rascal McGinty stood in the firelight, waiting for Hitch to speak. In time he gave up. "Well, Hitch, didn't change him none, did you?"

Hitch shook his head.

Bitterly Rascal said, "When a man gets money, he don't need old friends."

Hitch warned, "Go easy on Charlie; I won't have you talkin' him down."

"How about it, Hitch? You takin' us on strike like you promised?"

Only then did Hitch notice the heavy grounds in his cup. For a moment he thought he would choke. His voice sounded unnatural to him. "Boys, I can tell that some of you have already made your minds up. For them that haven't, let me say this: the whole idea of this strike goes against my nature. Another thing, there's a damned big chance it won't work. If you lose the strike, you lose everything; there won't be nothin' left to salvage.

"Now, havin' said that, and sayin' that I think any man who goes on this strike is a droolin' idiot, I'll say one thing more: if you still want to go, I've given my word and I won't back down. I'll ride with those who want to go."

Rascal declared, "Well, *I* sure do, and I think everybody else does."

Rascal was overconfident. About half the cowboys quickly came to his side. To Hitch's surprise and somewhat to his satisfaction, the rest held back. Talking it was one thing, but actually rolling up their beds and leaving was something else.

Rascal began to browbeat the men who hesitated. He grabbed a cowboy's arm and tried to pull him into the group with the others. Hitch laid a heavy hand on Rascal's shoulder, half threatening, half cajoling. "Hush up, Rascal. Let every man decide for himself. I don't want no man goin' on this strike with me that ain't doin' it of his own free will."

In the end only a little more than half the crew decided to go, including the kid jingler. To those Hitch said, "One last time, this could turn out to be a fool's errand, and you may cuss the man who took you. Are you dead sure you want to do it?"

No one backed out. Hitch half hoped they would. He turned to the men who had elected to stay. "No hard feelin's. To be honest, I think you're the only smart ones in the bunch. You-all stand by Charlie. He'll be needin' you."

He could see Charlie in the edge of darkness: the old rancher had worked back closer to the fire to listen. Throat tight, Hitch said, "I wish it had never come to this."

Charlie made no reply.

8

To Hitch the long ride to town was like going to a funeral. It was as if he were on his way to bury an old friend, as if he had come to a bend in the road and knew there would be no going back, ever.

He thought it a wonder that the jewsharp had not caused men to be murdered. The kid horse jingler was twanging on one as he rode, and it made Hitch wish Trump Tatum had done him the bodily harm he had always threatened. Some of the cowboys joked and cut up and watched their shadows like happy buttons on their way to a big drunk at the end of roundup. They were young, most of them, brimming and busting in the pride of their new manhood.

Hitch took the lead and held it, for he had no wish to mix with that funning crew. Walking Jack eased himself into a trot that he could maintain all day without a misstep. Hitch's eyes stayed on the gentle roll of the horizon line, but his mind was on everything he had left behind him, on all that lay wrecked by the damnfool stubbornness of other men, dragging him into a vague cause for which he felt no particular allegiance.

A familiar voice said behind him, "Cheer up, Hitch; there'll be better days." Rascal McGinty shoved a whisky bottle at him.

"Where'd you get that?" Hitch demanded.

"Never been a day a man couldn't find a little whisky on the Ws if he really needed some."

"Charlie's always forbidden it."

"Charlie never was hurt by anything he didn't know. Drink up, Hitch; you look like a pallbearer."

"I feel like one." Hitch turned away. Rascal kept awkwardly pushing the bottle at him, then pulled back and left him alone. If anything, the offer of whisky made Hitch angrier than he already was. He felt like stopping Walking Jack and telling Rascal and the others they could go to hell in a handbasket for all he cared, that he was riding back to the W and Charlie Waide. But he didn't do it.

Once you make up your mind to something, Charlie had told him more than once, *stick by it and don't drive yourself crazy wondering if it's right. You'll find you're right more often than you're wrong, and a man who ain't wrong once in a while ought not to be trusted noway.*

Hitch had already chopped down the bridge. No use tugging over it like a cat trying to spark fight out of a dead mouse. But a black mood settled over him, a feeling that in a moment of pinched pride he had thrown away something he could never regain. He wondered if the same thoughts tormented Charlie Waide. Hitch was haunted by a notion that if he had held things off for another day or two, he and Charlie might have come to some agreement and avoided all this. He beat the palm of his hand against the saddlehorn, angry at Rascal and the cowboys, angry at Charlie, angriest of all at himself.

He wished it were a hundred miles to town; he dreaded getting there. But in time he could see the ugly spread of it along the red sandy banks of the river, and he saw two chuckwagons camped on a little hill at the near side of the settlement, the cookfires sending up curls of gray smoke. Large groups of men idled in the shade of tall old trees. Horses stood staked or hobbled on the grass. He didn't count, but he guessed there must be fifty or sixty head, at least, scattered for a quarter mile up and down the river. Some of the cowboys got to their feet and left the shade, moving forward to meet the newcomers.

Rascal McGinty gave a long loud yell and spurred into a lope. He waved his battered old felt hat over his head as he passed Hitch, like some Rebel soldier galloping into his first battle before he had time to learn what it was really all about. Most of the other W hands took after him, yelping like coyotes. Hitch pulled on the reins and ate dust. Walking Jack acted as if he too wanted to move faster. Hitch felt they would get there too soon as it was.

He didn't know exactly what a strike was supposed to look like, for he had never seen one, but he had not expected to see it resemble a Fourth of July celebration; he had pictured it more as an angry funeral. Everybody here seemed to be laughing and talking at the same time; it was like a horserace where everybody had won. Men he had never seen before shoved their hands at him. One big red-faced boy perhaps a year off of the plow declared, "The more the merrier. We'll have them big outfits beggin' us to come back inside of a week."

Hitch felt like a fool, but he decided the easiest

thing was to agree. "Sure, a week." He listened to the whooping and shouting, and the thing he wanted to do most was to climb on top of a chuckwagon and yell louder than anybody, "Ain't there a man here that understands what he's done?"

There was no use dwelling on it; if they were fools, he was perhaps the biggest one, for he, at least, had some notion where all this might lead. He started looking for familiar faces. He saw Dan Truman of the Nine Bar; Hitch had had some pleasant set-tos of poker and had shared good whisky with him. Then there was Edson Biggs, one of the wagon bosses from the Snaketrack. Seeing them surprised him a little. He had considered them unlikely to get mixed up in a short-deck game. Edson especially. Edson was a smart fellow from Chicago or one of those other Eastern cities where the money grew, and he had a tolerable amount of schooling. He was a poor relation who had come out here to keep books for a wealthy uncle and learn the ranch business. He and his uncle had come to a parting of the ways, as kinfolks will, but not before Edson had rounded out his education and had become a pretty fair practical cow man. Some folks said if things went on the way they had started, he would own his uncle's ranch someday and the uncle would be working for him. Perhaps the uncle figured that out for himself, which could be why Edson was on the Snaketrack payroll when the strike came.

Guess Edson ain't any smarter than I am, Hitch consoled himself.

He saw sadness in Edson Biggs's eyes. Edson was a man who habitually shaved his chin clean every day of the world; right now he had a three-or four-day stubble and didn't seem to care. Edson said, "Can't say I'm glad to see you, Hitch. I hoped the W would manage to stay out of it."

"So did I," Hitch told him, sober as a hanging judge. "But I reckon we're all in it. Looks like some of the boys are havin' themselves a time."

"Like raw recruits just joining the Army," Edson said. He was a few years older than Hitch and could remember the war from a soldier's point of view. Hitch always suspected Edson had worn the blue, but he never said and Hitch saw no gain in asking him. Edson added, "The first shot hasn't even been fired yet."

Dan Truman obviously shared Edson's misgivings. He said, "It's a holiday to most of the boys. It ain't really sunk in yet that they're out of a job and got no money comin' in. They been paid off and got coin in their pockets. They feel like they got the ranchers by the tail and they're fixin' to tie a knot in it."

Hitch heard the shrill laugh of a woman. A cowboy—stranger to him—came to meet the W riders, a whisky bottle in one hand, a saloon girl in the other. It was easy to tell the pair of them had thrown the cork away.

Hitch didn't like it and said so. Dan told him, "Wait till night. There'll be a bunch of women up here from Gossett's and some of the other joints, or half the boys'll be down in town huntin' for them."

"It don't look like a strike to me," Hitch said. "Looks more like a spree."

"It is," Edson observed. "Most of the boys haven't figured out yet that there is a difference."

"How come you here, Edson?"

"Had a little cow herd started from when I was with my uncle. The company didn't give me any choice except to sell or leave. If there had been any alternative short of letting them have my cows, I wouldn't be here." He kicked angrily at a rock and sent it sailing. "I'll bet you-all are hungry. Come on over and we'll find you something at the Snaketrack wagon."

Hitch couldn't feature old John Torrington letting the Snaketrack cowboys use his wagon in a strike against him. Edson said he didn't, intentionally. When the trouble came the Snaketrack west division was camped not far from town, and every man in the crew decided to strike, including the cook. They couldn't go off and leave a good wagon deserted on the prairie. "He'll miss it by and by," Edson said. "Till then, we had just as well make use of it."

The other wagon belonged to a small rancher from north of the river. Beleaguered by big neighbors who made him feel as welcome on the range as a frog in a sourdough jar, he supported the cowboys and lent them his wagon to use as long as they needed it. "When this thing is over," Edson said, "we'll probably all be out there dogging him for a job."

This made Hitch feel no easier. "You don't sound confident."

Edson shook his head. "Are you?"

Word drifted down into town that the W cowboys had come. A while after Hitch ate, half a dozen men rode up on horseback, flanking a big man in a buggy. Hitch knew Fant Gossett by his bulk and by the wink of sunlight on his long gold watchchain. That chain, Hitch always figured, gave the cowboys a second look at their money.

Fant grinned like a possum. "Howdy, boys. Howdy, Hitch. My, it's good to see you W boys come in thisaway. Makes a man feel like all his good efforts ain't been in vain. I wanted to come out and personally welcome every one of you to town."

Hitch had gone to see a stage show that time he went to Kansas City with Charlie Waide. The actors had used the same broad gestures Fant Gossett did; Hitch wondered if Fant had seen the show. The saloonkeeper shook hands all around, teeth shining. "Brought you boys a little welcome-to-town gift," he said, and reached into the buggy to fetch out half a dozen whisky bottles. Some of his cheapest stuff, but a cowboy never looked at a gift horse's teeth.

Fant's coat swept back, and he shoved his big hands into the pockets of that broad vest. His voice went suddenly grave. "Boys, I'm sorry it's come to this. You-all got a just grievance here. You can be sure that ol' Fant Gossett is back of you all the way. Anything you need, anything us folks in town can do, just call on me and I'll see that you get it. In the meantime my saloon is open to you any time of day or night. If you find it closed, just come kick on my door. Man my age don't need much sleep. We'll all stand together shoulder to shoulder; we'll show these dollar-grubbin' big outfits that it's *men* who'll run this country, not money. They ain't goin' to buffalo you boys and they ain't goin' to buffalo this town. Ain't nothin' we can't do if we all stick together."

Dan and Edson didn't seem as impressed as the W cowboys. They had heard the speech before.

One of the horsemen with Fant was Asher Cottingham. He looked like somebody had lighted all his candles. "Glad you W boys done some thinkin' on what I told you. Even ol' Hugh Hitchcock. Must've took a big lever to prize you loose, Hitch. Bet ol' Charlie got a hankerin' after your little herd of cows, didn't he?"

Hitch knew no satisfactory way of answering him except by hitting him in the mouth, which seemed a pretty good idea the more he thought about it. Rascal sensed Hitch's mood and warned, "Go easy, Asher."

Cottingham went on, "Too bad you-all didn't bring along a W wagon. We could've used it, as many men as we got to feed here. But I don't reckon ol' Charlie would cotton to feedin' a bunch of men that had done quit him. He'll cotton to it a lot less when we make him start payin' us a decent wage."

"Us?" Hitch bristled. "You never worked for him, Asher. He don't owe you *any* wage. Come to think of it, you didn't have a job with anybody. Just who *are* you strikin' against?"

Cottingham gave him a glare that would wilt cotton. "By God, I'm strikin' agin *all* of them!"

Hitch, Edson and Dan Truman sat at the Snaketrack wagon awhile talking about horses, about cows, about everything except what was really on their minds. After a time Hitch decided he couldn't shove that off anymore. "I never been on a strike before. What're we supposed to do?"

Dan and Edson glanced at each other. "Do?" Dan asked. "Are we supposed to *do* anything?"

"Well, it looks to me like we got reasons for bein' here, things we want. Shouldn't we be figgerin' out just what it is we *do* want so we can tell the ranchers what it'll take to get this thing over with?"

Edson studied a while. "That's the way it ought to be done, only we haven't had anybody yet take the bit in his teeth and start."

Dan Truman made a weak grin. "Maybe what we been waitin' for is somebody to show us the way. You're the one to do it, Hitch."

Hitch didn't want the responsibility, but he could tell that if somebody didn't start things moving they could be here till Christmas. They called in the men who were around close and asked them to go out and fetch the others. After a while they had perhaps seventy or eighty men.

Edson Biggs had a way with words, so Hitch and Dan talked him into starting the discussion. "Boys," Edson said, "some of us have been here several days already; others are just now getting in. We've been at loose ends, and some of us think it's time we tied everything together. We think we should decide among ourselves just what kind of presentation we ought to put to the ranchers and then be about it so this affair doesn't drag on any longer than necessary. We've never all sat down and decided just what we want to ask for."

What happened then should have been predictable, Hitch decided, if he had stopped to think on it. Every man in the bunch tried to talk at the same time. Every man wanted everybody else to hear him out. The sudden rise of agitated voices caused two tied horses to break their reins and trot away. It seemed to Hitch the only men there who knew what they were doing were the two who went to catch the horses.

The hubbub didn't settle, and Edson Biggs became flustered. Sitting down, he told Hitch impatiently, "You wrestle with them."

Hitch had always been able to handle men at work, on the roundup or around headquarters, but he had never tried to handle a large group like this which included many men he didn't know. It took him a few minutes to get them quieted down to listen to him. Most of them seemed to be trying to convince the ones around them that they had the whole problem figured out.

"Boys," Hitch said when he thought they could hear him, "let's do first things first. We don't know how long we're goin' to be here, and we don't want any man hungry. We better pool some resources and build up a fund to feed ourselves." He thought this down-to-earth matter might pull them together awhile. He knew that up to now nothing had been done to organize a commissary. A bunch of the men, he was told, had chipped in various amounts, and a few people in town had brought out food. "Now," he said, "it ain't fair for some to carry the heavy load. Most of us are goin' to eat pretty much the same, and everybody in the strike ought to put in the same. How about ten dollars apiece for a chuck fund? Ain't hardly no way a man can eat ten dollars worth of food in less than a couple of weeks."

He felt that if they didn't take up that collection pretty soon, some cowboys might not have ten dollars left. The town was full of people who spent their lives seeing to it that a fool and his money were not long a burden to each other.

Most of the cowboys knew Edson Biggs, and it was quickly decided that he should take charge of the chuck fund. It could be locked in a safe in town and tapped as needed to keep the outfit in beef and beans.

That done, they went back to the first question, what to ask of the ranchers. For what they accomplished, they had just as well have been out racing horses on a grass flat. It seemed that almost every cowboy put in his two cents' worth, and a few like Asher Cottingham made it nearer a dollar-and-a-half. The wrangle went on for a couple of hours and seemed nowhere near a solution.

Hitch listened, frowning deeply. He had given up trying to talk. It became increasingly evident to him that many of the men were not even sure why they were here. They were dissatisfied, but the reasons for that dissatisfaction were so many and so varied that it was difficult to boil them down to a few clear and negotiable points. In frustration it was understandable that the men dwelt more and more upon the one point common to them all: a desire for more money.

Many tired of the argument and quietly slipped away until less than half the original crowd remained. The question was no nearer settlement. Hitch said finally, "Let's quit for tonight. Let's think it over amongst ourselves and make a fresh run at it tomorrow. Maybe we'll be thinkin' straighter."

That turned out to be a forlorn hope, for when the cowboys gathered after breakfast it was largely a repetition of what had already been said. Some had spent the night in town and were none too clearheaded. But gradually most of the loudest got themselves talked out and became more inclined to listen, or at least to keep quiet. Complaints against the ranchers boiled down mainly to two: wages and the written rules of conduct.

Rascal McGinty had had himself a royal time in town all night, and his eyes matched his uncombed red hair. "Boys," he said, his voice rough-edged from celebration, "there's more to it than just money." Asher Cottingham said money was the main thing *he* was after and pressed Rascal to be specific. Rascal couldn't put his feelings into words. "They're changin' things too much," he said. "They're changin' things that ought to've been left alone."

Some of the cowboys kept pushing him, and Rascal rubbed his hand across his face and his broken nose, trying to think clearly. "Well, now, you take that cattle rule. Main thing to me is they don't want no workin' cowboy to accumulate anything that would make him independent. Them owners, they got their pile made, and they want to keep the rest of us down to where we'll always have to work for them. I'd go on workin' for the wages I been gettin' if I knowed they'd let me keep ownin' cattle."

That roused a storm of argument. Asher Cottingham declared, "Damn it, Rascal, that's no more than I ought to've expected from you. Give an ordinary cowhand a few head of cattle and already he's thinkin' like an owner. You'd be willin' to take less money, and you'd hold down the rest of us who ain't lucky enough to own any cattle like you do."

Rascal's face reddened, but Asher Cottingham didn't let that faze him. "I can see where you rich fellers with cattle might be upset, but most of us here ain't got no cattle and don't ever expect to have no cattle. For us the big problem is money. That's what we're goin' to ask them ranchers for, is more money."

Rascal got awfully redheaded for a minute or two after Cottingham accused him of selfishness. It looked as if Hitch might have to step in and break up a fight.

The wrangle went on a long time. In the end the cattle rule somehow got lost in the dust and the smoke. There simply were not enough cattle owners among the cowboys. Those like Hitch and Rascal considered themselves poor, but to the men who had no cattle at all, they were too rich to be concerned about.

Edson Biggs said, "Asher, a little while back you yourself said there was more to it than money. There was the whole set of rules and of rancher attitude toward employees . . . there was the question of respect."

"By God," Cottingham declared, "when they have to pay us enough, they'll respect us."

The fevered discussion finally got down to a question of how much the strikers should ask for. Asher Cottingham said, "A hundred dollars a month!" That sounded good, and others took up the cry.

Edson Biggs had a bookkeeper's mind; he argued against that figure. "Boys, it's not realistic. It takes three cows to bring a hundred dollars, and there's never been a time a cowboy's labor was worth three cows a month."

Cottingham declared, "Maybe it's been worth that much; we just never had guts enough to ask for it before."

Biggs said, "Asher, you're supposed to shear the sheep, not skin it. If we break these ranchers, who will we work for?"

"I don't give a damn," Cottingham said. "There ought to be a law against them havin' so much anyway. If I was runnin' this country there couldn't no man have more than ten cows apiece. Then maybe we'd all have a chance."

Cooler men began to speak up, and some cowboys who had initially backed Cottingham seemed inclined to scale down the asking price. It settled awhile at a sullen seventy-five. Hitch saw they were angering at Edson, so he took up the argument in Edson's stead and convinced most of them that seventy-five was still too much to hope for. Somebody suggested a compromise on fifty. A lot of the cowboys seemed to regard that figure as satisfactory. Hitch thought it unrealistic.

He said, "Most outfits in this country are payin' hands twenty-five. A few pay thirty. We'll have snow three feet deep the Fourth of July before any of these ranches'll agree to double a man's salary. It's one thing to take a firm stand for somethin' reasonable; it's another to ask for somethin' plumb out of sight."

Cottingham was not convinced they couldn't get more. "We got them ranchers where the hair is short. We can get anything we want if we'll all stick together."

Hitch cleared his throat and spat. "Use your head for somethin' besides that hat, Asher. A good many cowboys didn't come with us; they're still workin'. Soon's the word gets out there'll be more men comin' into the country lookin' for the jobs we left behind. We ain't got *that* much leverage. Best thing is to get ourselves a settlement and go back to work before too many job hunters come driftin' in."

Cottingham clenched his fists. "We can go out to them ranches and make them other boys wish they *had* come with us. We can patrol the roads and throw back anybody who tries to come in from outside. If we bloody a few heads, folks'll sit up and take notice."

Hitch spat again. "For a man who talks all the time about his own freedom, you don't seem to give a damn for anybody else's."

"I say there's nobody else gives a damn about us; we got to take care of ourselves."

"There's always two sides to an argument. I figure if we've got a right to strike, other people have got a right not to strike."

"The other man ain't *got* no side when we're in a fight. The hell with *him*; the only thing that matters is to win."

Fifty dollars was as low as the majority was willing to go. Hitch had a cold feeling in the pit of his stomach; they would never get it. But perhaps the ranchers would make a counter offer and somehow reason would prevail to get this wagon out of the mud. A vote was taken and the decision was almost unanimous: fifty dollars.

Edson Biggs was given the task of tailoring the demand into good legal terms that would seem to give the whole thing a courthouse flavor and perhaps impress upon the ranchers that they were not dealing with a bunch of naïve, unschooled cowpunchers. He wrote:

We the undersigned cowboys of Canadian River do by these presents agree to bind ourselves into the following obligation, vis—First that we will not work for less than $50 pr mo. and we furthermore agree no one shall work for less than $50 pr mo. after 31 of Mch. Second. Good cooks shall also receive $50 pr mo. Third. Anyone running an outfit shall not work for less than $75 pr. mo. Those not having funds to pay board after Mch 31 will be provided for for 30 days.

Reading over Edson's shoulder, Hitch said, "It's too much money; it's just too damned much."

Edson Biggs laid down his pencil and flexed his writing hand, frowning at some of the cowboys who lay in the shade of the trees, or hunched over a game of poker on a saddle blanket. "I'll grant you, most of these men have been underpaid for their work and the hell they go through. But if you paid every man just what he's worth, there are a few who wouldn't be making twenty dollars."

"And they," Hitch said, looking for Asher Cottingham, "are generally the ones that holler the loudest."

He studied Edson's handiwork and decided it said what the cowboys had voted to say. But it said nothing about the underlying causes aside from money that had brought the conflict to the surface. It said nothing about the fact that the cowboy considered himself something unique, a breed apart and perhaps a little above the common man. He considered himself the instrument which had brought this country up from the buffalo range and made it flourish. The document said nothing about dignity, about pride, about respect. It said nothing about unwritten traditions and the unspoken trust which seemed violated when ranch owners felt it necessary to start writing down guidelines for a cowboy's conduct and slapping him in the face by posting them on a wall, making him seem irresponsible and less than a man, making him appear somehow unworthy of trust. But maybe these were things you couldn't adequately put into words, couldn't hope to capture on paper.

One by one as they got around to it the cowboys came and affixed their names. Somehow then, with all those signatures on it, the thing seemed more like a real legal document. In its own small way it was sort of a declaration of independence.

It was up to Edson to sit down and make enough copies by hand to go around to all the ranchers. While he did that, Hitch went to town to make a duty call on cowboy Joe Sands, still recuperating from his broken leg in a shack Fant Gossett was furnishing, for a fee.

He lay on a cot, the splinted leg propped. He shoved his hand at Hitch. They howdied and shook and swapped yarns awhile. Some of the W hands had been in to see Joe already, and they had thoughtfully carried him some whisky which still sat on a table unopened. Joe Sands was not much inclined in that direction.

When Hitch got through telling him about all the friends he hadn't seen, and about the horses he had left behind, Joe said, "I don't know much about this strike thing, Hitch, but if you'd like me to join up with you I will. Can a man strike with a broken leg?"

"You've got no cattle, Joe. Are you sore at Charlie Waide?"

Joe shook his head. "Charlie's always been a friend to me."

"Then you stay right where you're at. Stay on the payroll; don't be tippin' over the chili pot. You need Charlie and he needs you."

As Hitch stood up to go, Joe said, "Hitch, there's an awful lot happenin' these days that I don't understand."

Hitch frowned. "Neither do I."

Edson Biggs had finished making all the copies when Hitch returned to the campground. His right hand was so stiff from writing that he couldn't hold a coffee cup with it. A group from each outfit got together and decided who would take a copy to each ranch owner or manager. It was important that they choose men the ranchers might respect. Charlie Waide was Hitch's responsibility.

Hitch had rather take a rawhiding, but he went. First stop was Trump Tatum's chuckwagon, where cowboys told him Charlie had gone on to another camp. Some of the men from the other two divisions had left their wagons to join the strikers in town, so Charlie had regrouped what men he had left into only two divisions, both sadly short-handed.

"How is Charlie?" Hitch asked Trump Tatum.

The old cook was cool. In his view Hitch had betrayed Charlie. Perhaps even worse, Hitch had asked for Trump's advice and then had not followed it. He answered curtly by repeating Hitch's own question. "How is Charlie always? Same as ever, only more of it." Whatever that meant. Hitch looked regretfully at Trump, knowing he had lost a friend.

He knew he would lose other friends before this was over.

He found Charlie with the second roundup crew in the midst of the herd and cutting out cattle, something he hadn't done much in recent years. He had let younger men do it, for a cutting horse could move swiftly and shift direction in the batting of an eye, spilling a rider. Charlie saw Hitch, but he didn't quit until he had finished pairing up cows and calves to his satisfaction. He let Hitch wait on horseback at the edge of the herd for the better part of an hour.

He rode out slowly and raised his hand in a half-hearted salute. He appeared sad, much the way Hitch felt. They looked at each other, a strain between them. Charlie said, "You come back to work?"

"No, Charlie, I come to deliver this." Hitch handed him the strike declaration, careful so the paper flapping in the breeze wouldn't booger Charlie's horse and perhaps cause him to be thrown. At Charlie's age he didn't need that. Charlie held it at arm's length, face furrowed. He rubbed a hand across his big gray mustache and complained that it didn't seem like anybody could write worth a damn anymore, that a letter was no good if written in such a poor hand that a man couldn't read it. He would not have admitted that the trouble was his eyes. "You'll have to tell me what's in it."

Hitch told him.

"Wisht I could read it," Charlie said, "but it wouldn't make no difference anyway. The ranchers have all agreed they won't treat with any of the strikers; every cowboy who went on strike is fired for good. We've agreed that none of us will ever hire any man who took part, whether he was from our outfit or another. We're through with all of them."

Hitch had more or less expected that, but it hit him a little.

Charlie said, "Hitch, I'll make one exception, *you*. If you'll come back, you still got a job. And you can keep your cows."

The temptation was strong to grab Charlie's hand. Hitch said, "I never did want to leave here in the first place. Between you on one side and Rascal and them on the other, I found myself in a bind to where I couldn't do anything else."

"Will you come on back?"

Hitch wanted to shout *yes*. He came so near doing it, he didn't know exactly what stopped him. But something did. "Charlie, would you extend the same offer to the other boys?"

"I can't."

"I'd never be satisfied in my own mind if I took somethin' the other boys couldn't have."

"I've made my agreement with the ranchers."

The pain then was heavy; Hitch wished he hadn't come. "And I've made mine with the boys, Charlie. Looks like we're both stuck with somethin' we didn't want."

When Hitch returned to the strike camp, he recognized the old spring wagon, the tongue dropped slantwise in the badly beaten grass. Rascal McGinty strode out to meet him, all grin. "Looky who's joined up with us, Hitch."

Law McGinty didn't hump himself any to come

forward. He hadn't unbent in his feelings about Hitch firing him from the W. Because Law didn't offer his hand, Hitch didn't risk embarrassment to himself by trying to push his own hand forward. Hitch said, "Law," and Law said, "Hitch."

Rascal repeated, "He's come to join up with us."

Hitch had heard him; he wished he hadn't. "You think you ought to?" he asked Law. "Seems to me like you should be stayin' out yonder with Kate till she's delivered."

"Kate's had herself a boy."

Rascal laughed. "You hear that, Hitch? A boy! Law says it's the spittin' image of its daddy. That makes me an uncle, Hitch."

Hitch looked dubiously at Law. "She's doin' all right, is she?"

"Her mother is goin' to stay awhile, and you know how hard that old lady is to get along with. I felt like I could come over here and join up with the boys. The more there are of us, the stronger we'll be."

Hitch couldn't think of a thing that had gone right, and it wasn't getting any better. "Law, I ain't sure you got any place here. You were out of a job before the strike ever commenced. You can't strike against somebody you wasn't even workin' for."

"Your fault, Hitch. I figure my place is here with the boys. I'm payin' my way; even brought a beef." He jerked his thumb toward two halves of a beef hanging from a tree limb, one uncovered, the other wrapped in a bloodstained tarp.

Hitch had an uneasy feeling. "One of your own?"

"Was when I finished skinnin' him. I don't reckon ol' Selkirk will starve because of one beef. Especially when this one had a broken leg."

"How'd he break it?"

"When I roped him."

Hitch felt he ought to hit Law, but he didn't see how it would do anybody any good easing his own feelings a little. He turned to Rascal, thinking Rascal should be able to see the wrong in this for himself, but Rascal simply grinned. He turned back to Law. Sharply he said, "Right or wrong, we're into this strike with all we got. You bein' here puts a cloud over the whole bunch of us. Bringin' a stolen beef makes it worse. They're *wantin'* to call us thieves, some of them."

"The beef is here now. We can't just put the hide back on that critter and turn it out on the grass again."

It never did set well with Hitch to see meat go to waste; in the early days before the bonepickers scavenged the prairies, it had hurt him to look at the scattered buffalo bones and think of all the meat rotted there years ago because a man had a market for the shaggy hides. He said, "But if we're goin' to eat it, we're goin' to pay for it. Since you killed it, it's your place to pass the hat and take up a collection to pay Selkirk for it."

He reached up and took Law's hat from his head and handed it to him. Law hurled it to the ground. "The hell I will!"

Hitch picked it up and handed it back to him, crown down. "That's the way to hold it. The money stays in better." He dropped in a four-bit piece for a starter.

Law seemed likely at first to fight, but Rascal McGinty dropped a couple of coins in the hat, by that silently telling his brother to get moving. Sullen, Law moved among the cowboys, and most dug into their pockets. Presently he was back, eyes still angry. He shoved the hat at Hitch. "That ought to be enough."

"Law, you done right well." Hitch spilled the coins

onto a blanket spread on the ground and handed Law's hat back. Counting, he found almost thirty dollars. Hitch decided to make up the difference from the chuck fund and turn it in for a check that they could send the Figure 4. He wondered which would have given Selkirk the most satisfaction, getting the money or not getting it and thereby proving to his own satisfaction that the cowboys were the motley thieves he had been telling himself they were.

9

Most of those old-time ranchers lived by the adage that idle hands were the devil's workshop and saw to it that the devil had very little show with their cowboys. It pinched old John Torrington, not having all the help he wanted; it galled him to see so many men idle when he had work that needed doing.

Idle they were. As time became heavy on their hands, some cowboys spent most of the day and night down in town, keeping the cash flowing into Fant Gossett's till, and those of the red-lantern places in Hogtown.

The strike notice carried to John Torrington by two of his former cowboys was like a sharp goad used against an angry bull. He beat them back to town to wring out the sheriff, raising hell and putting a chunk under it. He could not see why the law did not arrest the whole bunch and throw them in jail. The sheriff, cowed by the fire in those sharp eyes, tried to explain that the jail had not been built that large; the county had been trying to keep taxes down for the ranchers.

Anyway, he had to wait until the cowboys broke a law.

"They're vagrants," old Torrington stormed for everybody in town to hear. "A man don't have a job, he's a vagrant. You go up there and arrest them or you'll be huntin' a new job too!"

A rumor had already gotten out that the sheriff was considering getting himself some long heavy chains and locking the cowboys to them, but he couldn't find that many handcuffs if he requisitioned from every Ranger west of the state capital.

Given no satisfaction by the sheriff, John Torrington rode up the hill with saddlegun in his lap to hurl the challenge where it belonged. It was said he had once ridden boldly into a Comanche camp to recover stolen horses; age had not dulled his sharp edge. He was flanked by four loyal cowboys, all pushing to keep up with him. He demanded fiercely, "Who's in charge of this heathen outfit?"

Hugh Hitchcock had seen him coming and had drifted down partway to meet him. "Nobody, Mister Torrington, and everybody. These are all free men." Torrington's narrowed eyes swept the crowd in contempt. "Free of work, free of responsibility. Bunch of damned thieves and radicals."

Hitch studied the four cowboys. Next to Torrington sat Slant Unger, whose nickname came from a misshapen shoulder; people said he had suffered it when a horse was shot from under him in a Mexican border battle fought for John Torrington. Two other cowboys Hitch knew by sight but not by name. Beside Unger sat Tobe Ferris, a Negro cowboy whose mother Torrington had owned before the war. Some people claimed they could see a resemblance to Torrington in some features of Tobe's dark face. Hitch had always regarded that as overactive imagination.

Torrington's hard gaze cut into Hitch. "Well, Hitchcock, Charlie Waide was sure as hell wrong about you."

Hitch said, "Somethin' you wanted, Mister Torrington?"

"Damned right! I want all you loafers down off of this hill, and I want you off in a hell of a hurry. This is my land you're squattin' on, and I won't have it. It's all my land, right up to where the town starts. If I'd had any sense I'd of never let them put the town there either."

Hitch wanted to avoid provocation. "As I remember it, Mister Torrington, this here land still belongs to the state. You just been usin' it for your cattle. You got no more claim on it than anybody else."

"I claim it by right of first possession. Wasn't nobody here when I come but a few Mexican sheepherders and a remnant of Indians with the butt end out of their britches. I took it and I'm keepin' it. I want you off."

Hitch made his voice sound calm, though he was much less than that. "I take it you've already talked to the sheriff. What does he say?"

"Never mind the sheriff; he's just a county employee. I do my own talkin'."

Hitch looked around to be sure of his support. He could tell by the strikers' faces that he had it. "Then I reckon we'll just have to tell you *no*, Mister Torrington. Respectfully, of course, but *no*. Anything else you wanted?"

Torrington pointed. "You got a Snaketrack chuckwagon up here. It belongs to me, and I'm takin' it."

"We been keepin' it for you. You're welcome to it.

You'll find some supplies gone from it. We'll pay you for those."

That threw the old man off for a moment; he hadn't expected it. His sharp eyes searched the crowd, fastening briefly on each striking Snaketrack hand he saw. "There was a team of mules with that wagon. Where they at?"

"Grazin' along the river. They'll be easy to find."

"Some of these men rode in here on company horses. I'm gatherin' up every Snaketrack horse I lay my eyes on."

"They're yours, Mister Torrington."

The old man seemed somehow disappointed. Perhaps, Hitch thought, he had hoped for physical opposition that would give him an excuse to cut the dogs loose. He turned to the cowboys on either side of him. "Go get the stock."

Hitch said, "Like to step down and have some coffee while you wait?"

Torrington's gray beard seemed to bristle. "Amongst *this* crowd? I wouldn't touch it."

He sat there alone and defiant in the midst of the opposing men while his cowboys spurred down the river and began working through the scattering of horses. It was evident he meant his presence to be a challenge; he seemed to hope someone would make a move against him. He wore an old six-shooter on his right hip, and he continued to hold the saddlegun ready.

The crowd of striking cowboys stayed, staring expectantly at Torrington or talking quietly among themselves. In a little while Unger and Ferris brought the mules. The other two men remained on the river, holding the horses they had gathered.

The striking Snaketrack cook moved to help harness

the team, but Torrington shouted at him, "You ain't workin' for us no more; you keep your grubby hands off of them mules!"

When the mules were hitched to the wagon, the Negro tied his horse on back and climbed up into the seat, ready to move. Slant Unger took his place beside Torrington, his eyes making a blanket challenge for any in the crowd to contest him.

Torrington looked back at Hitch. "I'm tellin' you, Hitchcock, I want all of you down off of this hill."

Law McGinty had walked up behind Hitch. Law said, "You heard what Hitch told you, so you just chase yourself up a stump, old man. There ain't nobody here afraid of you."

Hitch warned Law, "Stand easy."

Torrington's gray whiskers worked up and down. His eyes narrowed dangerously. "Seems to me I know you, cowboy, but I can't quite call your name."

"It's Law McGinty."

Torrington's gaze was so severe that Law flinched. "Oh, yes," the old man said, "you was the one caught sleeperin' cattle. I remember you now. And I'll keep on rememberin' you." He looked back at Hitch. "You're in bad company, Hitchcock. But I reckon it's of your own choosin'." His voice came up. "Now listen to me, every one of you! If the sheriff won't do nothin' about you, there's other ways. There's men left over from the Lincoln County war in New Mexico that'll do anything for hire. I bet it wouldn't take more than five-six of them to chase the whole damned bunch of you clear into Indian Territory. You think on it now, do you hear? You think on it!"

As Torrington rode away and the chuckwagon trailed dust down the hill, Dan Truman and Edson

Biggs moved to Hitch's side. Biggs said worriedly, "That old cougar means what he says, Hitch."

A chill played up Hitch's back. "Even if he does, it'll take him time." At the edge of camp he saw a woman a cowboy had brought up with him. Hitch said, "It may not take guns to bust up this outfit. Hard whisky and easy women will undo more cowboys than Torrington ever could."

Turning, he noticed a man talking to Law McGinty and Asher Cottingham. He looked like another cowboy—the working clothes, the battered felt hat, the boots and spurs—but Hitch knew he was not one of the striking group. "Edson," Hitch asked urgently, "is that who I'm afraid it is?"

Edson frowned. "That's Cato Bramlett."

Hitch cursed. Cato Bramlett carried the reputation of being the worst cow thief in the Texas Panhandle, working between here and the sanctuary of the New Mexico line. Hitch started to move toward him. Dan Truman caught his arm. "You better watch him; he's dangerous."

"In more ways than one."

Law and Cottingham watched Hitch curiously, but Hitch's eyes were on the thief. "Bramlett, I want to talk to you."

Bramlett's eyes showed instant challenge. "Talk away."

"You don't belong in this camp."

"I got friends here."

"If old Torrington saw you—and them sharp eyes see everything—you know what he must've thought."

Bramlett began to stiffen. "Maybe you'd like to tell me what he thought."

Hitch angered, for he sensed that Bramlett was

playing with him. "Torrington wants to believe we're a band of thieves. You bein' here makes that easy."

"You callin' me a thief?"

"You got that reputation."

Bramlett took a step forward, then stopped. Dan and Edson had moved up on either side of Hitch, and other cowboys silently came in behind him. Bramlett blustered, glancing back at Law and Cottingham. "This the man in charge up here?"

Nobody said anything, so Bramlett surmised the answer himself. "Well," he said, "then you boys are worse off than I thought." He got on his horse and rode down the hill.

Law McGinty turned angrily. "Now, Hitch, what did you go and do that for?"

"If you don't know, then it won't do no good for me to tell you."

Two men had been appointed to deliver the strike declaration to Prosper Selkirk at the Figure 4. They returned with the paper still in their hands. Angrily they related that they had ridden out to Figure 4 headquarters and had been met at the office door by Selkirk, bolstered on both sides by cowboys who had remained with him. Selkirk had refused to touch the declaration or allow the messengers to read it to him. Face red and voice embittered, he declared, "I will not treat with saddle tramps and chuckline riders who try to justify their idleness by calling it a strike, with men who demand more than a day's work is honestly due. It is the employer's duty and right to affix wages and conditions of work. Any employee dissatisfied with the terms is always free to leave. And you men . . . if you're ever seen on Figure 4 land again you will be considered trespassers and may very well be shot!"

Selkirk sent four men with rifles to escort them off the property in a fast trot.

The news spread through the strike camp like a grass fire. Hitch listened to the sullen messengers with Dan Truman and Edson Biggs. "It's no more than we ought to've expected," he said. "We didn't figure Selkirk would invite them in for a drink."

One of the messengers said, "They got some new hands out there. I seen men I never seen before."

Asher Cottingham jabbed his finger at Hitch. "I been tellin' you we ought to cut off the roads."

Rascal McGinty smacked his right fist into the palm of his left hand. "It's an insult, Hitch. It's a rotten insult to every cowboy that ever lent life and limb to these ranches. We're welcome as rain when they can use us and throwed off like old socks when they can't."

Hitch saw the ugly mood and tried to temper it gently. "You never worked for the Figure 4s a day in your life, Rascal."

Rascal was not to be placated. "Him and his kind . . . it ought to be open season on them big-city highbinders like on rattlesnakes and centipedes. They ought to be hung up by the thumbs."

Hitch kept trying to pour cold water on the threatening talk. "We didn't none of us expect them to take this strike and like it. In Selkirk's place we'd kink our tails a little bit ourselves."

Cottingham declared, "I told you the day you come here, Hitch, they'd be hirin' new hands to take our place. I say we ought to go patrol this country and throw all them stray cowboys out. Time we splash a little blood around, they'll stop comin' in."

Curtly Hitch told him, "The man who tries that is goin' to have to whip me first. Them others, they got rights too."

Cottingham cursed vigorously. "God damn a man's who's always talkin' about somebody else's rights! Hard to tell half the time whose side you're on, Hitch. It's *us* we got to worry about. Everybody else can go to hell!"

The atmosphere in camp became so thick it was a relief that night when Rascal and Law and a sizable bunch of men decided to go down into town to look for refreshment. "Time they've bought a few rounds at Fant Gossett's," Hitch told Edson Biggs, "they'll have more to worry about than cussin' Prosper Selkirk. I'm goin' to hit the soogans and catch some sleep while it's quiet around here."

He figured when they came in they would make enough noise to rouse Boothill, but he never heard a thing. He slept through till the rising sun hit him in the eyes. Pushing the blankets back, he raised up, put on his hat, then his shirt and his britches, and finally started feeling under the edge of the tarp for his boots, where he had stuck them to keep them from being wet by the dew.

Edson Biggs blinked the sleep out of his eyes and yawned. "Boys was sure quiet comin' in last night."

Looking around, Hitch saw a lot of empty bedrolls; they hadn't been slept in. "They didn't come in at all." It wasn't unheard of for some of the boys to drink so much that they went to sleep in the alleys, and a few had been finding beds down there, and somebody to share them. But this struck Hitch as being too many missing men. He couldn't feature Rascal snoring in an alley. He couldn't feature Law McGinty laid up in the arms of some wheeligo girl when he had a wife and new baby waiting for him out yonder at the claim, though on second thought Hitch realized it hadn't been long since he had suspected him of just that.

Dan Truman was up walking around worriedly and sharing Hitch's thoughts. "Reckon we better go down and hunt for them, Hitch? Could be they've went and got themselves throwed in jail."

That wouldn't surprise Hitch, knowing where the sheriff's loyalties lay. He took time for breakfast first, figuring the men were probably asleep anyway, wherever they were. Then he, Dan and Edson rode down from the hill. They made Hogtown first, riding out the streets and alleys. They found a couple of cowboys, but not the ones they were looking for.

They put off the crackerbox of a jail until last. When they didn't find the men anywhere else, they decided there was nowhere left. The sheriff was sleeping in the tiny front office, and it took him a while to come fully awake. He sat on the edge of his steel cot, bare feet on the earthen floor, his red underwear half unbuttoned. He yawned, a gold tooth shining, and he scratched under his armpits. He had probably been up a big part of the night nervously riding herd on cowpunchers who could, when the mood struck them, be to a town of this caliber like a bull set loose in a glass factory. Considering that, plus the pressure the sheriff was getting from the ranchers, Hitch saw no cause to envy him. The man had originally been a Torrington cowboy, not really good enough with livestock to keep on the ranch but too tractable to lose altogether.

"Yeah," the lawman said sleepily, "I got some cowpunchers in here. Say, ain't there anybody in charge up there at you-all's camp? Ain't there anybody got authority to tell some of these yahoos when it's time to quit? *Strike!* Hell, the whole damned bunch of you had ought to be in jail, is the way I see it."

Hitch nodded, knowing all that anyway. "Could we see about your prisoners, Sheriff?"

The lawman started to get up and changed his mind. "Hell's bells, go see them for yourself. You don't need to bother me about it. Take them with you if you've got a mind to; they probably ain't got any money left to pay a fine noway."

Only three men were in the cell, and it was plain they weren't going anywhere for a while. Hitch didn't disturb them. He backed out, and Edson said, "Wrong men. Sorry we bothered you, Sheriff."

The lawman looked like a bobcat with a foot caught in a trap. "Think nothin' of it. I enjoy bein' up most of the night quietin' down cowpunchers, then gettin' woke up at the crack of dawn. Makes me feel like I'm doin' somethin' worthwhile."

The three climbed back into their saddles and looked at each other uneasily. Dan Truman spoke the thought the other two had been afraid to express. "You reckon they rode off someplace?" When they didn't answer, he knew they were thinking the same. "Selkirk's."

Edson said, "We better go bring them back before they get in trouble."

Dread was like a cold hand against the middle of Hitch's back. "Whatever trouble they had in mind, I'm afraid it's too late now to stop them. They're already in it."

They rode through the scattered horses. Hitch didn't see Rascal's bay Sweetheart, and Edson and Dan missed some they knew belonged to men from their outfits. The three looked at each other in knowing silence and returned helplessly to camp.

A couple of hours later they heard horses plodding along. The riders slouched in their saddles, wearied and half asleep. They rode into camp without fuss and slipped out of the saddles. Rascal McGinty leaned against his bay horse to support his rubbery legs till the circulation got going. He took off his hat and ran his hand through his tangle of red hair. His eyes were watery and bloodshot. He looked at Hitch like a schoolboy caught turning over an outhouse. "Want to know where we been at, Hitch?"

"I'm afraid to ask you."

"We went out to hooraw ol' Selkirk a little and show him how the wolf went over the hill."

"Figured you did." Hitch looked past Rascal and saw frustration in Law McGinty's face. It struck Hitch that maybe they hadn't gotten anything done, which could have been a blessing. "I hope you-all didn't wind up in no trouble."

Rascal still held his hat in his hand. He rubbed it roughly across his stubbled face as if he itched. He pulled a bottle from his pocket, found it empty and tossed it away. "One thing you got to give ol' Selkirk, he's a cold, gutty bastard. I didn't think he had it in him. He stood up there like a man and told us exactly what he thought about us, which was considerable. You ain't been properly cussed till you've had it done to you by a damnyankee banker, Hitch. He purely knows the words. And you remember Dayton Brumley, that used to rep for him at the W wagon, the one I come near shootin' over that roan cow? He stood right by Selkirk. They got more guts than I gave them credit for."

"For God's sake, Rascal, I hope you didn't hurt anybody."

Rascal shook his head. "How could we, them standin' there on the gallery with all them guns pointed straight at us? Damn it, Hitch, you never seen so much cannon in all your life. Looked like enough to've shot their way through the battle of Bull Run."

Law's voice was brittle. "There wasn't but four guns. I kept tellin' you, Rascal, we could've took them."

"Could've got your fool head blowed off," Rascal snapped back. "You was too drunk to know how close you come to bein' killed. Damn fool button, I hope that baby boy don't take after you when it comes to sense; he'll never make it to be grown."

Hitch glanced at Edson and Dan and let out a long breath he had held as if it were the last he would ever have. "I'm glad, Rascal, there wasn't nobody hurt."

"We could've took them," Law said again, "if Rascal would've let us. We didn't have to stand there and take that cussin'."

"Better a cussin' than a funeral," Rascal said.

Law's jaw jutted. "At least it'll be a while before ol' Selkirk chases wolves with them hounds of his and gets some other cowboy's leg broke like he done Joe Sands."

Hitch caught that breath again. He saw a shamed look in Rascal's face. "What did you do?"

Law said, "I rode by the dog pen as we left. I shot them dogs."

Hitch hit him. Law staggered and went down on his rump. Hitch spat, "Goddamn you, Law, get up from there!" When Law did, Hitch knocked him down again. Law waved his arms in surprise and reached to his hip for a pistol he didn't have.

Rascal stood and blinked, glancing at his brother but making no move to help him to his feet. He spoke mildly, "Hitch, I had sort of intended to do that myself."

"Why the hell didn't you?"

"I tried, but I kept missin' him."

Law was on his feet again, swaying a little. Hitch knocked him down a third time. "I didn't miss him. Get him out of my sight, Rascal. Keep him out of my sight till you're both sober."

That time Hitch went down to town and bought a bottle at Fant Gossett's saloon. He took it over to the shack where Joe Sands stayed and let Joe watch while Hitch drank most of it.

Joe said, "You're goin' to hate yourself."

"I think I already do."

Looking back later, Hitch could see that from that point things went downhill. It would be hard to say the strike ended on any particular day, or even in a particular week, for it just dragged on and died away gradually in painful gasps. Some cowboys began straggling off, a few to seek jobs at their old outfits. They didn't find them.

A Nine Bar hand Hitch had known a long time came back cheerless and tired from a ride out to the ranch. "They wouldn't even talk to me, Hitch. I offered to work for the same wage I was gettin', and they're so short-handed it hurts to watch them. But they got themselves a blacklist . . . got all our names on it. There won't none of them ranchers give a job to one of us."

It was as Charlie Waide had said. The ranches would suffer in the short run, but new hands would keep drifting into the country and hiring on at the same wages the ranchers had been paying before the strike, or perhaps five dollars a month more. In that respect the strike would help some cowboys, but not the ones who had participated in it.

After the affair out at Selkirk's, Rascal McGinty stayed sober. He was good help, finally, when it was too late for help to matter much. Holding the strike together was like trying to grab a handful of water; it leaked out between all fingers.

Edson Biggs came to Hitch one day, expression dark. "We spent the last of the chuck fund today, and there ain't enough flour and coffee to go past tomorrow noon. We'll be out of beef pretty quick."

Hitch could feel the ground slowly sliding from beneath his feet. "We'll make another assessment. How much you figure we'll need?"

"We've already lost between a third and a half of the men. We'll lose the rest before long, I expect. Five dollars ought to do it. There might be enough left at the end for us to hold a wake."

They went among the cowboys. Some dug into their pockets without complaint. A few of the cautious ones declined. One said, "Hitch, I was figurin' on leavin' here in the mornin' anyway. Thought I might find somethin' over east, over in the Clarendon country or the Palo Duro."

Some turned their pockets wrongside out and found nothing. Some gave a dollar, some two dollars, all they had. When Hitch and Rascal and the other collectors turned the money over to Edson, it counted out to only enough for four or five more days. A few people in town might still contribute money or grub, but by now they knew what most of the cowboys did: the strike was a failure. The heart beat feebly, but the illness was terminal.

Fant Gossett came in his buggy, his weight mashing the spring seat way down. That fine broad smile he had used at first was gone now. He pointed a big stubby finger like a pistol. "Hitch, I need to be talkin' to you."

The tone was like a hoof rasp going to the quick. "Nothin' ever stopped you yet."

"Now, Hitch, you know that when you-all started this strike I told you it was all right with me, I was back of you all the way. I didn't think it was much of an idea; I always talked against it, but if you-all wanted to strike I told you you had ol' Fant Gossett's support. I always told you that, didn't I?" He paused, waiting for Hitch to agree. Hitch said nothing. Gossett went on, "Well, Hitch, I've always been a generous man; I'd give the shirt off of my back if it would help some poor soul to his feet. But on the other hand I ain't operatin' no charity institution down there. Now, there's three or four of them cowboys been givin' me a mite of grief, been comin' down there thinkin' because they'd spent all their money I ought to give them whisky on credit. You know credit's poison to a businessman. It's cash on the barrelhead, I always say.

"Now I don't want them boys troublin' me no more. If they do I'll have to call the sheriff into it. He's lookin' for an excuse to jail all you boys he can anyway. So you tell them boys for me, Hitch, if they ain't got the money to spend, don't be a-comin' down to the place and botherin' me for whisky. You do that, and it'll save us all a right smart of grief."

Hitch figured Fant Gossett had made enough money out of these cowboys to buy a quarter interest in the Figure 4 ranch if he had a mind to. "I'll tell them, Fant. And in return I want you to do *me* a favor."

"Anything reasonable, Hitch. You know I'll be tickled to."

"If I ever again show my face in your place of business, I want you to kick me out the front door."

Quickly Gossett was smooth as warm butter. "Now, Hitch, you know you're welcome down there any time, just any time atall. What I said about them others . . . I just got to take care of my business, is all."

"Then you go on and see about your business, Fant. I don't want to detain you none."

10

Hitch told Edson and Dan he was planning to leave come daylight. "The wise man realizes when he's whipped. He wipes his nose, picks up his hat and leaves while he can still walk. I don't aim to be the last one out."

Edson Biggs stared past Hitch toward the main part of camp, his eyes sober. "At least you have somewhere to go, Hitch. Many an old boy here doesn't have that, or the money to take him there if he had."

Hitch bent down to buckle his big-roweled spurs to his boots. "They're not all broke, Edson. There's some of these cowboys that sat on their money like they was tryin' to make it hatch. There'll always be the thrifty kind among us."

Edson said, "But there'll always be some of that other kind who can't see past tonight's poker game, who'll spend their last dime to pinch some empty-headed girl on the cheek, front or rear. Give one man a hundred dollars and pretty soon he'll have two hundred. Give another man a hundred and pretty soon he'll come back to you looking for more."

Dan Truman said sourly, "I been askin' myself a hundred times, where'd we go wrong? Where'd we come apart?"

Edson Biggs punched at the campfire, where a can of coffee was slowly coming to a boil. He glanced at Hitch, then back to Dan Truman, putting together what he wanted to say. "We lost it before we started. We lost it, for one thing, because we struck for the wrong reasons. We cheapened ourselves . . . we cheapened what we stood for when all we could agree to ask for was higher wages. We should have talked about dignity and freedom; those things count for more than money. Money's soon spent, and when it's gone it leaves no mark. But when a man loses dignity, that leaves a mark on him that stays. We didn't come apart; we never were really together."

Hitch said, "There didn't have to be a strike. Both sides had some right and some wrong. If we'd all been willin' to talk to each other, maybe we could've got around it. But the wrong people always seem to grab hold of things and holler instead of listen. I've never understood why it's always easier to fight than it is to talk."

Edson said, "Not many people can see more than one side to an argument. You have that gift, Hitch, if it is a gift; I'm inclined to think it's a handicap. You'll be miserable all your life because you see both sides. The man at peace with himself is the one who sees nothing but his own."

Much of what Edson was saying went over Dan Truman's head. Dan said, "All I know is that we lost and the ranchers won."

Edson shook his head. "We lost, but they didn't win. In the end they'll find out that they've lost too."

Dan said, "Damned if I see how you figure that."

"You will, in time. Hitch, where you goin' when you leave here?"

"I got a little money saved back that I can buy the necessaries with. I got me a section of deeded land and a little bunch of cows. I can plant me a garden, and I can hunt. I can live awhile on a little of nothin'. They'll play hell starvin' me to death."

Edson glanced at Dan. "Same goes for you, too. It goes for a lot of these men. The big ranches figure on them leaving the country, but they won't. They have a toenail hold here, and they'll stay. What's more, they're mad, and anything the ranches do to squeeze them out will make them dig in a little deeper. There are probably fifteen-twenty men who came to this strike as working cowboys and will leave it as small ranchers, mad at the big outfits and determined to stay. Some cowboys will find themselves a place in town, and the town itself is more against the outfits now than it ever was. The ranches will find out that instead of clearing this country they've broken a hornet's nest around their ears. They won't be able to control elections; they'll find people voting taxes on them like they've never paid before. They won't run this sheriff's office much longer, and they won't run the court."

He burned his hand on the coffee can and let it go. "I've had time to do a lot of thinking since we've been here. The old-time cowboy is finished, but the days of the big ranches are numbered, too. This is going to be a little man's country, and the little man is going to need himself a bank he can go to with dignity and trust. I think I know some money men back home who will listen to me. I'll get the backing and open a bank here that will serve men like you, Hitch, and you, Dan. A bank too small for the Figure 4 or the W or the Snaketrack but able to lend a man money to buy a section of land or fifty cows or groceries to help him survive till spring in a dugout winter camp. A lot of state land here is for sale if people can raise the money. I'll help them raise it. We'll crowd these big ranches off of the free range. Then we'll see who has lost and who has won."

Rascal McGinty had come up to listen. His jaw was working a little, though he wasn't saying anything aloud. Farther down in camp, Law McGinty and Asher Cottingham were still talking strike. But Rascal knew.

Hitch said, "Rascal, maybe it's time you was takin' Law home."

"Past time. He don't mean no harm, but seems like he causes it just the same. I wisht you could talk to him, Hitch."

"I'm done talkin' to him. From now on, Rascal, I reckon you'll have to do that yourself."

Rascal and Law and Cottingham were hunched over a coffeepot next morning as Hitch swung into the saddle at good daylight. Cottingham squatted on his spurs, nursing a hot cup in his hands and watching resentfully. "Desertin' us, are you, Hitch?"

Hitch considered some kind of answer but decided against it. Rascal muttered something to Cottingham.

Cottingham persisted. "It's your fault, Hitch. If they'd of listened to me instead of to you, we'd of given them ranchers hell. If you hadn't acted like some scared old woman . . ."

Rascal grabbed Cottingham's collar and jerked him

backward. Caught by surprise, Cottingham landed on his back. He rolled over on his side, frantically trying to brush away the hot, wet coffee he had splashed all over himself. Rascal said impatiently, "Asher, I told you to shut up." He looked then at Hitch. "Take care of yourself."

"I will." Hitch glanced at Law to see if the younger McGinty had anything to say. Law simply stared. Hitch spoke no more as he rode out of camp. But seeing Law set him to wondering about Kate.

It was not out of the way for him to go by the McGinty place; it lay only a few miles from his own. They had originally planned it that way, he and Rascal and Law, in a happier day when they had all been confident they would someday be rich and build fine mansions and have cows roaming over a thousand hills. It would be nice in their old age, they had thought, to be able to ride over and play cards and talk about the good old days when they were poor as a whip-poor-will.

Hitch led a dun packhorse he had bought as an extra animal to spell Walking Jack at the work. He had it loaded with supplies he would be needing. But he headed for the McGinty place instead of his own.

Kate stood beneath a clothesline she had strung between the corner post of a fence and a wooden cross post she had set up near the front of the dugout. Flapping clothes had always been a worry to Walking Jack, so Hitch dismounted and tied him a little way from the line. Hat in his hands, he walked up to Kate.

She was surprised. "Strike over, Hitch? Did we win?"

"It's over. We didn't win."

She was slender and small again like she used to be. He said, "You look real fine, Kate. Hope you been all right."

"Just fine. I want you to see my baby boy. He's in the house with Mother."

He remembered how astonished Selkirk had been to hear her call that dugout "house."

She said, "I'm sorry about the strike. What'll you do now?"

"Work for myself. I'm out of a job."

"Then I reckon everybody is . . . Law, Rascal . . . everybody." She frowned. It seemed to Hitch she looked pleasant even when she let her face wrinkle that way. Maybe Selkirk had not considered her pretty, but Hitch thought she was. She asked, "Law and Rascal, they behind you?"

"I expect they'll be comin' along. If not today, pretty soon. Not everybody's given up yet."

"I'm sorry, Hitch. But come on, let me show you the boy."

He followed her into the dugout. It was small and crowded but much cleaner than the name would imply. The floor was packed hard from people walking on it all the time, almost like cement, and a good housekeeper like Kate would sweep it clean a time or two every day, clearing up the dust that always seemed to filter down from the sodded-over roof. Kate's mother sat there, a time-worn, worry-torn woman aged beyond her years, embittered to the point that she trusted no one. That, Hitch feared, could be Kate by the time she was forty if life did not improve for her. It would be a pity.

Babies had always appeared pretty much alike to him, one and then another, but he bragged about this one being real special and already having its legs bowed to fit a horse as soon as it was a couple of months older and had its balance. This, of course, was an exaggeration. Most ranch boys didn't get put in the saddle till they were walking good.

Kate wouldn't let Hitch go until she had fed him, and he didn't really want to leave anyway on an empty stomach. He knew what it would be like, batching on his own place. But by and by there was no excuse to tarry longer. Kate followed him out to the horses. He must have looked worried, for she made a weak smile. "You'll do fine, Hitch. You've always been one to do fine. I hope you'll come over real often."

He hadn't told her about the unpleasantness between him and Law. He said, "I doubt there'll be much time, Kate; I'll have a right smart of work to do fixin' up the place. Besides, here lately since I had to let him go from the Ws, Law ain't been none too friendly with me."

"That'll pass," she said confidently. "You've always been good friends; anything wrong now, it'll pass."

"I hope so. I'm worried about you-all tryin' to make a livin' on a little place like this."

"Things always work out for people who have faith. I have faith in Law and Rascal." She made it sound cheerful, but in her eyes he saw a shade of doubt. She had seen many dreams go to dust in her father's time.

"Goodbye, Kate. If ever you need help, you know where I'm at."

"I'll remember." After he had ridden a long way he turned in the saddle to look back. She was still watching him.

He had told her he would have lots to do, but he hadn't realized how much there was. Working on the

W, he had had to let his cattle more or less take care of themselves. He had done very little toward building corrals to handle them in, or a dugout for him to live in. He had a small one, built for an overnight camp and hardly big enough for a man to stretch his legs. Even that little one was half caved in from last winter's rains. The more he looked at it, the more it seemed he would be better off to let it fall and build a new one. Meantime he slept outside and hoped it didn't rain more than was needful.

He decided to build what was known as a half-human, a dugout half under the ground and half above it. That was one step up in civilization, lying somewhere between a cave-type dugout and a frame shack in respectability. It took much pick and shovel work, which was a good thing because he brought up all the grievances of recent weeks and worked them out on the brown earth. By the time he had planted the garden and finished the dugout, he had pretty well rid himself of the pent-up angers. Spring was moving well along into summer. The rains came about as they were supposed to, the grass rising green and the cattle licking themselves, a sign they were doing well. The garden thrived, which pleased him in view of the fact that he had done little farming in his life. He had decided that until he had himself established financially, he would raise whatever he needed beyond coffee, flour and the like, and if he couldn't raise it he would do without it. That way he could conserve that tiny bankroll.

Rascal came by Hitch's place a few times. He still tried to be his old redheaded, grinning self, though he was more serious now. When Hitch looked for it he could see trouble lying behind the forced laughter in Rascal's eyes. Rascal was out hunting for work where he could get it, pitching in as day labor when one of the smaller ranchers needed help, one of the little men who had not been a party to either side in the strike and didn't give a damn about the blacklist. Most of these greasy-sack outfits weren't recognized at the big ones' roundups and couldn't send reps to watch out for their interests. They took care of themselves the best way they could. Rascal's travels kept him posted on the gossip. He knew where most of the striking cowboys had gone. As Edson Biggs had predicted, a majority were still somewhere around. Some had found work with small ranches not in the inner circle. The pay was small because these little ranchers didn't have the money. A number of cowboys stayed in town, some working, some showing no visible means of support.

A few cowboys simply squatted on open range and went to mavericking, trying to build themselves a herd. This was dangerous now, for the big outfits had outlawed it, though enforcement was difficult in a country so broad and open. A man who kept his eyes peeled could brand cattle under the noses of the big outfits' cowpunchers and not get caught at it. It was not illegal except in the eyes of the big ranches. An unbranded animal not following a branded mother was considered the property of the man on whose range it grazed. Since the big outfits did not own or pay leases on much of the grass they used, a man could make out a case that they had no solid claim on the mavericks. Any time Hitch came upon a maverick and felt to his own satisfaction that it did not rightfully belong to Charlie Waide, he shook his rope down and built a little fire to heat the cinch ring he carried in the pocket of his chaps. By summer his little herd of Two Diamonds was bigger than before the strike.

He made it a point to ride out the country diligently and keep his cattle thrown back close to their own home range. If a Two Diamond cow and calf were gathered in some big ranch's roundup, the cowboys were not likely to appropriate his calf, for that would be stealing; but on the other hand they would not brand it for him, either. They would simply throw the cow and unbranded calf back onto the open range. If Hitch did not happen to come upon them before the calf was weaned, it would be a maverick subject to branding by the first man who threw a loop on it. He supported the right of a man to maverick cattle, but he wanted to be sure none of them were his.

One day he saw a cowboy riding a horse that looked familiar. The cowboy was a stranger, but Hitch remembered the horse, a little W mustang named Chicken that Law McGinty used to ride. Hitch and the cowboy howdied and shook and introduced themselves. The name Hugh Hitchcock meant nothing to the young rider, though he worked for Charlie Waide and the W now. Hitch asked him how Charlie was and found the rancher was all right except, the cowboy said, grouchy as an old he-coon with the colic.

Seemed the cowboy had come up from South Texas with two dollars in his pockets. He had heard about the strike and the ranch jobs open. To him thirty dollars a month seemed a gold mine. Looking back on it, Hitch could see how futile it had been for the strikers to think they could bend the ranchers backward very long; too many needy people all over the country were ready and willing to take their jobs.

"Thirty dollars a month," the boy exclaimed, like it was a million. "I can't see what all them fellers went on strike for. Just got too big for their britches, I reckon."

"I reckon."

The cowboy went on to say they had been having trouble with maverickers and the like, and Hitch promised to keep his eyes open. Before he left, the cowboy said, "Them boys that lost the strike, I hear they're a desperate bunch that had as soon shoot a man as to look at him. I'm sure watchin' out that I don't run into none of them."

"You do that," Hitch told him.

He almost rode into one himself a few days later. He had finished looking through a string of cattle to see if any Two Diamonds were among them, or any mavericks. They weren't. He found several Snaketrack and Figure 4 cows with calves, and one weaned heifer yearling carrying a fairly fresh Figure 4 brand. Hitch wished he had found her before the Figure 4 men did, but that was water under the bridge.

Riding away through a clump of brush, he heard a stirring of hoofs and looked back. Another horseman had ridden among the same cattle, checking them over just as Hitch had done. He evidently had not seen Hitch. Out of curiosity, Hitch dismounted and watched him. The horseman shook down his rope, eased the heifer yearling away from the other cattle and threw a loop over her stubby horns. Then he put spurs to the horse and dragged the heifer jumping and bawling into the brush. Hitch could not see now, but he could tell from the popping of limbs and the angry bawling that the cowboy jerked the heifer down and tied her. Directly he caught a faint smell of burning wood, though the fire was kept so small that he never saw smoke. The tenor of the heifer's bawling changed; Hitch knew the horseman was burning a new brand on her hide.

Hitch swung onto Walking Jack and worked through the brush, coming up behind the man on the ground. The cowboy had a heated cinch ring and was changing the Figure 4 brand into an LR.

"Law," Hitch said, "if I was a Figure 4 man, I could kill you right now."

Law McGinty whirled, dropping the cinch ring and grabbing at a pistol on his hip. It was half out of the holster before he recognized Hitch. Breathing hard, face pale, he let the pistol slip back into leather. "Hitch, you got an awful bad habit of slippin' up on a man."

"You got a bad habit of makin' a man need to."

Law was trembling now. "You oughtn't to ever ride up on a man like that. It can get you killed."

Coldly Hitch said, "You killin' people now, Law?"

"You know better than that."

"Not necessarily. You've moved up from sleeperin' cattle to changin' brands. Why not move on up a little farther and kill somebody? Keep up this kind of business and sooner or later you'll have to. Can't you find enough honest mavericks to suit you?"

Law picked up the cinch ring from the dirt. It had cooled, and he dropped it back into his tiny fire to reheat. Defensively he said, "You throwin' in on the big companies' side now?"

"I got no side except my own, but I got eyes. That heifer had a Figure 4 brand on her before you got here."

"Ol' Selkirk ain't goin' to miss one now and again."

"Is it just one now and again, or are you changin' brands as fast as you can get around to them? Kate wouldn't be proud if she knew what you're doin'. Neither would Rascal."

"You figurin' on tellin' them?"

"It's not my place to."

"It ain't your place to tell *me* anything, either. We might've won that strike if we'd used stronger measures. You wouldn't stand for them, and we lost it."

"The strike's got nothin' to do with you changin' brands on somebody else's stock. We had some justice on our side in that strike. You got none with you in this."

"Justice is a useless word in this part of the country. What matters is how many cows you got. The LR is goin' to have plenty of them before I'm through."

"Even if you have to steal them?"

"You figure ol' John Torrington come by all his cattle honest, or Selkirk all his money? You can bet that anytime they got the chance, they just reached out and grabbed. Well, I'm grabbin' too." He frowned darkly. "Now, Hitch, suppose you just ride on out of here. You ain't seen nothin' and you ain't tellin' nothin'."

"I've seen," Hitch said, heavily disappointed, "but nothin' I'll ever want to tell."

One thing Hitch badly needed was a better set of corrals. He had only a couple of small working pens, and when he threw cattle into them he found some of the calves crawling out because the spaces at the bottom were too large. He didn't want to spend money on lumber that could better be spent on land or cattle, so he carried an ax down into the creekbottom and chopped brush. It took him all the time he could spare for some weeks, chopping and hauling trunks and branches big enough and long enough to serve as posts and fencing. He laid out the pattern on the ground, then set the posts in pairs, just enough space between them to wedge the branches in lengthwise, solid from the ground to a height of about five feet. This required a lot of digging and a lot of chopping; it was something a man could not do a-horseback, and it set him to longing for the good days on the W when he was never afoot except around the bunkhouse or the chuckwagon. It was hard to find dignity in work like this, at least dignity by cowboy standards.

He was chopping branches to fit the fence when he saw a buggy approaching from the west, two people on the seat. One was a woman, he could tell by the scarf flying in the breeze. The man he soon recognized as Joe Sands. Joe reined the trotting team to a stop by Hitch's half-finished fence. Hitch dusted his hands on his torn-knee britches and walked out to meet him. Joe extended his hand without trying to get down from the buggy. "Hitch, you probably don't know Maggie. This here is Maggie Horn, from town."

Hitch knew the buggy and team now; he had seen the saloonkeeper Fant Gossett use them several times. Though he didn't know the woman, he judged that Fant Gossett had probably used *her* a few times, too. Hitch said awkwardly, "Good to have you visit, Miss Horn." He touched the brim of his hat; he knew that if he took it off the sweat would immediately roll down into his eyes. "Joe," he said, "how's the leg?"

"Better, but I can't climb up and down from this buggy without help. That's how come I brought Maggie with me."

Hitch raised his hands. "I'll help you down."

Joe shook his head. "No time, Hitch. I come to warn you."

Hitch dropped his hands. "Warn me?"

"Bunch of the big ranchers are meetin' in town with

the county commissioners' court. John Torrington and Prosper Selkirk and some of them others, they've drawed up a list of what they call 'maverick brands.' The county court is goin' to order them seized and held."

"They can't do that; it ain't legal."

"Anything is legal if you're big enough, and if you own the court and the sheriff. Hitch, they got your name and brand at the top of the list."

"Why me?"

"They look on you as one of the leaders of that strike. The ranchers figured when the strike was over the trouble would be over, but it's only just started. They thought all the strikers would leave the county, but the biggest part are still around pesterin' them ranchers like horseflies, chasin' mavericks, runnin' brands . . . things like that. Them big outfits are like a snake mad enough to bite itself. They want to put all the maverick men out of business, and they consider you one."

"I never stole a cow in my life."

"They're fixin' to steal *yours*, Hitch, if you don't get the jump on them. They got the McGintys on their list and a bunch of others."

"We could get us a lawyer . . ."

"And fight them in their own court? It'd be like a banty hen fightin' a chickenhawk. You got to take care of your ownself, Hitch. Charlie Waide said he tried to head them off, but he was swimmin' upstream."

Hopefully Hitch asked, "Did Charlie tell you to come and warn me?"

Joe shook his head. "Not exactly, he didn't." He saw the disappointment in Hitch's face. "But he must of knowed I would, else he wouldn't of gone to the trouble of tellin' me about it."

"I don't know what to do, Joe. I can't fight the law, even *their* law."

"That's what I told Charlie. He said if he had a friend in that fix, he'd tell him this is a county court and it's got no jurisdiction anywhere else. Said he'd tell him that if he rounded up his cattle and pushed them across the county line, they couldn't touch him. At least not unless they got to the next county to do the same thing." Joe paused. "Mind you, if anybody was to ever ask, I couldn't tell them that Charlie told me to tell you that. He just said if he had a friend in that fix, that's what he'd say."

"Thanks, Joe. I reckon I'd best get busy."

"Wisht I could help you round them up, Hitch, but this leg won't let me get on a horse yet, and ol' Fant's buggy won't hardly operate off of a road."

"I'll do for myself." Hitch stepped back, then thought of one thing more. "You're goin' over to tell Rascal and Law, ain't you?"

"Hadn't figured on it."

"I'd take it as a personal kindness if you would."

Joe Sands considered soberly. "I been hearin' some things about Law . . ." He broke off. "All right, Hitch, I'll go."

After Joe left, Hitch stood around a few minutes trying to reason out what steps he should take. They couldn't do this to him, yet he knew Joc was right; legal or not, they *would* do it. It was a hard week's horseback ride from here to the state capital. The law here was whatever the big outfits chose to say it was.

He quickly gathered up a few necessaries such as coffee and cold bread and jerked beef and wrapped them in a sack, then caught and saddled Walking Jack. He rode north first, making a circle over that side of his claim and over open range well beyond, picking up what Two Diamond cows he found and pushing them southward. Giving them a long start, he rode off in another circle and made a second drag, picking up more cattle. They moved sluggishly, for the grass here was good, and they had no inclination to leave it. Whenever he let up pushing them, they slowed and began grazing again. When he finally had them strung out on a southerly course, he left them and went back to the first gathering. He found these no longer moving but spread and grazing. He bunched them, shouting and bullying them into a trot. After a long time he managed to join them with the other cattle. A quick count showed he had perhaps two-thirds of his herd. The rest were scattered to Kingdom Come. Frustration gnawed at him; if only he had a little help he could hunt while someone else pushed the cattle. He felt that in every swag, every creekbottom and brush motte he was missing a few, if only he could go get them. But whenever he left this herd it would quit moving forward and begin scattering to graze. It was better to save this many than to try for the rest and possibly lose them all. If he got these across the county line, he could come back for more.

The new calves quickly tired and fell to the rear of the herd. Anxious mothers missed them and dropped back bawling for their offspring. Hitch shook his rope loose from the hornstring and used it like a whip, sending it stinging across the hips of the cows. But he could do little about the calves. They were too young to be properly fearful of him, too tired to run even if they had been scared. One by one he began to let the smallest of the calves drop out, and he cut their mothers to stay with them. By late afternoon he had left ten or twelve pairs strung across the prairie as he bullied the rest of the herd along, shouting, charging them on the running horse, whipping them with the rope.

The county line was imaginary, not based on any geographical feature such as a creek or a river. It was a straight line arbitrarily drawn on some map years and years ago. Hitch thought he knew about where it was, and he felt some relief when he pushed the cattle over and beyond it. He let them slow a little, but he was not confident enough to allow them to stop. Safety lay in distance; the more he could get of it, the better. There was always a chance some of the cattle might try to return to accustomed ground, though as a general rule in this part of the country cattle drifted south, following the prevailing winds.

Dusk was upon him when he began to think of stopping and fixing some supper. This was open range just as in his own county, only a minor part of it yet deeded to individual owners. This county also knew cattle of the W and the Figure 4 and the Snaketrack brands, as well as those of other ranches big and small which headquartered south of here. Hitch's cattle had as much right to graze this grass as anyone's did, wherever he chose to turn them loose.

This, he decided, was as good a place as any. He stepped down from Walking Jack at a tiny creek where he found dead mesquite that would make firewood for his supper. He watered the horse, built a small fire in a sheltered spot where it could not spread out into the grass, and put a small can of coffee on to boil. Standing up from these exertions, he saw half a dozen riders bearing down upon him from the north.

Hitch was unarmed except for the saddlegun in its scabbard on his saddle. Not once did he even think of going for it. He stood uneasily and watched the riders approach. The one in front made a circular motion with his arm, and four men spurred out around Hitch's cattle. The remaining two rode up to Hitch. One was the sheriff he knew from town.

"Howdy, Hitchcock. Hope you're fixin' enough coffee to go around. I sure do need me some."

Hitch said, "You're welcome to coffee, Sheriff. But if you've come for my cattle, you can forget about it. I'm well over the county line."

The sheriff looked at his companion, the Torrington cowboy Slant Unger. "Slant, did you see anything back yonder markin' a county line?"

Unger gravely shook his head.

The sheriff turned again to Hitch. "Afraid you're mistaken, Hitchcock. Far as I know I'm still in my county. I got an order here from the commissioner's court that says I'm supposed to take custody of all cattle in the Two Diamonds herd and brand, among others. Them cattle you got yonder is all wearin' the Two Diamonds, ain't they?"

Hitch saw they fully intended to do it. He flashed into anger. "You're over the county line and know it. You can't do this."

Calmly the sheriff pointed to the four men bringing Hitch's cattle back. "Suppose you just watch me."

Irrationally then, anger drove Hitch into charging at the sheriff with his fists. He landed a blow that brought pain to his own knuckles but sent the sheriff staggering back. He sensed a quick movement behind him and tried to turn. Something struck him across the back of the head and sent him to his knees. He crouched in black, blinding pain. He sensed that Slant Unger had pistol-whipped him. He tried to push to his feet but instead went down on his stomach. Dizziness washed over him like a flood. The roaring in his head all but covered up the conversation above him.

"You oughtn't to've hit him so hard, Slant. You might've busted his head."

"He had his hat on."

"Lots of people look up to Hitchcock. They won't like us hurtin' him."

"A man that betrays the outfit he works for ain't much to worry about, to my notion. Anyway, this'll help teach them that nobody messes around with the likes of John Torrington."

"I got a bottle in my saddlebags, Slant. Go bring it here."

The sheriff helped Hitch to his feet, but Hitch was unable to stay there. He sank back to his knees. "Didn't go to do it like this," the sheriff said half apologetically, "but orders is orders, and I got mine. Here, have a drink of this." He held the bottle to Hitch's lips and tilted it. Hitch choked some of the whisky down. It set his stomach afire but gave him strength. The sheriff said, "It ain't exactly like we was takin' these cattle away from you. What we're doin' is sort of holdin' them in escrow till the court has made a final determination. You know what escrow means?"

Hitch wheezed, "You take them cattle back over that line and I'll lose them forever."

The sheriff didn't argue with him. He corked the bottle and started to place it back into his saddlebag. Then he changed his mind and put it into Hitch's hand. "Hell, you'll need this worse than I do. Keep it. Always kind of respected you, Hitchcock. Sorry things turned out thisaway."

Hitch attempted no answer.

The sheriff said, "Seems to me like you'd be better off if you went someplace else and started fresh. Be better for all concerned if we was to ride by your place sometime and find you'd pulled out."

It pained Hitch to talk, but he managed what he wanted to say. "You'll find me there."

He knelt, giving up for a time to the pain that all but blinded him, though he could see them driving his cattle away. He drank what was left in the bottle, hoping it would help. It didn't. He tried once to push himself to his feet, to get on the horse and go home. The last he knew, he was falling.

11

Hitch was vaguely aware that he had lain there a long time. Some inner consciousness kept prodding him to find his feet, but he resisted it as long as he could, his head pounding. A thought came that perhaps the sheriff had been right . . . perhaps that blow had fractured his skull. He tried several times to bestir himself, and finally he opened his eyes. It was dark; he had no idea how much of the night had passed. He blinked, and gradually he was able to see Walking Jack, standing there as if asleep on his feet. At least the horse had not run away.

It took Hitch some time to get to his knees, for every move brought blinding pain anew. He wanted to lie down, to find oblivion and end the pain, but that nagging drive would not allow it. He tried to get to his feet but could not. He looked at the horse and tried to think ahead. He did not know if or how he would be able to get in the saddle, but he knew that first he had to catch the horse. He began crawling on hands and knees.

Walking Jack lifted his head, ears pointed forward in doubt. He was not used to seeing a man move toward him on all fours. The horse tossed his head, trotted off a few steps, then turned again in curiosity.

Hitch stopped. If Walking Jack ran away, Hitch could lie here and die. He found voice. "Whoa, son," he rasped. "Be gentle now, son."

Jack watched him warily, but the voice was familiar. Hitch kept talking to him as he crawled. Jack seemed inclined to turn and run again, but the voice held him. Hitch reached cautiously toward the trailing reins, afraid his hand would frighten the horse and cause him to run. Jack held his ground, and Hitch's fingers closed on leather.

He stopped there a bit, breathing hard and painfully, resting from the exertion. He reached up and patted the horse's shoulder to set the animal at ease. Jack flinched but did not jerk away. Hitch rubbed the horse's foreleg and kept talking quietly until Jack seemed ready to accept him. He reached up and caught hold of the stirrup. Holding it, he slowly pulled himself to his feet and leaned heavily against the horse.

He thought of the whisky and wished he still had some of it for the momentary strength it might give him. He had also lost his hat. He kept leaning against the saddle, his hands on the horn. Presently he thought he might have the strength. He lifted his left foot and somehow fumbled it into the stirrup. He tried then to pull up and got about halfway before he slid down again. The left foot stayed in the stirrup, though, that much of a start for the next try. He waited and rested a minute, then tried it again. The third time he made it and brought his right leg across the cantle. Somehow he found the stirrup with his right foot.

"Old boy," he said, "don't you let me fall off again."

He considered tying himself into the saddle, but that was dangerous; cowboys lived with a fear of becoming entangled and being dragged to death. He knew it was up to him to find his way, for Jack was not yet used to the dugout camp. Turned loose and given his head, Jack would probably trail across to the W headquarters; Hitch was unlikely to be able to ride that far. Hitch sagged over the saddlehorn but turned Jack in the direction he knew led to the dugout. Every step brought pain, but gradually it became blunted to the extent that he was able to endure it. He clamped his teeth and made up his mind he was not yet ready to die.

Much of the night was gone when he reached his dugout. He knew he could not climb down. When he tried to leave the saddle, he was likely to fall. What if he could not then get up? He could lie here at the front of his own dugout and be as helpless as out there on the prairie. The more he considered it, the more convinced he became that it was foolish to stop here. Farther on was help . . . farther on was the McGinty place if he could stay in the saddle that long. He turned Jack away from the dugout door. The horse seemed reluctant to leave, for horses have the same resistance to physical effort that humans do; he had expected to be turned loose here. But directly Jack became resigned to the notion that he was not through working. Hitch had the horse moving in the right direction when he sensed consciousness trying to leave him, and the pain coming harder again. He took a tight grip on the horn and hoped that if he did lapse he would not fall; he had slept in the saddle many times, some subconscious instinct keeping him astride.

By summoning all his will he retained enough consciousness to stay in the saddle and to give Jack some vague guidance. It seemed they had been moving all night in Jack's easy walk when suddenly they dropped into a familiar trail.

Hitch sensed when the horse stopped in front of the McGinty dugout. It was still dark, but the east showed some promise of morning light. He tried to call. "Rascal. Rascal McGinty." There was no strength in his voice; he tried again. The voice was little better than a whisper. He shifted his weight and lost his balance. He grabbed vainly at the horn but could not hold it. He slid down the horse's shoulder and leg and piled limply on the ground. Jack stood a moment as if afraid he might step on Hitch, then pulled away a few feet, looking confused. Hitch tried to crawl but could not. He lay there and lapsed into either sleep or unconsciousness, he did not know which.

After a long time he was aware of a woman's cry from the flap of the dugout. He managed to open his eyes and saw that the sun had just come up. Kate McGinty stood at the dugout. "Hitch?" she called in surprise. "Is that you, Hitch?" She rushed up the hewn-log steps. Hitch tried to answer but could not bring out words.

"What's happened to you, Hitch?" she cried as she dropped to one knee beside him. Her fingers gently touched the back of his head where the pistol had struck him. "You've taken a fall or somethin'. You been hit a bad lick. I better get you inside." She looked around as if for help. "Can you hear me, Hitch?" He nodded. She said, "There's nobody here but me and the baby. Law and Rascal are gone. I'll try to get you down these steps and into the house. Think you can help a little?" He nodded again, though nod was about all he could do.

She put her arms around him and lifted him up; she was a strong woman to be so small. He tried to carry his own weight but could not. He managed only to get a little movement into his legs.

It took them a long time to get down those steps, and he was sure he cried out a time or two. But finally he was lying on his stomach on a bed. Her fingers gently probed the wound. "That's an awful nasty place," she said. "I'll have to clean it up before I can even see how bad it is."

She poured something over it that burned like coals from Trump Tatum's campfire. He passed out.

He awoke later to voices. Someone out front called, "You McGintys! Anybody home?"

Opening his eyes, Hitch saw Kate sitting in a rawhide chair beside the bed. She turned toward the dugout flap. The baby began to fret at the disturbance. The voice came again, "Rascal McGinty, you in there?"

A man pushed through the flap and stood in the gloom of the tiny dugout, staring in surprise at the woman. "Mrs. McGinty?"

Kate stood up. "I'm Kate McGinty, Sheriff. My husband is not here, and neither is Rascal."

A second man entered. The sheriff moved forward. "I got some papers for your menfolks, ma'am." He nodded toward the bed. "Somebody hurt?"

"It's Hugh Hitchcock. I found him lyin' outside when I went to feed the chickens. I don't know what happened to him."

The sheriff picked up the lantern for a closer look. He turned to the other man, rebuke in his voice. "Damn it, Slant, I told you you shouldn't of hit him so hard."

Kate's voice went sharp. "You hit him? But why?"

"He resisted a lawful and legal order, ma'am, but

we didn't go to use him that badly. You reckon he'll be all right?"

Kate was indignant. "Hugh Hitchcock is a good and honorable man. He's not one to be clubbed this-away. Now, what was this all about?"

The sheriff retreated a couple of steps in the face of her anger. "I served a court order on him takin' custody of his cattle. Same order I got here for your menfolks, an order for me to take all cattle in the LR brand into custody for the county court."

"So that's it!" She leaned forward belligerently, hands on her hips. "You stole Hitch's cattle and now you're here to steal ours. Well, Mister Sheriff, you've come too late. They're gone."

"We'll find them."

"Not in this county you won't."

The sheriff stared at her in surprise. "I'd sure give a pretty to know how everybody found out we was comin'."

Slant Unger said urgently, "Ol' John Torrington will nail our hides to the barn if we let them get away with them cattle."

"Your hide, not mine. I ain't workin' for him."

"The hell you ain't. Come on."

Kate McGinty followed every step of their retreat, her voice accusing. "You're thieves, is what you are. You talk about law, but the devil himself wouldn't have you. You won't catch Law and Rascal now because Hugh Hitchcock sent us word. You hurt Hitch and stole his cattle, but in the end he's beat you."

Unger said, "We ain't beat yet. You comin', Sheriff?"

The men went out through the flap and hurried up the steps. The baby was crying, disturbed by the sharp voices. Kate went to its crib and picked it up, cradling it in her arms and swinging gently to and fro, speaking softly and kissing its face. When the baby was quieted, she went back to Hitch. "You heard?"

He nodded, though it hurt.

She said, "When Joe Sands brought word, Law and Rascal and a friend of Law's started gatherin' cattle the quickest way they could. They drove them all night. By now they ought to be well across the county line. Ain't no way the sheriff can get our cattle now."

If Hitch could have talked he would have told her that might not be enough. All he could do was nod.

He was awake at times, but mostly he slept, fighting through a recurring bad dream of John Torrington and Prosper Selkirk driving him out of the country with a long cutting whip. Late in the afternoon he awoke to noise outside and a man's voice calling, "Kate, we're home."

Horses trailed past the dugout and moved on in the direction of the corrals and shed. Presently he heard heavy spurs ringing to quick-paced footsteps. The flap pushed open and Law McGinty stood there. "Kate, I see Hugh Hitchcock's horse out yonder." He saw Hitch then, lying on the bed, head bandaged. "What's all this about?"

Kate told him, voice crisp with indignation. "That sheriff said he would catch you too. Did he?"

"Not till we was ready to be caught."

Rascal McGinty came in. He bumped Law in his haste to reach Hitch's side. He turned to Kate. "How bad's he hurt?"

"I can't tell. They hit him with a pistol."

Law frowned. "He been here all day?"

"I found him when I went out this mornin'. He's been like this mostly, asleep or unconscious; it's hard to tell which."

Rascal bent low. "Hitch, you hear me?"

Hitch found a weak voice. "I hear you."

Rascal eased a little. "How do you feel?"

"How do I look?"

"Like pure hell."

Hitch nodded, letting that stand for an answer.

Kate had to explain it all again for Rascal. Rascal clenched his fists. "They get all your cattle, Hitch?"

"All I could round up in a hurry."

Rascal cursed. Kate glanced apprehensively at the baby, and Rascal told her it wasn't old enough yet to pick up the words.

"Ain't likely you'll improve much before he is old enough," she said reproachfully.

Law watched Hitch in silence. At length he said, "Me and you have had our differences, Hitch, but I owe you for sendin' Joe Sands. I owe you for what they done to you, too. If they hadn't been busy with you they'd of been after us a lot sooner. We wouldn't of got away with most of our cattle."

Hitch asked, "You *did* get away?"

Rascal said with angry satisfaction, "Got far across the county line before they come ridin' up wavin' their papers. We told them they was out of their county, and they said they hadn't seen no sign. But we was on the Matthews country, and the Matthews men rode up and gave witness to it. That sheriff, he backed off like a scalded dog."

"I'm glad, Rascal."

"It was you that done it for us. They probably drove your herd someplace to where somebody else picked it up before they come for ours. That gave us time." He put his hand on Hitch's shoulder. "You'll be needin' watchin' after till we see how bad hurt you are. Kate's the best watcher you'll nearly ever see.

You got a home here, Hitch, as long as you need it." He glanced at Law as if asking him to make it plain.

Law said, "Rascal talks for me too, Hitch."

Hitch feared he detected reservation in Law's voice, but perhaps it was on his own part; he hoped so. He nodded his thanks and wished they would go away awhile now and let him alone. His head ached terribly.

Then he saw a third man, silently standing just inside the flap. Law said, "Hitch, I believe you know Cato Bramlett."

Hitch did. He knew Bramlett's reputation, too. "I know him. I wish you didn't."

He managed to raise up and eat a little supper. He found after a while that he was too weak to stay up, and he lay down again. Kate very carefully removed the bandage and cleansed the wound. "It's swollen worse, Hitch, but I reckon that's to be expected. Been a full day now since it happened."

Her hands were gentle, and he warmed to their touch despite the pain they brought. The warmth roused a vague guilt, for it was in his rigid code of ethics that he had no right to enjoy another man's wife, even to this innocent extent. He found her looking directly into his eyes, and for a second came a fear that she might read his thoughts. He quickly looked down. She said, "I hope I'm not hurtin' you."

He said quietly, "You never hurt anybody in your life."

Bedtime came with darkness, for nobody spent more money than necessary on kerosene for lamps. It was proposed that Hitch be left where he was and that Law and Kate could carry the baby crib over to

Rascal's dugout and sleep there. But Hitch wouldn't hear of it. "When I'm dead you can put me where you want me. I'm not dead yet."

He had Law and Rascal help him to Rascal's dugout. They put him on Rascal's cot despite Hitch's protest that he could as well sleep on the floor. Rascal said, "The cot is yours, so hush up about it. I've slept on the ground so much of my life that when I do sleep on a bed I feel like I'm puttin' on airs."

Cato Bramlett followed silently, taking no part in helping Hitch, offering no conversation. He had a couple of blankets on the earthen floor. He pulled off his hat and boots and lay on one blanket in the rest of his clothes. He pulled the other blanket over him. He lay smoking a cigarette, the glow not strong enough to light his face. Presently Rascal was snoring.

Bramlett said, "You don't like me, Hitchcock."

Hitch did not feel up to an argument. "You and me don't see noways alike."

"Your way don't seem to've got you anywhere. They gave you a cow-puncher shampoo and took your cattle. They ain't took nothin' from me."

"They'll kill you someday, and maybe everybody that's around you."

Bramlett finished his cigarette in silence and flipped it into a corner, where it winked out. By his even breathing, Hitch knew he was soon asleep.

But Hitch could not sleep, not for a time. Maybe he had slept too much during the day. His head throbbed dully now but without the hard pain he had felt earlier. He decided that since he had not died by now, he would live. He would probably suffer through this constant headache a few more days, and he would probably have to avoid overexertion. But he would live, and if John Torrington thought he had run Hugh

Hitchcock out of the county, he was in for disappointment.

By and by, lying awake in the close stillness and quiet of the dugout, staring up at darkness, he let his mind drift to Kate. He put the tips of his fingers to the side of his face where for a few seconds he had felt the gentle warmth of her hand. Now, unbidden, came the thought of her and Law lying in each other's arms, giving each other love in the bed on which he had lain all day. It was a tormenting thought, a corrosive one, and he tried to push it away. He tried to force his mind to better days when he had ridden with Charlie Waide on the W, when he had shared the genial pleasure of a cowboy crew before trouble came prowling these hills. But always the picture came back, relentless, and against his will he wished it were him instead of Law.

The life of a cowboy had its freedoms; it had its many compensations to help offset the grinding hardships; but always there was this dark and lonely side, this troubling deprivation that Hitch had tried never to allow himself to dwell upon. Now he was unable to put it aside.

Then came the ugliest thought of all: *Law is a thief. Kate might be better off in the long run if something happened to him. I'd be better off, too.*

He denounced himself in silence for his weakness, his selfishness. He had not realized this effect the McGinty place would have on him. He decided that if tomorrow he could stay in the saddle, he would leave here. He could not spend another night in this dugout, these guilty pictures burning into his brain.

He arose next morning when he heard Rascal stirring. He sat up on the edge of the bed, the small room seeming to reel. He put his hands to his head. Rascal, hat on before either his shirt or his britches, said, "Lay back down, Hitch. We'll fetch you some breakfast."

Hitch reached for his clothes. "One baby here is enough." It took some effort, but he got himself dressed, and he stood up bracing one hand against the dirt wall. In a minute he managed a thin smile. "I believe I'm goin' to make it."

"Don't rush anything."

Hitch swayed to the flap and pushed outside. He struggled up the steps by bracing himself, and he stood alone, testing his strength. He turned his head carefully, looking back at Rascal and finding that the cowboy watched him worriedly. "Looks like my head was almost as hard as Slant Unger's gunbarrel."

Rascal was in no mood to banter. "Don't you overstep yourself. I'd as soon bury my own brother as to bury you, Hitch."

Hitch's eyes burned as he realized Rascal meant it. He moved toward the other dugout in short, halting steps. The farther he went, the stronger he became. Rascal helped him down the steps and called, "Kate, you ready for us to come in?"

"Come on, both of you." Hitch realized Kate probably had seen them through the tiny window which sat at ground level outside the dugout, shoulder level inside.

The smell of fresh coffee was good, and Kate's smile glowed. She was scrambling eggs, something a man didn't often have on a ranch unless there was a woman to watch out for the chickens. "Set him down at the table, Rascal. Breakfast'll be ready directly."

Rascal pulled a chair away from the table for him, but it faced toward the bed; Hitch couldn't look at that. He moved around the table. "If it's all the same, I'd rather sit where I can look out the window."

Cato Bramlett came along and they all sat down to breakfast. It surprised Hitch how hungry he was. The men ate without talking, the forks and knives rattling against the cheap tin plates. After a bit the baby stirred, tiny hands reaching beyond the top of the crib. Law smiled at his wife. "He wants his breakfast too." She smiled back. "Well, he's not goin' to get it while you men are in here."

When he had finished eating, Hitch said, "Rascal, you got my horse up close? I'll be goin' home today."

Kate protested quickly. "You can't do that. Who'll look out for you?"

"Same one who always does, me. I've made up my mind to it, Kate. I'll be all right."

Rascal seemed about to make an argument but changed his mind, seeing that Hitch would not be argued out of it. "I might just go over there with you and spend a day or two."

"No need in that."

"May be some of our cattle strayed in that direction. It'll give me a chance to find them before the sheriff does. Could still be some of yours left in the brush too, Hitch."

"I'm countin' on it. One reason I want to get on home."

Law frowned as he rolled a brown-paper cigarette. "Didn't figure on you leavin' so quick, Hitch. There was some business we wanted to talk to you about when you felt better."

"Business?"

"Bunch of us come up with an idea. We hoped you might like to join in with us."

Hitch glanced at Kate. The baby was fretting a little more. Hitch said, "Let's go talk about it outside. Not everybody has had breakfast yet."

A couple of short benches stood near the front of the dugout; there the McGintys sometimes sat to enjoy the cool of the evening. Law motioned for Hitch to take one of them, and he took the other. Rascal slouched on the ground, and Cato Bramlett squatted, silently playing mumblety-peg with a pocketknife.

Law leaned forward, face earnest. "Them big ranchers have got it in their heads they're goin' to run this country with an iron hand, but there ain't no reason we got to back away and let them, Hitch. There's ways for the little man to stand up and fight, and to earn himself a place here as strong as anybody. We can't do it standin' alone. We all got to stand together."

"We stood together once," Hitch pointed out. "We lost anyway."

"We lost a battle, but we ain't lost the war. There's one thing them big outfits understand and respect: size. They're strong because they got lots of cows, and cows mean money, and money means power. We can have lots of cows too, Hitch, if all of us combine what we got."

"You're talkin' about a pool outfit?"

Law nodded. "We already got us a name and a brand for it. The Three Cs, Cowboy Cattle Combine. Them of us that got cattle, we're throwin' them in for their value in stock. Them that got some money saved up, they're buyin' stock and givin' us some workin' capital."

Hitch could see Law was excited over the idea, and he thought Rascal showed a little of it, too. He frowned and pointed his chin toward the man tossing the pocketknife. "Is Cato a part of it?"

Bramlett looked up. "I got me an interest."

Law said, "So've lots of other people, Hitch. Ol'

Fant Gossett over in town, he's put money in and helped us figure some of the legal points like gettin' us a charter for the corporation."

"Fant Gossett too." Hitch mused. "If Fant puts his money into anything, he figures on a return."

"He'll get it; we'll all get it. I tell you, Hitch, pretty soon we'll have us an outfit big enough to hold its own against Selkirk or Torrington or any of them. They won't stomp on no poor cowboy anymore."

"The big outfits won't recognize you. They won't accept your reps."

"We'll have our own roundups; we don't need them. We'll be out there first, and with that many cowboys huntin' for them, there won't be many mavericks get away from us. Give us a year, Hitch, and there'll be ten thousand cattle runnin' these hills with the Three C brand on their hide."

"Takes land to run cattle."

"Them of us that've got places, we'll lease them to the combine. But there's all kinds of open range out here. The big outfits got no more right to it than we have. We'll take our share. And did I say ten thousand cattle? Give us two years and it'll be twenty thousand, or thirty. It's cows that make a man rich in this country, and we'll have more cows than anybody. We'll show them big outfits that they ain't so damned much."

"Cowboy Cattle Combine." Hitch said it quietly, getting the taste of it and finding it a little bitter. "Sounds more like the Get Even Cattle Company to me."

Law grinned. "I hadn't thought of that, Hitch. It fits; by God, it *does* fit. I wish we'd called it that."

"John Torrington and them others, they'll call it a lot worse. You think they'll be standin' still while all this goes on?"

"He'll be jumpin' around like a chicken with its head cut off, but there won't be a thing he can do."

"Don't you ever bet on it."

Law gazed intently at Hitch. "We'd like to let you in on the combine."

"I ain't got much left. You don't need me."

"A lot of people look up to you. Some of them on the fence, they'd join up with us if they seen you do it. Anyway, we owe you for helpin' me and Rascal save our cows."

"I like to know my partners, Law."

"You know us."

"I know Cato Bramlett, too, and Fant Gossett." He caught a look of threat in Bramlett's eyes as the man let the pocketknife drop.

Law showed disappointment. "I wish you didn't feel that way."

"I wish I didn't have to. If I was you, Law, I'd take a good look at the people I was throwin' in with."

"I've had a good look at the people on the other side. I like my partners better."

Hitch shrugged. Law was a grown man. "How about you, Rascal? What's your feelin'?"

Rascal's eyes were narrowed. "They done us awful dirty, Hitch."

That, Hitch decided, just about told it all.

12

Before Hitch was far down the trail he knew he had bitten off a large bite, trying to go home. At least the other night he had been unconscious part of the time and had not felt all the jarring. With each step Walking Jack took, it felt as if the top of Hitch's head was about to come off.

Rascal McGinty said, "You want to turn back, Hitch?"

Hitch didn't shake his head; it hurt too much. "I've come this far."

He was grateful when at last they rode over the final hill and he could scc his place below. Never had that dugout looked so good. But bitterness touched him as he looked down at the half-finished corrals where he had been working when Joe Sands brought him the news. It appeared he wouldn't need those corrals now.

Rascal hadn't been there in a while. He whistled. "You've put a right smart of sweat into this place."

"Maybe all for nothin'."

"You get down and rest yourself. I'll do up the chores."

There wouldn't be much to that. Hitch hadn't gotten himself a milk cow, though many settlers had done so, including the McGintys. He had gone so long at the W without the taste of milk that he had no use for it, not to drink, not even for making bread.

Rascal looked around curiously. "What come of the chickens you bought off of the Matthews?"

"I'm not around here enough to watch out for them. Seemed like every day or two I come up with one less. Sometimes I'd find a half handful of feathers, sometimes no trace atall. Them coyotes, they can sneak in here in broad daylight and raid you while you're lookin' off. Only got three or four chickens left. They're so wary that I can't even find their eggs. I wish the coyotes would get them too so I could stop worryin' myself over them."

"Messy anyway, a chicken is. I'd rather walk amongst cattle anytime than amongst a bunch of chickens. If it wasn't for Kate and her cookin', we wouldn't have a chicken on the place. She is a dandy cook, Hitch."

"I noticed."

"Kind of nice havin' a married brother. You get to be a bachelor and still have a woman do the cookin' for you. Ain't hardly any way to beat that. You never did have no brothers, did you, Hitch?"

"Got three, back home in South Texas. They've never come up here, though; I don't expect they ever will."

"Then you'll have to find a woman for yourself; you can't get by easy like I done. A woman sure does pretty up a place, Hitch."

"I noticed."

Hitch slept well that night and felt much better the

next morning. He and Rascal ate an early breakfast, saddled up and began riding out his claim and the draws and swales around it that might conceal cattle he had missed in his hurried roundup the other day. Among other things he hunted for and finally found the hat he had lost where the sheriff had overtaken him. They stopped in the shade of a big cottonwood at noon to chew on tough jerked beef and to rest awhile from the heat. Hitch still had a constant headache, but it was less than yesterday's.

They had gathered a small herd of cattle through the morning and now let them drift and graze along the banks of the creek where the cottonwoods grew.

Rascal said, "Twenty-two cows, fourteen calves is the way I count it. They didn't leave you much, Hitch."

"They won't leave me these either if I don't drift them out of the county before they make another drag through here."

"We'll run them over toward the Matthews place, where we took the LRs," Rascal said.

"We don't want to overstock that country. If it comes a dry summer and a hard winter, we'll all be in trouble."

"Them few you got left won't overstock anybody, and you're already in trouble."

Hitch kept looking back over his shoulder as they drove the cattle, half afraid the sheriff would come riding along about the time they hit the county line. But he didn't; he was probably busy gathering in other "maverick" herds. Late in the afternoon Hitch and Rascal turned the cattle loose along a good creek and sat awhile to watch them drift. Hitch hoped they wouldn't decide to drift back home.

The two men took advantage of range hospitality to go over to the Matthews ranch, knowing they would be invited to have supper and spend the night. The Matthews men had been buffalo hunters a decade ago, coming here from the Arkansas River country shortly after MacKenzie set the Comanches afoot in 1874 and forced them to the reservation. When the buffalo played out, Walt and Ben Matthews laid claim to one of their favorite hunting camps and took cattle there. They were only a nuisance size to big companies like the Figure 4 and Snaketrack, too small to consider as equals but too large to push around. They ran perhaps a thousand or fifteen hundred cattle, which was more than Hitch and the McGintys and several other cowboy operators combined. They had remained neutral and untouched during the strike; they never hired more than a couple or three extra cowboys. Their wives were fruitful, and they raised their own help.

The women's cooking was good and their sympathetic attention was pleasant, if only the youngsters' incessant running and shouting had not seemed to make Hitch's head hurt worse. Rascal took pleasure in watching the children, though. The older ones crowded around him and believed his outrageous lies.

"Hitch," Rascal said, "I hope Kate has a dozen kids. I expect Law'll be happy to do his part." He studied Hitch, frowning. "Did I say somethin' wrong?"

"Been a long day, and maybe I overdone it some. I'm goin' to find me a place to spread my blanket."

Next morning Walt and Ben Matthews suggested they had several days of work on which they needed help and offered standard cowboy wages if Rascal and Hitch would stay. Hitch figured they did it more out of sympathy than need; he declined. Rascal accepted.

"You sure you're able to be by yourself now?" Rascal worried.

"I'm all right."

"The cookin's good over here, and so's the company."

"I want to be home where I can think things out. I got some decisions to make, Rascal."

"You think some more about that combine deal. You'd be a good manager for the Three Cs."

"I'll study on it."

He did not have to give it much study; all he had to do was remember that Fant Gossett and Cato Bramlett each had a part in it. He regarded Gossett as a windbag and opportunist whose integrity was in serious doubt. He had no doubt whatever in regard to Bramlett's integrity.

He took his time going home, riding out some of the breaks in hopes he would find other Two Diamond cattle he had missed. He found one cow mixed with several carrying the Figure 4. One maverick heifer was running with the bunch. He knew within reason that she probably had been weaned by a Figure 4 cow, but there was no way for him or anyone else to prove it.

"One heifer," he said to himself. "They owe me a hundred times that many. But sis, you're a start."

He shook down his rope, touched spurs to Walking Jack and lined her out in a lope. He swung the loop over his head until he had her positioned just to the right and a few feet ahead of the horse. He sent the loop sailing around her half-developed horns and pulled up the slack. He slowed Jack gently, letting her reach the end of the rope without being unnecessarily rough. He flipped a little slack out to let it drop down over and around her rump, then spurred Jack away from her. The effect when he hit the end of the rope was to pull her completely around and flop her on her side hard enough to knock the breath from her momentarily. Hitch stepped down quickly with a short piece of rope, dropped the loop of it around one forefoot, then wrapped that foot and the two hind feet together before she had time to recover and get up.

The exertion was extreme for him, and he paused awhile, panting. When he had his strength again, he walked around and knelt by her head, turning it up and smelling of her breath. "No milk," he said in satisfaction. "Your ol' mammy has cut you off, all right."

To brand a calf that had milk on its breath was foolhardy for a mavericker; if that calf turned up following a cow that wore another brand, it was all the evidence needed to prove theft.

Hitch gathered dry wood from dead brush and built a small fire. Into this fire he dropped a cinch ring from his chaps pocket. Waiting for the ring to heat, he remounted and rode a circle, looking for sign that anyone was around. The fire was too small to create much smoke and draw attention, but there was always a possibility someone might ride by out of coincidence. Seeing no one, he went back. He cut a green switch from a tree and doubled it though the ring to hold it steady. Laboriously he ran his Two Diamond brand onto the heifer's spotted hide, pausing once to reheat the ring. Finished, he stepped back and dropped the ring into the sand, pushing it under with his boot to cool it. The stench of burned hair was strong. He dug out his pocketknife and notched her right ear with his own mark. Then he untied the rope and jerked it from her feet.

"Get up, sis. You belong to me now."

She was more frightened than angry and made no effort to fight him as she arose, hind end first. She trotted toward the other cattle, her hind end wobbling from partial cutoff of circulation while she had lain with her feet tied. Hitch poked his toe in the sand until he brought up the ring and found it cool enough to touch. He dropped it back into his chaps pocket, stomped out the little fire and remounted. He picked out his Two Diamond cow and the newly branded heifer from the others and drove them east, toward the Matthews country where his other remnants had gone.

He watched them trail away into the dusk after he turned them loose. Voice bitter, he said under his breath, "That's just maverick number one, Prosper Selkirk. You and John Torrington owe me a hundred more, and you're goin' to yield them up."

Hitch did not expect finding mavericks to be easy, and it was not. Main purpose of the big ranches' roundups was to brand the calves before they had a chance to become mavericks. Another thing, competition was keen, for many a cowboy left at loose ends by the strike had decided to go into business for himself. Hitch would get up long before daylight of a morning and ride to some distant point where he had not been, then spend most of the day combing the rolling hills and the draws and the creekbottoms for unbranded cattle. Many days he found none; other days he might find one or two. He found fresh brands he had never heard of, things like a Boxed Cross that he knew was probably a rustler brand purposely made out of the Figure 4; an RE connected, the R backward against the E and probably incorporating

Torrington's Snaketrack; an arrowhead, this likewise fashioned out of the Snaketrack.

The boys have been busy, Hitch thought, *and they've been bold.*

Increasingly he saw the CCC, most often in combination with some previous-owner brand, indicating the owner had put his cattle into the pool. But Hitch also found it sometimes on yearlings that carried no other brand; these were mavericks someone had caught and claimed for the combine. If any combine stock had been sold to cowboys still working on the big ranches—which he suspected was the case—it would be particularly easy for these cowboys to put the pool brand on company cattle when no one was looking. That was exactly the kind of thing that had prompted the ranchers to invoke the no-cattle rule against employees. By now they probably were prohibiting any interest in the combine, too, but stock ownership might be hard to prove if a man choose to remain silent about it.

Three weeks of hard riding netted him only nine mavericks. At this rate he would never be even for the cattle they had taken from him, for as time went on the mavericks would be even harder to find; the competition was severe.

One day he came across a scattering of Snaketrack cattle along a creek and gently rode through them. The wagon crew had worked this area within recent weeks, for the calves carried fresh Snaketrack brands to match the ones their mammies had. Not a maverick in the bunch. But Hitch did find a single bull calf following a Figure 4 mother. This calf somehow had escaped both iron and knife; had he not still been following a plainly marked mother, he would be free for the taking.

In his bitterness Hitch considered the various dodges he had heard of for forcing a calf to be weaned. He had known of men burning the calves' noses, making it too painful for them to suck, or of cutting the hoofs to the quick to lame the calf temporarily so it could not follow, then running the mother to hell and gone; or simply shooting the mother and driving the calf away. Hitch discarded such notions out of hand, for these were cruel, and anyway he was not a thief. He had never branded a calf that was not a true maverick.

But damn them, they owe me.

Then came the idea, a hair brand. It was not quite legal, yet it was not really illegal either. This was simply a brand made on the hair but not on the hide. Unless inspected closely, it would be regarded as a regular brand, and a company cowboy was likely to ride on by and give the calf no further attention. But through the long winter months the hair would grow out. By the time the calf was weaned there would be no sign of a brand, and the calf then would be a maverick.

The plan was so simple and easy that Hitch was surprised it had not come to him before. If the cow were a Selkirk, he could put a Figure 4 on her calf's hair; if a Torrington, a Snaketrack. Granted that other maverick men would have as good a chance as he to take that animal next winter or spring, at least he should be able to catch a good share of them. If he worked at it, for every two or three calves he hair-branded, he ought to be able to harvest one maverick later.

Even if caught, he could show that he had broken no law. The brand he placed on the calf would be the same one carried by its mother.

"Torrington . . . Selkirk," he whispered as he shook down his rope, "you'll pay me yet."

Catching the calf was easy, and he dragged it down into the brush where any chance rider was unlikely to see. He flanked the calf by hand and tied it, then gathered wood for a small fire and dropped in the cinch ring. He squatted on his spurs and studied the calf which lay vainly trying to kick. It bawled, and its anxious mother answered.

Ol' John Torrington would bawl too if he knew, Hitch thought. *Him stealing off of me was one thing, but me stealing off of him is something else.*

Stealing. The word did not sit easy. Hitch told himself that what he was doing was not stealing; it was simply recovering the equivalent of what he had lost.

But what he was doing here was the same, in effect, as what he had fired Law McGinty from the W for; he was artificially creating a maverick, knowing full well the brand its mother bore.

I don't know what's so bad about it anymore, he told himself in justification. *Everybody does it; the big take away from the small, and the small take away from the big.*

The cinch ring began to glow. Hitch tried to grip it in a green switch and burned his fingers. He dropped the ring into the dirt and shook his hand. He pushed the ring back into the fire to heat again. This time he got a heavier switch and a good hold. Carefully he ran the brand, burning the hair down to the hide but not marking the hide itself. He backed away a couple of steps to check his work. It looked good.

He castrated the calf and put the Snaketrack mark into its ear, knowing he could replace it later with his own larger one and no one be the wiser.

He stood up and looked at the brand again. Nobody would ever know.

A sobering thought chilled him. *Nobody? I'll know.* This was the first time in his life he had ever stolen anything. *I never thought any man could force me to this.* He tried to shrug off the depression that came over him. *Hell, it's their own fault; they brought it on themselves. I'm only taking back what they stole from me.*

He tried to dismiss the doubts by telling himself there was a good chance someone would beat him to this calf anyway, as soon as it was weaned. The hair brand was no guarantee he would personally profit. But it was virtually guaranteed that Torrington would lose.

He reached for the tie-rope to let the calf up, but he could not bring himself to jerk the knot. He knelt, cursing himself for weakness and indecision. "Aw," he swore finally, "what the hell?" and dropped the cinch ring back into the fire. When it was hot he branded the Snaketrack well into the hide, where it would stay. He let the calf up and hollered "Git!", sending it running. "Git before I change my mind." But it was too late to change his mind.

"No charge, Torrington. But damned if I'll ever do it again."

He mounted Walking Jack, recoiled the rope and started home, hunched in anger at himself.

John Torrington, he thought, *you and Selkirk may break me; you may take away all I've got but one thing, and that's my pride. Be damned if I'll let you turn me into a thief.*

The incident left him in a ill humor for hunting cattle. The coyotes had finally gotten all the chickens but one hen, which relieved him of any worry about eggs. But they hadn't hurt his garden, and it needed tending if he was to eat this winter and not have to spend much from his meager bankroll. The garden work caught up, he went back to building his corrals. True, he had no cattle here now; he could not afford to bring any and risk their being taken into "escrow" like the others. But a man had to show faith in the future.

One day he looked up from digging postholes and was shaken to discover a man sitting on a blue roan horse, silently watching him from perhaps thirty yards. Hitch didn't know how long he had been there; he had been so busy cussing and fussing with rocks in the postholes that he hadn't noticed him riding up. He rubbed his sleeve across his face to stop the sweat from running into his eyes, and he tried to clear those burning eyes long enough to tell who the man was. He was no one Hitch had seen before. Hitch said, "Howdy. Come on over."

It had been a week or ten days since he had seen anyone. He hadn't realized how lonesome it would be out there by himself after working with a cowboy crew for years and having people all around him. He was ready for company. But the man just sat there.

Hitch thought he might not have heard, so he hollered again. The man still sat there staring at him. Though Hitch didn't know him, he became increasingly afraid that he knew the type. "Howdy," he said a third time, without eagerness now.

The sweat was running down his chest and back, the shirt sticking to him, but nevertheless he felt a hard chill. He saw the pistol in the holster at the man's hip, and the sun caught the shiny stock of a saddlegun in a scabbard under his leg. Directly the man touched spurs easily to the roan horse and moved up in what seemed like the slowest walk Hitch had ever seen. Hitch looked at that pistol and that saddlegun, and the thought kept running through his mind that his own saddlegun was in its scabbard in his saddle beneath the shed fifty yards away. He had never owned but one pistol in his life, and he had swapped that a long time ago for a pair of chaps, a good bridle and a saddleblanket. Those were much more practical for his use.

The rider came so near that with one good stride Hitch could have reached out and touched him; he wouldn't have made that stride for a thousand dollars. The man looked down at him with cold eyes the color of steel. His mouth lay flat and hard beneath a gray-salted mustache that curved grimly around its corners. A small badge shone on his shirt pocket. He said, "Whichaone are you?"

"My name is Hugh Hitchcock."

The man nodded. "Hitchcock. I remember. They said you was wagon boss for old Waide, had lots of men workin' under you. You was really somebody come." He looked over the dugout, over the still unfinished brush corrals, then back to Hitch in sweat-crusted old clothes patched and ragged. "The mighty do fall, don't they?"

Dread came to Hitch, dread like he had once felt when he had to enter a house where a man had died of smallpox. "What can I do for you?"

The rider said, "I'm the new deputy sheriff for this county. Name's Lafey Dodge."

The chill came again. Lafey Dodge had been mixed up in that Lincoln County trouble over in New Mexico. Some said he had been a friend of Billy the Kid, some said he had been an enemy. It didn't matter; neither way was any recommendation. It was said he hired out the use of those guns to whoever offered his price. He called himself a shootist, which was a way of saying he was an artist with a gun. He had the reputation of being an undertaker's friend.

His age surprised Hitch a little; he had not expected Lafey Dodge to be a man this old. Dodge appeared to be in his fifties, and a little softness was pushing over his belt. But there was no softness in his eyes.

Hitch said again, "Somethin' I can do for you?"

"You could move out."

Cold sweat was breaking on Hitch's face. "This is my place."

"I know a couple of men who would buy you out. If I was you, I'd be in a notion to sell."

"You meanin' to threaten me?"

The man's expression never changed. "I never threatened nobody. I've never had to. I always been one just to state the facts and let a man make up his own mind whichaway he stands. The facts are that there's some people that don't cotton to a lot of squatters settin' theirselves down on the river."

"I'm no squatter. I got the papers."

"That makes you a higher-class squatter than some, but still a squatter just the same."

Hitch decided if Lafey Dodge intended to kill him now he would already have done it, for the man obviously derived no satisfaction from this talk. Hitch sized him as a cold, methodical man who took no pleasure in taunting or baiting. Whatever he came to do, he would do it without talk and fanfare. Dodge was unlikely to shoot an unarmed man; he had the reputation of staying close enough to the law that he could stay around and spend his money in the same place he had earned it. Hitch said, "We're all squatters in this world, when you look at it that way.

The land belongs to the Lord; we just use it a little while."

"I wouldn't know about that. I just know there's some taxpayin' citizens worried about *this* bunch of squatters. The trouble with a squatter is, he don't generally have much of his own, so he uses that which belongs to the other man. Land, cattle, all of it."

"Has somebody accused me?"

"Can't say as I know. I was just sent here to deliver a message. If they decide they got another message for you, I'll be back."

Afterward Hitch thought of many brave things he could have told Dodge had he had the inclination, which he did not. He could have said he figured the big difference between Selkirk and the little people was that he was a big squatter and they were little ones. If the Figure 4 or John Torrington had had to keep all their cattle confined on the land their papers covered, they would not have amounted to much in the cow business.

But it seemed a waste of time to point this out to Lafey Dodge; he was not looking for that much information. Possession was nine points of the law, and his bunch had all nine.

13

Lafey Dodge would have made an easy target, riding that blue roan horse away in no hurry at all, back turned as if he were trying to tempt Hitch to move toward his rifle. More likely, Hitch decided, he was walking that horse to give Hitch a long time to watch him and contemplate so he would not soon forget him. Dodge need not have troubled himself over that.

Hitch had to finish building those corrals, but now it was a nervous, unpleasant job. Because Dodge had caught him digging postholes the first occasion, each time Hitch went back to it he kept thinking he might look up and see Dodge there again on that big roan. He kept expecting to.

One day he looked up and saw a rider coming, and the breath caught in his throat. But he knew the horse, and he knew the man by the way he rode, shoulders cramped as if they hurt him with every step the horse made.

Charlie Waide.

Charlie was by himself, which didn't particularly surprise Hitch. What surprised him was that Charlie came at all. He hadn't seen the old rancher since he went to deliver the strike notice, and that had been three or four months. Charlie looked older now.

Hitch laid aside the "idiot stick" and raised his hand. "How do, Charlie? Git down."

Charlie dismounted as if it hurt him. The two men shook hands and went through the amenities, but they were awkward about it, like strangers cautiously making themselves known to one another. Charlie asked how everything was, though he could see for himself that prosperity had not found Hitch's address. Particularly he inquired about any aftereffects of the pistol whipping. Hitch asked how Charlie had been, and Charlie told him about all the trouble he had had lately with his arm.

"Come on up to the house, Charlie," Hitch said, "and I'll fix us some coffee." He had gotten in the habit of calling his dugout a house, something he had caught from Kate McGinty. Even yet, it was more camp than home.

Charlie Waide shook his head and dug into his saddlebag for a bottle of whisky. "Coffee don't do much for the pain." He passed the bottle, and Hitch took a shot of it, his first swallow of whisky in a long time. Charlie took a long, long drag like he was trying to find the bottom of the bottle. Then he squatted in the loose earth where Hitch had been digging. He rambled awhile about the fact that Hitch had done a lot to bring the place up, that his fences looked good and square, and that sort of thing. He expressed his regrets over the taking of Hitch's cattle and said there hadn't been a thing he could do.

Hitch said, "Anyway, I thank you for sendin' Joe Sands."

"If anybody ever asks you, it was a hoot-owl whispered in your ear."

Hitch decided Charlie was not here by chance; he had come for a purpose, and he was putting off talking about it as long as he could.

Charlie finally blurted, "Selkirk's got me by the short hair. Been talkin' about callin' in my loan. I reckon if he knowed that I told Joe Sands, he'd of called it already."

Hitch let a long breath go out slowly. "That's too bad."

"He's been mad ever since the strike; says I didn't give him and Torrington enough support. If he calls that note, he'll bust me to a splinter."

"That's rough, Charlie." Hitch wished he had stronger words of comfort, but that was all he could think of to say.

Charlie's eyes were bleak. "Goddamn Yankees . . . they been after me all my life, seems like. Tried to kill me in the war; left me crippled. Been after my hide ever since I come up here and started spreadin' out and lookin' like I might overtake them. Don't seem like they can stand to see a native man pull himself up and amount to somethin'. They'll slap him down ever chance they get."

Hitch knew that was more Charlie's prejudice than fact. John Torrington, for one, was a Texan, born in war and weaned on border troubles that had left him tough as a rawhide boot. But there was no gain in arguing with Charlie Waide. Hitch said, "At least you'd be free of Selkirk then, free from all of them. Whatever you had left would be all yours; they couldn't touch you."

Charlie nodded his gray head, and some of the old spark flickered in his eyes. "That's the consolation; I'd pay them off and then I'd tell them to bend over and kiss my left hind cheek. At least I own a right smart of my own land, and some of them don't. From now on every dollar I lay my hands on, I'll use it to buy land with. One of these days that free-grass bubble will bust, and then we'll see who's who. We'll see how them damnyankees like havin' their faces rubbed in fresh doin's."

The anger and the hate came boiling up. Hitch understood better than ever now that in a way Charlie had gone on fighting the war long after it had ended, and he seemed to think everyone else was fighting it too. He had kept trying to prove that even in military defeat he was still much of a man. He was trying in his off-center way to make up for the wound that had crippled him, to keep hurling defiance into the faces of old enemies who had long since forgotten the fight.

Charlie's voice was gritty. "By God, I'll whip them yet before I die."

Hitch managed a smile. "Charlie Waide, you'll never die. You'll just turn into an old gray mule and kick some *young* man to death."

That seemed to please Charlie; he eased a little. Presently Hitch told him, "They're a long ways from bein' whipped yet. They sent me a visitor the other day." He told about Lafey Dodge.

The news was no surprise to Charlie. "I swear to you, Hitch, I been no party to that. Old John Torrington was the one who wanted to hire professionals and break up the strike by force, only him and Selkirk wanted to make an assessment against all us ranchers to pay for the guns. I told them hell no, and some of the other ranchers done the same. Way I heard it,

Torrington and Selkirk wound up havin' to pay for Lafey Dodge all by themselves. You know Selkirk; he got the sheriff to deputize Dodge so the county has to carry part of the load." Charlie poked aimlessly in the dirt. "You'll want to be careful of him, Hitch; he's a bad one."

Hitch said he had no intention of stirring Dodge up.

"If ever he comes after you," Charlie said, "don't be foolish and give him a chance. Take every advantage. Kill him any way you can."

He kept scratching in the dirt, and Hitch noticed he had made a Figure 4 brand, then altered it into a McGinty LR. Charlie said, "Ain't really you I'm so concerned about, Hitch. I feel like you'll take care of yourself the way you always took care of me. But I *am* worried about Law and Rascal McGinty." He looked off toward the McGinty claim, away yonder and out of sight. "You ever see them?"

"Sometimes."

Charlie frowned deeply. "I wisht you'd go talk to them. They wouldn't listen to me, I'm afraid. I try not to remember what Law done; I try to remember the good cowboy he used to be. I'm worried about him, Hitch. He's puttin' himself in shape to get killed."

Hitch stared.

Charlie asked, "Hitch, you bought any interest in that Three Cs outfit?" When Hitch said he hadn't, Charlie said, "That's good. But Law is in it up to his neck. Somethin' bad has got into that boy to make him throw in with the likes of Cato Bramlett. Law's been runnin' Figure 4 cattle down into the breaks and changin' them over to the LR. Been changin' the Snaketrack into one of them other pool brands."

Hitch shook his head, hoping Charlie wouldn't see that he already knew.

"He don't know it, Hitch, but Law's been watched. Remember, what John Torrington said about catchin' somebody and makin' an example of him? They got Law McGinty's name wrote at the top of their list. They're watchin' him, and sure as a spotted calf follows a spotted cow, they'll spring the trap on him. Then you'll know what they hired Lafey Dodge for."

Hitch sat on his heels, staring at Charlie's cattle brands in the sand. His hands were wet with cold sweat, but his mouth was dry.

Charlie said, "Maybe Rascal knows, maybe he don't. I don't believe he'd be a party to it, but he might know and not stop it. If he's around when they come for Law, they're liable to kill him for bein' in the way."

"I doubt Law would listen to me."

"Talk to Rascal then, if you got any feelin' for them boys and for that little girl over there. Make Rascal bend a gunbarrel over Law's head if he has to, but stop him. Them people want blood."

Charlie started to go, but he kept hanging back, wanting to say something more. "Worst day I've had since the war was the day you boys all up and left my wagon. Hitch, we still friends?"

The need for friendship was heavy in his eyes. Hitch said, "We'll always be friends, Charlie."

But somehow he knew it would never again be the same.

Hitch found Law and Rascal shoeing horses behind their shed. He didn't see Kate. She evidently hadn't been aware of his coming, and he was glad for that. She would ask the reason for his visit; he didn't want to lie to her.

The McGintys said they would finish the job in a few minutes and go "up to the house" for a drink. Hitch said, "I'm not here for social reasons. I got somethin' you-all need to hear."

They studied him curiously; the deadly seriousness of the matter must have shown in his face. Rascal said, "If it's Lafey Dodge you're talkin' about, we already seen him. He scared Kate half to death."

That, Hitch thought, was probably part of the strategy. Get a man's woman scared enough and the man was likely to leave. "Ain't Dodge I come about, at least not altogether." He didn't know how to phrase it gently, so he just threw it out there like a loaded gun. "Law, they all know you been swingin' the wide loop."

Color rushed into Law's face. "What you been tellin'?"

"I ain't told anybody nothin'." He recounted what Charlie Waide had passed on to him. Law appeared more angered than worried, but Rascal's face seemed to turn gray.

Law said, "If you're spreadin' stories, Hitch, you ain't no friend of mine."

"I came here because I *am* a friend."

Law's voice was angry. "Like hell you are. You better go!"

Rascal McGinty turned savagely on his brother. "Damn you, Law, shut your mouth and listen to somebody for once in your life!" He so startled Law that the younger McGinty rocked back on his heels, silent. Rascal said tightly, "Hitch, we're doin' all right; we don't have to steal . . . not from nobody. I got a little outside work with some of these little ranchers now and again, and if we're careful on what we spend we'll make it through. We don't have to steal."

Hitch had the feeling Rascal was talking more to his brother. Hitch didn't have to ask outright; he could read it in Rascal's eyes that he knew Law was guilty. Hitch said, "What you're doin' ain't necessary, Law. You got a start here, you and Rascal. Keep all your heifer calves and you'll be surprised how soon you'll have a herd as big as Charlie Waide came to this country with. You got no need to throw in with the likes of Cato Bramlett. This other way is slower, but it'll get you there."

"When?" Law demanded. "When I'm an old man with a beard down to my navel? I ain't waitin', Hitch. They owe us for what all they've done, and they'll pay. The Three Cs is goin' to have forty-fifty thousand cattle before I'm done. They'll wish they'd never tried to mess with Law McGinty. You can cringe and bow if you want to, but I'm standin' up and spittin' right in their coffee."

"In their eyes you're a thief."

"And in your eyes too, I suppose?" Law seemed to answer that question for himself. "I told you already, you better go."

Hitch wasn't ready. "Don't underestimate them, Law. They mean business; that's why they hired Lafey Dodge. You got a wife to be thinkin' about, and a baby."

Law flared, "I'll take care of my wife; I don't need you to help me. Seems to me like you been more concerned about her than you got any business bein'."

Rascal exclaimed, "Law!"

"It's the damned truth," Law said bitterly. "He wanted her himself, only I beat him to her. He knows he can't ever have her and it eats at him. Don't believe me? Look at his face."

In the moment before he turned away, Hitch knew his eyes betrayed him.

Rascal said reproachfully, "Law, Hitch come to help you."

"By makin' me out a thief? If you believe him, why don't you just go on along with him?"

Rascal's face was splotched, and for a moment it appeared he might strike his brother. "Hitch tells the truth, Law. I've known it a long time. Now, I believe I *will* go with him."

Hitch heard a sound, a tiny whimper. Turning, he saw Kate McGinty. The baby in her arms was making some soft noise, but Kate made no sound at all. She stared, eyes wide with hurt and surprise.

Hitch's mouth dropped open. He wondered how much she had heard.

She tried to speak, and her voice broke. Tears shining, she tried to say, "I was . . . goin' to ask you-all . . . up to the house . . ." She broke off and hurried back to the dugout, crying.

Rascal silently riding beside him, Hitch left there feeling like a whipped dog.

Rascal didn't stay long; he found another short-term job at the Matthews place. Hitch bided his time, living out of the garden and off of stray beef, the custom of the country. He spent most of his days riding the Canadian River country in an almost futile search for mavericks.

The green grass made its seedheads and stood gold against the summer sun, then began to cure with all the strength that once made it the great buffalo range it had been for uncounted generations of Indian hunters, and the cow range it had lately become. The hot wind was always there, searching a man out wherever he went. It came sometimes like a friend and sometimes like it sought to punish, but always it came.

And one day as it came it brought the sound of running horses and turning wheels. Even before Hitch went to look, he thought he knew. He had sensed the inevitability of it that day Charlie Waide had talked to him.

Kate McGinty drove the wagon as if she were trying to wreck it. Her baby was tied in her lap so both her hands were free for the lines. She shouted at the lathered team, and as she rolled into Hitch's camp she was screaming.

"They're killin' him, Hitch! They're killin' him! Help me, Hitch, for God's sake help me!"

The team had stopped by the corrals, bellies heaving, their mouths open and their nostrils flared. Kate's face was flushed red. Even as she blurted the story, Hitch was throwing the saddle on Walking Jack.

"They came to get him, Hitch. They let me and the baby go, but they cornered Law in the dugout. He's trapped."

"Where's Rascal at?"

"Gone on a job. You're the only one can help us."

"How many are they?"

"Seven or eight."

Hitch considered the odds and felt a chill. "They didn't hurt you none, Kate?"

She shook her head. "Please do somethin' to help Law. He can't stand against them long."

Hitch pointed east. "You know where Dan Truman's place is, and the Matthews outfit just past it?" She did, and he told her to go get Dan, get the Matthews men. "Get anybody else in reach!"

He spurred Walking Jack into the hardest lope the horse had struck in a long time. As he looked back he saw Kate slapping the lines at the team, driving them into a run again. She would likely kill them, or run them into the ground.

Hitch pushed the horse as hard as he dared, the hot wind burning his face. Seven or eight men, and one of them certainly Lafey Dodge.

What in the world will I do when I get there? he asked himself urgently, and he came up with no answer, no earthly idea. All he could do was keep urging Walking Jack with the spurs.

A sick feeling washed in his stomach; he had a fear that whatever he did, he would be too late, and he dreaded what he would find when he got there. He tried to think of something he could do, but he had no more plan when he neared the McGinty place than when he had left his own.

He saw a lone horseman moving west, slumped in the saddle. The rider spotted Hitch but kept his horse in a trot. Angling toward him, Hitch recognized the sheriff. The lawman appeared badly shaken. He started trying to wave Hitch back, but Hitch stayed on course and pulled Jack to a halt in the dry grass.

The sheriff said, "Hitchcock, go back to where you come from."

"What's happened?"

"I had me a prisoner. They took him. Don't go over there, Hitchcock. It'll already be too late."

"Law McGinty?" Hitch demanded, though he knew before he asked.

"I tried to arrest him and he got into his dugout. His wife and baby come out and then we tried to smoke him loose. Finally we brought the dugout down around him and drug him into the open. Then they taken him away from me, Dodge and them others."

"You mean you *let* them have him!" Hitch shouted. "What kind of a sheriff are you?"

"I'm an ex-sheriff, that's what kind I am."

"You're not a sheriff and never was. You're a coward."

"There's worse things than bein' a coward; there's bein' dead. When I taken this job they told me there wouldn't be nothin' to it; just a drunk cowpuncher now and then was all. They don't pay me enough to fight Lafey Dodge. If you're smart, Hitchcock, you'll wait a while before you go down there. Don't go amongst them while their blood is hot or they might do it to you, too."

Hitch stood in his stirrups, wanting to strike the man with all the strength that was in him. "If they've done what you say they have, I'll be in to see you, Sheriff."

"You better be quick about it. Soon's I can get my plunder together there won't be nothin' left but an empty office."

Hitch still had no idea what he was going to do, except keep riding. He spurred Jack into a hard run over the hill and down to the McGinty place, a cold knot drawn tight in his stomach.

He found what the sheriff had told him he would. The dugout lay in ruins, two ropes still looped around the center pole to pull it down. The dog had been killed. A milk cow lay dead in a corral gate, struck by a stray bullet. Hitch saw no men, but he quickly found the tracks of the horses. They led down to the river, where the trees were.

14

Hitch had no plan; he wasn't even thinking ahead now. He simply gave full rein to a cold rage that took over. He pulled his saddlegun out of its scabbard and rode in a walk. He saw the men clustered in the timber on the river, a couple on horseback, the rest afoot.

Hitch cocked the hammer back and kept riding. The tall cottonwoods swayed and threshed in noisy struggle against the high north wind. The men stared in morbid fascination at the result of their work and did not notice his approach. Lafey Dodge was the one Hitch watched closest; he stood on the ground. Old John Torrington, in the saddle, looked up at Law in satisfaction; this was not his first hanging. Slant Unger was also a-horseback and equally unmoved; whatever suited John Torrington was always all right with him.

But on the ground Prosper Selkirk was drawn up tightly, probably even trembling. It surprised Hitch that the man was here at all. Two Selkirk cowboys stood back to themselves as if ashamed. Tobe Ferris, Torrington's Negro cowboy, was the only man not looking up at Law. He stared at the ground; he might have been silently praying.

Ferris caught Hitch's movement from the tail of his eye and turned quickly. Hitch was almost close enough to have struck him with the gunbarrel. The other men turned then in surprise. Hitch was too choked to tell them to raise their hands. He motioned with the muzzle of the rifle, and they easily got his meaning. He held the saddlegun on the ready; in his rage it was all he could do to keep from picking one of them and shooting him. He glanced up and felt sickness come over him. He forced his eyes away from Law.

Lafey Dodge did not speak; he stared at that saddlegun. Prosper Selkirk was pale. John Torrington glared at Hitch with more impatience than fear. "This man was a thief," he growled.

Hitch's mind was afire with things to say, but he could not say them. He motioned the gunbarrel toward Unger, who was nearest the body. "Cut him down!"

Unger did not move. Torrington glanced at the hired gunfighter. "Do somethin', Dodge."

Dodge shook his head, not for a moment taking his eyes off the rifle.

Torrington growled, "Dammit, what do you think we're payin' you for? He don't know how to use that thing. He's nothin' but a cowboy."

Dodge said evenly, "That's the most dangerous thing there is, a mad cowboy with a gun in his hands. He'll kill somebody sure as hell."

Slant Unger said, "I ain't afraid of him," and spurred toward Hitch.

In cold rage Hitch shot him out of the saddle. He levered another cartridge into the chamber.

Unger writhed on the ground, clawing at a shattered arm. Dodge glanced down at him, then up at Torrington. "Goddammit, old man, I told you."

Hitch said to John Torrington, "*You* cut him down!"

Torrington looked at the smoking rifle and with care not to let his hand come anywhere near his gun, he fished a knife from his pocket. He cut the rope, and two men on the ground caught Law and laid him out on the grass.

The fallen Slant Unger began moaning. The sight of the blood brought Hitch to a realization of what he had done, and the bad position he was in. If Lafey Dodge was all his reputation implied, he could probably draw his pistol and kill Hitch any time he wanted to. Hitch's chance of bringing that saddlegun up to his shoulder and taking aim against a fast-draw man was not the kind a good gambler would bet his poke on. Hitch had shot point-blank at Unger without consciously trying. That he had even hit him in the arm was probably an accident.

But Lafey Dodge just stared at that saddlegun and gave it full respect. Gradually Hitch came to a conclusion that surprised him a little: at this moment, Lafey Dodge was afraid of him. He wondered if the man's reputation as a shootist might not be somewhat exaggerated.

Old Torrington's face was ablaze. "We're a legal posse, duly sworn."

"You ain't no court," Hitch told him. "You lynched a man without a trial. That makes every man here a murderer!"

Hitch watched all the men, but he continued to

watch Lafey Dodge most. John Torrington had been a hellion in his day but was too old now to do much real fighting for himself. Prosper Selkirk's being here didn't seem to fit; best Hitch could figure, his and Torrington's presence was meant to make it clear that the big ranches' full weight was behind this. The other men were simply cowboys . . . two Selkirks, three Torringtons. Hitch knew them every one.

Dread was cold in his stomach as he faced the eight men. It was like having a wildcat by the tail and being unable to turn loose. If all suddenly came at him, he might have time to shoot one, but he would certainly go down.

They were not going to rush him, though. He saw in every face what he had seen in Dodge's. As a mob hanging a helpless man they were one thing, but facing a gun they were eight uneasy individuals, each pondering the awful possibility that he might personally be the next shot down.

Hitch had a strong feeling he was about to throw up. If he did, he wouldn't want these men able to take advantage of his helplessness. He motioned with the saddlegun. "One at a time, you-all drop your guns."

They did, until the turn reached Lafey Dodge. Hitch said, "Not you, Dodge. You keep yours." The men looked at him in surprise, but Hitch was afraid to let Dodge touch a gun, even to shed it.

"What you fixin' to do with them guns?" Tobe Ferris asked cautiously.

"I'll throw them in the river."

"Mine cost me better than two months' wages."

"Spend the next two months thinkin' about the man you killed here. Now all of you, get on them horses and move out."

He held the saddlegun aimed at them until they

rode over the hill, Ferris and another man supporting Slant Unger. Hitch had seen a couple of saddleguns and wished he had made them leave those, but he had been afraid a man could pull a horse around to cover himself and bring a rifle into play. He had left well enough alone.

He considered the possibility that someone might circle back and try to pick him off. Gradually he decided they would not come back. They had done what they came to do. He slumped. Throat tight, eyes afire, he looked down at the cowboy he had known for most of ten years. "Law," he whispered half accusingly, "you never would listen to a man, would you?" He noticed for the first time that Law's britches were wet. He realized with sudden force what terrible fear the cowboy must have suffered in those last moments.

"Goddamn them!" Hitch cried. "Goddamn them all!"

It was more than an hour before Dan Truman got there. He took a long look at the collapsed dugout, then rode over to Hitch, standing beside the saddleshed. His face showed that he knew. "I'm too late."

Hitch nodded. "We're all too late." Dan dismounted. Hitch led him into the shed and motioned toward the corner where he had carried Law out of the sun, covering him with a tarp he had found there.

Awhile later the Matthews men loped in. Far behind them came Kate McGinty's wagon with a fresh team. Mrs. Walt Matthews was driving so Kate could hold the baby. As the wagon stopped, Hitch strode out to meet it. Kate McGinty sat looking at him, her face grave. In her eyes he saw that he didn't have to tell her anything. She slowly handed the baby to Mrs.

Matthews. Hitch raised his hands to help Kate climb down. She leaned into his arms and sobbed quietly. He held her, helpless to speak. He knew not a word that could change a thing.

Finally she asked, "Where is he?"

Hitch motioned toward the shed. Kate reached up and took the baby from Mrs. Matthews. She started to go into the shed but stopped and looked back at the ruins of the dugout she had so carefully kept. Hitch helped Mrs. Matthews to climb down, and together the women went into the shed.

The men remained outside, silent and grim. At length Dan Truman asked, "What we goin' to do about this, Hitch?"

Hitch was a long time in attempting a reply. "What they done was murder in the eyes of the law."

"Anywhere else, but not here. So what do we do now?"

Hitch shrugged. "I don't know. We'll do somethin'."

Later, when Kate was composed, Hitch suggested they could probably all work together and raise the dugout's center pole so that it could be repaired and made livable again. Kate shook her head. "Thanks, but no. If we can rescue some things out of there that we need, that'll be enough. I couldn't stay on this place again."

Hitch thought he knew her feelings. There would be Rascal's dugout for a night or two, if she needed it. After that she would probably go stay with her mother. He said, "First thing we have to do is put Law decently away. Do you want us to take him to town?"

Again she shook her head. "And bury him in Boothill? No, Hitch, this is his place; I want him buried on his own land."

"All right. I'll go to town and find a minister, and get your mother. While I'm there I'll see what I can do to have justice done."

She reached out and touched his hand. "Don't get in any trouble."

Dan Truman said, "I'll go with you, Hitch. You ain't goin' there all by yourself."

They rode straight to the sheriff's office. Hitch had little hope of getting satisfaction there, but he would try. He stepped through the door and stopped short. In a rawhide chair, feet propped up on a desk, sat Lafey Dodge, the silver deputy badge catching light from the window. He held a pistol in his lap, and a cleaning rag. But Hitch suspected the rag was only to give him some apparent reason to have the pistol out. Every chamber was probably loaded.

Dodge said coldly, "Figured you'd be in."

Hitch's stomach drew up, much as when he had faced Dodge and the other men earlier. His saddlegun was out yonder on the horse, a safe place for it, beyond temptation. "Where's the sheriff at?"

"I gather there ain't no sheriff. Wrote out his resignation and left town. Want to read it?" Dodge paused. "Suddenly decided town life was bad for his health, which looks to me like a good idea for some others. Town's hard on a boy who's used to the good clean country air. Feller like you, out of the country, ought to come to town as little as he possibly can. *Never*, if he can help it."

Dan Truman demanded, "You takin' over the sheriff's office?"

"Reckon there ain't nobody else to do it. They'll have to call a special election to fill the vacancy. Looks like I'm all the law they got till then. Hope you boys don't figure on makin' no disturbance."

Defeated, Hitch went to Kate McGinty's mother. Her reaction was a bitter mixture of condemnation for "that wild boy" and sympathy for "that poor little helpless girl of mine." Hitch told her he would borrow a buggy from Edson Biggs, or perhaps Biggs would take her out there himself.

At the small adobe building in which Edson had set up his new banking business, Hitch reviewed what had happened. Depressed, Dan Truman stood in the open doorway, leaning against the jamb and smoking cigarettes as he watched the sparse foot and horse traffic moving up and down the dusty street. Edson said with sadness, "Law didn't have to steal. I told him and Rascal if they wanted to borrow some money to buy cows, I could get it for them. But Law thought he could get big faster through the Three Cs. Maybe he figured that way he didn't have to pay anybody back."

"He paid." Hitch held silent a while, his throat too tight for talk. Presently he said, "We got to have a preacher. I never been much to go to church, but I was hopin' you'd know one."

"Sure, Hitch. First thing a banker does in a new town is to join the church."

Dan Truman came erect and threw his cigarette out into the street. "Hitch, it's Rascal!"

Hitch jumped to his feet. "My God! Where?"

"Headin' for the sheriff's office hard as he can go."

Hitch passed Dan Truman on the plank porch and hit the street running. "Rascal!" he shouted. "Rascal, wait!"

If Rascal heard him he gave no sign. He reined in at the front of the sheriff's office and dismounted. Even at the distance Hitch could see the pistol in his hand. "Rascal!"

He lost a stride, expecting gunfire, expecting to see Rascal stagger back out that open door. But there was nothing. Rascal strode out again, the pistol still in his hand. By now Hitch was almost up to him.

Bitter tears flowed down the red face. "Where's he at, Hitch? I'm fixin' to kill him!"

Lafey Dodge had left the sheriff's office. But it wouldn't take Rascal long to find him in this town.

Breathing hard, Hitch could barely speak. "Rascal . . . wait up. We got . . . to talk to you."

Rascal shouted, "You seen him, Hitch?"

Hitch held off answering until he had most of his breath. "You're no match for him. He'll kill you."

"Not if I get the first shot."

Hitch saw there was no hope of arguing Rascal down; he had gone into a fury that would stop for nothing except blood. Hitch grabbed the pistol and gave it a sudden wrench. Caught by surprise, Rascal reacted to the pain by loosening his hold. Remembering what Slant Unger had done, Hitch jerked the pistol from Rascal's hand, brought it up and fetched Rascal a hard blow on the side of the head. Even through the felt hat, it was severe enough to send Rascal to his knees.

I *fractured his skull*, Hitch thought for a moment, then decided he hadn't. He grabbed the cowboy to keep him from dropping on his face. Dan Truman caught Rascal's left arm. Edson Biggs came running, not far behind. He said, "He'll be sore at you, Hitch, but he'll be alive."

They lifted the half-conscious Rascal onto his horse, and they had to hold him on till they got him to Biggs's bank. There they cleansed the wound with whisky. Rascal would have to go back to the ranch in the buggy with Biggs and Kate's mother.

* * *

Hitch did not expect to see many people at the funeral. He assumed that most would take Law's death as a general warning and would want to avoid displeasing the powers responsible. The crowd surprised him, families arriving in wagons and buggies, single men a-horseback. Before time for the service he estimated between seventy-five and a hundred horses tied around the dugouts and down by the river.

Biggest surprise, perhaps, was the quiet arrival of Charlie Waide and many of the W cowboys. Some of the river settlers and veterans of the strike edged back uneasily to give them room. Charlie Waide stood by his horse until he picked Hitch from the crowd, then handed the reins to a cowboy and walked to meet Hitch. His eyes were bleak.

"I come to pay my respects to Kate."

Hitch pointed his chin toward Rascal's dugout. "She's in there, Charlie. I'll take you to see her."

Charlie hesitated at the steps that led down to the door. "I'd sooner take a whippin'." But he came on. The canvas flap had been laid open, and Hitch let Charlie go in ahead of him. Kate McGinty sat in a rawhide chair, her mother and some of the neighbor women clustered in painful silence around her. Charlie crushed his hat in his hands, plainly afraid of the reception. "Kate . . ."

"Mister Waide," she said in little more than a whisper. "I didn't expect to see you."

"Took me a while to get the nerve to come. Kate, I want you to know . . . I didn't have nothing' to do with what happened. Done all I could to stop it."

She nodded. "I knew that all the time. I'm grateful to you for comin'."

"Kate, if there's anything you need, anything at all . . ."

"What I need, there's no way to bring back. But I'll always remember that you asked."

Charlie turned to leave, avoiding Hitch's eyes. Kate said, "Mister Waide, one thing I want you to know. Law always respected you. Even after he left the Ws, he never had a bad word to say about you."

Charlie didn't look back. He went up the steps. Hitch followed him. Charlie walked a short way from the dugout, then turned to look back. "Hitch, I meant what I told her. If she needs the borrow of any money . . ."

"Sure, Charlie. But it seems to me like there's somethin' else that's badly needed here. What're we goin' to do about them that killed Law?"

Charlie clenched his fist. "You got to remember, Hitch, he was stealin' cattle."

"A man goes to jail for stealin' cattle: he don't get hung."

Charlie looked Hitch in the eyes, a warning in his voice. "You had judgment enough to know when the strike was over. I hope you still know when to turn aloose of somethin' you got no chance to win."

When the time came, Hitch and the other pallbearers carried the pine coffin out of the shed and up the slope to a place Kate had picked. There were Dan Truman, Edson Biggs, the Matthews men, the ever-complaining Asher Cottingham. The minister followed, Bible in hand as he walked beside the black-veiled Kate. She carried the baby in her arms. Behind them walked a solemn procession of people many of whom could not possibly have known Law McGinty but whose presence could be taken as silent protest against the manner of his dying. That the message would quickly reach Torrington and Selkirk, Hitch had no doubt. There were many people here whom he did not know; certainly among them must be someone who would report to the ranchers.

They set the coffin on the ground and waited for the crowd to work around in a circle. The minister bowed his head for a prayer, then raised his chin. He looked at the people.

"It is always painful for me to perform a service like this for one so young, for one whose life should have spanned far more years, who should have been allowed to live to see his children grow to manhood, who should have lived to see the seeds of his labor bear fruit and yield their harvest to him. It is always tragic to see a life cut down just as it has come to flower.

"But there is an element of even more tragedy here, for this man was not swept away by some illness over which no man had control, nor was he victim to some accident which no man could have avoided. No, he was willfully put to his death by plan, by men who assumed unto themselves a power which the Scriptures plainly reserve to God alone. Had Lawton McGinty died of illness, or of some accident, we could have consoled ourselves that God's will was somehow served. But the act of murder is contrary to the will of God. Therefore as we weep today we weep in double anguish, for this death should not have been. This fine young woman should not be dressed in mourning clothes, and this baby should not have lost a father it will never be able to remember.

"So we come here today to mourn for Lawton McGinty, but let us do more than simply mourn. Let us pledge ourselves to seek some way of assuring that no other widow shall be left mourning in this manner, no other child left fatherless. There was a time, perhaps, when we could have shrugged our shoulders and said this was simply a thing that should be expected on the raw frontier, that harsh conditions somehow justify harsh actions. But my friends, the frontier is gone. We are a civilized people now, with laws and courts and established methods of justice. There are still some among us who live by the old ways, and this is a shame upon us as much as upon them, for we do not have to allow it. We must rise up in righteous anger and declare to them that this shall not happen again, that we shall not be silent nor stand fearful in the presence of their power. We must show them that we have come into a new time, that we intend to see this land pleasing to the sight of the Lord, and bountiful in His service. We need not bow to anyone but God."

The hymns started then, and it seemed to Hitch they would never stop. He did not know the words to most of them, even if he could have brought himself to sing. He watched Kate and wished for her sake that the service were over. The baby cried much of the time, and Kate cradled it tightly to her bosom. Perhaps, Hitch thought, it was a blessing the baby gave her concern, for it kept her distracted and did not let her dwell entirely upon her grief.

Finally the last amen had been said, and the coffin was lowered slowly by rope. Friends filed by and dropped a little sand into the grave. People moved back down the slope without the order they had shown on the way up. A few women repaired with Kate into the dugout, and many of the people left. But many stayed, talking among themselves. They still simmered in the quiet anger roused by the minister's words.

Charlie Waide acted for a moment as if he wanted to say something to Rascal and Hitch, but the words wouldn't come. Hitch asked, "Charlie, did you listen to what he said?"

Charlie frowned. "He's just a preacher, Hitch. A preacher don't have to answer for anything." Charlie climbed stiffly onto his horse, his cowboys trailing after him. Some of the other men gathered in awkward silence around the saddleshed, staring at each other, staring at the ruins of Law and Kate McGinty's dugout.

Rascal wore a bandage around his head, as Hitch had done a few weeks earlier. He had withdrawn into himself and had spoken little, seeming like some wild creature wounded and bewildered and seeking solitary retreat in his misery. Now suddenly he let the grief begin to spill out in talk. He spoke to no one in particular, unless possibly to himself.

"Pa died first, and then Ma, and then it was just me and Law. He was a little dickens then, ten-eleven years old, and me just a button myself to look after him and try to raise him. Law would tag along behind me like a colt followin' after a grown horse, only I wasn't grown either. We wandered around a long time before we found us a place with ol' Charlie. Seemed like there was always a little hell in Law. It ain't like he meant no harm by it, though; he was always just funnin'. There never was no real harm in that button, just a little more than his fair share of hell, was all." Rascal's fists clenched, and he cried out in a pain that was close to tears. "They could at least of shot him instead of hangin' him thataway; that's no fit way for a man to die. Even a cow-killin' wolf is given that much of a show."

He looked around bitterly. "And where's the people at that got him into this mess in the first place? Where's Fant Gossett? Where's Cato Bramlett?"

Asher Cottingham spat. "Fant couldn't afford to shut down business. You know how it is with a rich fat man. Cato Bramlett slipped out of town in the night, headin' west. Figured he was likely to be next."

Rascal cursed Gossett and he cursed Bramlett. The men listened, letting him work off the grief by talking. When Rascal was done they looked at each other uncomfortably. Rascal finally walked out to be alone awhile. Edson Biggs's eyes followed him. Sorrowfully shaking his head, Edson said, "Law was born twenty years too late."

Hitch asked what he meant by that.

"I mean that Law had a lot more in common with John Torrington and Prosper Selkirk than he ever realized. Old man Torrington, he's greedy after land. Selkirk is greedy after money. Law was greedy after cattle: he couldn't get them together fast enough. If he'd been here twenty years sooner, when all a man needed was a fast horse and a long loop, he'd have been as big today as John Torrington. And probably just as mean."

Rascal McGinty came back presently, subdued. All eyes went to him in silent sympathy. Dan Truman cursed under his breath and said, "Men, we got to do somethin'."

Hitch hunkered, eyes on the grieving Rascal McGinty. He had nothing to offer.

At length Edson Biggs spoke. "I've given this thing a lot of study, and I've got an idea. It's not a total answer, but it's a start. This county doesn't have a sheriff now; it has to call an election. The big ranchers'll hand-pick themselves a man. I doubt they'll go so far as to put up Lafey Dodge: his reputation would stir suspicion as far away as Austin. But they'll choose a man they can control."

A small rancher said, "That leaves us no better off than we've been."

"I said *election*, and an election is supposed to have more than one candidate. Why don't we put up a man of our own to run?"

Several men spoke at once with reasons that occurred to them on the spur of the moment. Edson let them speak their piece, then said, "I think the strike brought changes in this country that you-all haven't realized yet: I don't believe the big ranchers have, either. Most of the men who went on strike had always voted however the ranchers wanted them to. A lot of those men are still here in the county, and thinking for themselves now. Give them a man to vote for and I think they'll hand these ranchers a surprise."

Hitch wished he had thought of that himself. The idea stirred him. The longer he mulled it over, the better he liked it. "You sayin' you'll run, Edson?"

Edson Biggs demurred. "Not me; I'm not the man for it. But I know a man who's been here a long time and won respect for a clear head and leadership. I believe if we put his name on the ballot he'll stand a good chance." Edson paused, looking at Hugh Hitchcock. "I'm talking about *you*, Hitch."

Hitch's mouth dropped open. "Edson, you've lost saddle, blanket and all."

"I don't think so. The sheriff idea came to me first, then I started trying to think of the men who would qualify. I kept coming back to the same one."

Hitch saw that hope had stirred among the other men. Dan Truman spat an oath that would curl mesquite bark. "He's right, Hitch. You're the one can do it."

Hitch swallowed, thinking of all the reasons he didn't want the job, and there were plenty of them. He pointed out that he had his place to worry about and work on, that he had never carried a gun in his life, except the one on his saddle. "What if I had to shoot somebody? I've never even shot *at* a man except a couple of Indians, and I never done *them* any harm."

Edson said, "There's already one too many *gun*-men in this country. We want a man."

"Find somebody beside me."

Edson kept pressing him. "We need a man who'll stand up for the plain people and put a stop to the oppression we've had here. The only way to do anything about what happened to Law McGinty will be to get a sheriff who represents our way of thinking and not that of a few big outfits. Longer this thing goes on, the more chance somebody else will be killed."

Hitch said, "I'm no fair opposition to Lafey Dodge."

Dan Truman declared, "You won't have to face him by yourself. Comes time, there'll be lots of men behind you."

Hitch had reservations about that, remembering the strike.

Edson argued that Hitch could use the sheriff's salary to buy land and cattle and fix the place to his liking.

At length Rascal McGinty spoke, and everyone else stopped talking. "Hitch, you listen to Edson; he's right. And remember you promised me that somethin' would be done about Lafey Dodge and them. It won't be unless you see to it that we have fair law in this county. I'm askin' you as a friend, Hitch. Run!" He pointed his finger. "One more thing: if you win you'll need a deputy. I want to be him. I got a sore head that says you owe me that."

Even as Hitch argued, he knew they would pin him against the wall.

The minister said, "Mister Hitchcock, I'll pray for you."

Hitch said, "You'd damn well better."

15

Filing for sheriff required more paper-signing, it seemed to Hitch, than he had put into filing for his land. He couldn't put aside the nagging concern that he was making a mistake. He told Edson Biggs, "I never realized how much work a candidate does before he gets in office."

Biggs nodded. "More, like as not, than after he gets in office."

"I got a lot to learn. What I know about politics I could write on my hatband."

"Nothing to it," the banker smiled. "You just have to get more votes than the other man."

"Sounds easy."

"Just have to get out and see the people, that's most of it. Those who don't know you have to be given an opportunity to see you have an honest face. I'll go with you as much as I can and help you electioneer. When you have a banker with you everybody will give you a hearing. Some of them are borrowing from my bank and the others know they may someday want to."

When the legal necessities had been attended to, Edson suggested that he and Hitch have a drink to seal the commitment and bring good luck. Hitch observed that the drink would have done him more good *before*, but it was never too late. They walked into the Buffalo Bar, which charged more than Fant Gossett but carried a better grade of sipping whisky. Edson raised his hand in greeting to the saloonkeeper. "Tending bar yourself, Luke?"

Lanky, sad-faced Luke Gannaway wiped a damp cloth across the mahogany, then set up a bottle and two glasses. "Way business has fell off since the strike, I can't hire much help."

Edson said, "I'll buy *you* a drink too, Luke. We're celebrating a new candidate for sheriff."

Luke looked around as if to see who might be listening, but the three had the place to themselves. "Got him all signed up, did you?"

Edson nodded. Luke said, "Then I'll buy the drinks, and I'll join you."

That surprised Hitch a little, for the big ranch-cowboy trade was the backbone of Luke Gannaway's business. Luke poured the glasses full and raised one in salute. "Whup them good, Hitch."

When the glasses were empty, Edson poured them full again. "This is my round."

Gannaway's eyes narrowed in concentration on Hitch. "You really figure you got a chance, any chance atall?"

Hitch shrugged. "I don't know enough about . . ."

Edson put in, "He'll win it if enough straight-thinking people decide we've had all the big-man rule we need around here. There's a new day coming, and we'll do all we can to rush it along."

"Three months ago," Luke declared, "I'd of said you're crazy. I'll still say I don't think you got a Chinaman's chance, but I'm tickled to see you try. It'll take money to keep you runnin'. I ain't no Fant Gossett when it comes to that, but I'll chip in my share if you won't say where it come from."

That surprised Hitch again. He stammered that he didn't know, but Edson cut him off. "I'll be around in a day or two, Luke, and we'll talk about it."

As they walked out Edson said, "Feel better? You already have support you didn't know you had."

"One bartender. That's a long ways from prosperity."

Edson agreed that as soon as he could get ahead on some work at the bank, he would join Hitch to spend several days riding over the country shaking hands and drumming votes. Accordingly, he showed up at Hitch's dugout just before dark a few days later, still more cowboy than banker as he swung down from the saddle.

Hitch looked up from his wood-cutting, drove the ax deep into a chopping log and leaned on it to rest. "You bein' a financier," he said dryly, "I thought you'd be travelin' in a nice black buggy by now, or at least in a buckboard."

"I'm in business to lend money, not to spend it." Edson looked at the Spartan place Hitch called home. "Doesn't look like you've spent much either."

"It'll surprise a man how much he can get by without. I expect you're dry."

"You expect right. Coffee if that's the best you can do, stronger medicine if you have it."

"I've got it. I knew a money-changer was bound to show up."

They saw to the horse first, an unwritten rule of survival around any cowcamp. Edson untied a rolled blanket from behind the cantle of his saddle and unstrapped a pair of saddlebags. "Brought my own medicine," he said, hefting the bags, "just in case. But I'll drink yours first."

Hitch conceded, "You'll prosper in the bankin' business."

Hitch built a fire, pinched biscuits off of sourdough he kept in a crock, and put a small pot of beans on to reheat for the fourth or fifth time. "I got a slab of salt pork here that I traded off of a farmer up the river."

"After years around a chuckwagon, I can eat anything."

Hitch had seldom seen an old bachelor cowboy living alone who wasn't skinny as a whip-poor-will. After a few months of doing his own cooking, he knew why.

Edson said, "I don't suppose you've heard who the ranchers are putting up for a candidate."

"All I've heard out here is the coyotes howlin'."

"They're runnin' Dayton Brumley."

Hitch pondered that news without emotion. "I know Dayton. He was Figure 4 rep at our W wagon awhile. Him and Rascal McGinty like to've burned powder last spring. But he's always been a good honest company man."

"That's what they want, is somebody who'll do what he's told."

They ate in silence, Hitch pondering the campaign ahead and not caring for the prospect. "I been thinkin', Edson; maybe we ought to go by the McGinty place and have Rascal ride with us."

Edson frowned. "I was hopin' you wouldn't suggest that."

"Why not?"

"Rascal is a brother to Law McGinty."

"If it hadn't been for what happened to Law, I wouldn't be in the race."

"There's another side to it. Folks'll remember that no matter how much they regretted the way he died, Law was stealin' cattle. I wonder if Rascal being with you might not do you as much harm as it does good? Some people might take it as a sign that you condoned what Law was doing."

"Rascal's my friend. What kind of a man would I be if I denied my friends?"

"Not deny him, Hitch, just kind of stay away from him till this race is over with. Sometimes in politics a man has to compromise a little."

Hitch angered. "They'll take me as I am or pass me by. I don't intend to try to look different than I am. If they take me they'll have to take all them that go along with me, them that believe in me."

Edson shrugged. "A suggestion, Hitch, that's all it was. Let's go see Rascal."

Rascal was pleased at the invitation to go along. Hitch watched him shave a week's growth of whiskers at a tiny cracked mirror nailed to a log in front of his dugout. "Where should we start, Edson?" Rascal asked.

"Some merchants have a theory that if they can make a sale to the first customer who walks in, they'll do all right the rest of the day. Gets their confidence up. I'd suggest we take a couple of easy ones first to get everybody in the right frame of mind."

Rascal aimed the tip of his straight razor at Edson. "I know just the place for that . . . ol' Morey Shumm."

Morey Shumm was one of the many cowboys who had lost his job as a result of the strike. He had a small claim out in the middle of the rolling prairie, far from wood and water. Like Hitch's and Rascal's places, it was devoid of comforts, any indulgencies of personal pleasure. His water supply was in a barrel at the front of his mud-daubed dugout. From an ash-blackened pit and scattered pots and Dutch ovens a few steps from the dwelling, Hitch deduced that the man did most if not all his cooking outside rather than in the cramped quarters of the dugout. He was probably used to spending most of his time in the open anyway.

Shumm eagerly shook Hitch's hand. "Man alive, I sure was tickled when they told me you'd agreed to run, Hitch. I'd all but given up on any future for me in these diggin's. Ol' Torrington, he's been lookin' at me kind of cross, and I figured sooner or later he'd find some excuse to come and take me over. And if not him, then maybe Prosper Selkirk. You're the biggest hope we got. Maybe the only one."

Flustered, Hitch mumbled an acknowledgment of the compliment and wished he knew better what to say. Shumm didn't give him time to worry about it much.

"I bet you fellers are hungry, and I got fresh beef that was runnin' around yesterday on four legs eatin' grass. I'll get a fire started and we'll just have ourselves a feed."

As Hitch expected, Shumm kindled a fire in the outdoor pit, using dried cowchips. He kept the beef hanging in the dugout, where it was cooler than here on top. Pretty soon he had sliced steak sizzling in deep grease and sourdough biscuits browning with glowing chips both under and atop the black Dutch oven that held them. "The beef's my own," Shumm said, "in case you're worryin'. Couldn't hardly feed a sheriff candidate stolen beef. Though I expect you ate more stray beef over at the Ws than you ever ate of Charlie Waide's."

Hitch only smiled. It was widely known that even the big ranches which protested about cattle theft were more likely to kill stray animals for meat than their own. It was said of many a rancher that the only chance he ever had of eating his own beef was in visiting a neighbor's wagon. To Charlie Waide's credit, Hitch remembered no time that Charlie had ever ordered the killing of a stray except those rare occasions when one suffered a broken leg in the roping and would otherwise have gone to waste. Waste was one thing Charlie Waide would not abide.

"Hope you fellers don't mind eatin' outdoors," Shumm said. He pointed his chin at his rough dugout. "Never have been able to get used to stayin' in a house. Place smells like damp earth all the time. Man wakes up in the night and it's pitch dark and like bein' in a grave. Found a rattlesnake in there with me the other day and almost decided just to give it to him."

Shumm had provided a scanty shade by building a small brush arbor, though he must have had to drag the materials for miles; Hitch saw no brush around here . . . nothing but miles and miles of wide open plains and summer-brown grass. If a cowboy wanted to nap in the shade he had to have a horse that would stand mighty still. Beneath the arbor Hitch saw a roll of blankets. Shumm must be sleeping outdoors, except perhaps when the weather was bad.

Shumm noticed that Hitch was looking his place over. "Ain't much of a layout, is it, Hitch?"

"No worse than mine," Hitch said, stretching it a little.

"No, it ain't much, but at least I got a toenail hold on somethin' that belongs to me." Shumm looked across his open land, and affection showed in his eyes. "I come up here from the brush country, Hitch, where a man couldn't see a hundred yards through the mesquite and chaparral. First year or so up on these plains, I thought this open country would run me crazy. And this everlastin' wind . . . But it grows on you. I can stand here on my own little parcel of land and see two-three hours' ride in any direction. I can see and count every cow I own, peart near. I loved a woman once, Hitch, and I lost her. Now I've come to love this country the way I used to love that woman. I'd hate to lose it, too."

Hitch knew some people would consider that Shumm didn't have much here to lose, a poverty claim like this. But those people never would understand that Shumm didn't really live in this cheerless dugout, this crude cowcamp; this was just a place to come for the night. He *lived* on that big prairie, and there he spent the time that really mattered to him. Some people would never understand the hold this land could take on a man if he stayed rooted long enough in one spot to develop a communion with the grass-blanketed earth, to begin to feel and fall in with the rhythms of the changing seasons. There was a pulse in this land, like the pulse in a man, though most people never paused long enough to sense it.

Shumm said, "Every man has a right to what belongs to him. I got nothin' against Torrington and Selkirk if they would just stay in their own yard.

But me and you, we know that ain't in their nature. They're *reachers*. That's why I'm with you, Hitch. They'll have to break my leg to keep me from votin'."

Edson had been right; the visit to Shumm lifted Hitch's spirits, made him feel better about the campaign. The reception was similar at the next couple of camps the three men went to. But they came finally to a small ranch operated by a man with whom Hitch had had a nodding acquaintance the last two or three years, a man who reminded Hitch uncomfortably of Kate McGinty's late father. The woman and four children were out hoeing a garden which appeared to be withering under the hot sun. The horsemen rode up to the smooth-wire fence that surrounded it, and all took off their hats.

"We're lookin' for your husband, Mrs. Free," Hitch said.

She pointed toward the house. "He's yonder, diggin' us a well. You-all be stayin' for supper?"

Hitch couldn't tell whether she really wanted them to or not. Playing safe, he said, "I reckon we'll be movin' on directly."

She appeared relieved, though she said, "That's a pity; there's aplenty for everybody."

Hitch doubted that; not one of the children showed much flesh. Mrs. Free herself was skinny as a cedar post. "We're obliged anyway, ma'am." He pulled away.

Free's oldest son, about twelve, operated a windlass, drawing up the dirt that Free dug from the bottom of the hole. Hitch winked at him, then leaned over the rim and called down, "Mister Free, it's Hugh Hitchcock. I'd be obliged if I could talk to you."

Hitch and Rascal relieved the boy and turned the windlass to draw Free to the top. The man, as hungry-looking as his family, had mud and dirt on him from his ragged felt hat down to his cracking old boots. He made a useless effort to brush a little of it off, then extended his soiled hand to Hitch. "You'll excuse my looks; I ain't on my way to church. I figure there's water down yonder someplace if I just go deep enough."

Rascal smiled. "You're liable to find hell down there if you go too far."

"I've found hell up here; that's why I'm huntin' water." Free wiped his arm across his sweaty face and pointed his whiskered chin toward a picket shack he had built of small trees, standing them up and lashing them tightly together to form the walls, the roof also of pickets, covered by dirt. "Cooler over yonder in the shade. You said you wanted to talk."

Free paused long enough to tell the boy he had better move some dirt he had spilled too near the edge of the hole. Hitch followed Free's example in squatting on the shady side of the shack, his back against the rough wall. "You may not have heard, Mister Free; I'm runnin' for sheriff."

Free showed no enthusiasm. "I heard. You're runnin' against the ranchers."

"I'm a cowboy, Mister Free, not a politician. I reckon you know why I decided to do it."

Free cast a quick glance at Rascal. "I believe I do. But I also believe you might be mistaken in your thinkin'."

"How is that?"

"You've took on men like Torrington and Selkirk; you've put the challenge to them. Anybody that backs you up, it means *he's* took them on, too. And anybody the ranchers think *might* back you, whether they really do or not. That's a big thing for a man to have hangin' over his head if he intends to stay in this country. A man wants to think twice before he goes to angryin' up the likes of them, and the power they got behind them."

"It's bad for anybody to have that much power over somebody else, Mister Free. But if we don't make a stand, they'll get even more powerful. We think we can draw up the string on them."

"You *think*? You ain't real sure of yourself."

"We got no cinch."

"You sure don't. So what if you try and don't make it? What happens to them that get their necks stuck out there with you?"

"If a man believes in a thing strong enough, he takes a risk."

"I've already took enough risks in this life, Mister Hitchcock. I got a wife and five kids that can't afford me to take anymore. From now on anything I get my hands on, I'm hangin' onto. I ain't takin' no chances of losin' the little I got. Look around you; what do you see?" He didn't give Hitch time for an answer, and Hitch didn't know what he was expected to say anyhow. Free said, "It's damned little better than starvation, but it's cost me and my family an awful lot, and I got no wish to throw it away."

"A man has got a responsibility to his neighbors."

"He's got a lot more responsibility to his own family." Free's mud-smudged face furrowed deeply. "I'll grant you, there's truth in what you say; them big outfits have done things I don't personally approve of. But on the other hand I'm just a little feller, and them thieves, they steal off of me just like they do off of the big ranches. Difference is that I ain't big enough to protect myself. And even if people like Torrington and Selkirk may step on me a little now and again, at the same time they're protectin' themselves they're protectin' me too."

He looked regretfully at Rascal. "Sure, I was sore distressed about that hangin'. They oughtn't to've done it. But I will say that some shady characters left this country right afterwards, and I doubt they're ever comin' back. So you see, I made some net gain out of what them ranchers did, bad as I hated the way they done it. It helped me like it helped them." Free pushed to his feet, indicating the visit was over as far as he was concerned. "I'm sorry, Mister Hitchcock; I'd like to help you. But things bein' like they are, and us needin' law and order so bad, I just can't go along with you."

Hitch stood up, hands shoved deep in his pockets as he tried to think what to say. "I can understand the way you feel, Mister Free, even if I don't agree with you. Thanks for listenin' to me, anyway." He turned to leave but couldn't. There was one more thing that had to be said. "You mentioned about law and order. I notice that lots of people who talk about law and order don't mean it for anybody but themselves. When somebody was stealin' cattle off of Torrington and Selkirk, that was a crime. But when Torrington and Selkirk stole mine off of me, they called that justice. Someday they may come for yours, Mister Free."

"Not if I make sure they know I'm on their side. This country has got to have strong protection. If a few people get run over in the process, they shouldn't of been standin' there in the way."

Hitch knew there was no point in staying around arguing over it; nobody's mind would be changed. He went to Walking Jack, mounted, then pointed. "I believe I saw another house over yonder-way."

Free nodded. "Elijah Neihardt. You'll want to talk with him."

Hitch rode off without looking back, Edson and Rascal silently flanking him. Edson had no problem reading his thoughts. "You can't expect to get them all, Hitch."

In frustration Hitch exclaimed, "Don't he know that Torrington and Selkirk are no friends of his?"

Edson Biggs shrugged. "He's like a child that hides behind his mother's skirts. He doesn't realize that if she makes a wrong move she'll step on him."

Rascal rode in brooding silence a long time. Finally he asked, "Did you-all notice the way he kept lookin' at me?"

Hitch glanced at Edson, then at Rascal. "I didn't notice anything." Edson looked down at the horn of his saddle.

Rascal said, "I seen it. He kept thinkin' to hisself, 'That's the brother of the man they hung for stealin' cattle.'"

"He never said any such of a thing."

"With his eyes he did."

Hitch said, "You're imaginin' things, Rascal," and looked to Edson for help. He received none.

They could hear angry shouting before they reached the Neihardt place, and Hitch thought uncomfortably that they might be riding in on some kind of fight. But through the dust he could see a man struggling with a pair of young mules, evidently trying to teach them how to work. One would pull ahead and the other balk or try to kick free of the traces. The man would curse and slap at their rumps with the reins and try again. Hitch looked at the piece of ground the stockfarmer was trying to break and wondered idly if it should ever be turned over by a plow; he seriously doubted it was cropland, and farming it might ruin it for the grass God must have intended it to grow.

Neihardt saw the visitors but gave the mules one more minute of disgusted effort before cursing loudly and bringing them around. He let the mules stand and blow while he walked toward the horsemen.

"Hugh Hitchcock," Hitch said, extending his hand. "I take it you'd be Mister Neihardt?" When the man nodded, Hitch introduced him to Rascal and Edson. Neihardt frowned, giving Rascal a moment of special attention, then turned to Biggs. "I believe I've seen you in town. Banker, ain't you?" When Edson said yes, Neihardt added frostily, "I doubt as you'd ever lend me any money. A banker never will loan a man unless he knows he don't really need it."

Edson made an effort to be pleasant. "You might be surprised. Come see me sometime if you're ever in need."

"I always been able to take care of myself." Neihardt turned back to Hitch. "You'd be the man that's runnin' for sheriff."

"Yes, sir. I came to ask you for your support."

Neihardt glanced again at Rascal. "And suppose you tell me why you think I ought to give it to you."

Hitch reviewed the same general case he had made to others before. Neihardt listened without comment, his eyes boring into Hitch. At length Neihardt said, "You come from the direction of Doug Free's. You talk to him?" When Hitch nodded, Neihardt asked, "What did he tell you?"

Reluctantly Hitch told the truth. "Said he couldn't support me."

Neihardt nodded. "Me and Free, we talked it over a couple days ago. I notice, Mister Hitchcock, you never said nothin' about the rustlers, though you done a lot of talkin' about how the ranchers had done wrong. Them cow thieves been more worry to me than the ranchers have; they don't respect no man, big or little. Awhile back they took off half the cows I owned." He turned his eyes to Rascal McGinty, though he went on talking to Hitch. "Seems to me like you ought to've said what you're goin' to do about them rustlers."

"Well, you know I'm against them. I'll do whatever I can to see that they're put a stop to."

"I always been a man to call a spade a spade, Hitchcock. Seems to me like this man here is a brother to the man the ranchers hung for a cow thief; ain't that true?"

Rascal answered before Hitch could. "They *said* he was one. There never was no trial." Rascal's eyes hardened.

"There don't seem to've been no doubt that he was guilty. I judge this country is better off without him; better off than it might be with a sheriff who rides around the country with the brother of a known thief."

Neihardt never saw Rascal's fist coming. Suddenly the farmer was flat on his back, his hands up defensively, his nose bleeding. Rascal stepped forward angrily to grab him and pull him back to his feet, but Hitch and Edson caught the cowboy and shouldered him aside. "Damn you, Rascal," Edson said harshly, "you trying to get Hitch beat?"

"You heard what that farmer said!" But Rascal loosened a little. Hitch turned back to help Neihardt up, and the farmer angrily waved him off, rubbing his nose and cursing the three men the way he had cursed the mules, ordering them off the property and warning that he had a gun in the house. Rascal stood with fists clenched, ready to pursue the conversation, but Hitch and Edson pulled him to his horse. Red-faced, Rascal kept looking back as they rode away. He talked awhile, then muttered, then was quiet.

Hitch said, "Rascal, we come onto this man's place without any invitation. He had a right to say what he thought whether we agreed with him or not."

Remorse was beginning to set in on Rascal. It always did, after the sudden storm. Rascal said. "Well, I reckon I cost you a vote."

Hitch shook his head. "I never had *that* vote to start with."

Soberly Edson Biggs said, "By the time Neihardt gets through spreading the story around, it's likely to cost a good many votes."

"Depends on what his neighbors think of him. Way I sized him up, he ain't no easy man to be neighbors with."

Rascal watched their shadows reaching out across the thick turf of curing grass. "I tried to tell you somethin' while ago, Hitch, and you wouldn't listen. This goes to prove that I ain't doin' you no good. I'm goin' home."

"You're takin' it too personal."

"It is personal." Rascal lowered his head. "He's right about Law; I know that. But I still can't stand by and hear somebody else say it. So you give them a good fight, Hitch, and I'll see you about election day." Rascal shoved his hand forward, and Hitch took it unwillingly. Rascal turned to the banker. "Edson, you keep Hitch out of trouble." The cowboy struck out across the prairie, shoulders slumped in melancholy.

Hitch sat on Walking Jack and watched until Rascal

was only a speck far out on the flat tableland. "Edson, I wouldn't of hurt him for the world."

"The *world* has hurt him, Hitch; you didn't."

For the next three days Hitch and Edson hunted out farms and small ranches, line shacks and cowboy batch camps all over the county. Hitch disliked the electioneering part; pleading for votes was somehow demeaning, a little like going from door to door and begging for money, though he considered his reasons worthy. It went against the grain for a man who had been self-sufficient since he was fourteen or fifteen. But the visiting itself was pleasant. It surprised him, meeting settlers he didn't even know were there. He enjoyed finding cowboys he had known and ridden with in years gone by.

The sedentary life of a banker had not yet set in on Edson Biggs; he rode as tirelessly as Hitch the long miles up and down both sides of the river, meeting people, speaking his piece. At one point Hitch suggested they were probably several miles across the county line. Edson said, "For all we know they may want to come over and vote with us. It's been done plenty of times in the past."

One day they rode onto range claimed by old Allie Clay of the Nine Bar. Hitch felt uneasy about being there, for he knew within reason that as a large rancher Clay had allied himself with Torrington and Selkirk even though Clay and John Torrington had feuded for years over water and grass. But Hitch felt he had nothing to lose by talking to the old man; there was always the longshot chance that Clay might throw his support to Hitch simply out of enmity for Torrington. It wouldn't cost anything to find out.

Clay had had lumber hauled all the way from Colorado to build himself a house bigger than John

Torrington's. Actually, he needed it, for he was married and had brought up a family, which his rival had never done. Mrs. Clay, a gray-haired woman of sixty, was lonely to talk to someone new, and Hitch could have spent the day at the ranch headquarters if he had been in no hurry. But as Edson pointed out in a whisper while the old lady went to fetch coffee, women didn't get to vote and they had better move on where the votes were. Mrs. Clay told them her husband was with his west division wagon and reluctantly bid them farewell, standing behind the oval glass window of her front door and watching them as long as they were in sight.

Clay should have built that house in town, Hitch thought, where she could see people. But these plains ranches were not established with a woman's comforts and needs in mind. Someone had said this country was fine for men and horses but hell for women and dogs.

About midafternoon they came upon a young cowboy having trouble drifting a string of Nine Bar cows and calves in his chosen direction; they were led by an old spotted cow of an independent longhorn strain that had never accepted man's domination. Their home was a brushy little header a couple of miles back, and she meant to return there, incidentally taking the others with her. She made a break past the cowboy, and he spilled a loop trying to rope her. Hitch shook his own rope loose from the hornstring and built a loop in it. As she came by him, he swung it over his head and sailed it out around her horns. He let her skid on her rump, then come over hard on her back. When she tried to rise up hind quarters first, Hitch brought her down again. The cowboy got off of his horse, a short length of rope in his hand.

Kneeling on her shoulder, he tied the rope around one forefoot, then the other, bringing the feet close together. He slipped Hitch's rope off of her horns and stepped back.

She got up slinging her head and wanting to fight, but as she attempted to charge, the hobbled forefeet crossed her up and brought her to her knees. She slung her head in anger and frustration, trying once more and going down again. A calf bawled, and she turned to see. She gave the men one more menacing look, then hopped awkwardly to her calf.

Hitch recoiled his rope and hung it on the hornstring. The little exertion had warmed and pleased him; he had liked the feel of the rope in his hand, the sudden violence of the cow at the end of it. It was a challenge he had always enjoyed as a cowboy, a man's prowess against animal strength, and the feeling of pleasure at a skill well learned.

The cowpuncher—a stranger to Hitch—raised his hand in belated greeting. There hadn't been time before. "That'll give ol' Sis somethin' to think about besides runnin' off. An outlaw like her ought to be sent up for beef."

Hitch said, "No, it'll be a sad day when all the wild things are gone." He introduced himself and Edson Biggs. "Whichaway's the wagon?"

The cowboy pointed. "Yonder. We'll be throwin' the gather down by the Kildee Lake. You lookin' for somebody in particular?"

"Allie Clay."

"He'll be with the gather. You-all had as well ride along with me if you'd like. You're a pretty good hand with that rope."

"Had aplenty of practice."

"I can tell that by lookin' at you."

Hitch didn't know if that was meant as an indication he was looking old. To a youngster like this one, seventeen or eighteen, he supposed he did, but the thought was not reassuring.

The lake was one of the playa variety so common on these plains, wide but shallow, fed by runoff waters in the rainy seasons and doomed to recede toward a stagnant center as heat and dry weather set in, its edges grown up in rank weeds and grasses that parched brown as the water gradually withdrew toward the middle. At this side of it, where Hitch knew buffalo must once have congregated by the thousands or tens of thousands, several hundred cattle were being gathered into a dusty, milling, bawling mass. He had to rein up and look. It was a sight he had watched more times than he could count, and he had not realized how much he really had missed it since leaving the W. It was a joy to watch, and yet it brought an ache as well, for he sensed that he would never be a part of this again.

He and Edson stayed back a little from the herd and the busy cowboys, because an outfit like this usually had evolved a place for everyone without new orders being given, and two outsiders unexpectedly riding in had no particular usefulness. They watched the cowboys and the cattle. The longing must have shown in Hitch's face, for Edson remarked, "Makes you want to go back, doesn't it?"

Hitch nodded.

Edson said, "Just remember that it was always for somebody else, never for yourself."

"I reckon that makes a difference. But I miss it all the same."

As the sun dropped down toward the brassy edge of the prairie sky, most of the cowboys rode away from the main herd, letting it spread some to graze. The smaller "stray" herd was moved farther to keep the cattle from coming back together. These would be the animals belonging to other brands; other ranches' representatives would periodically take them home. Seeing that most of the cowboys were on their way to the chuckwagon, Hitch and Edson followed along.

Old Allie Clay was taken aback, seeing them here. He shook hands civilly enough but without warmth, for he well remembered that they had been regarded as leaders in the cowboy strike. "I expect I know what you men come for. I'll have to say that I didn't expect it."

"We kind of surprised ourselves," Hitch admitted. "Maybe we oughtn't to've even come. But we wanted to talk to you. We wanted to let you know where we stand."

"I reckon I already know where you stand." Clay looked around at his curious cowboys, probably wondering if he was risking strike talk again by letting Hitch and Edson stay in camp. "We'll have us some supper, and then we'll talk. An empty stomach always distracts a man."

The cook was a red-faced fellow with all of Trump Tatum's irritability and only a modicum of his cooking ability. The beans had rocks in them, and the sourdough bread hadn't been given enough time to rise; it had been baked on the squat. But the meal beat the ones Hitch had fixed for himself, so he guessed he was ahead.

After supper he put forward his case. "I suppose this race has taken on a look of the big ranches against the little people, Mister Clay, but it shouldn't have. I'm not against anybody for bein' big; I'm only against people usin' power in an unfair way against other people who can't protect themselves. I've never heard anybody complain about you bein' unfair to neighbors, any more than I ever heard them complain about Charlie Waide. My bein' sheriff won't mean trouble for anybody except them that *make* trouble. And that includes cow thieves, Mister Clay. I hear some people sayin' I'll take up for the cow thieves, but you know me well enough to know that ain't so. I'll bear down hard."

"And you came here thinkin' I might come out in your favor?"

"I been hopin' you might."

Allie Clay smiled thinly. "It'd tickle me to do it. I can imagine what old John Torrington would say, how he would cuss. I'd like to be the one to tell him, so I could watch him go into a fit of apoplexy." The smile died. "The hell of it is, Hitchcock, that politics makes a man do things he never thought he would, makes him join up with people he'd rather crawl into a snakepit than be associated with. Like me and ol' John. I always figured you for a good man, Hitchcock, because Charlie Waide wouldn't of put up with you if you hadn't been. I take it you're honest, and I'd like to help you. But you can see how it is: we've all had sides chosen up for us whether we like it or not. We've had our friends picked out for us whether we like them or not.

"When you was a button, Hitchcock, did you and your friends ever have a cowchip battle? I did, lots of times. I always liked to find and throw the freshest ones, that hadn't been long out of the cow. Them kind, when you hit a man with them, they splattered. You got everybody around him. It's like that now; whatever you hit Torrington with, it's goin' to splatter. There's people yellin' for Torrington and Selkirk to be pulled down, but they'll pull down some of the rest of us with them if they do. We been dealt a poor hand, and there's nothin' to do but play it out and play to win. Some other time, some other situation, I'd support you and ask my men to support you. But the way it is . . . well, Hitchcock, that's the way it is."

Hitch nodded soberly. "I guess I knew all the time, but I thought I'd try."

"A *man* always tries, Hitchcock. We'll beat you, but nobody can take away from you the fact that you tried."

16

Though Hitch dreaded it, he inevitably had to move his campaign into town, for that was where the largest number of people lived. He found he disliked town more than ever, and the thought that if he won he would have to spend most of his time there was no comfort to him.

The place to see most people who came in was the saloon. That, for most cowtowns, was the place to rest one's saddlesores, to see one's friends and enemies, to swap off a horse or to sell ten thousand steers.

Hitch made it a point to avoid Fant Gossett's place. One night he sat in Luke Gannaway's Buffalo Bar, not drinking but simply visiting with people who came in. Some were cowboys from the big outfits, and they spoke to him self-consciously, most of them, then pulled away. Eventually a familiar face showed in the doorway. Dayton Brumley spied Hitch and came on in.

"Howdy, Hitch. I'd like to have a drink with you. I'm buyin'."

Hitch shook hands with his opponent. "I'd be tickled," he said, though he wouldn't.

Brumley signaled Gannaway for a bottle and glasses, and he motioned toward a small round table, shoving a brass spittoon aside with his boot. Brumley studied Hitch, troubled. "Hitch, we always used to be friends."

"Far as I'm concerned, we still are."

"I'm glad. I was afraid under the circumstances . . ." He poured the drinks but didn't pick up his glass. "This election, Hitch, you really want to go through with it?"

"Hell no, I don't want to. But I reckon I'm stuck."

Brumley raised his glass. "Here's to a clean race."

"I'll drink to that."

Brumley fingered his glass, frowning. "They're usin' us, Hitch, both of us."

Hitch tried to cover his surprise. "What do you mean?"

"People used you for that strike, and they're usin' you now. As for me, Prosper Selkirk has always used me, and now all the big outfits are doin' it. Difference between me and you is, Hitch, that I always knew."

"There's another difference."

"What's that?"

"I'm bein' used for a better cause."

Brumley shrugged. "Maybe so; I give up thinkin' a long time ago. I think me and you if we was smart would both pack up and leave this country and let everybody else fight their own battles."

"We won't, though, neither one of us."

"I suppose not." Brumley finished his glass. "One

thing I promise you, Hitch. I'll do what I can to see that it's a straight election."

"That's all a man could ask for, Dayton."

Lafey Dodge stayed in town most of the time, walking up and down the streets in his dark, grim silence, making sure the voters fully recognized the power for which he stood. He never overtly threatened anyone; in fact, he had little or nothing to say. But his ominous presence itself was a threat, a reminder that the men who had always controlled the country intended to continue and that any who opposed them were likely to be quietly marked and their transgressions remembered, perhaps to be called up for accounting on some future day when all this foolishness was over and relationships had returned to normal patterns.

As the campaign went on, Hitch found himself increasingly discouraged. He was sure he had visited every little ranch, every dugout, every bonepicker camp in the county and for several miles beyond on all its perimeters. He had knocked on every door in town.

"Way I see it," he told Edson Biggs disconsolately, "I ain't got the chance of a three-legged rabbit in a wolf den."

"You've made lots of friends."

"I always been a good hand at countin' cattle, and I been carryin' a pretty good count of people in my head. Now you figure up all the big ranches, and you figure up the cowboys workin' for them. Then you add to that the people here in town who'll follow the ranchers' lead because they want to protect their trade or they got some other personal interest in keepin' the courthouse like it is. Tote them all up and you got defeat written there plain as daylight."

"Election's not over till they count the ballots."

"I've already counted them."

Two days before the vote, Hitch unexpectedly came face to face with Prosper Selkirk, walking self-consciously with Lafey Dodge on the street. Selkirk paused in midstride, blinking uneasily at the sudden confrontation.

Hitch nodded civilly. "Mister Selkirk." He neither spoke to nor looked at Lafey Dodge.

"Hitchcock," said Selkirk. Just plain Hitchcock, still no *Mister*. The two men looked at each other a nervous moment. Selkirk said, "I was somewhat impressed with you once, when you were at the W. I didn't think you would be dragged into this kind of mistake."

"Sir?"

"I know this is a free country and every man has a right, but I hate to see a man completely waste his time and energies and make unnecessary enemies in a hopeless cause."

Hitch didn't intend to betray his lack of confidence. "We'll pretty soon know if it's hopeless."

"In spite of all that has happened, I've always had a certain respect for you, Hitchcock. My impression is that you entered the strike out of some misplaced loyalties and more or less against your will. I dislike seeing an honorable man hurt. I'd like to help you."

"You could start by releasin' my cattle from 'escrow.'" Hitch knew that was unlikely to happen; even if it did, it would be a hollow victory because the county had taken poor care of his Two Diamond herd. Thieves already had made off with most of it;

those cows were probably far across the New Mexico line, beyond retrieving.

Selkirk said, "You can't make anything on that little amount of land you own. I'd like to buy it from you at a fair price. Even more than fair. With that money you might do better for yourself elsewhere."

"You makin' me an offer?"

"I would. But first I would have to ask what you would take."

"If I sold out, I suppose you'd want me to leave the county."

"You would have no reason to stay."

"That'd be an easy way for you to win the election."

"We'll win that election anyhow. The offer is made in good faith."

Hitch figured they didn't want him staying on even in defeat, a *reminder* to his backers and perhaps an encouragement for them to try another round. "And I'm turnin' it down in good faith."

Selkirk shrugged. "It's your choice. You may wish you had taken it." He walked away, his back stiff.

Lafey Dodge remained a minute, his eyes without emotion. "Sounded to me like the man made you a good offer."

Hitch tensed, searching the man's words for a threat but not sure he found one. "Me and you, we both know why he done it."

"His kind naturally thinks of money first. But always remember, if he can't buy you off, he can buy you killed."

A chill went down Hitch's back. "You'd be the one to do that."

"I'm just a workin' man. I do what I'm paid for."

After that encounter, Hitch had had all of town he

could stand for a couple of days. He saddled Walking Jack and rode east to his own place. There he found a good many Snaketrack cattle grazing his grass and figured Torrington had his cowboys drift them there on purpose. Hitch circled them, bunching them the best he could, and pushed them off his land onto the Figure 4. *Let Selkirk wrestle with Torrington over the grass,* he told himself.

Resting, watching the cattle drift away, it occurred to him he had not seen Rascal McGinty since the cowboy had left him and Edson on the electioneering venture. It would be pleasant to ride over to the McGinty place and *augur* awhile, and not ask anyone for a vote.

He noticed many Snaketrack cattle grazing McGinty grass, just as they had been grazing his. *Greedy old bastard,* he thought, *won't even let our land alone.* He would help Rascal push them off.

But he found no one at home. Evidently Rascal had found temporary day-work somewhere. Disappointed, Hitch prowled around the little place, as if hoping Rascal might come riding over the hill. But he knew somehow that the cowboy wouldn't. Without wanting to, Hitch found himself looking down toward the river. He could see the tall cottonwoods rocking in the wind as they had done the day Law died. The memory came back in a rush that made him suddenly cold. He turned away, trying to shut it from his mind.

But the image would not go away, and now he looked toward the gentle rise where they had carried Law to bury him, safely above the occasional floods that sent angry red water sweeping this valley. He felt a compulsion to ride up there.

When he allowed himself to think about it, which

was seldom, he felt guilt for the fact that just once—that night he lay suffering in Rascal's dugout—he had told himself it might be better for him and Kate if something *did* happen to Law. That unbidden thought had been on his conscience of late. It was as if, even for a moment, he had willed Law to die.

Dan Truman had put up a simple plank headboard with Law's name on it. As Hitch approached the grave he found the board lying flat on the ground. An angry thought came that somebody had contemptuously done it on purpose. But cowtracks on the mound made him realize that a wandering cow had knocked it down, or perhaps some itchy-hided bull trying to scratch himself.

Hitch dismounted and removed his hat, remembering Law in another time, a wild, impetuous kid who would ride anything that pitched or rope anything that would run. He began talking quietly, partly to himself, partly to the man who would never hear. "Law, I'd figured we'd set things right for what happened to you, but now it don't look like we can. Far as I can tell, we're beat at that election before we start. Don't look like there's any way to even the score except to take the law in our own hands the way *they* done, and you know that ain't our style. So it looks like it was all for nothin', Law. All for nothin'."

He stared at the cow tracks on the grave. "Don't look like you'll even have peace here till we put a fence around this place. I'll see what I can do."

He rode down to the shed and corrals. He found a stack of posts that had been cut for corrals but never used, and long branches cut for rails. He tied a rope onto several of the posts and snaked them up to the gravesite, then made several more trips dragging poles. When that was completed he got the diggers and began digging holes for the posts.

He was so absorbed in the work that he didn't hear the horseman until the shadow fell across him. He turned, startled, and his eyes went wide. Sitting on a big blue roan was the solemn-faced Lafey Dodge.

Hitch's heart hammered. He had no gun except the short rifle in the saddle scabbard, and Walking Jack stood tied fifty or seventy-five feet away. Hitch stood with the diggers in his hands and tried not to let his fear show through. At length he managed to speak. "Looks like you always catch me thisaway."

Dodge nodded. "I make a point of it. But don't worry yourself about the gun. I ain't here to kill you. Ol' Man Torrington just wanted me to follow along and scare you."

Hitch's tongue explored his dry lips. "You've done that."

"I been trailin' you at a respectful distance ever since you left town, curious to see what you was doin'. Thought you might be leavin' the country."

"Disappoint you that I didn't?"

"Some. I hate to fight a man I respect. Damned few men I *can* respect anymore."

"If I ran, you wouldn't respect me."

"A pity, ain't it? This way we're both in a bind." He nodded curiously at the grave. "What you fixin' to do?"

Hitch showed him the cowtracks. "I was goin' to put a little fence around it to keep the livestock out."

Dodge pondered a moment. "Good idea. I believe I'll help you."

Hitch stared, dumfounded. He was inclined to refuse but knew he was in no position to make an issue of it. "But you killed him."

"I take no pride in what happened to this boy. It was a poor piece of business."

"Then why did you do it?"

"It was a job of work. I always deliver what I'm paid for. I told Ol' Man Torrington I'd rather just shoot the boy; that's the businesslike way. Hangin' a man never went well on my stomach. The old man felt like folks wouldn't learn much from a shootin'. Hang a man, though, and they'll sure take notice."

Dodge hung his belt and six-shooter across a pile of posts not far out of reach. "I want your word you won't do nothin' foolish."

Hitch nodded, still surprised. "I'm in no hurry to get killed."

"See that you remember." Dodge picked up the diggers and attacked the soft earth with a vengeance. He dug a pair of holes, then Hitch took the diggers and started to move to the next post location. Dodge pointed. "Thataway would suit me better." Hitch's direction would have moved him closer to Dodge's pistol. Dodge tamped dirt around the two posts, spaced just far enough apart for the poles to wedge between them.

Sweat running down his face and soaking his shirt, Hitch paused in wonder. This didn't fit his mental image of a man coldly singleminded in Dodge's profession. "Dodge, I thought I had you figured. Now I don't understand you atall."

Dodge wiped sweat from his face onto his sleeve and stopped. "I don't know what you mean. I'm just me. I always been just me."

"You act like you've done this kind of work before. You didn't always make your livin' with that gun."

"I was a farmer once, a long time ago. The big war

come on and by and by I was a soldier. Folks cuss the war, but them was pretty good days in some respects. There was room for a man to find out if he *was* a man. But finally the war was over and all of a sudden there wasn't no call anymore for Confederate soldiers. People was sick of the fightin', and of them that done the fightin'. A little while then I tried packin' a star for the State Rangers, but that was a carpetbag outfit of Unionists and scalawags that a man couldn't take no pride in. Besides, it didn't pay much; you had to steal most of what you got. So I become a free agent. Somebody wanted a man caught and was willin' to pay, I went out and caught him."

"Like you done Law McGinty?"

"A job of work, that's all it was. I never took no pride in the hangin'."

Hitch saw that Dodge had no remorse over the killing, only for the method. He said, "One thing always puzzled me a little. I can see you bein' there, and Torrington bein' there, but I never did picture Selkirk havin' the stomach for it."

Dodge frowned. "He didn't want to. Said he'd done his part by payin' his money in. But Ol' Man Torrington, he said it wouldn't mean nothin' if they wasn't both there. He cussed Selkirk for a yeller-legged pothound and browbeat him into goin' along. Selkirk throwed up his dinner after we left you and that boy down on the river." Dodge spat. "Torrington's a mean one, but you got to respect him for his guts. Never could have no respect for Selkirk and his caliber. Them kind, they think when they hire another man to do a dirty job, they keep their own hands clean. Seems to me like I've made the biggest part of my livin' workin' for cowards."

Together Hitch and Dodge finished the fence. If it was not a pretty job, at least it would keep the cows out. Someday somebody might put up a better one.

Dodge strapped his pistol back on his hip. His shirt was soaked with sweat, his hands and face grimy. "You know, there's somethin' about work like this that sort of frees up a man's blood, makes him feel good. Makes him sort of wish . . ." He broke off, perhaps not really knowing just what he *did* wish.

Hitch sensed that for a little while Dodge had reverted to a better time when a man's honest labor had counted for something. He sensed a vague satisfaction in Dodge, but it was a fleeting thing soon gone. Dodge drew the pistol, and Hitch's breath stopped. But Dodge only turned the weapon over in his hand, examining it. "Almost forgot this gun for a while. Afraid we might've throwed a little dirt on it." He slipped it back into the holster. "Well, Ol' Man Torrington will want to know if I scared you enough to change your mind about runnin' for election."

"You scared me," Hitch admitted, "but I ain't quit."

Dodge nodded. "That's what I told the old man, but he ain't much judge of people. You take care of yourself, Hitchcock." Lafey Dodge shoved a foot in the stirrup and methodically swung up onto the roan. He rode off, taking his time. He must have known Hitch could have gotten his saddlegun and shot him in the back, but Dodge neither hurried the horse from its easy trot nor looked around.

Hitch stared after him, his mouth open.

"Law, how do you punish a man who don't even know he's done anything wrong?"

17

Election Day. Hitch sat in a rawhide-bottomed straight chair in front of the Buffalo Bar, bootheels hooked over the bottom brace, the top leaned back against the adobe wall. Directly across the hoof-churned street stood the little courthouse where the polls had been set up. The saloon was not allowed to sell liquor during election hours, but it would be considered cruel and inhuman to close the doors and deny the visiting public a place to go and sit for brief shelter from the hot summer sun. For the duration of the day, at least, service at the bar would be limited to hot coffee and cold lemonade, or water dippered out of a wooden barrel.

Rascal McGinty strode up the dusty street and onto the plank porch, slapping his dusty hat against his clothes. He grinned. "Thought I'd wait till late in the day, but I couldn't sleep, so I rode most of the night. Mind if I sit down with you?"

Hitch gratefully shook hands. "Anything you want to do. Where you been hidin'?"

"Had a short job drivin' some horses over east to Clarendon. Got back yesterday. You're winnin', ain't you, Hitch?"

Hitch didn't answer, and he could tell that Rascal could read the answer in his face. Rascal ran his sleeve over his forehead and into his red hair. "I swear, Hitch, but it's hot. Whose idea was it that they can't sell a man nothin' to drink?"

"State law. Politicians don't want people gettin' drunk and killin' anybody that ain't had a chance to vote yet."

Rascal said, "Hitch, you just got to win."

Hitch looked back toward the courthouse. "Don't count on it. Looky yonder." He nodded his chin toward a dozen riders. By the horses, some of which he remembered, he knew these to be part of Allie Clay's Nine Bar hands come to vote early. Dust on the trail behind them showed more were on the way. "I been sittin' here watchin' ever since the polls opened. Ain't seen many friends of mine ride in."

"Day's young yet. Things'll look different by sundown."

As the morning wore on, he saw little to change his feeling. In small bunches and big ones, cowboys drifted into town and tied their ponies around the courthouse, walking up to the steps with spurs jingling in lively concert. After they had voted, some hung around the courthouse to talk in the shade; others made for the saloons and were quickly disappointed to find the well dried up for the day.

A little before noon, Kate McGinty walked up the street toward him. He thought she probably would pass by him on some errand, and he watched her surreptitiously, still finding it difficult to look at her without an old tightness building in him, a sense of wanting and of loss. She came directly to him. He stood up as she neared, the front legs of the chair dropping noisily. He took off his hat.

She spoke first to Rascal, then turned to Hitch. "You've avoided us, Hitch. We haven't seen you much."

He tried to make light of it. "Women can't vote. Been doin' my visitin' with the voters."

"Well, you'll do some with us for a little while. We've fixed a special Election Day dinner. Neighbor killed a couple of chickens."

"Wait till tonight and I'll probably eat the neck."

"Come along, Hitch. You too, Rascal. The only thing poorer fed than a cowboy at a chuckwagon is a cowboy doin' his own cookin'."

The attention of the women—Kate and her mother and a couple from a nearby house—was embarrassing. But Hitch ate his share of the chicken and watched Rascal hungrily stack bones at the edge of his plate. Rascal didn't leave the table until the baby awoke from its nap. Rascal seemed always to melt when he looked at his nephew. That baby had him tied in a helpless knot. "Look there at Punkin', Hitch," Rascal insisted, "don't you see the McGinty in him? Lookin' more like me every day."

"If so, God help him."

The women other than Kate busied themselves clearing the table. Hitch walked outside under a little arbor that substituted for a porch on the pitifully poor shack that Kate's mother called home. Out back, respectfully far from the privy, Hitch could see the blackened wash-pot that served as the old lady's only means of livelihood. Kate's coming here had given her some help but probably had not added greatly to the revenue.

"Kate," Hitch asked worriedly, "you made any plans?"

"Plans?"

"You said you didn't ever want to live out at the place again. You figurin' on stayin' here with your mother?"

She shook her head. "A while, maybe, but not forever. It's a strain on her, and the baby's sure no help."

"You got anywhere else to go?"

"Been thinkin' I might go to one of the cities and try to find me a job of work. I could cook in a cafe or sew or take in washin'. Bigger the town, the better the chance."

It hurt him to consider these alternatives. In time Kate would be another bitter, wornout woman like her mother. He said, "Don't be in too big a hurry, Kate."

"What do you mean?"

He knew exactly what he meant, but he couldn't say it in so many words. There hadn't been enough time yet since they had put Law in the ground. "Maybe somethin'll turn up here close by. Maybe if you'll stay around . . . somethin' else will come along."

She touched his hand, then pulled away. "Hitch," she said evenly, "I know what you're tryin' to say. Don't."

"I'm tryin' not to. But when you talk of leavin' . . ." His face burning a little, he looked straight into her eyes, trying to find an answer there.

Rascal McGinty stood in the door. Hitch didn't know if he had heard. Rascal said, "You ready to go, Hitch?"

Hitch nodded, giving Kate one more quick glance.

They thanked the women for the good meal, then walked together awhile in silence. Presently Rascal said, "I remember readin' somethin' in the Book one time, somethin' that if your brother dies, you should take his widow to wife. You ever read that, Hitch?"

Uneasily Hitch shook his head. "I always meant to read the Bible, soon as ever I had time."

"It's in there someplace. I done a lot of thinkin' on it here lately, since Kate and that baby been alone."

The town was filling up with cowboys, for once they had come to town and cast their votes they had no intention of leaving dry. Hitch took up his station in front of the Buffalo Bar, moving the chair only enough to keep it out of the afternoon sun.

The single bit of excitement came when most of the cowboys had found dinner one place or another and were sitting around in the shade to rest and belch. A lone cowboy in a hurry to get to town from some outlying camp, and probably not realizing the place was dry until the polls closed, carelessly dropped a match to the ground without being sure it was out and the stick broken. The sun-dried grass flared up. Jumping to the ground to try to stamp out the blaze, he let his frightened horse jerk loose and run away from him.

Sight of brown smoke a mile from town aroused the idle cowboys and brought a mass rush for horses. In a rain-shy time like this, a prairie fire out of hand might race for miles and miles, leaving the range a huge stretch of black ashes, useless for grazing next winter and possibly dooming hundreds or even thousands of cattle to starvation unless they could drift far enough south to find grass; even then they would be doubling the grazing load on someone else's range.

Hitch and Rascal had their horses in a corral, and it didn't take them long to saddle up. By the time they reached the blaze, they found a dozen or so cowboys had pretty well stamped and beaten it out. It had had time to spread only a hundred or so feet, leaving ragged fingers of black as it had raced along in the dry grass trying to build momentum and heat. Left alone in those first minutes, it would quickly have gotten beyond control except by major measures and an army of men. Old buffalo hunters said that in Indian times huge prairie fires occasionally swept across these vast plains, burning wildly until they finally reached a river. That was one reason so little brush grew here.

Slapping each other on the back, the smoke-smudged cowboys rode into town again. A thing like that made men thirsty, and they loudly propounded a view that the Election Day saloon rule ought to be suspended in return for the service they had performed for the community. But the law was the law, and most of them settled for cool well water.

As the afternoon passed, Hitch saw a few townsmen drifting in to vote, taking time away from stores, jobs or whatever they had to do. A few stray riders came in, people Hitch remembered from the strike and with whom he had visited to ask for votes. But they weren't enough; nowhere near enough. A time or two Edson Biggs came down from his little bank to sit with Hitch. Rascal would stray off restlessly. Edson said, "Don't give up. All the voters haven't been heard from."

"Some of them may not ever be. All those big-ranch cowboys sure don't encourage them none. And Lafey Dodge is no help to us, either."

"He may be more help than you think."

Dodge had been in strong evidence all morning, quietly walking the streets, gravely studying all who came into town. Now, in afternoon, he was back at it.

Hitch said, "I'd just as well go home."

Edson said, "The polls are still open."

John Torrington came in, flanked by a dozen or more of his riders. Slant Unger was not among them; his wounded arm was proving slow to heal, Hitch had heard. Torrington's gaze touched Hitch and then cut away. Torrington gave no orders; he simply dismounted, tied his horse and walked straight to the polling place. His men followed after him.

The stockfarmer Free came to town, riding a plowhorse. As John Torrington came out of the courthouse, Free met him on the steps. Nervously Free announced for everybody to hear, "Thought you'd want to know, Mister Torrington; I'm votin' for your man Brumley. I've been tellin' everybody, I think he'll make us a good sheriff." Torrington did not reply; he only stared at Free as if he were a worrisome gnat. More nervous now, Free said, "Just wanted you to know, Mister Torrington." Torrington only nodded at him, then came on down the steps.

Prosper Selkirk came with the headquarters contingent from the Figure 4. Most of the Figure 4 wagon crews had been in town since morning, but the headquarters men had probably been too closely under Selkirk's thumb to waste more of the day than necessary in town. Selkirk studiously avoided looking directly at Hitch as he rode by.

Rascal waited until the cowboys had all come back out from the polls. "Well, Hitch, me and you ain't voted yet."

Hitch let the chair go forward and arose, stretching his legs. "Might as well. That's the only two votes we're sure of."

Many of the cowboys watched in idle curiosity

as Hitch and Rascal went up the steps and into the courthouse. Marking the ballot took only a minute; it seemed almost too simple for the importance it carried. Even so, Hitch had to wait some for Rascal. Together they walked out into the courtyard. Another set of horsemen had just arrived, Charlie Waide in the lead. He looked dusty and tired. Limping beside Charlie, his leg mending, came Joe Sands. Cowboys from the other outfits were watching, and Hitch noted that Prosper Selkirk was, too. Hitch decided it was best to let Charlie make the first move.

Charlie took Hitch's hand. "Hitch," he said solemnly, "you know you're goin' to lose."

"I figure that."

"Then why keep on?"

"Why do some horses fight the rope even after they know they're caught?"

"I've always wondered." Charlie moved painfully up the steps.

Hitch turned his attention to Joe Sands. "What you doin' these days, Joe?"

Grinning, Joe glanced across the street toward Selkirk. "Watchin' out for greyhounds, mostly. Good luck, Hitch."

Late in the afternoon Hitch began to see what Edson Biggs had meant about waiting. The "little men," the stray cowboys left at loose ends by the strike, the handful of nesters all seemed to hit town at the same time. Almost in a body, as if by consent and perhaps for a measure of mutual protection, they advanced on the courthouse to register their votes. A string of them led by Edson Biggs marched up the steps past the lounging cowboys from the big ranches. Hitch could see John Torrington peering darkly at them from the wide-open doors of his favorite saloon. Beside him stood a grim Lafey Dodge. Torrington was talking to the old gunman, and pointing.

Edson Biggs came out presently and walked briskly over to Hitch. Edson was dressed now in a town suit and a derby hat; he already looked more banker than cowboy. "See what I told you, Hitch? They came."

"But not enough, Edson. Like I told you, I was always pretty good at countin' cows. I been countin' people all day. There just ain't enough."

His somber appraisal seemed to sap the optimism from Edson. Frowning, the banker took a cigar from his pocket, bit off the end, then forgot about lighting it. He walked away, the cigar still in his hand. Hitch watched him, idly thinking that Edson was beginning to put on a little weight; if he stayed in the banking business, he would probably weigh three hundred pounds someday.

Word quickly swept through the crowd when the polls closed, and most of the cowboys made a rush for the saloons. Hitch sat glumly and watched a dozen or so Figure 4 hands push into the Buffalo Bar. "Well, Rascal," he said quietly, "we done the best we knew how."

Rascal seemed finally to have come to the same conclusion as Hitch. "It ain't over for Lafey Dodge," he gritted. "Not by a damn sight."

Hitch glanced at him in quick concern. "Rascal, without the law behind us we can't do nothin'."

"I can do somethin'."

"You can get yourself killed, is all. Let him alone."

Presently Dayton Brumley came along smiling, carrying victory in the set of his shoulders. "Hitch, I'd be tickled to buy you a drink." He looked at Rascal, forgiving past differences. "And you, Rascal. I'd be right proud."

Hitch shook his head. "Another time. You got a victory celebration started in there, Dayton, and we'd be out of place. Another time, maybe."

Dayton nodded his understanding and went on in.

Lafey Dodge came along, walking by himself. He didn't go into the saloon, for the cowboys were never at ease in his company, nor he in theirs. He was a man long used to being alone. There was no mocking in his eyes; he was not a man for that. His brief gaze seemed simply to say, *I told you so*, without any reproach, and he went on. Rascal McGinty got to his feet and seemed inclined to follow. Hitch caught Rascal's arm.

"Come on, Rascal. Let's go someplace."

As they left the front of the saloon they could hear some of the Figure 4 cowboys addressing a toast to Sheriff Dayton Brumley. Hitch walked aimlessly down the street, the taste of defeat like ashes in his mouth, even though he had expected it. He gazed awhile at Fant Gossett's saloon, about the only one the big-outfit cowboys hadn't taken over, and he thought how much good a stiff drink might do him. But he didn't enter.

"Maybe we ought to go tell Kate we've lost," Hitch said. Loss of the election meant there would be no retribution for Law.

Rascal said, "You go tell her, Hitch; it's your place to do it."

Hitch hesitated about leaving Rascal, thinking of Lafey Dodge. Rascal read his worry. "I won't hunt no trouble, Hitch."

"I take that as a promise."

"It is."

It was a good way over to the shack, and Hitch could have saddled his horse again, but he preferred to walk. Walking sometimes helped work the anger and frustration out of a man. After a while he stood under the arbor, facing her, and he found again that he didn't have to tell her. She knew by his face.

"It doesn't matter, Hitch. Truth is, I'm glad."

"Glad?"

"I didn't want to tell you before, but I always hoped you'd lose. If you'd won you'd likely tangle with Lafey Dodge."

"It ain't right, us not able to do anything about Law."

"I can live with it, Hitch. Vengeance won't bring Law back; it's just apt to get somebody else killed . . . more than likely you. A man like Dodge always gets his wages sooner or later. Let somebody else pay him." She touched his hand, then beckoned with her chin. "Come on in. We'll have supper directly . . . what we had left over from dinner."

Hitch tried to smile. "I'll eat that chicken neck."

He sat down at the plain pine table to sip coffee from a tin cup. He watched Kate bustling about, and he watched the baby in the cradle Rascal had made for it, reaching up and grasping at the air, flexing its tiny fingers. For a while the simple comfort of this poor little house reached him through the disappointment, and he felt almost content. The sting of the loss was almost gone.

He became aware of voices outside, shouting his name. Rascal burst excitedly through the door. "Hitch, they've done with the countin'. You didn't lose after all. You won, Hitch, you won!"

Hitch let the cup tip, and some of the coffee spilled. "You're lyin'."

Edson Biggs came in behind Rascal. Outside, Hitch could hear several more shouting for him to come on out and take his victory. Edson reached into the pocket of his suit coat and thrust a cigar at Hitch. "From now on you stick to counting cows and let me count the votes. You won it by a fair margin, Hitch."

Hitch pushed to his feet, looking back at Kate. To his surprise he saw dismay in her eyes. Kate cried, "No, you must be wrong!"

Edson was bursting with cheer. "The ranchers were wrong, not us. A lot of their own cowboys voted for you, Hitch; they don't like Lafey Dodge. Do you understand what this means, Hitch? They've lost control of their own cowboys."

Kate cried, "No, Hitch, no."

Before he could stop them, the men outside surged in and he found himself being rushed out the door. He glanced back and saw the anguish still in Kate McGinty's face. Then the men were sweeping him down the street in a loud, boisterous, shouting parade. They shoved him through the open door of Fant Gossett's saloon. The broad-bellied Gossett hove out from behind his bar, both big hands outstretched in a wide, beaming welcome. "Hitch, boy, you come on in this house. First drink for everybody is on ol' Fant Gossett. I knowed all the time you was goin' to win; told everybody you'd come through for us honest folks."

Next morning at eight o'clock Hitch was knocking on the county judge's front door. Behind Hitch were Rascal and Edson Biggs and several townsmen. The wizened judge peered unhappily at them; his watery eyes indicated he had drunk quite a bit last night, and not for celebration. "What can I do for you?"

"The oath," Hitch told him. "You want to administer it here or do it down at the courthouse?"

Judge Wilkins looked like a man being led to prison. "Courthouse is the proper place. I'll get my hat."

They walked back down the street, the judge swept along unwillingly but without protest, for he had seen the handwriting scrawled all over the political wall. Additional spectators fell in behind the original crowd, swelling its size. The judge looked back once, plainly distressed, and afterward never looked any direction but straight ahead.

Prosper Selkirk kept a small house in town for his convenience when he had business here that kept him overnight. Hitch glanced that way and saw Selkirk soberly watching from his front door. *That's good*, Hitch thought; *I'll know where to find him easy*. John Torrington had left town last night shortly after the vote was counted, breaking short his cowboys' planned celebration.

Hitch's hand rested on a black-bound old Bible as he repeated the oath. When it was done the judge declined to pin the badge on him but simply placed it in Hitch's hand. Edson Biggs said, "Here, Hitch, I'll do the honors." He shined the star against his trousers leg, then pinned it on Hitch's shirt. He stepped back in satisfaction. "That's a sight I've wanted to see since the day we buried Law McGinty."

Hitch said, "You got a deputy's badge, Judge?"

The judge rummaged around in a corner drawer and came up with one. Hitch said, "I want you to administer the oath to Rascal."

The judge argued, "You're legally entitled to do that."

Hitch stubbornly insisted, "I want you to do it." That was like rubbing salt into a wound, and Hitch did it with malice aforethought. Once Rascal was properly deputized, Hitch said, "Now, Your Honor, I have some complaints to file with you, and some warrants I need you to write out."

The judge knew what was coming. Eyes narrowed, he asked, "You know what you're asking me to do?"

"I'm on solid legal ground."

"There's no question of the legality. I'm thinking of the advisability. It wouldn't matter so much if they were simply cowboys, but substantial men like John Torrington . . ."

"He made a substantial mistake. I want those warrants, Judge."

He had some of them in his hip pocket when he walked up to Selkirk's town house, Rascal beside him. Dayton Brumley stood on the porch. As Hitch mounted the steps, Brumley moved to meet him, extending his hand. "Congratulations."

Hitch felt no animosity toward Brumley. "Hope it didn't hurt too much."

"Main thing hurtin' me right now is a headache from that *victory* party we was havin'. It ended kind of sudden."

"No hard feelin's, Dayton."

"Never no hard feelin's between me and you, Hitch." He glanced at Rascal. "Or us either."

Rascal shook his head. "That old roan cow died anyway."

Prosper Selkirk did not come to the door, but Hitch knew he was inside even before he asked Brumley. He knocked on the door and then walked in, motioning Rascal to stay on the porch. Selkirk sat at a table, some papers spread out in front of him. Hitch noted that a couple were upside down. "Mister Selkirk," Hitch said, "I've come to see you."

"Obviously." Selkirk's hands trembled a little on

the table. "Sit down, Hitchcock . . . *Sheriff* Hitchcock. We have some things to talk about." He offered a drink, which Hitch declined. Selkirk didn't take one himself and probably wouldn't have even if Hitch had accepted. Hitch sensed that this would have been a subtle way of showing superiority. "Well, Sheriff Hitchcock," Selkirk said evenly, "the impossible seems to have happened, and I can well imagine the business that has brought you here. I've always believed you to be a reasonable man: I think we can come to some understanding."

Hitch frowned. "Maybe you ought to clear that up a little."

"I realize now we made a mistake when we—the court, that is—confiscated your herd. I know now that you were not one of those who stole from us. I think I could prevail upon the court to release that herd to you."

"There's no herd to release. Most of them've been stolen and run off."

"How many have you lost?"

"Accordin' to the receipt I got, the county took eighty-four cows and fifty-seven calves and three bulls. How many of them are left we can't know unless we round them up and take a count. There won't be many."

"I've always tried to be a reasonable man myself, Hitchcock, and a fair one. I'll buy your interest in those cattle. Whatever are left, we'll vent to the Figure 4; any loss will be ours, not yours. I'll pay you a decent price. What do you think they are worth?"

Hitch hadn't considered it, but he quickly priced the cows and bulls at fifty dollars apiece and the calves at twenty. He expected to haggle and finally settle for forty. Even that would have been forty dollars more than he had ever expected to recover. To his surprise, Selkirk totted the figures on a piece of paper, then wrote him a check for the whole amount. Selkirk wrote a bill of sale describing the cattle and the brand. "There, Mister Hitchcock, and I hope you'll accept my regrets for a rather unpleasant incident."

Hitch said, "I got some Two Diamonds cattle that the county didn't seize. I want it wrote on there that all Two Diamonds not vented to the Figure 4 brand within thirty days revert to me; that'll protect me on the others."

"Done," said Selkirk, and added that provision to the bill of sale.

Hitch took the check and signed two copies of the bill of sale, keeping one. "I sure didn't expect this."

"I daresay you didn't, but I've always been a man who faces up to his debts."

"I'm glad you feel that way, Mister Selkirk, because you still got another one to pay." He handed him the warrant.

Selkirk's face fell. "Really, Mister Hitchcock, I thought we had come to an understanding."

"I understand *you*. You thought you'd bribed me with my own cattle. Much obliged for the check. I'll deposit it with Edson Bigg's bank right away."

Quick anger showed in Selkirk's face. "I've been trying to understand that election. I think it was Charles Waide who put you across. Charles Waide and his men."

Hitch remembered the financial hold Selkirk had on Charlie. "It wasn't Charlie; he told me he couldn't support me."

"Then who was it?"

Hitch shrugged. "It's your right to ask for a recount."

"In the meantime, do you actually think you're going to put me in that dirty little jail?"

"No, I know you're not goin' to run off anywhere; you got too much at stake here. Judge Wilkins'll set bond for you. Knowin' him, I doubt it'll be much."

It was a long ride out to Torrington's headquarters. Hitch and Rascal moved in an easy trot to spare Walking Jack and that wicked mustang bay named Sweetheart. They came finally to the place. Four cowboys stood by the barn, watching as Hitch and Rascal approached. One came forward and volunteered, "The old man's up at the house."

Hitch asked, "What about Dodge?"

"Up there with him. You fetchin' warrants?"

Hitch nodded. The cowboy said, "I'm sorry it come to this for the old man. Lafey Dodge, now, I don't care nothin' about him; you can throw him in jail and forget what you done with the key. But I almost didn't vote for you, worryin' about the old man."

Hitch stared. "You voted for me?"

The cowboy looked around carefully. "A lot of us did. We want Lafey Dodge and his kind of trouble cleared the hell away from here. But don't you tell the old man."

Hitch edged his horse toward the simple two-room frame that the cowboys gratuitously called "the big house." If Torrington had ever married, no one knew of it. He spent so little time indoors that all he wanted of a house was something to keep the rain off, and that was about the most which could be said of this one. It was in nowise a match for the one Allie Clay had built. Hitch did not dismount. He sat in the saddle and called, "Mister Torrington!"

On second call the old man stepped out onto the little porch, the breeze lifting his short gray beard and ruffling his uncombed thatch of frosty hair. His eyes were defiant as a wounded hawk's. Lafey Dodge came out and stood on one side of him; the Negro Tobe Ferris stood on the other.

"Mister Torrington," Hitch said, "I brought some warrants."

The old man stared antagonistically without reply.

Hitch said, "I got warrants here for you and Lafey Dodge, for Slant Unger, Tobe Ferris and Hobson Clark."

The old man's jaw trembled in anger. "Warrants. *Warrants?* What right you got to be talkin' to me about warrants? Me, the first white man into this country with a herd of cattle? What right you got to be a-wearin' that badge?"

"You was there; you know how the election came out."

"You-all *stole* it, is what you done. You stole it from us that settled this country, us that built it and put all we had into it. Now all you people who waited till it was safe are doin' your damndest to take it away from us."

"Nobody's takin' away anything that's rightfully yours, but you can't take away what's rightfully somebody else's, either. It's not enough anymore that you was the first one here. There's other people now, and other rights. Time don't stand still for anybody. I'd of liked to've seen it stay just the way it was for us cowboys, but you didn't let it. It won't stay the same for you, either."

He saw no sign in Torrington's face that the old man understood what he was saying. Torrington never would understand; it wasn't in him.

"About those warrants, Mister Torrington . . ."

Tobe Ferris stepped down off the porch, face somber. His black hand reached up. "I'll take them. Mister John's legs is got too much of the miseries to be a-troublin' himself comin' down them steps."

Hitch said, "The warrants mean you'll have to come to town and make bond, Tobe. You understand?"

Tobe Ferris nodded. "Whatever Mister John says, that's all right with me. And somethin' *you* better understand. Ain't no no-count strikin' cowboy goin' to lay a hand on Mister John." Tobe's eyes carried a strong threat.

Hitch looked at Lafey Dodge for sign of trouble. Dodge gave none. John Torrington abruptly turned and walked back into the house.

As Hitch and Rascal rode away, Rascal said, "That old man don't know it yet, Hitch, but he's headed down the hill."

Hitch nodded. "Mean as he is, give him credit. He was a gritty old bastard in a time when grit was what it took to stay. The country needed him then. Without him, the rest of us wouldn't be here." Remembering Selkirk he said, "One other thing about the old man."

"What's that?"

"He might kill us off, but not in a hundred years would he ever think of tryin' to *buy* us off."

18

The defendants arranged to meet in town and make bond together. Selkirk did most of the talking, John Torrington standing by in defiant silence, Lafey Dodge showing no emotion at all. The involved cowboys watched the two bosses and said nothing except to answer a brief question or two.

Hitch had not seen Slant Unger since he had put a bullet through the man's arm. Unger had lost weight and his face was pale, for he had not been outdoors much. The arm was still bound. Someone whispered that Unger's arm might be impaired for life. Hitch was uncertain whether to feel sorry for him or not; at least he was glad he hadn't killed him.

The attitude of the county judge and county attorney Zachary bothered Hitch. He had never paid much attention to legal matters and had not understood until now whose job it would be actually to prosecute the case. By his action, Zachary seemed more a defense attorney than a prosecutor.

"Now, Mister Torrington," the attorney said apologetically, pushing some papers forward, "we hate to trouble you with so much detail, but we must meet all requirements of the law. The judge and I agree that you and Mister Selkirk are men of substance who will not leave the county, so we have agreed that the bond should be set on a nominal level, a hundred dollars per man."

That wasn't much, Hitch thought critically. Selkirk would let a thirty-dollar cowboy kill himself chasing a thirty-dollar cow, but he would spend a hundred on himself and never look back.

Judge Wilkins impatiently scanned the charges, reading glasses at half-mast down his nose. "I've half a mind to throw this whole damned case out of court."

Stubbornly Hitch said, "Then I'll find me a court someplace that won't."

The judge peevishly began to lecture him about contempt, but Zachary raised his hand. "The sheriff has a point, Your Honor. It is to the advantage of all concerned to bring this case to trial and see it properly disposed of. If these men are found guilty, so be it. If they are not, a verdict of innocence in a proper court renders them free of jeopardy forevermore. Until we have such a verdict, this matter will always hang over their heads. Disgruntled persons and a hostile court could use it against them years from now."

The judge frowned over his glasses. "You got a recommendation?"

"Yes, that we convene a grand jury at the earliest possible date, have indictments drawn and call the case to trial. The sooner we finish the entire matter, the sooner this community gets back to normal."

Judge Wilkins glared at Hitch. "That would suit me better than anything I know . . . for things to be normal again."

The legal manuevers left Hitch confused. The grand jury was called into session the following week and evidence presented. All defendants appeared, but none was called to testify. Selkirk watched the action with confidence. John Torrington's narrowed eyes focused on the window most of the time, his mind probably on the work he needed to be doing instead of wasting his time in this hot, cramped little courtroom. The grand jury signed the indictments as Zachary wrote them, and Judge Wilkins set trial for two weeks from Monday. "That," he pointed out to Prosper Selkirk, "should give you time to get a competent defense attorney."

Selkirk smiled without humor. "Adequate time, Your Honor."

After everyone else had filed out of the courtroom, Zachary took another look at the signed indictments. "Well, Sheriff, you've gotten everything you wanted so far."

"So far," Hitch said grudgingly. "But I get the feelin' you're about to drop a wagonload of rocks on me."

"We're interested only in seeing that justice is done fairly and impartially, to the least as well as to the largest."

"And then turn them all loose," Hitch said dryly.

Rascal McGinty waited for him at the door. Rascal said, "I don't understand what *indictment* means, Hitch. Ain't they goin' to jail?"

Hitch shook his head. "It just means they'll go to trial."

"But I thought *this* was a trial."

"This was more like the roundup, Rascal. The brandin' comes later. Only, I'm afraid somebody has run off with all the irons."

"There ain't no question that they done it. Why ain't they in jail?"

"The law is set up to make sure they get their rights."

"The law wasn't around to see that they gave my brother his rights. How come it's so bothered about theirs?"

Hitch shrugged.

Edson Biggs looked up from a ledger and flipped a black eye-shade out of his way as Hitch and Rascal walked into his small bank. "How did it go?"

Hitch said, "I get the feelin' it's *me* on trial, not them." He related what had happened in the grand jury session. "I always figured when a man committed a crime and the sheriff caught him, that was the end of it."

Biggs's brow furrowed. "One lawyer can turn loose more men than ten sheriffs can jail. Selkirk has already sent to Kansas City for a good defense attorney. It'll be him against Zachary."

Hitch gritted, "And Zachary won't half try, so we already know how the trial will come out." He clenched his fist. "What did we go to all this trouble for if nothin' is to come of it? How come me wearin' this badge? What good was it for people to vote for me if the court throws out everything I do?"

"We've made a start, Hitch. Regular elections come next year. Sooner or later Zachary and Judge Wilkins are bound to go down."

"That's no help to us today."

"But we've made a start, that's what counts. And if they can send off for a good lawyer, so can we. We can see to it that when the trial starts, Mister Zachary has help whether he wants it or not."

* * *

Selkirk and several Figure 4 cowboys were in town to meet defense attorney Loring DeWitt as he arrived on the mail hack. Hitch watched curiously from across the street to see what caliber of man Selkirk's money would buy. DeWitt was something spectacular for a cowtown like this, his fine tailored suit dusty from the long ride but his dignity not the least impaired as he stepped down with a flourish. The whole town quickly knew he was there.

The special prosecuting attorney hired by Edson Biggs arrived on horseback from Austin so quietly that hardly anyone noticed him. His name was Allan Baucomb, and he put up in the adobe house where Edson lived. Hitch took him out to the McGinty place to familiarize him with the scene of the crime. Baucomb talked to a few people and stayed out of sight. Not until two days before the trial did the Torrington-Selkirk side even learn about him.

When Hitch introduced him to Zachary, the county attorney sat down heavily and stared like a calf knocked in the head. Judge Wilkins began leafing furiously through his lawbooks, looking for a way out. Baucomb calmly cited him page and paragraph, establishing his right to participate. Zachary immediately got himself a buggy and team and disappeared from town in a hard trot.

By nightfall Prosper Selkirk was in town. He wasted no time getting over to Edson's house and introducing himself to Baucomb. Resentfully glancing at Hitch and Edson, he asked Baucomb if the two of them might go somewhere in privacy and talk business. It occurred to Hitch that Selkirk might have brought someone with him, and if his talk with Baucomb did not end as he wished it, Baucomb might not get back. Hitch said, "Me and Edson will go have us a smoke, Mister Selkirk. You can visit here with Mister Baucomb."

Hitch and Edson did not stray much past the front door; they kept an eye on the house. In twenty minutes or so, Selkirk strode out stiffly and rode away in the Figure 4 company buckboard.

Baucomb explained, "Tried to hire me. Said he had a good attorney from Kansas City but thought it might be well also to have a man versed in Texas law. I told him it wouldn't be ethical for me to change now; I already had my clients."

Edson said, "We should've known he'd try to buy you."

Hitch frowned. "And now that he knows he can't, maybe he'll let Torrington use his ways. Mister Baucomb, you better not leave this house anymore unless some of us go with you."

Hitch did not sleep much the night before the trial. Court was set to convene at nine o'clock in the morning. Hitch lay on his cot listening to Rascal snore. All night Hitch mentally gave his testimony against a hostile judge, a hostile county attorney and defense attorney. By daylight he was up, poking a fire into life beneath the coffeepot in the office's small stove. He could hear horses moving outside, and he walked to the window. Against the glow of the eastern sky he saw half a dozen sleepy-looking horsemen riding up the street from the cottonwood-lined river, a thin trail of late-summer dust slow to settle behind them. At the head of the street were five or six more.

Gathering early, he thought.

By the time he had his clothes on and finished his first cup of coffee, he saw more riders in the street. He knew some of the faces, but mostly he went by the brands on the horses. Snaketrack. Figure 4. Rascal McGinty was up now and standing in the doorway, looking outside. He said, "Looks to me like Selkirk and Torrington must've sent word to every camp, every wagon. Looks like every man they got is in town."

Hitch worried, "I wonder if I got the authority to close all the saloons while court is in session?"

Rascal said, "You'd have to ask the judge. If he sees you want it, he'll probably rule against it on principle."

"Best leave well enough alone," Hitch nodded. He picked up his carbine; he had never gotten used to wearing a pistol. "You stay close and keep out of trouble, Rascal. I'll go see how Edson and Baucomb are comin' along."

Walking out into the street, he became uneasily aware that he had the full attention of every cowboy. None spoke to him, either friendly or otherwise; they just watched him. He tried to keep his step steady and even, showing no outward sign of the nervousness growing inside him. He knocked on Edson's door, and the banker hollered for him to come in. The two men were eating steak and eggs. Biggs motioned for Hitch to help himself. Hitch tried, but he couldn't get much breakfast down. "You-all looked outside yet?"

Edson said, "More people than the Fourth of July."

Allan Baucomb commented uneasily, "Surely they wouldn't try to disrupt a trial. It's to their interest to settle this right here rather than risk the outcome in a court where they lack influence." Baucomb was in his mid-thirties, wearing black muttonchop whiskers and a heavy mustache, already trimmed this morning. They gave him an appearance of severity. "Surely they are intelligent enough to recognize that, Sheriff. Selkirk, at least, if not Torrington."

Hitch abandoned any attempt at eating. He poured a cup of Edson's coffee, which he found weak to his taste, and stood in the doorway where he could watch the street. It was an hour now until time for court. The town was full of horses and men. Hitch finally mused, "We got a long ways to walk. Reckon we ought to get a buckboard?"

"It's not very far," Edson argued.

Hitch nodded toward the gathering cowboys. "Could be the longest walk any of us ever took."

Presently he sensed that something had happened, for word began passing down the street, and men started mounting their horses and riding toward the courthouse. "I reckon Torrington's here, or Selkirk. Maybe both of them. Right now might be a good time for us to go."

Edson went for his coat and Baucomb for his satchel. Hitch stepped out into the street, holding the carbine at arm's length, the other men stepping briskly to catch up with him. They began walking. They had not gone far before the horsemen started moving down toward them. Every few feet a couple of men would drop out, forming lines on each side of the street. Hitch glanced uneasily at Edson, then at Baucomb. "Boys," he said, "we're alone out here like a pigeon on a post."

They could have turned and run back to the house, but neither man beside him showed any disposition to do that. They kept walking. Whatever came, they would meet it head-on.

Hitch knew John Torrington by the way he sat straight and proud in the saddle, and Selkirk by the way he slumped in his. It struck him as it had before how ill-matched the men were to be caught up together like this. Lafey Dodge was there, too, on one side of Torrington and opposite Selkirk. Torrington reined in twenty feet from the three men afoot, as did Selkirk. By now their cowboys lined both sides of the street all the way up to the courthouse. Torrington spoke to Lafey Dodge, and Dodge pushed his horse forward in a walk. He gave a moment's attention to Edson and Baucomb, then nodded impassively at Hitch. "Mister Torrington says court's ready to commence. You ready, Hitchcock?"

"Ready."

Dodge pointed his chin at Baucomb. "I reckon that'd be the Austin lawyer."

"That's him."

"Mister Torrington says tell him he ain't needed up at the courthouse, or wanted."

Hitch's breath began to tighten. "He's got a legal right."

"I ain't a lawyer, and I ain't talkin' about *legal* rights; I'm talkin' about facts. He stays here. You come on, Hitchcock, so court can start."

Hitch's hands were turning sweaty against the carbine. Up and down the street, townspeople were beginning to come out cautiously, watching the horsemen. Hitch said, "We're all comin'."

"You'll be the only one that gets there."

Hitch knew Dodge was not making idle talk; that was not his way. Hitch's mouth was dry, his heartbeat picking up. He looked hopefully along the street for help from the people of the town. They watched, and a few might help if someone would but start. Nobody started.

Far up the street, Rascal McGinty came running, pistol in his hand. Hitch froze, not breathing. Lafey

Dodge would kill Rascal as coldly as he might kill a beef.

He never had to. Some cowboy swung a loop and sent it snaking out to catch Rascal by both feet. Rascal sprawled. Before he could get up, a couple of cowboys had the pistol. Rascal was out of it.

Hitch trembled now; he was scared, and he knew he showed it. But he remembered that Law McGinty had been scared too. Hitch stepped forward, thumb on the hammer of the carbine. His heart was pounding. He stared straight at Torrington, and everything else seemed to blur away as if Torrington sat at the mouth end of a funnel. Hitch walked past Lafey Dodge, half expecting to be struck by Dodge's pistol, or shot by it. It didn't happen, for Dodge watched him in wonder. Hitch cocked the carbine hammer back with his thumb. As he walked up close enough to reach out and touch Torrington's leg, he swung the muzzle of the carbine up. He aimed it point-blank at the old ranchman.

His voice sounded like someone else's, and far away. "It's loaded, Mister Torrington."

Torrington glared down at him. "You think I'm scared of that?"

"You ought to be. I am."

The old man's mouth was hard and flat behind the gray whiskers. "What do you mean?"

"I mean I'm within a hair of shootin' you. I don't want to, but there it is."

"There's two dozen, three dozen men would cut you to pieces."

"That wouldn't put you back together."

The beginnings of uncertainty stirred in the hard eyes. "You ain't got the guts to shoot me."

"I don't know, Mister Torrington; I honestly don't

know. I don't think either one of us really wants to find out. We're goin' up that street, me and Edson and Baucomb, and you're ridin' along beside us."

Torrington swayed, but he did not yield. "Like I said, he ain't goin'. If you ever intend to fire that thing, go ahead and do it now."

Hitch already had taken up the slack in the trigger. One tiny squeeze now and it would shoot. He didn't breathe. His hands were cold and wet; he could feel his pulse drumming against the wooden stock.

A commotion started at the upper end of the street, and he glanced that way, blinking, trying to refocus. A new group of horsemen came toward him in an easy trot, passing between the lines of Snaketrack and Figure 4 cowboys. There weren't as many of these as of the others, but there were a respectable twelve or fourteen. In the lead rode Charlie Waide.

Charlie reined up, his men coming about and forming a semicircle around Torrington and Selkirk, Lafey Dodge and Edson and Baucomb. Charlie gravely sized up the situation, then said, "We come to see that court starts on time. You ready, Hitch?"

Hitch lowered the muzzle of the carbine, his knees suddenly feeling as if they would give way. He wanted to smile, but it wasn't in him. He gave Baucomb a quick nod of summons. "Ready, Charlie."

Torrington's angry eyes bored at Charlie Waide. "This don't noways concern you, Charlie."

Waide's voice was even. "It concerns me, John."

Selkirk found voice. "Charles Waide, you're forgetting that I'm in a position to ruin you."

Charlie gave him a look of contempt. "You damn near did already. You damn near took away what self respect old age had left me. Let's go to court, Hitch."

Some of the townspeople were emboldened by

Charlie Waide. Gathering in, they and the W cowboys formed a protective circle around Hitch and Edson and the lawyer Baucomb. Together they walked up the street to the courthouse, moving safely between the lines of cowboys. Rascal hurried up to join them, dusty and angry. Someone had given him his pistol back.

Few besides the veniremen could get into the small courtroom at first. Hitch stationed Rascal at the door to take up all the pistols and put them in a clerk's office; there wouldn't be a gun in the courtroom except those of the sheriff and his deputy.

When Judge Wilkins gaveled court into session, the eight defendants sat at a table in the front of the room. Selection of the jury took time, defense objecting to any cowboys who had participated in the strike, prosecution objecting to any who now worked for a big ranch. In the end the jury was made up mostly of farmers, of townsmen, of a few cowboys from small outfits which had not been involved. All in all, Hitch thought the opposing attorneys had obtained as fair a jury as could be gathered here. There was no way to obtain men who had no detailed knowledge of the recent months' events, or opinions about them.

Hitch studied the defendants' faces. Selkirk was ill at ease; this might have been the first serious situation he had not been able to buy his way out of. Torrington stared resentfully at the jury, shamed at having to submit himself to the judgment of ordinary men for whom he felt no kinship, no particular regard. Dodge seemed untouched and unworried. Slant Unger sat hunched, his good hand gripping his crippled arm as if it still brought him pain. Tobe Ferris was visibly disturbed, looking out upon the curious crowd, then back to John Torrington as if for assurance. The other cowboys were quiet and worried, a little at bay as they had been that day under Hitch's carbine.

County attorney Zachary made a brief introductory comment about the subject of the trial but carefully avoided any accusations. He stated several times that "you will hear it alleged that these defendants did willfully" do so-and-so, seeming to reflect some doubt on his own part, adding that "It will be up to you gentlemen of the jury to decide based upon clear evidence and upon your judgment of the circumstances leading up to and surrounding this case."

Hitch figured Zachary was giving them an out should they decide that Law had deserved killing. He thought it would have been more seemly for the defense, not the prosecution, to say so.

Kansas City attorney DeWitt laid out the groundwork for the defense: "Gentlemen, I have been here but a few short days, and already I am greatly impressed by the beauty and the bounty of this high-lifted land. I ask you gentlemen to gaze upon this man, this hardy pioneer John Torrington, who dared bring the first herds into this region before the dust had settled behind the horses of the wild Comanche. This man and the brave cowboys who rode beside him opened the way for all of you to share the vision with him, to make this no longer a wasted land grazed only by the buffalo and traversed only by the savage. I ask if any one of you would be here today but for the sacrifice and hardship endured by these intrepid men? I daresay you would not. So now that all of you have shared in some measure the fruits of his labor and the fulfillment of his brave dreams, can you now turn upon him and betray him to his jealous accusers?"

He gave the jury a long, challenging stare. "Consider next the man seated beside him, Prosper Selkirk, who brought to this area the capital it needed to nurture the growth begun by John Torrington and the valiant men around him; who brought business acumen and sound managerial judgment for all those who wished to observe and learn from it, and thereby profit this entire land. Let me assure you that in the financial community from which I come, the name of Prosper Selkirk stands high in honor and respect.

"And lastly let us consider these gallant cowboys whose loyalty has stood the test of fire, men who have ridden unflinchingly through summer heat and bitter cold, asking not selfishly for themselves but rather selflessly giving their best for the ranches they proudly serve, and for this region they have helped to build. Slant Unger, once injured in a border battle alongside John Torrington, now perhaps crippled for life at the hands of a man more inclined to defend the thieves among us than the upright and the builders. Shorty James, Hobson Clark, Reston McPhail, loyal cowboys all. And this black man Tobe Ferris, a credit to his race, in his way perhaps the most loyal of all because once freed from slavery he chose to remain the lifelong friend and aide of his beloved master John Torrington when he might easily have followed the blandishments of those hypocrites who so often used members of his race for political purposes of their own."

Hitch kept waiting to see what the lawyer would say about Lafey Dodge. DeWitt never mentioned Dodge at all. He passed over him as if Dodge had been one of the cowboys, as if the jury could not count and did not know him.

Allan Baucomb took over for the prosecution. "Sheriff, would you please bring Mrs. Lawton McGinty into the room?"

Kate waited in the clerk's office, face pale, her hands nervously twisting a handkerchief until it had begun to tear. Hitch said quietly, "Kate, it's time."

She looked up, tears in her eyes. "Do I have to?"

"I'm sorry, Kate."

"Revenge isn't important to me, Hitch. It never was."

"It's not just for revenge, Kate; it's to be sure no other woman is ever widowed here again the way you were."

"I don't know if I can stand up to it."

"You got friends in there, Kate. And I'll be there."

"If you weren't, I *know* I couldn't stand up to it."

Baucomb began with innocent questions about Kate's name and place of abode. She spoke so softly at first that the judge had to admonish her to talk louder. When she had eased somewhat, Baucomb gently led her into telling how Law had ridden to the dugout in a hard run, closely pursued, and had ordered her to take the baby and get away. When Baucomb was finished, Loring DeWitt began his cross-examination.

"Mrs. McGinty, I do not believe in the course of his questioning Mister Baucomb ever got around to asking you where you lived before you came to this region."

She told him East Texas, over in the blacklands.

"I have been told your father was a farmer."

"Yes sir, that he was."

"A successful farmer, would you say?"

"He never did have much luck."

"An unsuccessful farmer, then?"

"I suppose he was."

"It would be easy for an unsuccessful man, struggling, to be jealous of those who were doing better, would it not?"

Kate blinked. "I don't understand what you're tryin' to say."

"A man so afflicted might well pass that jealousy—that resentment—on to his children."

Baucomb stood up. "Your Honor, I do not see that this has anything to do with the case at hand."

DeWitt said, "Your Honor can see where it has everything to do with this case, can't you, sir?"

The judge nodded quietly. "Carry on."

"Mister Torrington and Mister Selkirk are considered successful men in this region. Might you, Mrs. McGinty, feel a little resentful over their success in view of the very little your own people have achieved?"

Kate sat looking at him, not knowing what to say. DeWitt gave the jury a long glance which said her silence showed she agreed with the truth of his statement. He went on, "Since you have been widowed, Mrs. McGinty, what is the means of your livelihood?"

"I help my mother take in washin'."

"The pay for such work is very meager, I would assume."

"We eat."

"But not very well, do you?"

Again she failed to answer him.

"It would appear you are again trapped by the *hard luck*, as you put it, which seems to have plagued your family all along. Hard luck which it would be easy to blame on someone more fortunate." He paused, facing the jury and allowing time for effect. "I sympathize with your distress, madam, and I have no wish to prolong your ordeal here today. However, there are some points I feel we must clear up in the interests of truth. You testified to the identity of the men who rode up that day in pursuit of your husband. I must ask you if you are positive you recognized them."

"John Torrington was there, and Lafey Dodge."

"Did you actually see them?"

"Yes . . . yes, I think so."

"You think so? You are not certain?"

"Well, Law said . . ."

"You did not yourself actually see them?"

"I saw them, only things happened so fast and I was so scared . . ."

"Then you cannot for a certainty say that it even was John Torrington or any of these other men sitting here?"

"It was them, all right. Everybody knows . . ."

"Not everybody, Mrs. McGinty, for even you yourself obviously do not. You are acting upon supposition, and supposition is notoriously unreliable. The facts are that you saw a group of men but in your very natural and understandable fear were never sure, even, who they actually were. They might have been anybody. And quite probably your resentment of men such as Mister Torrington and Mister Selkirk—successful where your kin never were—made it easy for you to tell yourself it was they you saw."

Kate insisted, "It was them; I know it was."

DeWitt turned away a moment, then back. "Now, Mrs. McGinty, I have another question . . ."

"It was them," Kate said again. The judge admonished her to speak only in reply to a question.

DeWitt glanced at the jury. "Mrs. McGinty, have you ever known a man named Cato Bramlett?"

Lips tight, Kate nodded.

DeWitt said impatiently, "I did not hear you, Mrs. McGinty."

"Yes, I know him."

"And did your husband know him?"

"Yes."

"Are you aware, madam, of the reputation of this man Bramlett?"

Baucomb said, "I object, Your Honor. Bramlett is not being tried in this court."

DeWitt said, "He *should* be tried in this court. I believe Your Honor will find that I am working toward a key point in this case if you will but allow me."

"Objection overruled."

DeWitt frowned at Kate. "Again, Mrs. McGinty, are you aware of this man's reputation?"

"I've heard things. I never did like him."

"But it would seem your husband liked him, for they had business dealings together. Is that not true?"

Baucomb stood up, and the judge cut him off. "Overruled."

Kate said, "I don't know about their business. Bramlett was there three or four times, is all."

"Three or four times?" DeWitt made it clear he did not believe that. "I submit, Mrs. McGinty, that your husband and Cato Bramlett were in league in a cattle-stealing enterprise. If this was done without your knowledge, then you are a naive young woman."

Kate looked at the floor. Hitch thought across the room he could see her shoulders shake a little.

Baucomb protested, "Your Honor, Lawton McGinty was the *victim* in this case; he is not the defendant."

DeWitt said, "My reasons will become clear as the trial progresses. For now, however, I am through with this witness."

Kate looked accusingly at Torrington and his group. "I know they're the ones who killed Law."

The judge told her she was excused; she could go on home.

"It was them. All the rest of this is just talk," she declared.

The judge said, "Mrs. McGinty, the bench always tries to be lenient with a woman. Now will you please go home?"

Hitch met her at the courtroom door and walked with her to the outside door of the courthouse. She was still shaking.

"I'm sorry, Kate," Hitch told her gently, "that you had to go through that. I hope it won't be for nothin'."

She leaned into his arms a moment for strength, then pulled back, blinking away tears. "I just want to see an end of all this."

He heard a sound and turned to see Rascal, surprise in his face. Hitch watched Kate walk down the street, his heart heavy. Rascal McGinty said quietly, "Hitch, they want you on the stand now."

19

No doctor had seen Law McGinty to certify his death. It was for Hitch to establish the fact that Law had indeed died, and that he had been hanged. "And now," said Baucomb, "would you simply recite for the benefit of the jury the events leading up to the final act of violence which has brought us together today?"

Hitch reviewed Kate's arrival at his place, her near-hysterical story. Attorney DeWitt arose when Hitch started to relate what Kate had told him. "Your Honor, I object to introduction of hearsay evidence."

"Objection sustained."

Hitch rubbed his hand across his face and proceeded to tell about rushing to the McGinty place, and about meeting the sheriff on the way. The Kansas City attorney objected again, and the judge warned Hitch against repeating any statement the sheriff might have made to him, for this also would be hearsay. Hitch gritted his teeth, then proceeded to tell what had happened on the river.

Baucomb said, "Sheriff Hitchcock, would you please point out to the jury the men you saw at the scene while Law McGinty's lifeless body was still hanging there?"

"Yes sir." Hitch began to point out the defendants one by one. "John Torrington . . . Prosper Selkirk . . . Lafey Dodge . . ." He named them all.

"There is no possibility of any mistake on your part?"

"No, sir. I had plenty of time to look at every man."

When Baucomb had finished his questions, DeWitt arose, giving Hitch a long, careful study. "Now, Sheriff Hitchcock . . . you *are* sheriff, I believe." When Hitch acknowledged that he was, the attorney continued, "But you were not sheriff at the time these alleged events took place. Therefore, Mister Hitchcock, upon that occasion you were merely a private citizen, even as I, or any of these good gentlemen in the jury. You had no legal authority to give commands, make arrests or use a firearm against anyone."

"I went there to stop them from hangin' Law. I was too late."

"You've spoken at length about this so-called hanging. Did you actually see anyone hang this man?"

"You mean to actually pull him up there? No sir, he was already dead when I got to him."

"Are you a physician, Sheriff Hitchcock?"

"No sir."

"Then can you say with certainty that this alleged hanging was even the cause of death? Might he not have been shot, stabbed or otherwise done to death? Might he not, for all you or I as laymen can know, have even suffered a stroke and died a natural death?"

"I saw the body. There wasn't a bullet in him, or a

knife mark. They had him hangin' up there. He died from hangin', and that's a pure fact."

"Even if we specified that this is so, you have already stated that you did not see these defendants actually perform the act."

"They was there."

"Might they not have happened innocently upon the scene after someone else executed this cattle thief?"

Baucomb said, "Your Honor, I must object. The victim is not on trial."

"Objection overruled." Judge Wilkins tore off a chew of tobacco with his teeth. "Everybody knows he was stealing cattle."

DeWitt said, "Mister Hitchcock, I have heard a great deal of talk in the days I have spent here, but I do not propose to deal in someone else's suppositions. I want to know if you ever personally saw Lawton McGinty in the act of taking someone else's cattle."

Hitch glanced at Baucomb, and Baucomb objected that this was irrelevant to the subject at hand. He was overruled.

DeWitt pressed, "Well, Mister Hitchcock, did you?"

Hitch looked to Rascal, wishing he weren't here, glad Kate had gone home. Reluctantly he admitted he had once found Law changing the brand on an animal that belonged to someone else.

"Did you do anything about it, Mister Hitchcock?"

"I told him it wasn't right."

"That was all you did?"

"I wasn't an officer then."

DeWitt nodded. "This establishes beyond question that Lawton McGinty was a cattle thief. Now, Mister Hitchcock, do you know a man named Cato Bramlett?"

"I've run into him."

"Again, I hate to deal in suppositions, but I am told he is a notorious cattle thief."

"He has that reputation."

"Have you ever seen him in the company of Lawton McGinty?"

Hitch hesitated, wondering where DeWitt was trying to lead him. DeWitt pressed relentlessly. Hitch said, "Yes, I seen them together."

"And now, sir, have you ever heard of a Three C Cattle Company, also known variously as Cowboy Cattle Combine and Get-Even Cattle Company?"

"I have."

"Do you now or did you ever own stock in it?"

"No sir."

"Were you ever offered the opportunity of buying such stock?"

"I was."

"And why didn't you?"

Hitch was slow in deciding how to answer. "I didn't want any."

"You didn't want it because you knew it was a company of thieves, designed specifically to prey on the big ranches and take revenge for loss of the strike. Isn't that true, Mister Hitchcock?" When Hitch didn't answer, DeWitt said again, "Isn't that true?" Hitch gave no answer, but he knew everybody could read it in his face. DeWitt read it. "It is true, gentlemen of the jury." He paced a little, staring at Hitch. "Now, sir, you have already stated that you saw Lawton McGinty and Cato Bramlett together. Did you ever hear cross words pass between them?"

Hitch said he hadn't.

"Have you seen this Cato Bramlett at any time since the death of Lawton McGinty?"

Hitch hadn't.

DeWitt nodded. "I understand that no one else has. He has disappeared like a man in flight. Now the natural question which arises next is: in flight from *what?* Could it be, Mister Hitchcock, that he and Lawton McGinty quarreled over the division of spoils? This is known to happen among robbers. Could it be that he and some of his henchmen hanged Lawton McGinty?"

Hitch flared. "Now, you know better than that. We all know . . ."

DeWitt cut him off. "We all know you did not see McGinty hanged. You came upon Mister Torrington and Mister Selkirk and these other men at the scene and took it on circumstantial evidence that they had done it. In actual fact, you have no way of knowing it was not done by Bramlett and some of his robber band."

Old John Torrington began to squirm.

Hitch declared, "Lafey Dodge himself told me . . ."

"I did not ask you what Lafey Dodge told you, Mister Hitchcock. I asked you what you had seen with your own eyes. Your Honor, I am through with this witness."

DeWitt sat down, and immediately John Torrington went into a whispered argument with him.

Baucomb stood up. "Your Honor, before you dismiss this witness I would like to ask counsel if he intends to have any of the defendants to testify."

DeWitt seemed glad to break away from the insistent Torrington. "In interest of time, Your Honor, and because of the constitutional guarantee that a defendant need not subject himself to the ordeal of questioning, we have agreed that these men will not be called to the stand."

"Then," Baucomb said, "since the question of Lafey Dodge's statement has come up and Mister Dodge will not personally testify so that we may explore the question to its full potential, let me ask Sheriff Hitchcock just what Lafey Dodge did tell him."

DeWitt protested that this would be hearsay. Baucomb countered that it was not hearsay in that it involved a statement by one of the defendants. Confused, the judge stammered. Hitch did not wait for him to make up his mind. "He told me they done it, Your Honor. He told me . . ."

Wilkins hammered. "Objection sustained. You will not answer that question, Hitchcock."

"I already answered it, Your Honor. I said Dodge told me they done it."

DeWitt protested angrily. Judge Wilkins threatened that if Hitch persisted in giving testimony contrary to the rulings from the bench he would be jailed for contempt. He told the jury it was to disregard what Hitch had said because this was inadmissible testimony; they were to forget they had heard it.

Hitch smiled thinly. He had made his statement, and the jury would play hell forgetting it, especially when DeWitt's and Wilkins's anger tended to underscore it.

DeWitt said crisply, "Your Honor, I am through with . . . no, just another moment. There is something else." His eyes narrowed. "Sheriff Hitchcock, I believe you have a deputy. Would you mind stating his name?"

"Ra . . . Michael McGinty."

"I believe you were about to say Rascal. I would assume he is better known by this name than by Michael."

"Ain't many people know his real name."

"Do you know how he came to be called Rascal?"

"Can't say as I ever heard."

"Perhaps simply because the name fits, Sheriff. He is a brother to the cattle thief whose death precipitated this entire unhappy affair. Given the oath of office, you immediately hired the brother of a known thief. One might wonder about your loyalties, Sheriff. One might wonder about *you*."

Hitch pushed halfway to his feet in a flush of anger, then checked himself. Baucomb immediately lodged an objection, and DeWitt backed off, looking satisfied. He had made his point with the jury. "I withdraw the comment, Your Honor."

The prosecution called Charlie Waide to the stand. Charlie stiffened in surprise, then limped reluctantly up the narrow aisle to the front of the room. He took the oath and sat heavily in the witness chair. He glanced at Wilkins. "I don't know what I'm doin' up here, Judge. Ain't nothin' I can tell anybody about this case."

Baucomb asked a few questions to establish Charlie's identity and the length of time he had spent in this part of the country. "Now, Mister Waide, it is my understanding that shortly before the cowboys went on strike, you attended a meeting of ranch owners at the Figure 4 headquarters. Am I correct?"

"That's a fact: I did."

"Do you recall the tenor of the discussions there that day?"

"There was a lot of talk; everybody had somethin' to say."

"Do you recall a suggestion by John Torrington that perhaps the way to assert rancher control would be by way of a few hangings?"

"There was lots of things said."

"But specifically, do you remember such a declaration by John Torrington?"

Charlie watched the jury warily. "I remember somethin' like that."

"If my information is correct, you argued against the Torrington point of view. What was the nature of your objection?"

"Just that we don't need to do things that way these days. There's other ways now."

"Did you have any part—in the planning or in the act itself—in the hanging of Lawton McGinty?"

"No sir, I did not."

"Why not?"

Charlie's hands rubbed nervously against the arms of the wooden chair. "I always liked that cowboy. Contrary, but I liked him."

"What if you had not even known him?"

"It still wouldn't have been right."

"Some would argue that such a course is justified in the defense of one's property."

"We have laws now, and men to enforce them."

"Did you know that someone had designs against Lawton McGinty before the hanging occurred?"

Charlie thought over the question. "I went and told Hugh Hitchcock that he better talk to Law, that somethin' bad was fixin' to happen if he got caught changin' brands."

Prosper Selkirk gave Charlie a look of hatred.

Baucomb turned to the jury. "Gentlemen, Mister Waide is known to all of you as one of the 'big' ranchers. Despite this, you have heard him state that he does not subscribe to the notion that owning property gives a person a right to circumvent the due process of law. He does not believe that one man's property rights are superior to another man's right to life. And I do not believe you gentlemen subscribe to that theory either."

Baucomb indicated he was through with Charlie. Prosper Selkirk was whispering in DeWitt's ear. The defense attorney stood up. "Your Honor, I have a question or two for this witness."

Charlie's hands rubbed the chair arm faster.

DeWitt said, "Mister Waide, have you ever participated in the hanging of a man?"

Charlie Waide looked at the floor, face coloring. DeWitt repeated the question. Charlie said, "Yes, I have."

"Would you please describe the circumstances?"

"It was a long time ago."

"We would still be interested in hearing about it. For what crime was this punishment exacted?"

"One time was for murder. Another time was for horse stealin'; in them days takin' a man's horse could be the same as killin' him."

"More than once, then." DeWitt nodded gravely. "And yet now you declare such a thing to be wrong. What has brought the change, Mister Waide, a guilty conscience?"

Charlie's gaze was on the floor, his voice soft. "There wasn't no law then except what we made for ourselves. If we hadn't done what we done, them people would have overrun us. Even so, I ain't proud of it; I've woke up many a night rememberin' and wishin' it never had happened. Them days we had an excuse, of sorts; now there's no excuse at all."

Baucomb called Allie Clay of the Nine Bar to corroborate what Charlie had said about John Torrington's comments at the ranchers' meeting. DeWitt made some effort to discredit Clay by bringing out the fact that he had feuded with Torrington a number of years and thus was not an objective witness.

The prosecution had no further witnesses. The defense brought out several people to vouch for the character of first one and then another of the defendants.

It came time, finally, for the opposing attorneys to present their summations. Baucomb had entirely taken over the prosecution. County attorney Zachary sat alone in resentful silence. Baucomb approached the jurors.

"Gentlemen, I want all of you to take a long and careful look at the defendants. Most of these men are simply cowboys, working for wages and doing the bidding of the men who pay their hire. It might be argued that since they were simply following orders, they should be held blameless. But obeying an order to rope a cow is one thing; blindly obeying an order to put a rope around a man's neck and to murder him is something else entirely. One does not surrender his conscience, his soul, when he accepts a job. Each of us is still a man, and individually accountable for his sins.

"Consider then the two men who ordered this outrage. Prosper Selkirk, an arrogant product of the Eastern financial community, a man to whom all things reduce to a question of silver and gold, to whom no man's rights are as sacred as his own quest for the dollar. John Torrington, a feudal lord, an anachronism in this enlightened time when the poor man's aspirations are to be valued as highly as those of the mightiest landholder.

"Now, the time has come for you to go and consider a verdict. We all know there is traditionally a certain amount of rhetoric and a certain amount of showmanship in a trial of this sort, but now let us put all this behind us and try to sift rhetoric from fact. And the facts in this case are plain. We will specify that Lawton McGinty was indeed stealing cattle from the two principal defendants. They wanted it stopped. They wanted it stopped in a manner so chilling that others tempted to steal from them would be afraid; that even honorable men who seek only their just rights would not dare press the matter, might even become discouraged and leave the country. Torrington and Selkirk wanted no interference. When interference came, they met it with savage force.

"And the principal instrument of this force was this final man you see before you, this Lafey Dodge. I ask you gentlemen to remember what your own feelings were when first you learned that Lafey Dodge was in the county. Was it not fear, was it not a cold dread? His is a name, his is a reputation that automatically brings this reaction. To this man this reputation is a tool of his trade, as your saddle or your plow are the tools of yours. His gun and his loyalty are for hire. He kills not in the heat of passion but in cold, mechanical calculation. His is a legacy left to us by a lawless era which, thank God, is over. Men of Texas no longer settle their differences with guns in the streets. Men of Texas no longer hire the services of mercenaries like Lafey Dodge to do for them with force that which they cannot do for themselves by legal means. At least, few men do, and those few men have outlived their natural time; they have not seen that we have entered a new era of law, of justice, of human rights. They have not learned that Texas has outlived the swaggering arrogance of occasional large property owners who would walk roughshod over smaller neighbors.

"Most of you here remember the recent cowboy strike. Whatever your personal *opinion* of it may be, you will all concede that it was an expression of popular resentment against the same blind despotism which led to the hanging of Lawton McGinty. Despite the transparent attempt of the defense to lay a false trail, you and I and everyone else in this courtroom know where the truth lies. With the professional Lafey Dodge to lead the way, they entrapped Lawton McGinty; and even as the anguished cries of his unfortunate young wife echoed in their ears, they did drag him away and hang him without pity. Now, I have conceded the guilt of the victim in taking these men's cattle. Nevertheless, his guilt should have been determined by a jury of twelve men in a courtroom, not by eight men on horseback beneath a cottonwood tree.

"Remember this: if you free these men, it can all happen again. If you free Lafey Dodge, you will be loosing a savage wolf among you. All this can happen again, and next time it can happen to an innocent man. As you deliberate, consider this: that innocent man may very well be *you*."

Whatever had stirred Torrington earlier, he was still dissatisfied when DeWitt pulled away from him and stood up. DeWitt paced in deep concentration, eyes first on the defendants, then on the jury, "Gentlemen, at this point I can think of many things that perhaps I should say; yet in retrospect it seems to me that I have said most of them before. I would remind you first of all that the man over whom this ill-advised trial has been waged was—by the admission of his friends and the prosecutor himself—a thief. A low, common thief. I would remind you once more of the hardships and sacrifice endured by this fine old pioneer, John Torrington, and his faithful cowboys, in opening this region for settlement; of the vision of Prosper Selkirk in bringing needed capital into this area to allow growth and prosperity to be shared by you all.

"I would now remind you that you are charged to find these men innocent if you are not certain of their guilt beyond all reasonable doubt. I have shown that the charges against them are based upon suppositions, fed perhaps by the bitterness and jealous hatreds which some men . . ." he looked directly at Hitch ". . . have carried since the collapse of their abortive strike, that ill-conceived uprising of the lazy, the malcontent and the misled. Shall we perpetuate this petty legacy or shall we cast it away with the disdain which it deserves? Shall we listen to these mean and strident voices and persecute these men whose farsighted leadership and devotion have brought this region to where it is today, or shall we respect and honor these wise and good and gallant men and stand together shoulder to shoulder with them in building toward an even greater future?

"I submit again that no eyewitness has come forward. I submit again that these men are the victims of circumstance, that the hanging was done by parties unknown, very probably led by the notorious Cato Bramlett, and that . . ."

He never got to finish. John Torrington stood up angrily. "Goddammit. Judge, this has gone far enough. It's a damned lie, every bit of it!"

Judge Wilkins pounded the gavel. "John, you set yourself down."

"The hell I will. I paid enough money for this Kansas

City lawyer to've bought me four good sections of land, and be damned if I intend to see all of it thrown away in a lie."

Attorney DeWitt grabbed the rancher's arm. "Mister Torrington, you're out of order."

Torrington shoved back. "*You'll* be out of order if you keep a-pullin' at me." Tobe Ferris arose as if to aid Torrington. DeWitt backed off, agitated.

Torrington looked at the jury, then at the bench, defiance in his eyes. "Judge, what he said ain't the way of it at all. It wasn't no two-bit Cato Bramlett that done the hangin' and I don't want him gettin' the credit for it. It was us that hung Law McGinty. We done it because he was a cow thief, and we done it as a lesson to anybody else who might be thataway inclined. Now if people get to thinkin' maybe we didn't do it, then all that is wasted, don't you see?" Prosper Selkirk sat stunned, face draining of color. Torrington turned to the jury, in no way apologetic. "We done it because a man ought to stand up for himself, not wait for some slow-footed court to do it for him at public expense. You think this country was built by tiptoein' lawyers and a shelf full of lawbooks? No sir, it was built by men with guts, men who done whatever had to be done and didn't fool around about it. It's been that way and it's that way now; it'll be that way as long as I got strength to climb into a saddle. And if it ever stops bein' that way you can mark it down that this country has gone to hell.

"Law McGinty was a damned thief; he needed hangin' and we hung him. Better to hang one man as a lesson than to wait and have to hang a dozen. That's why I couldn't sit quiet and let the lie go without bein' answered. I didn't enjoy hangin' that boy; anybody says I did is a liar. I wouldn't want to do it again. But I *would* do it if I had to, and these good men of mine would help me.

"Now, if times has changed so much that a man can't take care of his own troubles anymore, then I say Texas is the worse off for it. And if you folks on this jury think you got to punish somebody, don't you do it to these good loyal men here who just done what we told them to. They are not responsible. If you got to punish somebody punish me and Prosper Selkirk." He glared at the jury. "But I want you to know one thing: I ain't in noways sorry, and I ain't in noways ashamed. And remember this is still our country. You don't have to keep on livin' here. If we was of a mind to, we could put you out."

He sat down. Prosper Selkirk's face was hidden in his hands. The courtroom was in shocked silence a moment or two. The judge hoarsely read his charge to the jury, and the jury was led out into another room to deliberate. John Torrington sat at the head of the defendants' table, nervous as a wild stallion trapped in a pen. Prosper Selkirk's face was still half hidden. He did not look at anyone. The cowboys were quiet and troubled. Lafey Dodge stared at John Torrington, and Hitch thought he saw a new respect in the gunfighter's eyes.

Presently Judge Wilkins arose from the bench. "If counsels would like, I might find a bottle in my chambers." Baucomb, DeWitt, Zachary, and the judge disappeared together through a door at the rear of the room. That surprised Hitch. He would have thought the heated differences during the court session would preclude any friendliness between opposing attorneys. But, he decided, there was a lot he didn't know about law.

He had a notion the jury would deliberate a few

minutes, then come back with its verdict. Hitch had no watch, but he judged after a while that the jury had been out an hour, and he saw no sign of stirring in that direction. He was beginning to ache a little from sitting so long, and he stood up to stretch. He glanced at the defendants and found none of them looking his way except Lafey Dodge. He couldn't read what—if anything—was in the man's thoughts.

Rascal McGinty came up from the back of the courtroom, his patience gone with thin. "Dammit, Hitch, how long does it take the jury to find them guilty?"

"We don't know that it will."

"What else can they do? You heard what the old man said. He pulled the cell door shut on himself."

Hitch shrugged.

Rascal said, "I still blame Lafey Dodge more than any of them. He's the one who kills people for hire. Without him, they wouldn't likely of ever done it."

"Main thing is to be sure it don't ever happen again. It's not as important to say who was to blame."

"It's important to me," Rascal insisted.

Darkness came, and still the jury was out. Hitch could not sit long at a time now; a nervous prickling started in his rump every time he went to the chair. Mostly he paced the floor or stood leaning against the wall, watching the lamps and lanterns being lighted around town. The same uneasiness stirred most of the defendants. Half of them were up looking out the windows, the rest slumped at the table patting their feet, drumming their fingers, smoking cigarette after cigarette. Selkirk started to say something to John Torrington and the old rancher turned on him in fury. This day had done something to Torrington. It had humiliated him to sit here like a common criminal in the dock, to be stared at and speculated about by people whom he held in contempt.

The Negro Tobe Ferris stayed protectively near John Torrington, staring out at the onlookers with angry eyes that seemed to rebuke them for this disrespectful treatment of the old man. It struck Hitch that there was a faint resemblance between John Torrington and Tobe Ferris, despite the differences in their skin.

The judge went into the jury room several times, and always he came out impatiently shaking his head. Often Hitch saw him pull a heavy watch from his pocket and hold it out to arm's length, squinting to read it.

Much of the original crowd gave up and went home, though other people came in to take their places. Allan Baucomb sat down wearily beside Hitch. Hitch said, "Does it always take this long?"

"Sometimes."

"Is that a good sign or a bad one?"

"You never know."

Hunger gnawed at Hitch, but he had no intention of leaving so long as the issue remained in doubt.

The lamps had been burning at least an hour when word came from the jury room. Judge Wilkins went out for a brief conference, then came back to the bench and rapped for order. "I will remind everybody that this court is still in session." The jury filed into place. The judge leaned forward. "Has the jury arrived at a verdict?"

A tall farmer designated as foreman stepped forward. "Like I told you back there, Judge, we been havin' some trouble. There's some says guilty, and there's some says we owe John Torrington too much to do this to him. We've talked and argued with each other till we're wrung out. We still don't come to any agreement."

"You're deadlocked, then?"

"Sure looks like it, Judge."

"What would happen if you took a little more time?"

"A fight, more than likely. Ain't been a man changed position in two hours."

The judge evidently had known this from his several visits to the jury room. "That being so, I declare that we've got a hung jury and this court is dismissed." He pounded the gavel.

The defendants looked at each other in confusion. Tobe Ferris whispered a question to John Torrington, and the old rancher stood up. "Judge, I'm figurin' on goin' home, and takin' my boys with me. Is there any reason I can't?"

Wilkins shook his head. "You're still under bond till there's a decision made on whether or not there'll be a retrial. That depends on the prosecution." He looked past the county attorney and fixed his gaze on Allan Baucomb. Baucomb said, "We'll have to take it under advisement, Your Honor."

The judge frowned. "Well, you know what *my* advice is. I rule that bond be refunded to those men and that if there's ever another trial—which I doubt—new bond can be set for them. Anybody wants a drink with me, they'll find me at the Buffalo Bar." He rapped the gavel one more time for emphasis and got up from his seat.

Some of the Snaketrack and Figure 4 cowboys began crowding around the defendants, laughing and slapping them on the backs.

Hitch looked at the floor, his frustration sour as

clabbered milk. To Baucomb he said, "I reckon we lost."

"Depends on how you look at it. Two years ago . . . one year, even . . . you would not have ever gotten them to trial."

Hitch said hopefully, "How about a retrial? Maybe next time . . ."

Baucomb shook his head. "You've made your point, Hitch, that's the main thing. Even a hung jury is a sign of change, and a warning. This thing would never be stood for again. In another year or two the whole bunch would stand convicted. I'm sure Selkirk realizes that. If the old man doesn't know it now, it'll soak in on him. What happened to Law McGinty will never happen again . . . not here."

Rascal McGinty's eyes were bitter. "Does this mean they don't even get punished?"

"They've been punished just bein' here," Hitch said.

As a deputy, Rascal McGinty had not had to leave his pistol outside. He drew it, his eyes afire. "Well, Lafey Dodge ain't gettin' away."

Before Hitch could move against him, Rascal leveled the pistol. Lafey Dodge, unarmed, stood rigid, almost resigned. Hitch leaped at Rascal, striking his arm just as the pistol fired. It made a thundering noise in the small courtroom. Black powdersmoke billowed in a choking cloud. Hitch wrestled Rascal for the pistol while men dived excitedly for windows and doors, under tables and chairs, behind the cold pot-bellied stove.

Hitch got Rascal down onto his back and drove his knee into the cowboy's stomach. Rascal relaxed his hold, and Hitch flung the pistol across the floor. Lafey Dodge stooped and picked it up in his left hand.

Expecting retaliation, Hitch shouted, "Dodge, don't you do it!"

Dodge made no move to aim the pistol at Rascal. He held it out butt first. "Here, Hitchcock, I expect you'll want this thing. I've never killed a man for pleasure."

Hitch saw then that Dodge's right arm hung limp, blood beginning to soak the sleeve and run down his hand. Hitch glanced back at Rascal, expecting more fight from him. But Rascal had made his try and was through. He sat on the floor with arms tight against his stomach while he attempted to regain the breath Hitch had knocked out of him.

Hitch said to Dodge, "We'll get the doctor for you."

Dodge said, "I been hurt worse than this tryin' to open a can of tomatoes."

Hitch shoved Rascal's pistol into his own boottop and helped Rascal to his feet. "I'm takin' you to jail, Rascal, for your own protection."

Rascal made no protest. He still didn't have all his breath back. Hitch told the bystanders to get Dodge to the doctor. "I'll be along directly," he said. Hitch took Rascal to the jail and unlocked a cell. Rascal walked in without protest and sat on the iron frame meant for a cot. "Hitch," he said heavily, "he didn't get off scot-free. I drawed blood on him."

"You did that," Hitch admitted. "I hope you're satisfied."

"Not particularly, but I reckon I'm through. What you fixin' to do now?"

"Go see that Lafey Dodge gets patched up, then first thing in the mornin' ride along with him till I make sure he's plumb out of the county. Till he's gone, you're stayin' in here."

"Am I still your deputy?"

"I don't know. I'll have to think on it."

"It don't matter. I done what I wanted to be a deputy for. I drawed blood on him, at least." Hitch turned to leave. Rascal called him. "Hitch, you be careful with that Lafey Dodge. He'll kill a man as soon as look at him."

"I'll watch out."

"Before you go, Hitch, I got somethin' that needs sayin', somethin' I want you to think on."

"About Dodge?"

"About Kate. Ain't good, her bein' alone. I been thinkin' maybe after a proper time I ought to marry her myself."

Hitch made no reply; he didn't know how.

Rascal said, "But I can see now that I couldn't do it. I couldn't touch Kate in no way except as a brother. The time'll come when she'll need a man again, and not just a brother. I seen you two at the courthouse, and it come to me. You're the one to marry her, Hitch."

Hitch let go a silent sigh of relief. "It's a way too early for us to be talkin' thisaway. We need to wait a proper time."

"If you go with Lafey Dodge, you better think on it now. I don't want nothin' happenin' to you."

20

They crossed the wide, shallow river shortly after sunup, following the marker stakes to avoid the quicksands, then started across the rolling hills toward New Mexico. Lafey Dodge rode that big blue roan of his. Hitch rode Walking Jack. Dodge's right arm was tightly bound. Anger pinched his face.

"That son of a bitch Selkirk," he grumbled. "Still owes me a thousand dollars. You mark it down in your book, Hitchcock: a man like that ain't to be trusted."

"I never did."

"Give me an old fire-eater like John Torrington anytime. Bullheaded, stupid sometimes, but he's every inch a man. He's got his honor. If he's ever said he'll do somethin', he'll do it. Paid me all he had promised and a little extry besides. But not Selkirk. He says the whole thing turned into a fiasco and he didn't see where he owed anybody another nickel. That son of a bitch!"

Hitch listened without particular interest. He did

not care whether Dodge was paid or not; he simply wanted him gone.

Dodge said grimly, "But he just thinks he's done with me. One way or another, he'll damned sure pay."

Hitch's eyes narrowed. "You wasn't thinkin' about comin' back and doin' somethin' to him, was you, Dodge? I could lock you up for makin' threats, but I'd rather just see you out of the country."

"No, I promised you I'd leave, and I'm like ol' John Torrington; I keep my word."

"Then I don't see how you'll make him pay."

"There's ways."

They did not talk for a while. Hitch felt no worry about treachery from Dodge. For one thing, Hitch had the man's pistol, and he did not intend to return it until he was ready to turn back. He looked at the cattle, most of them Torrington's, and at the dry, cured grass which blanketed the ground like some huge light-colored buffalo robe.

Dodge tried rolling a cigarette one-handed and spilled his tobacco. When Hitch started to help him, Dodge shook his head. "I got to learn or quit smokin'. This right arm ain't goin' to be much use to me for a while."

Dodge finished the cigarette and struck a match to it. He started to flip the match away and Hitch warned him to be sure it was out. "This country's dry enough to go up in smoke."

Dodge nodded. "Wouldn't want to hurt ol' man John." He pinched the head of the match between his fingers, wincing from the heat.

Hitch said, "Where are you goin' from here?"

"There's some good Mexican people over close to Anton Chico that I done a favor for once. Thought I'd stay with them till this arm's healed. I can't afford to be out in public as long as I'm in this shape. You ever see what a bunch of wolves will do to a crippled buffalo?"

"It's lucky Rascal didn't do a damn sight worse to you."

Dodge shrugged. "I reckon he felt like he had a right. You goin' to do anything to him for this?"

"Without you here to press charges, I don't suppose anything'll come of it."

"It's just as well. I never did favor jails much . . . for me or for anybody else. Tell him I hold him no grudge."

"When your arm heals, what then?"

"I don't know. By that time there'll probably be another job."

"Times are changin'. There may not be."

Dodge blinked, not comprehending. "There's always a job for a man that knows his business."

"Not if time runs out for his kind of business. And for yours, it's runnin' out fast."

Dodge still didn't understand. "I always gave a man his money's worth. There's always been more work than I could get around to."

Hitch saw that there was no reaching Lafey Dodge, no more than there was any real way to reach John Torrington. Neither had recognized a change since the Civil War.

It's a pity, in a way, he thought. *Somebody'll shoot him, more than likely, or put him away in a prison, and that's just another kind of death for a man like Lafey Dodge.*

They rode all morning. By now the Canadian River hills were behind them and the prairie rolled gently, solid dry grass as far as a man's eyes could see. Dodge pointed to some cattle. "That's the Figure 4 brand on those. Selkirk's, ain't they?"

"We been on Selkirk country since we come through that last set of breaks. It goes yonder way for half a day's ride. There's a little creek just ahead of us. We'll stop and fix us some coffee, then I reckon I'll turn back."

They drank the coffee and ate cold biscuits and bacon Hitch had brought along. Finished, Hitch said, "You take the coffee can and what food we got left. You'll likely need it."

Dodge nodded. Hitch rolled it up in a canvas sack and tied it behind Dodge's cantle, along with his bedroll and small warbag. The last thing he did was hand Dodge his cartridge belt and pistol. "It's unloaded," he said. "I figure you got cartridges someplace. I just don't want you usin' them around here anymore."

Dodge said, "I won't. I promise you I ain't comin' back."

"And you leave Selkirk alone, you hear?"

"I *didn't* promise you that." Dodge studied Hitch intently, not seeming to want to pull away. "There's somethin' been botherin' me, Hitchcock, somethin' I'd purely like to know."

"What's that?"

"If old Charlie Waide hadn't come along on that street when he did, would you of really shot John Torrington?"

Hitch pondered. "I'll never know."

"I'm bettin' you would have. And the old man thinks so, too. He'll hate you as long as he lives, but he'll never look down on you." Dodge shoved his left hand forward, offering to shake. "Been a pleasure to know you, Hitchcock."

Hitch hesitated, then accepted. "I'm sorry I can't say the same."

He sat a long time, watching Dodge ride away. He had a feeling Dodge meant to keep his promise about not coming back, but he felt compelled to stay and see him out of sight. After a long time, Dodge disappeared into the heatwaves that shimmered over the distant brown grass and that melted the vague horizon line into the clear summer sky. Only then did Hitch swing up into the saddle and head Walking Jack back toward town.

A long time later the prairie wind brought him the vague smell of something burning. He turned in the saddle and brought Walking Jack to an abrupt halt, wheeling him around. Light brown smoke billowed in the west, clouds of it climbing up into a sky of burnished brass.

Instantly he knew. "Lafey Dodge!"

Old-timers always remembered that fire as a curly wolf. With the north wind to push it and all those miles and miles of dry grass to feed upon, it swept across much of the Figure 4 range, taking out a big percentage of Prosper Selkirk's grass and leaving him without half enough for the next winter. It covered parts of John Torrington's and several other ranches, too.

The sight of such a fire strikes fear into the heart of a brave man, the angry smoke boiling higher than a circling hawk, the noise fierce as screaming eagles. All the animals flee ahead of it in panic. At night the bright red flames reflect on the rolling smoke above, invoking visions of the hell so dreaded by the believing man. Times when wind and ground conditions are right, a prairie fire can outrun a man afoot. This one swept over a nester's place north of the Canadian, and he saved himself only by jumping into his own well. Even so, he almost drowned.

Cowboys turned out from all the ranches, and many who were unemployed joined in, though they had nothing personal at stake. So did many of the people in town. It was not that they worried about Selkirk and the Figure 4, or about old John Torrington, but the fire was hurting other people. There was a danger that it could sweep on to God knew where if they did not stop it.

For a time Hitch found himself fighting fire side by side with John Torrington, and on either side of them were jobless cowboys set adrift after the strike. Some no doubt had been mavericking Torrington cattle, yet the old man asked them no questions and they asked him no favors. The rabbit and the wolf will run side by side to get away from a fire; human enemies will stand together to fight one.

Some of the men fought the blaze half out on the western line, then had to run for their lives when the wind whipped it around them and caught them in the middle. All the nesters who had plows went ahead of the flames and cut deep furrows. Hitch helped Charlie Waide kill a Torrington cow, split her open with an ax and flatten her out. Hitch tied onto one hind leg, Charlie onto the other, and they dragged the whole juicy mess up and down the front line of the flame, smothering it. Other cowboys were doing the same.

One way and another, after two days of fighting they brought the blaze to a standstill. A rainstorm thundered down from the north and finished putting out the fire, the first minutes of rainfall sending clouds of steam rising up from the hissing ashes.

The danger gone, from the east came the wagons and the buggies and hacks, and women from the scattered ranches and from town, bringing food and fresh water and pots to boil coffee in.

Charlie Waide sank to the ground, totally exhausted. He was holding the bad arm now. He had ignored it the last couple of days and had forced it to do things certain to bring him pain later. They watched John Torrington, weary and bent but still riding up and down the line. His slicker had been lost somewhere in the fight against the fire. The old man still hoarsely barked orders, though the men were so tired they did little but nod acknowledgement. They were far more interested in the food and coffee.

Hitch said, "You know where we're at now?"

Charlie Waide looked around. "Figure 4."

"We didn't save much of Selkirk's grass for him."

Charlie shook his head. "He'll never make the winter out, Hitch. Come spring he'll probably be broke flatter'n a stepped-on centipede."

"He's got it comin' to him."

"But he'll take me out along with him. He'll have his bank call me in."

"Why? That won't save him."

"I took your part against him. He won't let me stand while he falls."

"I'm sorry, Charlie."

Charlie shrugged. "It'll hurt like hell, but they can't get it all. I ain't so old and wore out but what I can't start fresh. I'll beat them damnyankees yet."

"Sure you will, Charlie." Hitch stared at him, the words coming easy but the doubt strong. "How about me goin' to the wagon and bringin' you some coffee?"

Charlie looked, and his eyes softened. "Go to the

wagon, Hitch, but don't be in no hurry. Come back in your own good time."

Hitch turned. He saw Kate there at the wagon, face smudged by smoke and ash. Through the ash, she was smiling.